King's Wolf

Michelle Wingfield

Contents

A note from my journal

Quinton, home to the sullen creatures known as Humans, was also my home.

Nevertheless, Home is not always where the heart lies. And seldom is it really a Home. Human as I may be, there are parts of me that never were, nor ever will be, and there would come a time when I was more so a beast than human. Most would believe it so, but only few know better than to adhere to the lies Humans are so willing to spread.

In this land so vast a treasure, and so vast a wreck simultaneously, there are tales of Dragons and Elves and Magicians, Dwarves and Mermaids and Winged People. None proven, yet all told to be among the world. If I ever come across any of these Peoples in my ventures, you'll be the first to hear of it. These accounts of my toils, ventures, and life, I write now, by candlelight, under a full moon in my favorite place. My fingers tremble around the pen, neither from age nor frailty, but from eagerness to pass on the things I've learned.

Whether you consider my accounts fictional tales written by an ambitious, exuberant novelist, with a simple longing to entertain or to create fanciful illusions to distract you of your realities, or whether you find truth in my words and take to heart the lessons on these pages– I am unconcerned.

Simply, I wish that you listen carefully, and that in these pages you might find a piece of yourself. I cannot promise these accounts will bring comfort or pleasure to you, merely the opposite. And yet I do not doubt the courage of those willing to take up these pages.

If you are one, I bid you well and good tidings. Nonetheless; Be warned. Difficult is the path that lies ahead, and more so the knowledge you might gain. But strength isn't only measured by what the eye can see.

Remember that.

Remember.

Chapter One

Jala

I died.

Or, at least I should have.

But there is a place in the human mind, rarely discovered, that when the body fails, the consciousness flees into. A very last resort, but one that few come to find available. This place is beyond reach for most, beyond understanding, and those who learn or come upon this place that survive, either rise to greatness, or dwell in utter reticence.

Yet most are executed. Or rather…disposed of. And either there have been so rare a person to use this place of mind, or there are too many that are afraid to admit it. The place, or ability, for lack of better words, has been known as the Keen to wiser, older generations long before. Now it is known far and wide as the Demise.

Funny, be that, Demise. And yet it is the Demise that kept me from meeting my demise.

My mother, a woman of high rank, a Princess of the Highland Kingdom, befell a fate so far below humane at the hands and manhood of a
long sought after criminal. It happened on the eve of the Solstice.

Princess Tira was traveling with the royal's caravan to the neighbor-
ing Kingdom of Lowland to be betrothed to the Prince Grevan. Their
marriage would unite the two kingdoms as allies and the Prince and
Princess would become the King and Queen of both kingdoms when
the kings of both passed on.

This did not come to pass. The Princess never reached the Lowand
Kingdom, and she ever become Queen.

That bleary winter night as the snow billowed around their night
camp, Princess Tira, bundled in her woolen travel clothes, was just finishing her evening meal when she fell at the mercy of Cordon Greyver,
wanted for multiple counts of murder, treason, assault, and legends
have it that he bore the ability of the Demise.

The Princesses' guards were ambushed by a lot of men, criminals
long wanted and ruthless, loyal followers to Cordan. No one knows
how many, exactly, but enough to overpower the guards and raid and
squander the caravan of its royal goods.

The royals had chosen the winter season to send the Princess for the
sole reason of a lesser chance of being raided, and yet, that is exactly
what had happened.

Among the survivors were the Princess and her maids, and a few
young ones who were responsible for the animals.

But the cost was great. Cordan and his men didn't have any intentions to kill the royal. Merely, they intended to plant a seed that would later grow and bring chaos and division in the Kingdoms.

And so it was.

Together with the few survivors, Princess Tira was found near–dead on a path that led back to Quinton, her King's city, by some travelers and merchants. Recognizing the Princess, they took her home where she swiftly recovered.

She spoke nothing of what had befallen her that night. Nevertheless, the seed had been planted.

Nine months later, she bore twins. Her betrothal was called off, and Tira was hanged, for she was too afraid and ashamed to speak of how she had come about these two little ones, so the royal family assumed she had had an affair. But with whom, they did not know.

But as the children began to grow, it became evident who had sired them.

Cordon Greyver.

The royal family was horrified, utterly downcast with themselves that they had taken the Princess's life for something that she hadn't been able to stop. And yet, the act had been done, and there was no reversing it.

Of the twins were a boy and a girl. They resembled both their late mother and the one who had sired them so much that the royals were unsure of what must be done with them. But since the two were the only heirs that the Princess had borne, they came to a decision on the children's third birthday.

The boy they kept, named Sabian, and would raise as an heir to the throne, learning the ways of a prince, but the girl they had no use for.

It would be bad enough having one heir that resembled the crown's most wanted criminal, but two? They could not have it.

So they hid her away, keeping her out of sight from her brother, for they wanted no memory of her to taint his mind. Disposing of her completely would not have been a good omen to the crown, nor an honor of the late Princess, and sending her away would only make her a threat to the crown, so they kept her in the stables and animal keep, where they could keep an eye on her and where she would learn to care for and train the beasts, from dogs, to horses, mules, and messenger birds. She lived and worked there, scarcely setting foot in town unless it be for supplies. A few certain palace guards and townsfolk took pity on her and kept her somewhat fed. In exchange, the girl would care for any sick animals the folk and soldiers had.

It became evident that the girl had a way with animals, and could tame even the wildest of stallions over the course of a few short days, and could bring back to health any sick beast brought to her. She became known simply as Stablegirl by the handful of those who cared enough to speak to her. None except the royal family were aware that she was Prince Sabian's twin sister. And Prince Sabian himself was told he never had any siblings save the other royals.

When Stablegirl was ten, the head of the royal guards sought to take her on as his apprentice. He argued that the girl was fit and strong and even more so wiry, and would be a waste to the crown unless she became a King's soldier. So after some time and much hesitation of the royals, it was arranged that the girl be apprenticed in the art of defending and fighting for the royal family.

From then on, she learned the ways of swordsmanship and combat with a staff. Alongside that, she learned formation and to stand well and long out in the cold on guard duty, hours without moving a muscle. By day she did these, and by evenings and nights she tended to her stable duties. All this she excelled at, and was soon much respected by the other soldiers and palace guards, so much that it came to the attention of the King, Rubarb.

So it came about that King Rubarb placed the girl under his royal spy's apprenticeship so that she may be of further use to him. The Queen, Hersha, did not approve, and saw to it that suspicions were raised about the girl. Still, the girl worked her other duties, but she quickly mastered various forms of sneaking about without being seen or heard, listening and memorizing conversations and people's habits and ways, and various other things that make one a royal spy. She soon became a young woman, more so in mind than in body, and though she still lived the life of one shamed by her siring, she also became a skilled warrior, and even more so a skilled spy.

From when the girl turned eleven to when she was thirteen, she was given many spying tasks, some by Prince Farlay, the King's son, some by Queen Hersha, and some by King Rubarb himself. She saw and reported many things, from simple thievery amongst the servants, to royal disputes, to even plots against the crown.

The girl found these tasks to come naturally, and she didn't realize it, but she had a way of knowing where people were without seeing or hearing them, knowing someone was going to come before they did, and sometimes even knowing what someone will say before it is even said. Thus it was also so with any beast, if not more so.

It was brought first to Prince Farlay's attention, and suspicious that the girl had the Demise, the Prince sought forth the Queen.

Queen Hersha had been discontent with sparing the girl's life from the beginning. In court, the Queen had voiced her displeasure, distrust, and especially anger more than once over the situation. When the girl had become guard and spy, the Queen had rested back for a while. But it was no secret that she sought to make the girl's life miserable. More so than the girl could have counted, the Queen sent her on the most dangerous suicide–type missions she could come up with. And yet, she became ever more angry everytime the girl returned alive and having had completed the mission.

So when Prince Farlay brought forth suspicions of the girl's abilities, the Queen was delighted. She quickly swept up the chance.

One evening, the girl was summoned to the Queen's chambers while Queen Hersha was readying for bed. Tomorrow was Prince Farlay's birthday, she informed the girl, and she wished to send a gift to him. But, she wanted it to be a surprise. So she gave the girl a bottle of the finest wine, imported from across the sea, and instructed the girl to take the wine to the Prince's chambers and leave it there. "You must only be seen by the servants, never by the Prince, for he will wake to a fine bottle of his favorite drink. Say to the servants and guards, the Queen sends a gift to her son, but do not wake him so that when he wakes, he may be surprised."

The girl obeyed despite the oddities, and brought the wine to the Prince's chambers. When his guards questioned her intentions, she repeated to them what the Queen had told her. "A gift from the Queen. She wishes the Prince wakes to find this in his bedchambers that he may be surprised."

They allowed her entry, and using her skills, she placed the bottle of wine and a glass on the Prince's nightstand without waking him. Then, she slipped away, informed the Queen of the successful mission, and returned to the stables.

The next afternoon, the Prince fell dead after drinking a glass of wine, and after it had been examined by the royal assassin, it was announced that the wine had been tainted with a deadly poison. The guards were questioned thoroughly, and it was brought to sight that the girl had been the one to bring the wine. Immediately blame was brought upon the girl for tainting the wine. For poisoning the Prince.

She had done no such thing, and yet she knew no one would believe her. Before the palace guards could find her and bring her in for execution, and before anyone could take action against her in any way, the girl fled. She took to the shadows of the town quickly, using every bit of skill she had to avoid those who searched for her, and intended to flee into the forest.

With just the clothes on her back, the only things that she had ever been able to call her own, she headed towards the wild hills and mountains, not along the paths of travelers and merchants and hunters, but along the rabbit and deer trails that threaded through the woodlands like illusive networks of life.

But before she was far enough from Quinton, the King's city, for it to be safe, the girl crossed a merchant path in order to get further up into the mountains. It had only been a few days since she'd fled, and the search for her had continued on. But even though the girl didn't sense anyone nearby as she cautiously stepped onto the path and made her way to the other side, a voice behind her said, "Stop right where you are."

The girl froze, inwardly scolding herself for being unable to sense someone following her, and slowly turned to face the person. He stood a few feet away on the other side of the path, holding a blowgun in one hand and a dagger in the other. The girl recognized him as the crown assassin, Kelgare. His eyes were dark from all the things he'd seen and done, and darker yet with the duty that weighed him. His hair was darker still, jet black and long, tied back with a cord. Clad in matching black dyed attire and boots, he looked his part.

"Stablegirl," he said calmly, with a coldness about his tone that sent shivers down the girl's spine. "You've been charged for treason and the murder of Prince Farlay of the Highland Kingdom, and have been sentenced to death under King Rubarb. You must face the royal court so as to be judged on what form of death you merit. Under command of King Rubarb, you will comply. However," he continued, "If you do not, I am under orders to bring you in dead."

The girl bowed. "Sir, I am aware of the Prince's murder, but not at my hands. I swear by my mother's grave I did not poison the Prince. I have no knowledge of poisons or herbs or the such, and so have no way to have committed the act even if I had intended to do so."

A moment of silence, then Kelgare spoke again, dismissing the girl's words. "I have given you the King's orders. Comply."

Her heart racing, the girl turned and fled into the trees. But the assassin was well trained in his art, and hastily lifted the blowgun to his lips. A moment later, a whistle through the air and a sharp sting to the girl's neck. And yet, she kept running, even as the poison from the dart flooded through her veins.

Yes, the assassin was well trained, but he was not as wiry and quick as the young woman. She outran and lost him soon, and faded into the forest. She ran until the poison no longer let her, and collapsed. Fire burned through her veins, paralyzing her, and her vision failed her completely. Her limbs grew numb and lifeless. She convulsed and shook with seizures. And as she lay there under the stars and towering forest canopy, she knew she was breathing her last breaths because of a crime she didn't commit.

Through the burning and agony, an instinct tugged at her, from deep inside. Her mind folded into itself, tucking her spark of consciousness into the place rarely reached by most but one that was all too familiar to her. Retreating, all sense of her surroundings faded away. For how long, she knew not.

Nearby, a mother wolf heard the girl's struggle and thought it to be an orphaned cub's cries. So she found the girl, sniffing her and examining her. And though she was first perplexed by the strange 'cubs' appearance and convulsions, she felt a closeness with her, a sort of connection that would soon blossom into a fierce protectiveness over her. She took the girl's garment in her jaws and dragged her to the nearby river. It was a lazy river, one that snaked slowly throughout the mountains without much of a current. But the water was fresh, and by some instinct, the mother wolf knew that that is what the girl needed.

She submerged the girl into the river, once, twice, thrice, and then held the girl under until she tried to breathe and inhaled the water. Then, the wolf dragged her back to the bank and placed her paw into the girl's mouth to cause her to gag and cough up the water. The girl did so, coughing up the water from her lungs and stomach along with enough of the poison to spare her life.

The wolf then cared for her until she came back to health, and after, the girl became a natural part of the wolf's pack. She used the skills she had been taught to hunt using a bow and arrows she'd made. She played with the other cubs, hunted with the wolves, and patrolled their territory with them. She could feel the minds of the animals in the forest, especially the wolves and the wolf-birds, better known as ravens. She was one of them.

Motherwolf loved the girl as if she was her own cub. Alphawolf respected her. And all the others trusted her with their lives and the lives of their cubs. Through their minds and senses, the girl and the wolves understood each other well.

There came a day when Alphawolf gave the girl a name. He noticed her keen senses and light footedness, along with her incredible hunting abilities. Most importantly, the way she could move through the forest without making a single sound. The name could not be properly translated to this language, for it came not through a language but through feeling and speaking of one mind to another. The closest translation of the name is Tala, meaning, Stalkingwolf.

Tala thrived with the pack, and though it hadn't killed her, the poison had affected her permanently. It caused her to have tremors and seizures at random, putting her in extremely vulnerable situations frequently. So she never hunted or strayed from the pack alone.

And all the while, the assassin reported her dead, loosely, since he didn't have the body for proof.

That girl was me.

Chapter Two

Some things just cannot be explained. And some things are better left unexplained, even if there is an explanation. Some things one can never speak of. And some things can only be held in the depths of one's heart. Some of these things you know of, some things you don't. But it is one thing to feel, and another thing to understand, and yet an entirely different thing to know, with certainty, those things that trickle through your heart and deep within your mind. Truths never uttered from the lips, yet truths that all are aware of. From the birds in the air to the grass on the ground, from the largest beasts and purest souls, to the water flowing through the mountains to the blood coursing through your veins— all feel those truths.

But it is one thing to feel, another thing to understand, and another to know.

All feel. Not all understand. And rarely ever does someone know.

My name is Tala, cub of Motherwolf. Named by Alphawolf, I strove to live up to my name. I'd never had a name before, save Stablegirl, the name the palace guard called me. But I'd never had an attachment to that name. In order for one to have a name, it must hold meaning and truth to the one. One should be able to hear a name and know whose it was by their character, skills, and heart.

Motherwolf is mate to Alphawolf, and she mothered many of the pack cubs. She was best at it, better than the other female wolves, obvious by the healthy, strong, long–living pups she produced and raised. Alphawolf is alpha, leader to the pack, and that was clear by the way he carried himself and by the sacrifice and courage he displayed for his pack. Omegawolf is second to Alphawolf and his mate, and he would be successor if something were to befall Alphawolf. There were many others in the pack, but each lived up to their name and status in the pack. Each were part of the web–like network that is the pack– many individuals, one mind.

I shared a den with the other wolves: Swiftwolf, Songwolf, Wise-wolf, Strongwolf, Moonwolf, Slywolf, Nightwolf, Omegawolf, and Alphawolf. Motherwolf stayed in the small alcove of the den with all of the pups who hadn't earned their names yet. I liked spending time with the pups, and they quickly took a liking to me. A little too much of a liking, Motherwolf often complained when they tried to venture after me when I hunted.

Often, when I'd venture closer to the paths of the Highland King-dom, I had to make sure a certain pup didn't follow me there. She was the youngest of the pups that year— sharp sky eyes and dark fur much like Nightwolf's. She had spirit, reminding me of myself, and I believed she had already earned her name. The other wolves didn't recognize it yet, because of her youth, but I called her Spiritpup, though I made certain to keep it under wraps so as not to disrespect Alphawolf. But I knew Spiritpup was thrilled with her name. Many times I reminded her not to trail along with me when I hunted close to the Kingdom, but frequently I found her at my heels anyway, reaching her mind to mine.

Wait, Stalkingwolf! Watch you hunt, I must. Learn I will! Quiet I'll be!

No, Spiritpup, I shoot back. *Not safe for a young one like you. Go back to Motherwolf.*

Motherwolf warm, but hunt I want to learn. Make kill, good food. Fun! Be with you I want also.

Well...alright. Just stay close and listen. Next time you stay back.

When I'd seldom cross the Kingdom's paths, I'd notice the wanted flyers pinned to the trees, with a reward of high pay advertised if found dead or alive, and a sketch of my face. They remind me of who I am, but they also remind me of what I was blamed for. Though I knew the Prince's death wasn't my fault, guilt weighed on my heart. I had brought that poisoned bottle of wine to his chambers. I had been the one that hadn't sensed the deceit in the Queen and stopped her before she murdered her own son. Me. A spy with the Keen— the Demise.

And no one would ever know the truth. Only I knew it. They have a woman ruling them who murdered her own kin. Her child. And they'll never know.

I had been with the pack for two years now, and was almost sixteen winters old. I was woven into the finely knit network of everything around me, and was content. When something was stirred, I felt it.

But I also knew what I left behind. And I still felt the dwindling connection to him.

Prince Sabian. My twin brother.

Though I had no memory of him, I've always felt him. And since he'd been ripped from me, I felt a piece was missing from myself. But I still felt him. I knew when he was in danger, or having a strong emotion, was in pain, or anything of the like, I felt it. Many times I've reached to his mind, but every time I was blocked. First, confusion. Then, an impenetrable wall of guardedness. So, I soberly pulled back, regrettably aware of the sever between us and unsure if it would ever be amended or restored.

Brother or not, we were connected. And I knew he possessed the Keen just as I did, though if he was aware of it, I did not know.

I only wished to know him one day, and share the connection we were meant to have. I longed with all my heart that he didn't believe me to be a murderer. Even if he didn't know we were siblings. And most of all, I hoped he didn't allow others to diminish who he was, or to break him down– or even worse– break him into something he's not.

Stalkingwolf.

I was pulled from my thoughts as Motherwolf padded to my side. I adjusted my position against the oak I was leaning against and slid down to crouch next to her and meet her eyes— amber, deep and reading me.

My cub, your mind wanders.

I smiled. *Yes, Motherwolf. My mind wanders.*

She tucked her haunches beneath her and placed a paw on my knee, her white tipped fur glistening like snow in the sunlight.

Calm. Stay present to what is around you. That is what matters. Not what suffers your mind.

I nodded. *Wisewolf.*

Motherwolf snorted what can only be named a laugh. *Wisewolf is Wisewolf's name. Though folly would have it that my mate did not name me with wisdom.*

He should have.

Hush. She tilted her head knowingly. *You've had another fit. Haven't you? That is why you lean on this tree and your eyes droop.*

Yes. I avoided her gaze. *I tire of them, Motherwolf. They seize me without a moment's warning. When I'm hunting, sleeping, patrolling our territory. . .I cannot go on this way.*

You must. You have no other choice, young one.

I know. It doesn't make it any easier, though.

Motherwolf got to her paws and nosed me to my feet. *Come. Fresh, cool water will do you good. This summer heat is bound to make you worse.*

And yet the winter cold makes it worse, too.

Stop complaining, Stalkingwolf. As a pack we bear your burdens with you. You are not alone. Complaining will change nothing. Now come.

She was right. I got up and followed her on shaky legs. True, the summer heat made my tremors and seizures worse and more numerous, likewise with the winter cold, but it was also true that the pack made my life possible. Motherwolf was right; I shouldn't complain.

The river was swift and cold as it always was, regardless of the temperature. It did do me good, and I laughed and thanked Motherwolf as she splashed me while I drank.

The evening coolness was welcomed by the pack. During the day, the pack spent most of their time lying in the shade. Evening and night— and when the moon was bright— was when the pack was most active.

Motherwolf and I found all of the pups out of the den, chasing and nipping each other, yipping and annoying the older wolves. Ravens hopped about with them, enjoying the play, but when Motherwolf entered the midst, the pups grew still and shook out their coats, and the ravens scattered, squawking.

Spiritpup came and nuzzled my leg. *Finally! Stalkingwolf, hunt will we?*

Later, young one. If Alpha permits.

She snuffed. *He won't. I'm too young, he says. Too small.*

Hush. He can understand you as well as I.

No, he does not. He does not understand me like you do. Not at all.

I mean he can hear you as well as I. Don't disrespect him.

She fell silent, but she stayed at my side as she always did when I was near. She caught a bit of my buckskin pant leg and began pulling at it. I scolded her, but to no avail. The other pups bowled her over and began tugging at my pants as well.

Enough, Motherwolf barked. *Stalkingwolf needs rest.*

Reluctantly, they obeyed. All except for Spiritpup. She continued on, but I didn't mind. She was quite tiny compared to the other pups, and her pull was not strong and didn't bother me. She tagged along as

I followed Motherwolf to the den per her demand. I sat down against the stonewall of the den and sighed. I did need rest.

No hunting tonight, Stalkingwolf, Motherwolf commanded. *Sleep until sunrise. I will tell Alphawolf, do not worry.*

She left me alone, save Spiritpup. She pranced around me, her tongue lolling. *They leave, then we hunt!*

I laughed. *I need sleep.*

She tilted her head. Confusion. *More shaking? More pain?*

Yes. But I will be okay.

Finally, Spiritpup laid down beside me and rested her head on my lap, relenting, understanding. *With you, I stay.*

I didn't have the strength to reply, but I knew she felt my gratitude as I slipped into sleep. With her at my side, I never felt alone. I had a connection with all the wolves, all the animals. But Spiritpup was special.

Once, last winter, a hunter had been spotted by Slywolf, and the pack all had to go further into the mountains for a while. But as we were heading away, I started having tremors again, and fell behind. Soon, the tremors turned into a seizure. Up ahead, Spiritpup, who was just old enough to walk, stopped where she was and sat down facing my direction. She refused to move, and that was when the others realized my absence and came back for me. That was only one of many things the young pup had done for me, and proved our deep connection.

No, your other left, Spiritpup. Around the pine, not the oak.

Oh! My mistake!

I was hunting with the pup, teaching her how to properly stalk and surround prey with a hunting partner. Typically, it was easier for me to hunt alone. My human scent tended to scare off prey, and so for the sake of the pack, I usually stuck to hunting alone, because I was more successful that way. As were they. But Spiritpup always insisted on coming along, and she prefered my teaching to her father's, despite my human hunting methods.

Crouch, and wait. No! I said wait!

The pup took off towards the rabbit, on light paws, but she made the mistake of carelessly storming through a cluster of bush, scaring the prey. Her legs were still too short to be able to catch up to the swift hare, so I drew back an arrow and let it fly.

I plucked the arrow from the prey a short moment later. *You must have patience. Patience is key.*

Patience? I know not that human word.

Right. It was easy to forget that there were some concepts only humans perceived. I did my best to explain in a better way.

Waiting is patience. Be eager, but do not rush. Strike only when the time is right.

She understood that. But I could feel the impatience in her, even if she didn't know the word for it. She was growing quickly, in both mind and body. She mirrored her father's determination and fierce loyalty, but she looked like his littermate, Nightwolf, with her sleek obsidian pelt— a shadow among the pack. But Spiritpup's sky blue eyes were uniquely her own, echoing only the sky. Her legs faded into a silver gradient. She would grow into a beautiful, wild thing.

I hadn't talked or interacted with any humans since I left their territory. Really, this land was theirs according to maps and borders with other Kingdoms, but it wasn't truly. This land– the forests, the mountains, the trees and rivers and lakes– it all belonged to the animals. Occasionally, hunters came. But they never strayed far from the trails. They had patterns, too. They hunted in practically the same places, at around the same times. It was easy to avoid them.

Once or twice, I spotted the Crown Assassin from a distance, flanked by someone smaller than him, on horseback. My senses told me that they searched for someone, likely me, but I couldn't know for sure. And I wasn't planning on finding out the hard way.

Sometimes I daydreamed and my mind wandered. I'd think about the animals at the animal keep, and my duties as part of the royal guard. I missed the warm shelter of the barns and horse stalls during the winter, but I didn't miss the way most would treat me. I did wonder sometimes what it would be like to have a place there again, though I knew that could never be.

But I was content within the pack, part of the oneness of all things, part of the balance of nature. I continued to grow in skills, and continued to have seizures. Spiritpup grew to near full size, and was soon called Spiritwolf. Our bond was seamless, almost as if we were one. Things stayed within the routine of the pack, and I didn't expect anything to change.

But balance makes sure the things you least expect come to unfold the moment you least expect them.

It was spring, and I had out-grown any sort of clothing I had come up with. The pack and I were passing near a village of the Lowland Kingdom, and I decided I'd take a risk.

I fell to the back of our pack, where Alphawolf was, keeping it together from behind and guarding from any attacks. *Alpha.*

Stalkingwolf.

I did my best to explain to him my intention. *I wish to find my littermate in the warm season, but I cannot do so without a proper pelt, lest I be seen. I will go into the human place near here and find myself a good pelt.*

I could sense the confusion in him as he paused and shook out his gray and white fur from the spring rain.

I do not understand your wish to find your littermate, for surely it is a dangerous quest? I do understand your wish for a pelt. You are human, and do not have reliable fur to protect you. Just be alert. Pack will be west of human place when the sun falls beneath the sky.

I thanked him for his approval and then tracked off away from the pack and towards where I knew a trail into the village lay, though I would only follow it from the cover of the forest. No sooner was I out of sight from the pack, I sensed Spiritwolf close behind me.

I waited, and she stepped out from the brush.

Not this time, Spiritwolf. I have to go alone.

She snorted droplets from her nose. *You know I won't obey you.*

I know. But I know you will be wise. And following me into the village is not wise.

She shifted her weight on the melting slush underpaw. *I will be near. Will not follow. Only be near. Village dangerous for you as well as it is for me.*

I sighed, but I relented. *Stay out of sight.*

She bounded away and was invisible within the time it took me to blink twice. But I could feel her keeping very close as I made my way to the village. I needed to be careful about this. I was dressed in my makeshift buckskin clothes, but they didn't do much for warmth or covering, especially with how much I had grown. And I didn't want anyone to recognize me.

I found the edge of the village, where squat cottages were scattered here and there, and then slowly clustered more and more together the deeper into the village one went, smoke billowing from their chimneys. I caught the scent of human food– baking bread, cooking soups and vegetables, frying meats, and sweet herbs, seasonings and pastries, making my mouth water. Since I left to be with the wolves, I'd only ever eaten rabbit, deer, quail, and the occasional wild berries that I picked– plainly cooked over a fire without any seasonings. The memories of the human food tastes were renewed with the scent wafting on the breeze.

I crept past the houses, careful to avoid anyone outside or their tethered dogs, and I put my mental shield up to keep the dogs from sensing me nearby. I managed to get to the marketplace part of town without being spotted and caught sight of a fabric stand selling fabrics of all kinds and a few simple sewn tunics. I locked on my target and moved in while the stand's owner was busy helping customers. I snatched one of the tunics, a forest green one with a dark brown leather belt, and got out of there quickly. I didn't let down my guard even as I left the village and I made sure no one was on my tail before I finally stopped. I wasn't out of breath from running, I had grown adapted to running long distances without growing breathless, so this was an easy, simple task.

I paused beside an old, battered down, abandoned hut. Part of it looked burned down, and clutter of what had been inside was strewn about on the ground beside what was left of the door as if its former inhabitants had tried to save as much as they could. Broken glass lay shattered on the ground at the base of where a window used to be. I saw my reflection and studied it. I couldn't remember the last time I had seen a reflection of myself.

I had somewhat forgotten how I looked. Wow, I'd definitely grown. My auburn hair was to my waist, and though I hadn't brushed it in who knows how long, I'd somewhat kept it, and it didn't seem too unruly. My skin was tanned from my constant being in the sun, and my eyes were hazel brown– in the light they looked almost rusty. I'd never been very concerned about what I wore, unless it was my uniform back while I was still a royal guard– but what I had on now was simply unacceptable. Even to the most tomboyish, careless gal.

Quickly, I changed into the tunic and discarded my scrap clothing. It went past my knees, and the leather belt fit perfectly. Good, it wouldn't get in the way of my hunting or going about through the forest.

Next, I ran my finger through my hair and sighed at my reflection. I rolled my eyes at myself for caring, but I did. I looked terrible. Dirt and grime smeared my face and legs, and my arms and legs were scraped and bruised. I trembled almost constantly, and the whites of my eyes had a yellowish tint from the sickness that the poison had brought me.

Finally, I clenched my jaw and opted to braid my hair. I still remembered how to do it, which was satisfying. Once my hair was braided and tied with a scrap of leather, I felt a little better. It wasn't like anyone was going to see me anyway.

I went through the scattered things on the ground to see if I could find anything to add to my collection of useful things– which only consisted of a dagger, staff, bow, and arrows that I made myself. I found nothing worth my attention, so I started to head back into the forest.

Spiritwolf, I reached out.

Nothing.

Strange.

I stopped in my tracks and stood still, reaching out with my mind, feeling for the wolf. I felt our bond at the back of my mind, as always, but I couldn't feel her nearby physically. And she wouldn't respond to me. It wasn't like her at all.

Maybe she just returned to the pack? I thought. But I knew she hadn't. She wouldn't. Not without me. And tethered to our bond, I felt a tug of fear from her, and pain, but she was too far away from me for her to respond to my calls.

I tilted my head in concentration.

East. She was somewhere to the East of me.

I started off, confused to find that the further I went, the further she felt from me. But somehow I knew I was going in the right direction.

It pained me when the sun dipped below the horizon. I knew that the pack would be too far from the village now for me to catch up before tomorrow, even if I were still in the village. But I was about thirty miles from it now. By morning it would take me at least three days to catch up with them. Besides, I would not abandon Spiritwolf.

So I continued on, keeping my senses sharp. My bond to Spiritwolf brought me back into the Highland Kingdom territory.

I ventured for four days, with just a few hours to rest every night, and to stop to hunt for something to eat. But I kept my breaks short, because I was worried. It perplexed me how quickly Spiritwolf had gotten so very far, and how it felt like she kept moving further the closer I got to her.

On the dawn of the fifth day, I was drawing uncomfortably close to the palace grounds and the city, Quinton. I had just finished a small grouse that I'd hunted, and was sliding the arrow back into my leather quiver. I slung my bow over my shoulder and got to my feet with a stretch.

Suddenly, I grew lightheaded with a strong sense of Spiritwolf nearby. Very close. My heart soared. Finally! I relaxed with relief and opened myself to her, letting my mind guard down so that we could reach each other, and so that I could sense where exactly she was. That's where I made my mistake.

A force crashed into my mind like a tidal wave, startling me. I gasped as the force deepened, penetrating my mind like a hot knife through butter, searing at me. It felt as though someone was rummaging through all exposed parts of my mind. I stumbled around blindly, grasping my head and gasping, desperately forcing the other from my mind and pulling my shield back up.

It was like struggling with a bear, the force was so strong and unwittingly persistent. I'd never experienced anything like it before. It was draining me physically, and I gripped a low branch of a tree and leaned on it.

Back! Get back! Leave me alone!

Ah, but there is something I must do first.

As it responded, I pushed at it in panicked defense. I blocked it away, and for a moment, it worked. I sensed surprise and frustration from the other as I pushed it away. But then it pushed back at me again with tripled force, piercing my mind so much that I physically stumbled forward in pain as if someone had pushed me from behind.

I heard an ear piercing *snap*, and then pain like I'd never experienced before shot up my leg. I shrieked in agony, looking down to find that I'd stepped directly into a small bear trap. Blood already glazed the melting slush around the trap, and more seeped from around the trap's teeth sunken deep into my leg.

The force in my mind was satisfied and fled from me.

Pain took over my consciousness, and I collapsed, the blackness at the edges of my vision taking over completely.

Soft fur nuzzled against my face, bringing me back to consciousness.

Stalkingwolf. Stalkingwolf!

I opened my eyes and found Spiritwolf at my side. She tilted her head at me, concern in her sky eyes. *You were straying so far! Wandering around as if in search of something. I kept trying to reach you but you kept pushing me away so that it was difficult for me to follow you. From a distance I heard you yelp in pain and finally found you.*

Confusion gripped me. *But. . .you were in danger. I was trying to find you. But you kept moving further and further away. . .*

No. I was fine. You *were moving further and further away.*

I blinked. *So it wasn't you, in pain and danger? I could feel it.*

No. It wasn't me.

Someone had orchestrated the whole thing. On *purpose.* I shivered as chills traveled down my spine. Someone out there had the Keen and was very skilled with it– more so than I. They had targeted me. But why? And. . .

I forced myself to look back at my trapped, bleeding leg. It was a gruesome mess. They had caused me to end up directly here, in this trap. And so close to the Royal Grounds.

I had to get out of here. Now.

I managed to sit up, and studied the bear trap. My bone wasn't broken, but the teeth of the trap had definitely bit into my bone in more than one place. So fractured, at least. But the teeth were embedded there. The circulation was cut off, leaving my foot numb and purple. It made me terribly nauseous, but I forced myself to take a deep breath and tried to pry it open. No luck. It only caused the pain to worsen and I gritted my teeth to keep myself from crying out.

Spiritwolf whined with concern, feeling my pain. *Don't. You'll only hurt yourself more.*

But danger is near. I have to get away.

I was trembling, and breathing laboriously. The trembling quickly turned into another unavoidable seizure. I faded in and out of consciousness, shaking violently and unaware of my surroundings. The pain that wracked my body, from head to toe, that I'd experienced when I'd been poisoned returned every time I had a seizure. This time was no exception. Oil boiled inside my head and insides, while fire seared my veins. I drowned from the inside out, lucky to get in the few gasping breaths I could manage.

And then, nothing. Just a void of darkness.

When I awoke, all I was aware of was my throbbing head and sore, completely exhausted body.

Then, I heard a horse snort, and I started. I realized that Spiritwolf was standing over me in a defensive stance, her ears pulled flat against her head and her teeth bared. I was aware of a human mind, close by, as well as a horse's. I panicked and managed to sit up, leaning my back heavily against the tree.

Before me, a few yards or so away, stood a young man, holding on to the reins of his saddled horse. He was dressed in the simple way of the royal servants, in leather boots, woolen leggings, and a gray tunic with a leather belt. He also wore a woolen cloak against the early spring cold. His gray eyes were concerned as they stared at me, and his black hair hung past his ears, but not quite to the shoulder.

"Miss?"

My heart raced, and I forced myself to steady my breathing. It felt strange to hear someone speak the human language directly to me. But though I could feel genuine concern radiating from him, I did not trust him. I had mistaken my attacker's prods in my mind for genuine feelings, and they had been entirely false. . . .wait, how long had it been since I was trapped?

Two days, Stalkingwolf. Spiritwolf snarled at the man, but she kept her mind focused on me as if to stabilize me. *I was afraid the shaking and pain had killed you.*

The man gave no notice of the exchange between us. He stepped closer, reaching out. "Miss, has the beast harmed you?"

Spiritwolf took a stride towards him, driving him back.

"Stay away from me," I croaked. The words felt foreign on my tongue after going so long without uttering a single human word.

He tilted his head, his eyebrows furrowing. "But. . .Miss, you're bleeding terribly and are trapped there. I wish to help you." He took a tentative step towards me, and I felt Spiritwolf hesitate.

He does not wish harm, Stalkingwolf. I do not trust either, but perhaps he is the only way to save you from the trap.

No. Out loud, "I said stay away from me!" I slid my dagger from my belt and held it out in front of me defensively, but my leg protested at the sudden jerk of movement. I groaned in pain, nearly dropping the dagger.

Keep him away, Spiritwolf. Please.

Spiritwolf didn't protest. She leaped at the man, but not to cause harm. Simply to invoke fear. He stumbled back, sprung upon his horse and sped away.

I steadied my breathing, hardly relaxing. Now they knew I was here. I didn't think the man recognized me, as I had changed in appearance quite a bit, but even so. I was trapped here until they came and realized who I was. I figured my head would not still be part of my body by the end of tomorrow.

For hours, I shifted from being conscious to only partially conscious. I startled at every slight sound.

My anxiety drew itself up to a peak as I finally heard the sound of horses drawing near through the trees. It was almost dusk, the sun brushing against the horizon and turning the sky deep orange and scarlet like so much blood.

There were two approaching this time, I sensed. Both had their own horse. One of the men was the one from before, but the other was not. But as I dared to try to sense who it might be, I realized with a jolt that the mind connected to mine, reaching tentatively just as I was doing. But not in a latching, forceful way. But more like how a button fits perfectly into a button hole.

Even before we saw each other, we considered each other. The person felt confused and tense at the connection of our minds, but there tugged at him a sense that this was familiar. To me, the mind was so familiar, so warm and comforting like a memory from long ago. A piece I had been missing and longing for for so very long. And I sensed he felt this, too. But he did not understand it as I did.

It was my brother.

They rounded the thicket of brush in front of me and unmounted their horses. The man with the black hair held the reins of both horses as Spiritwolf stood over me like she had before. Prince Sabian was dressed similarly to his companion, but his fabrics were clearly finer and more appropriate for royalty, and instead of gray, were dark Carmen. A sheathed sword hung at his belt. His auburn hair was shorter than his companion's, cut close to his head, and his eyes were a brilliant emerald green.

He studied the situation carefully, his eyes widening as he saw my leg. Then he locked eyes with me. He was confused at the familiarity between us, since he had no memory of me. The royals had wiped my name and existence from his life like a drought to a well. But there he was, and there I was. It was not simple, and yet it wasn't complicated.

Spiritwolf snarled, but she was confused. *I feel him. He is aware as you are. He can feel. He is a kindred spirit.*

He is my brother, I responded. *We can trust him. Allow him to pass. And go, so as not to scare them, but stay nearby.*

She relaxed her hackles and turned to look me in the eye, then trotted away into the undergrowth reluctantly.

Cautiously, Sabian approached, looking baffled for a moment over the exchange he had felt between the wolf and I, and her sudden departure. But he came steadily to me, his hands held out in a placating gesture.

"I do not wish to harm you. I only wish to help."

I didn't have the strength to reply just then, between my pain, exhaustion, and the shock at finally meeting my brother.

He came to me and crouched, while behind him his companion said, "I said the same thing, but she and that beast wouldn't let me near."

Sabian and I exchanged a knowing, wordless look. Then he called over his shoulder, "Aiden, bring me the satchel with the supplies, would you?" He began to study the trap while Aiden went through the saddlebags, then came over to us with a cloth bag and crouched beside the prince.

"That is sunk deep," he observed, wincing, as he watched Sabian gently run his fingers over the different parts of the trap.

"Indeed."

Aiden gave me a sympathetic, concerned look. "How did you end up in this thing? And why have you wandered so far from town on your own?"

"Don't batter her," Sabian chided him. He looked up at me and warned, "I'll do my best, but this is going to hurt an awful lot."

I nodded in resignation, gritting my teeth.

Sabian pulled a knife from his belt and inserted it into the trap. It didn't touch or cut my leg, but I tensed. With the knife and his other hand, he began to pry the trap open slowly. I was ashamed at how I cried out. I could feel each of the trap's metal teeth as they grinded bit by bit from my bone. My vision blackened at the edges, and I slammed my head back against the trunk of the tree, crying out.

Finally, Sabian's strained, rushed voice said, "Get her leg out now! Hurry! I can't hold it open any longer."

Aiden gently but quickly pulled my leg out and rested it on the ground as Sabian let go of the trap, which slammed shut with a horrible, metallic *snap*. My leg was in agony, a painful, terribly bloody mess, but it was free. I went limp with dizziness for a long moment.

Sabian went straight to work. He cleaned the wound and applied ointment, and then bandaged it well. It seemed as if he'd done this more than once before. When he was finished, he asked quietly, "Are you in much pain?"

I didn't answer, afraid that I'd answer truthfully. He understood.

"Where is your residence? I can help you there," he offered. I simply met his eyes. There was confusion in them.

"Maybe she is in too much pain to respond?" Aiden suggested.

Sabian didn't answer him, he just kept his eyes on me. "I have a place nearby where you could shelter until you heal." Without waiting for me to respond in any way, he pulled my arm around his shoulders, to which Aiden did the same. They helped me onto Sabian's mare and he mounted behind me, saying, "Aiden, go on ahead of us to the shepherd's cabin and get a fire going at the hearth. Also, boil some water." He kept me steady as he reined his horse and started after Aiden.

His hand gently brushed the back of my neck as he draped his cloak over me. "You're burning up."

I didn't respond. It was all I could do to keep myself conscious.

I was hardly aware when we arrived at the small cabin. Sabian carried me inside and laid me on a bed opposite the hearth which was warm from the fire burning inside. Immediately, I fell asleep despite myself.

"No, that wouldn't be wise. If I encouraged King Rubarb to do that, then I'd be putting a target on my back."

"But if what you said is true, then it might be the only way to survive the war."

"No, Aiden. It's too risky. I won't. If I reveal myself, then I'll always be in danger."

"But—"

"No. I won't do it."

Their voices woke me. My senses told me that it was still nighttime. I could feel Spiritwolf just outside the cabin, prowling and worrying.

Calm, friend. I am alright.

I could sense her relief. *Safe?*

Yes, safe.

Good. I shall hunt. And she was gone.

I rolled onto my side, careful of my leg, which had clearly been freshly bandaged since when I'd fallen asleep. Sabian and Aiden were both staring at me, having noticed that I was awake. Sabian asked, "How are you feeling?"

I took a deep breath. I was safe. I didn't have to worry. . .and yet I did. Cautiously, I answered, "Sore."

Sabian and I locked eyes once more. I reached to his mind, gently, *You can feel this, too.*

He physically started, his eyes widening. *I. . .no! I–* He stopped. Out loud, he said, "Aiden, go check the trap line. And bring something back for us to eat. Don't let anyone see you."

Aiden looked confused, but he nodded in obedience to his prince and put on his cloak. He stepped out into the night, closing the cabin door firmly behind him.

I sat up and let my good leg down to dangle over the side of the bed, but kept my injured leg stretched out straight. Sabian stood from where he was sitting at the table and brought a chair over to the bed, sitting down.

"The other day," he began, "I was going about my duties and my leg erupted in pain. Terrible, excruciating pain. I collapsed, crying out, but had no visible injury. The pain faded shortly afterwards. A while later, my friend and stablehand, Aiden, came to me, telling me that he found a girl who had stepped into a trap. I kept it between us, because I found it strange. And I'm glad I did."

I stared down at my hands in my lap. "Why?"

Sabian swallowed hard. "Because. . .When the pain came, my surroundings changed. I seemed to suddenly be somewhere else. Someone else." He shivered. "I was a young woman, and I had stepped into a trap. When the pain faded, so did the vision. That's why when Aiden told me what he found. . .I felt it was best to keep it to myself."

"You've felt things like this before." I looked at him. "Haven't you?" More as a statement than a question.

He blinked, as if I had struck him. "Yes," he said, finally. "Yes. Ever since I can remember. As if I were connected to someone. Sometimes, I feel a prod at my mind, but I push it away." His emerald eyes pierced mine. "That was you, wasn't it? We're connected. I felt it as soon as I saw you. I knew. . ."

"Yes," I said simply. "We are."

"But. . ." He stood up in denial, shaking his head. "But that means you have the Demise." He looked ill. "I have it."

I didn't say anything as he paced around, gripping his sword hilt so tight his knuckles turned white. Finally, he took a deep breath and sat down again, composing himself.

"So, you've known this since. . .?"

"Since forever."

I could feel him teetering on the edge of knowing the truth. He rocked back and forth, considering everything over and over again. Remembering things, feelings, and truths he felt from within.

Quietly, he said, "You're my sister."

My eyes stung with tears of joy from hearing those words. "I never thought I would hear you say that."

He met my eyes. "I always had this feeling, like–"

"A piece of you was missing," I finished for him. He nodded, then continued softly, "I always thought I was just strange. Then I learned about the Demise, and I was angry with myself for having it. I was terrified someone would find out. But. . ." He gave me a pained look. "I have a sister. And they never told me."

"Twin sister," I managed a small smile. "You know who sired us, right?"

"Of course," he sighed. "I can't go a day without being reminded of that."

"The royals didn't want any extra reminders of that than necessary," I said quietly. "I was near you, though. I even worked at the palace for a while. And I tried to seek you out, but you were always surrounded by people and guards. I never got a chance."

Sabian covered his mouth with his hand, taking in a shaky breath. "I. . .I can't believe I never saw you. Surely. . ."

I shook my head. "They made sure to keep everything about me far away from you. They kept me busy, as they did you. And they kept me away, always keeping an eye on me." I shivered, and I could feel the beginnings of a tremble coming on. I prayed I wouldn't go into a seizure now. "Help me to the fire?" I asked. "I've a chill."

He helped me to the hearth and into a chair, propping up my leg gently onto a soft pile of furs to keep it elevated. The warmth from the fire helped, but I felt the nagging ache in my veins that I got every time I was about to have a seizure. Or maybe it was leftover from the last one I'd had.

Now in the brighter light from the fire, Sabian studied my face. Concern was once again in his gaze.

"Must you look at me that way?" I complained.

"Your eyes," he leaned a bit closer so as to see them better, "they've a tint of illness to them."

I averted my eyes from his. "We just met, and already you're so concerned for me."

"I feel as though I've known you all my life," he whispered. Then, more audibly, "What ails you?"

I swallowed. "Prince Farlay was poisoned, you remember. But I was blamed."

"That was you?"

"I didn't poison him, if that's what you're at. But I was blamed. No one would believe me. So I ran. But the assassin came after me. Poison dart to my neck. I survived, but I haven't gone a day without having a seizure since."

"You're still ill," he stated the obvious. "And you've been on your own since. How did you survive?"

"What you call the Demise saved me. And I've been with a wolf pack. They care for me, and I them."

"Wolves. . ." he marveled. "That's why that wolf was there, back at the trap with you."

I nodded.

"Well I know you didn't poison Prince Farlay. That much I can assure you." Sabian handed me a tin cup of water. "And I will not mention anything about you to anyone. And neither will Aiden."

I gave him a doubtful, worried look, to which he responded, "He is trustworthy. He is more so my best friend than my servant."

"I trust you," I said. "So I trust who you trust."

Silence stretched between us for a moment. Then, I asked, "So what is a prince like you doing out here? What if they ask that?"

He managed a sly smile. "I'm out hunting with Aiden."

I snorted. "They'd believe that?"

He shrugged. "As long as we come back with something. He and I have gone hunting before, just the two of us."

I shook my head. "You shouldn't be helping me. If anyone finds out, they'll–"

"No one will find out," he promised.

I was still uneasy. "No," I persisted. "I was trapped on purpose. Someone got into my head. They know where I am."

Sabian narrowed his eyes. "That's possible? A mental attack? On purpose?"

"I didn't know it before now, but yes." I looked him dead in the eyes. "Have you felt anything like that lately? Anything like that at all?"

He shook his head. "No. I thought I was the only one alive with the Demise. Other than you. Ever since I was little, they always taught me how terrible and wicked the Demise is, and how each person who has it must be slain lest they become mere beasts. So I just. . .I just denied that I had it. I hid it. It is my most guarded secret. But you've learned its ways. You had to in order to survive. You understand how it works."

I struggled to explain it. "It is something one can really only understand when one experiences it first hand. Most of it is instinct. The rest comes with openness towards the ones you wish to Keen to. That is the hardest part. Staying guarded, yet open."

"The Keen," he repeated as the firelight danced across his face. "I've read that term before. In the old scrolls about the Demise, that is what they called it."

"The ones of the past were wise," I said quietly. Suddenly, my hand began to shake, and soon it took over my arm, and then my whole body was convulsing as I slipped into a seizure. I was hardly aware as Sabian managed to carry me back to the bed and hold my flailing limbs down. I could feel the panic in him. But he kept himself composed. Darkness swept over me once again.

When I woke, sunlight was spilling in through the cabin window. Aiden was adding more wood to the fire while Sabian was cleaning a hare. I sat up, groggily rubbing my eyes. The pain in my leg was less, but the fatigue from the seizure was overwhelming.

"You know what this means, right?" Aiden was saying, not having noticed that I was awake. "She's a princess. Another heir to the throne."

"Indeed," Sabian answered. "That hardly matters though. She can't show her face there. They'll finish what they didn't two years ago."

"Still," Aiden brushed off his hands, "This could change things."

Sabian looked up from the hare, who's scent was making my mouth water, and gave his friend a hard look. Aiden held up his hands reassuringly. "But I swear I won't speak a word of this."

"Good," I said, to which they both jumped and jerked their gazes at me. "Because if you do, just remember that I'm a trained spy. There isn't anywhere you can go that I won't find you."

Aiden raised his eyebrows and shot Sabian a look. "Never in my life did I ever imagine hearing those words out of a princess."

"I'm not a princess," I growled. Actually growled. I realized, then caught myself. Quietly, I said, "I'm not, nor ever will be."

Aiden studied me, then Sabian. "I can see the resemblance. Auburn hair and. . . woah! You both have the same glare!"

Sabian and I exchanged annoyed glances. He sighed, then formally introduced his friend. "This is Aiden, my best friend and my servant. Though he usually forgets the last part. And," Sabian gestured to me, but then stopped. "I actually don't know your name."

I cracked a smile. *Really? Look deeper inside yourself. You know.*

He stared at me for a moment, hesitating. I added, *There aren't any royals here to punish you for it. Use your Keen.*

He bit his lip, then focused for a moment. I could sense him groping for a memory or even the tiniest knowledge inside himself regarding my name. When he opened his eyes, he whispered, "Stalkingwolf."

Aiden scrunched his eyebrows. "I'm sorry?"

"The name Alphawolf gave me," I smiled. "In our language it translates to Tala."

"Tala," Sabian repeated, testing the name on his tongue. He smiled warmly at me. Meanwhile, Aiden was struggling for a foothold in the conversation.

"Back up," he said. "Stalkingwolf? Alphawolf?"

"Her name is Tala," Sabian offered. He put a hand on his friend's shoulder. "Just stick with that. How are you feeling, Tala?"

"You don't have to ask, Sabian," I chided him. I wanted him to get used to having his ability instead of pushing it away and disgracing himself.

He reached out with his mind tentatively, as if reaching toward a flame that might burn him. *It's okay,* I reassured him. I couldn't blame him for being so hesitant. Hate for what he was was engraved in his soul by those around him. I assured him that he was in a safe place. He could be who he was.

I felt our consciousnesses entwine. He felt me, I felt him.

A moment or two, and then the connection loosened a bit. But I felt it dwindle, and I knew the bond was permanent, just like mine and Spiritwolf's.

"You're tired and sore," Sabian said. "And your leg is causing you pain. But it isn't as bad as it was before."

I nodded. "Good."

"Good?" Aiden exclaimed. "What is going on? Sabian, why do you keep closing your eyes?"

We both looked at him with a laugh. Sabian asked him, "Did you not pay attention to *anything* I told you about?"

Aiden looked back and forth between us. He did a visible double take. "Oh. You did *that*." After another hard look from Sabian, he added, "I won't tell anyone I swear."

"Do you give all your subjects that look?" I asked Sabian. "Very *princely*."

For a moment he looked confused. Then he shrugged. "Habit, I suppose."

"As long as you don't give *me* that look." I stood up and carefully put some gentle weight onto my foot. It protested painfully, but it wasn't as terrible as it had been yesterday, though the bandages were stained scarlet. I ignored the tempting rabbit meat on the table and limped to a chair, taking a seat. "Do you have more clean bandages? I need to change this before I leave."

"Before you leave?" Sabian joined me at the table. "You can hardly walk. And. . .we just met. I finally feel whole. We're finally together again. You can't just leave."

"I know, I feel the same way." I sighed. "But I told you; I can't stay here. Whoever attacked me mentally. . .they *wanted* me to get hurt. I don't want to find out why. And they know where I am. I'm not safe here. And neither are you as long as I'm around."

"You have to heal first, at least." Sabian pulled clean bandages from a satchel on the table. "You can't get by on your own with an injured leg."

I knew there would be no use arguing with him.

I clenched my jaw as I unwrapped the soiled bandages. Sabian crouched to help. The wound was still gnarly looking, and my whole lower leg was terribly bruised, but wasn't bleeding as much anymore. We got it rebandaged, and then Sabian and Aiden cooked the hare over the fire and made stew. While they did, I reached out to Spiritwolf. I hadn't sensed her nearby since yesterday, which I found strange.

She didn't answer me. So I closed my eyes and felt for her senses. Our bond allowed me to do that if she let me. She always did.

The warmth of the sun soaked through her fur as she zig-zagged through the trees. Her heart was racing, and she was breathing hard. She heard horses galloping close behind her, and human scent was strong in her nose. Fear. Urgency.

She sensed me in her mind and warned, *They're coming! Run!*

At that moment, an arrow struck her shoulder, and she yelped in pain, our connection severed.

I cried out as my shoulder screamed with pain so sudden and sharp that the force of it knocked me off my chair as if I had also been struck with an arrow.

Sabian jumped to his feet. "Tala!" He rushed to my side and helped me back up. "What happened? What's the matter?"

I gripped my shoulder, wincing. "They're coming. I have to leave *now*."

"*What?*" he exclaimed. "They're coming?"

I was still breathless, so I just nodded. I stumbled to the door and opened it, stepping into the warm sunshine just as Spiritwolf came into view. An arrow was embedded in her shoulder, and blood seeped out around it. She limped to me and leaned against my good leg. Sabian and Aiden were at my shoulders, looking both afraid and confused. I did my best to radiate calm and reassurance to my wolf, despite the panic and fear rising like bile in my throat.

I held her down by the flank. *Be still. This will hurt.*

I yanked the arrow out, and she yelped. She turned and lapped at the wound, licking away the blood.

I could hear the people coming now, their horse's heavy hooves thundering on the trail just around the bend to the cabin.

Go! I urged Spiritwolf. *Go, now!*

But—

For once, you must obey me! Go! I pointed at the forest. *Now!*

She crouched with her tail between her legs and stared at me for a moment. She could feel my fear and didn't want to leave me. But then the horses came into view and she ran, disappearing into the forest like a shadow.

Seven men astride stallions came and surrounded us. I was trapped. Out of time.

All were king's soldiers, Royal guards. All except one. Prince Rayden. Son of King Rubarb and Queen Hersha, and brother to my mother– the first heir to the throne. A tall man, slender but not as fit as Sabian. His hair was dark umber that hung to his shoulders in pampered curls, and his mustache was small and thin above his lip. He wore regal outdoors clothes in shades of red and oak, and jewels decorated his neck and fingers.

"What goes on here?" he demanded at the sight of Prince Sabian, Aiden and I. I trembled with fear, and I desperately hoped he wouldn't recognize me.

"Prince Sabian, what is it that you're doing out here accompanied only by one stablehand and a peasant girl?"

"I was hunting," Sabian responded coolly. "I came across this girl who had accidentally stepped into one of our traps. I couldn't very well just leave one of my people there, injured, could I? So I've been caring for her injuries."

Prince Rayden unmounted his horse and crossed his arms over his chest, peering at me. "Why do you look so familiar, girl?"

I curtsied as well as my leg would allow and avoided his gaze, looking down at the ground in front of me. "I suppose I just have one of those faces, my Prince."

He came uncomfortably close. "Stop mumbling, girl, and look at me."

Sabian stepped forward. "Uncle Rayden–"

"Shut up, Sabian," the older prince commanded. "Girl, heed me!" He gripped my arm and shook me roughly, forcing me to meet his gaze. His eyes widened, and he let go of me. "You're the girl who murdered my brother."

I shook my head. "No, I–"

He backhanded me so hard that I was knocked to the ground. I tasted blood in my mouth, and my hands and knees were splattered with mud. He hissed, "Don't think you'll get away with it, like you have these years. You will pay for what you've done."

I sensed Sabian's anger and fear for me and that he was about to do something really stupid, so I told him, *Don't. Don't let them think that you know who I am. We're both safer that way.*

Prince Rayden pointed at me. "Bind her."

His guards unmounted their horses and yanked me roughly to my feet, binding my hands behind my back so tightly that they cut off the circulation. Rayden came nose to nose with me, hatred in his eyes. "I can't believe you're my niece. Your death *will* be a painful one," he vowed, but quiet enough that Sabian wouldn't overhear.

Sabian put a hand on Rayden's shoulder roughly. "You've no proof that she murdered the prince."

Rayden turned his attention to him, and pointed an accusing finger. "You are nothing more than a fool. You should not be around this *beast*, lest she taint you." He turned to his men. "Back to the palace."

"No," Sabian said firmly, using his princely tone. "Do not–"

Rayden rounded on him, his voice rising. "*I* am your uncle, and the first heir to the throne. You are merely second. Therefore, my orders precede yours." He mounted his horse. "Prince Sabian, get back to the palace. You must be present for her trial."

"I won't–"

"You *will* obey, *nephew*. Guards, make sure the young prince follows closely behind me." Rayden nodded to guards holding on to me, and they turned me to face them just as one of them hefted the iron hilt of his sword and slammed it into my head. The force knocked me off my feet again, and my vision went scarlet, doubling, and then tripling.

The guard bent down and slammed the sword hilt into my head again, in the same spot, and then again. And finally, all went black.

Chapter Three

There is a thing about pain, whether that be physical or mental, that numbs a person from emotion. Many folk live with diseases that weigh heavy on their shoulders. They go about every day in pain most couldn't bear. Not only do they bear it, they work with it. They live with it. But there are days where they cannot feel anything but the pain, numbing them of all emotion.

When one who has had little to no pain suddenly feels pain, they flee into panic like a frightened hare. And yet, they compare themselves to those who feel that pain every day of their lives, as if the glimpse of pain they had felt could possibly compare to that of theirs.

And yet, those who know pain— really know pain— stay silent. We stay silent, knowing that no one could possibly understand. We diminish our own pain to ease the pain of others, and yet we always come back and remember that we are the ones who are ill.

We rejoice in the health of others, despite knowing that health will always be a foreign concept to us.

One seizure after another. I couldn't remember the last time I had so many in a row. It probably came from my fear. When I finally came to, I was still trembling from the aftermath of a fit, and fire coursed through my veins. I was lying on a cold stone ground in a dark dungeon cell. The only light was that of torchlight filtering in through the cell bars of the window in the cell door. The only sound I heard was the steady *drip, drip, drip* from somewhere down the corridor.

I sat up groggily, swaying as my head pounded painfully. I felt blood oozing from the wound that the guard had inflicted on me with his first few attempts to knock me unconscious. My leg hurt, too. One of my wrists was chained up on the wall. Both of my wrists were rubbed raw from the tight binds from earlier.

I wasn't sure how much time had passed. Hours? Days? I couldn't tell. I was weak with exhaustion, and I was hungrier than I'd ever been. My stomach kept turning into itself painfully.

I tilted my head back against the wall with a sigh. What had I gotten myself into? Surely, they were going to kill me. Why wouldn't they? They believed I killed their Prince. I wouldn't be surprised if they used some painful form of execution. But I couldn't help but think, *Is this it? Is this what I'll be known for when I'm gone– a crime I didn't commit?*

Despair threatened to creep up on me. It would be. All my skills as a spy, as a royal guard, as a caretaker of animals– all wasted. Even if they somehow decided I wasn't guilty of murder, they would still kill me just because I had the Keen. The Demise.

A tear traced down my cheek.

I remembered my earliest memories, when I lived and worked in the stables with the animals. I had been happiest there. I had a roof above my head and furry bodies around me to keep me warm during winter. The few townsfolk that would give me food were kind. I liked taking care of the sick and injured animals.

Training to be a royal guard, and then a spy, had been difficult, but most things had come naturally to me. And the Keen made spying missions much easier, because I could sense someone around a corner, or when someone was heading my way, and I could hide.

I enjoyed the spying missions, and reporting to my grandfather, King Rubarb. It gave me a sense of importance and usefulness. He was kind. And though everything he asked of me was more than difficult, I felt honored to fulfill my duties for him. I was thankful to him for allowing me a part of the royal life, even if it was in shadow.

I hadn't liked living in the royal guard's quarters nearly as much as I liked the stables, but again, a roof over my head was more than I could ask for. So I took it. And I took every opportunity to be at the stables caring for the animals that had grown so fond of me.

And then the incident happened, and I lived with the wolves. It was something to get used to, but get used to it I did. And I loved my life with them. They felt like the family I had never had.

I was only sixteen, and yet I felt like I had lived a whole lifetime already. Ironic, since it was coming to such a bitter end. I could do nothing except hope it would be a quick end.

Finally, I heard footsteps coming down the corridor, and then the cell door swung open. Three guards came into the cell. One came over to me and unchained my wrist, then said, "On your feet."

I obeyed. They handcuffed my hands behind me and roughly shoved me out of the cell. They led me down the corridor as I stumbled between them, their fast pace hard on my leg.

Corridor upon corridor, and then out into and through the courtyard. It was just the way I remembered with its center fountain, well, and cobblestones beneath the shadow of the palace. I could see the places I would stand guard with my sword for hours at a time, sometimes whole nights.

The guards took me into the palace itself, and straight to the throne room, where court was usually held. It was a grand room; candled chandeliers hung from the ceiling, colorful, intricate tapestries hung along the walls, and the royal thrones graced the central dias with their bright velvet. Usually, rows of tables piled high with feasts was the main purpose of the Grand Hall, but they were all cleared as was protocol for court.

King Rubarb was sitting upon his throne, looking disgruntled and regretful. He was a wise, muscular older man, his short, well groomed beard gray. He was dressed well in simple wealthy clothes the way he preferred. He wasn't one to primp just because of his status. The only charms that indicated his status were his simple gold band for a crown, and his royal seal ring. His wife, Queen Hersha, sat beside him on her own throne. In contrast, she seemed like a peacock in her lucious skirts and folds in all shades of violet and indigo. A crown that looked to be too big for her head and too heavy with jewels weighed upon her graying head. Eagerness was bright in her eyes, and she tapped her fingers on the arm of her throne with anticipation. Prince Rayden was pacing impatiently in front of them, while Prince Sabian stood to the side with his arms crossed and a worried, anxious expression on his face.

The King's advisor stood at his king's shoulder. A few court witnesses sat to one side, whispering to each other. And lastly, Princess Teyqa, daughter of the King, and Princess Joy, daughter of Prince Rayden, sat in one corner dressed as princesses do, with floor length gowns and silk elbow gloves. Teyqua looked utterly distressed, her eyes red and puffy from crying. Joy, the younger princess, comforted her with gentle murmurs. Typically, princesses and minor princes didn't attend trials unless they were directly involved, but apparently they had all been summoned. I was surprised not to see the king's assassin.

All of this I took note of by the time it took me to blink twice. It came from my instincts as a spy. Or, *former* spy.

As the guards shoved me into the hall, all eyes were on me. The queen cracked a sly smile, clearly excited to see me punished for something she had set up. King Rubarb looked on me with disappointment and regret, which pained me deeply. He thought me the murderer of his own son. Prince Rayden's eyes sparkled with hate at the sight of me, and quite clearly, eagerness, just like the queen's. The princesses watched me enter, their faces falling expressionless. Prince Sabian met my eyes desperately. He was worried and distressed, and he was scared. The court witnesses and advisor fell silent as the guards forced me to stand in front of the dias.

I bowed respectfully to the king that I had once served, then I held my head high and glared defiantly. They would not see me cry. I refused to glance at Sabian. I would keep him out of this and keep him safe.

For a moment, all were silent. I was painfully aware of the way I swayed on my feet as my head wound pounded and made me dizzy. My leg kept shooting pain up to my hip in agonizing twinges. I did my best not to wince.

"Girl," King Rubarb started. "You are charged with the murder of my son, Prince Farlay. It is regrettable. I thought you to be loyal and trustworthy." He leaned forward in his throne and his gaze hardened. "But you poisoned my son. Your past loyalty and achievements will not protect you now."

I took a deep breath and forced myself to hold my tongue.

King Rubarb sat back in his throne again, addressing his court. "We know the form of murder this girl used upon Prince Farlay, and we know that his death was less than quick, and was painful. But there are still things to take into consideration before we make any decisions."

"What else is there to consider?" Prince Rayden exclaimed. "She murdered him. For that alone–"

"And," the King interrupted him, "hasn't there been rumor that she possesses the Demise? We must also take into account her motives and anything she wishes to say for herself."

Prince Rayden clenched his fists until they turned white. "Yes, my liege."

The King nodded to his advisor. "You may begin, Lord Drake."

Lord Drake stepped toward me. He was a lanky man, tall and skinny and pale. "What name do you go by, girl?"

I didn't answer.

"Very well," he muttered. "Girl, then. What was it that led you to murder Prince Farlay of the Highland Kingdom?"

Instead of looking him in the eye as I answered, I locked eyes with the King. "I didn't have any motives. I've never had any reason to dislike or wish to harm the Prince. And I have no knowledge of poisons. The night before Prince Farlay was found dead, I was ordered by Queen Hersha to use my skills to bring a bottle of fine wine to her son's chambers so as to surprise him. I swear, I did not taint the wine. I did not poison Prince Farlay. If the wine was tainted, then it was before I laid my hands on it."

"Nonsense!" the Queen exclaimed. "Are you accusing me of poisoning my own son?"

I didn't answer. I simply held the king's gaze. My heart thumped wildly like a cornered animal's, and I felt clammy with sweat, fear lacing every inch of my body.

Queen Hersha reddened with fury, rising from her throne. "How *dare* you! This is preposterous! Surely you wouldn't consider believing her, would you, Rubarb?"

He was silent for a moment. Then he said, "Of course I wouldn't."

She sat back down, blanching. I suddenly realized how afraid she was that she would be called out. But I had no power against her whatsoever. I could only stand by and watch as she accused me of her crime.

"You, my dear, are a liar," she pointed at me. "Everyone here knows that." No one argued with her as she swept her gaze round the room at all those gathered there. Sabian looked close to bursting, and he was paler than a ghost, but remained silent. Finally, she gestured to Lord Drake. "You may continue," she said as she cracked another smile. "Ask her about her Demise, Lord Drake."

It felt as though the room had dropped by a few degrees by the way everyone's faces hardened.

Lord Drake narrowed his eyes at me. "We have reasons to believe that you possess the ability of the mind known as the Demise. In fact, we are certain of it. Is there anything else you wish to say in defense?"

I held his gaze steady, despite my swaying. "I do not wish to say anything else."

"There," the Queen said. "She won't even deny it. My poor son probably knew about this, and so she silenced him."

I glared at her. How could someone be so conniving?

The court witnesses, princesses, and princes– all except Sabian– nodded and murmured their agreement with their Queen.

"These are the charges, my liege," Lord Drake finished. "The court has found her guilty of both murdering the heir to the crown and of possessing the Demise. What is your verdict?"

The King and I locked eyes for a moment. I could sense him considering everything, even the things everyone else wouldn't. He remembered everything I'd ever done for him– from caring for the beasts of his kingdom, to guarding his palace, to going out on dangerous quests to spy for him. He couldn't wrap his head around that I would do such a thing as murder his own son, but all the evidence was pointing toward me. And I possessed the Demise. I was dangerous and of the beasts, and no good could possibly come of that.

"Guilty," he decided. "Penalty for possessing the Demise is death. Likewise for murdering an heir to the throne. I will hold by the laws. It shall be so."

I had been expecting this, but I still felt my heart race, and my stomach drop. Or was that Sabian's?

He swiftly stepped forward despite my desperate commands to stay put, and stood in front of me protectively. "No, my King. I cannot stand by and watch as you sentence her to death for a crime she didn't commit."

King Rubarb leaned forward again, narrowing his eyes. "Is that so, Prince Sabian? What has led you to believe that she is not a murderer? And what have you to say about the disgraceful ability that she possesses?"

Sabian was silent for a moment. Then he said, "I–I just know, my King. And what is it about the 'Demise' that has you convinced she is evil? One shouldn't judge someone on what they may or may not do until they have done it."

"You just *know*?" the King asked. "Tell me, Sabian. Why are you stepping up for this girl?"

Don't, I told my brother. *Do not. Do you hear me? Don't–*

"Because she's my *sister*," Sabian answered. His voice quivered and he sounded close to tears.

The King's eyes widened, and the Queen raised an eyebrow. Prince Rayden grew red in the face with fury as he faced me. "You *told* him?"

The Queen was on her feet, aiming a quivering finger at me. "Prince Sabian was free of you! He would have been better without any knowledge of you. But now you've tainted him."

I opened my mouth to say something, but King Rubarb spoke before I could. "Prince Sabian. Yes, she is your sister by blood. However–"

"Why have you kept this from me?" Sabian demanded. "Why–"

"*Because,*" King Rubarb rose from his throne. "It would have been impossible to keep you apart if I hadn't. It was bad enough, your siring. But to have two of you? I spared her life and put her to good use. But she's betrayed me. Us. I won't make that mistake again."

"No," Sabian shook his head. "No, don't–

"You have no say in this," Prince Rayden interrupted. "Do not speak against the wishes of your King."

Sabian took a step back, then turned to me. "Tala, I–"

"Sabian," I poured as much feeling out to him as possible. A tear traced down his cheek as he felt it all. "You have to be okay. Alright? Don't lose yourself when I'm gone." Quieter, I added, "Prove them wrong about the Keen."

From behind him, Prince Rayden shoved Sabian away from me. "Great gamble, *stop talking to her*!"

The Queen was putting on a show of tears and sniffling. She clung to Rubarb and wailed, "First she takes my son, and now she's trying to taint my grandson!"

King Rubarb held her. "Sabian, stay away from the girl. It will only hurt you to grow close. And you cannot risk her tainting your mind with the Demise. She must pay for her actions." To everyone, he said, "I do not want attention drawn to this situation, so I sentence her, daughter of Princess Tira and criminal Cordan Greyver, to death in the dungeons below." He turned to his wife. "You may do as you wish to bring about this sentence. I will have no more part in this. Court dismissed."

He left the Grand Hall without a glance behind him.

The Queen gave commands to the guards that I couldn't hear over the roar in my ears. The despair I felt was indescribable. I felt as if a deep pit had opened up inside of me, dark and cold, and I was being shoved into it. My mind had long retreated to someplace I couldn't account for, numbing me against the paralyzing fear, but somehow, I still felt it all the same.

Somewhere far away, a wolf lifted her head and let out a long, soulful cry to the moon.

The things that followed I will not speak of. If I ever speak of them, it would be to the one that holds my heart, if ever I meet that someone.

The only thing I will tell of it is pain. Oh so much pain. The dungeon, men kicking; hitting. Their fists and boots against me over and over and over again. And when I couldn't protect myself or stand any longer, then came the lash. Whenever I fell unconscious, the pain woke me, and they continued on.

When they were finally finished with me, they tied me to one of the support beams of the dungeons, where I sat with my head lolling against my chest and the world a thousand miles away in darkness. One of my eyes was completely swollen shut, and the other wasn't too far behind. I couldn't count every pain on my body; it was everywhere. I was Pain. But it was my back, where the lash made the most contact, that kept pushing me under my stream of consciousness like a raging current. My clothes were torn, but the lash had torn away the back of my tunic completely. I could only imagine how my back looked; I felt the blood. But mostly just pain. That was all I was aware of when I managed to come to consciousness.

I had no idea how long I had been unconscious. And I wasn't sure if the pain had roused me or if something else had. My face was wet with a mix of blood and tears. I was unaware of my surroundings, blinded by pain. It would have been a mercy to die then, but I didn't. I willed myself to slip back into unconsciousness, but another mind penetrated mine.

No, listen to me.

I felt part of myself startle and come back to consciousness fully. I opened my eye a miniscule crack, enough to make out the boots of someone standing over me.

That's it...

His presence in my mind was familiar, but it wasn't Sabian. For a moment, I was confused, unable to think through my pain. But then it struck me. It was the same voice from out in the forest, the same presence that had made me stumble into the trap.

Yes, Tala. It is I. No need to fear, he added, *I will not harm you.*

It didn't reassure me. But there was nothing I could do as he crouched in front of me and gently took my chin in his hand and tilted my head up to look me in the eye and examine me. Somehow, through the pain and my darkened, double vision, I realized it was the Royal Assassin, Kelgare. He furrowed his brow as he examined me, clenched his jaw, and murmured, "By my grave..."

I sensed pity in him, but I turned my head away from him. *Leave me alone. Do not pity what you caused.*

He let go of my chin, but stayed crouched in front of me. "It is true that I caused you to come into harm. But for good reason..."

His voice trailed off as I began to drift under again, my consciousness hardly a wisp within me, my essence fading. Kelgare took my shoulders gently and said, "Tala, stay with me. You must listen."

I came back, hardly. *Let me die. Is that too much to ask?*

He still held my shoulders, keeping me from having to lean my wounded back against the beam, to which I was thankful. "I too am one of the Keen, Tala, as you have surmised. But King Rubarb took pity on me when I lay there beaten, just as you are now. He promised me my life as long as I serve him. My skills made me a remarkable assassin, and I proved myself. I am going to speak to him about you. I brought you here because I think you could be an important tool in turning the tides of this war."

War. . .?

"Just hang on while I speak to him. I cannot promise or assure you, but I will do my best. If he is in favor of it, will you cooperate? You must be prepared to face. . ."

Again, I faded. He brought me back, my pain growing. "Tala."

Yes. . .I a–agree to the terms.

He nodded. "Very well. If I do not return, then take that as a no from the King." And then he was gone, and I slipped into darkness completely.

"Tala. Tala, you must awaken." Kelgare's voice.

I managed to open the less swollen eye and look up at him. He stood in front of me, and beside him stood King Rubarb. The King swallowed hard when I met his eyes, and I thought I saw him wince.

"My King," Kelgare stated. "As you can see, she *is* still alive. But she won't be if we don't act swiftly."

"I *have* acted swiftly, *Kelgare*," the King responded. "I sentenced to death my son's murderer. What less should I have done? I took you in and allowed you your life in exchange for your skills and to put to decent use your. . .abilities. But you did not murder my son."

Kelgare was silent for a moment. Then, quietly, "Do you trust me, my King?"

"I do. You have proven yourself time and time again."

"Likewise has she," Kelgare pointed out. "Never once has she turned against you or refused to do as you asked. Evermore, she succeeded on every mission you sent her on. Every. Single. One. I ask you," he pleaded, "trust me. She is *not* your son's murderer."

King Rubarb looked at me once again while addressing Kelgare. "Does your Demise. . .does it confirm your belief?"

"Yes."

The King considered for a few heartbeats. "I do trust you, Kelgare. That is the only reason I am hearing you out. In the event that I do spare her life, how do you propose she would be a useful tool to me in the war?"

I struggled to remain conscious, the stone floor like ice beneath me, while Kelgare explained. "She has been the best spy that we've had for a really long time. I have read the recordings of her missions, and her work is exceptional. To add to that, the Demise only amplifies her skills by a hundredfold in contrast to any other spy's. This war has lasted us years, and the enemy is only getting stronger and bolder every day. We need to know where they draw their power from and how they use it so that we can have a better chance in this war. We need someone to infiltrate them discreetly and survive to report back to us." He gestured at me. "She is more than capable, and she is the *only one* capable. I cannot do it because you won't allow me. I am too valuable to you to risk losing me. But she is expendable, and it wouldn't come at a great cost to lose her. But if she does succeed as she always has, then we will actually have a chance to win this war."

Expendable.

The King stared at me for a long moment. Then he said, "Very well." He turned towards the door.

"Very well?" Kelgare sounded astonished.

"Yes," King Rubarb faced him again. "You are fully responsible for her and her recovery– if she is even *capable* of recovery. In five weeks time, I will assign her her mission. Make sure she is ready by then. Don't make me regret this decision."

Kelgare bowed deeply to his King. "Yes, sire."

After King Rubarb left, Kelgare crouched at my side and unchained my hands. When I was free of my bonds, I slumped sideways, unable to keep myself up. Kelgare caught me and, with a gentleness I had never experienced before, picked me up. The man who had poisoned me years ago now held me as if I were his own child.

I don't recall much of the days that followed.

But when I finally came to permanent consciousness, I was lying on my belly on a bed beside a warm hearth. It was a fairly sized chamber, with a bed, table, wooden chest, and shelves against nearly every wall that were lined with bottles, books, and many things I couldn't recognize. The smell of ointments and herbal medicine was strong in the air, and I could feel that I was covered in it and in bandages like a mummy. My hair was loose and thoroughly combed, and cleaner than it had been for a long time. My lower half was covered up with blankets, and I had on a soft button up shirt, but it was on backwards, with my back fully exposed. I dared not move; I was in enough pain as it were.

"Yes, stay still. You don't want to re–open the wounds." Kelgare came to my side and crouched so that he could look me in the eyes. "How are you feeling, Tala?"

I blinked a few times, and managed. "Alive."

"Alive is better than dead, though death may seem appealing at times." He went over to the hearth and pulled the pot of water from over the fire. He crumbled dried herbs into it and then stirred it with a wooden ladle. Then he sat down on the bed beside me and helped me sit up just enough so that I could sip from the ladle.

"Good," he murmured. "This will help restore you and relax you. I also added something to lessen the pain a bit."

"Why are you doing this for me?" I asked, my voice croaky. I honestly wondered.

"I obey my King."

"No," I pressed. "I mean, why were you so willing to help me in the first place? You could have just let me die, or tell one of your servants to restore me. And I can feel the care you have for me radiating from your mind like a furnace."

"First, I don't have servants," Kelgare replied. "I am an assassin, not a prince. Second. . ." He gazed into the fire, the flames dancing in his dark eyes. "You remind me too much of my daughter for me to let you die."

"Your. . .daughter?"

"Don't look so surprised," he laughed. "I have a life outside being an assassin."

"How do I remind you of her?"

He thought about it for a moment. "Your age. The fierceness in your eyes. But mostly the way you hold your head high, even in the face of torture and death."

I clenched my jaw. "I hope your daughter never has to do that."

"She has," he said softly. "She did."

I suddenly realized. "Oh, she's. . .?"

He nodded, his gaze distant. "Scarlet fever and pox. It was her own torture, and she held her head high through it all for weeks before it took her, after my wife. It was her own personal hell. And her death was mine." He met my eyes once again. "We each have our own hell."

I held his gaze, realizing that underneath the dark surface he displayed, there was sadness deeper than an ocean. "I'm sorry."

He let a small smile tug at the corner of his mouth. "Helping you was the least I could do. I couldn't save Maya, but I could save you."

"Thank you." And I meant it full heartedly. I didn't hold his poisoning me against him anymore. He was only following his King's orders, and besides, he was making it up to me.

He studied me. "There is sickness in your eyes. From the poison dart. Do you–"

"I have seizures. A lot of them, every day."

"That is regrettable. I can heal you from most of its effects, but I cannot heal you completely."

I nodded, then regretted it as my pain grew worse. "Where are we?"

"In my chambers, in the palace. Prince Rayden and the Queen are your only threat here, and even they have minimal power over you since you are now the King's. His wishes precede theirs. No harm will come to you, as long as you are here and are careful."

"What of Prince Sabian?"

"He keeps coming to my door," he sighed. "He worries himself mad, and his scattered mind has no boundaries. I have been unable to sleep with his loud thoughts over mine constantly, even when I bring up my shields."

"Where is he now? Can I speak to him?"

"If he comes here, yes. But you aren't getting out of this bed until you heal enough to do so."

I closed my eyes and concentrated on the tether that bonded my brother to me, and called. It took him a moment, but then I felt him startle and leap up. *I'm coming.*

"He will be here soon," I told my new guardian.

He let out a miniscule snort. "Then I shall go to the storeroom and retrieve more herbs. Far away from his screeching mind."

As he stepped out of the chambers, my brother pushed inside. "Tala!" He rushed to my side and when he saw the wounds, his features turned the color of snow. "Oh Tala. . ." He knelt down beside the bed and took my hand. "I'm sorry, I–I couldn't stop them. I tried, but I only made things worse. And now you're. . .so hurt. They did worse to you than to even male criminals. Tala, I'm so sorry. I–"

"Hush," I interrupted. "What's done is done. I'm alive, and that is what matters." But my voice quavered at my own words.

He took a deep breath. "I thought I lost you. Already. *Again.*"

I squeezed his hand. "The King allowed me my life, so long as I serve him once again. Tell me Sabian, what war were they talking about?"

He swallowed hard. "We've been at war with the Northland Kingdom since you ran away. They are powerful. Magicians."

"Magicians are real?"

"Yes, humans corrupted by magic. We don't know where they draw their power from, but they are currently unstoppable. Every attack we've managed to keep them at bay, but barely. With each attack, they weaken our forces and drive us back. Most of the Lowland Kingdom has been taken over already, and they only keep getting stronger."

I managed a nod. "Yes, the King is going to send me into their midst, into the Northland Kingdom, to find the source of their magic and power. That makes more sense now."

Sabian's face dropped. "But–"

I gave him a look of warning. "I know what you're going to say. But if I don't do it, then I die."

"Yeah," he sighed, sounding helpless. "What are your chances, though?"

"Of succeeding?" I forced myself to breathe, stifling a sigh. "It depends. But even if I don't succeed, I'll survive."

Silence stretched between us for a few heartbeats.

"Are you in much pain?" Sabian asked quietly.

I dodged the question, not willing to talk about it and surface the memories that were so close to pulling me under again. "We'll be in close proximity, at least for now. That will be nice. Though Spiritwolf won't be very happy about it. How has the food been as of late? Has Cook made those raspberry pastries since I left?"

Sabian smiled. "She has. But only once. Raspberries are a rare delicacy as of late, because of the war. So are a lot of fruits, vegetables, and spices that we don't grow locally. A lot of things here are hard to find lately."

"The war has been worse than the others let on, hasn't it?"

"Yes."

I sighed, feeling the weight of what I was going to deal with weigh heavy on my shoulders. I wanted to live, was responsible for finding the reason the Magicians were so powerful and unstoppable. But I had a feeling it would come to much more than that.

For the next four weeks, I stayed in bed, unmoving for the most part to keep my wounds from reopening, both the ones inside and out. Nightmares plagued me, of what had happened in the dungeon. The drip of the water down the corridor and the flicker of dim candlelight. The roaring laughter of the guards as they beat me to death. The overwhelming fear as I lay in a ball, trying to keep my vital organs safe. The crack of the lash as it hit my skin. The scent of my own blood. The despair. The hopelessness. The humiliation. The pain. I would wake up screaming from a nightmare, fully drenched in sweat, breathing hard, shaking, my heart racing. I startled easily. The simple sound of boot scuffs outside of Kelgare's chambers paralyzed me with fear as my mind related it to the same sounds I heard in the dungeon.

Kelgare took care of me and my wounds. Everytime he would touch me to re—bandage a wound, I would jump. I drifted from the present continuously, and when I would come back, I would find that I lost time. Kelgare said it was expected, after what I went through. But he didn't truly understand the extent of my internal wounds. I knew they would be harder to heal than my outer ones. And my feelings, emotions…I felt them. But everything was drowned out, as if underwater. I felt numb.

By the first day of fifth week, I could finally walk and move around without opening most of my wounds. The lash wounds on my back and my injured leg still hurt terribly, along with my other more major wounds. Those I kept bandaged even as I dressed in the clean, embroidered, dark violet tunic that Kelgare brought me to wear when I would have an audience with the King to discuss my mission.

Along with the tunic, Kelgare provided me with a belt and leather boots. When I was dressed in my new attire, I brushed my waist–long hair and braided it down over my shoulder. I studied myself in Kelgare's mirror. My posture was crooked from pain, a streak of white hair was now amongst my auburn hair where I had been hit with the sword hilt. I was still bruised, and a long scar ran from my forehead to my cheek, and another across my nose and to under my eye. I knew those would be permanent, along with all the scars the wounds would leave, especially the ones on my back. I looked different. I'd been broken, inside and out, and the proof of that would forever haunt me.

I stepped out into the corridor outside his chambers where Kelgare was waiting for me. He nodded approvingly as I limped to his side.

"You look very presentable. You aren't healed yet, but you are well enough to get around. You're just going to have to take it easy for now. How are you feeling after that seizure?"

It was true, I'd just had another seizure. They had become more often and more severe since I'd been. . .hurt. Kelgare had been doing his best to treat it, but nothing was working for now.

"I'm alright now."

"I can sense you putting a shell around yourself. What is the matter?"

I held his gaze steady. "If I do not, I fear I will fall apart. I must face the man who had me tortured to death, and if I do not keep myself inside this shell, I will lose control. Surely you agree that I must, lest I cry and tense into a ball before the King?" I did not say my King. I was already shaking, tearing up so that my vision was blurry and it was difficult to see.

Kelgare's eyes held sympathy. "Do as you must," he said quietly.

We made our way down the corridor in silence. Tapestries of common color and history hung here and there along the walls between the cressets and doorways. We turned a corner and entered a much wider corridor, decorated much more elegantly. The tapestries and hangings here were of bright, costly colors and displayed scenes of coronations. Instead of cressests, brilliantly carved braziers stood firmly and gracefully with their dancing fires. An immensely long red carpet lined the floor under our feet, and guards stood at every door. I knew immediately that this was the corridor of the Royal chambers.

We came to the largest doors. The design of an oak tree and an eagle were carved into it, giving it a three dimensional look that was beyond me. I'd seen all of this before, back when I still worked here as a guard and then King's Spy. Many times I stood outside these very doors, either guarding or waiting to be admitted to report my mission to my King. Yet still, the grandness of this hall dazzled me.

Two guards stood on either side of the doors, looking tired but vigilant nonetheless. Kelgare knocked twice, then the doors were opened from the inside by two more guards.

Kelgare and I were led by a well-dressed servant into the King's chambers. The dressing room, the bathing chamber, bedchamber, and finally, we entered a warmly lit office. All of the rooms were grand, but this one was most of all. Massive oak bookshelves lined the walls, a beautifully carved pine table, and a stone fireplace with a swirling marble mantle. All too familiar.

The King sat behind the table in a red velvet chair, dressed in his loungewear. He sipped from a large, steaming mug, looking tired. Maybe even fatigued. I sensed he was growing ill of hearing the two princes in front of him arguing.

Prince Rayden was standing with his fists and jaw clenched, facing Prince Sabian with a stern look on his face. My brother was going on about something.

"—too dangerous. Someone has to go with her."

"Sabian," Rayden growled. "I've told you before, and I'll tell you again. You do not have a say in this. Remember your place."

"Enough," King Rubarb commanded quietly but firmly. "I am King. I am also wearied with a headache. Not another word out of either of you."

Kelgare bowed deeply as we stepped fully into the room and the servant announced our presence, bowed, and hurried away. I didn't bow. It was difficult enough to stand. Besides, I wasn't in the mood to bow to this King. I stood where I had stood every time I reported to him, years ago, and wondered what I was really feeling. It was all too much, and I was too numb to tell for sure. My expression was slack, devoid of all emotion except for the burn in my eyes.

"Kelgare," the King greeted him, looking genuinely glad to see him. He turned his eyes to me. "Tala."

Sabian smiled in an attempt to encourage me, and offered his hand to support me. He could sense I was in pain. I transmitted to him, *No. I won't show weakness.*

He narrowed his eyes. *Accepting help isn't weak. It's courageous.*

Kelgare cleared his throat. *Take his arm, Tala. He is correct. You do not want to fall in the presence of your king, do you? And both of you, stop jabbering.* Out loud, "My King, you summoned us?"

I took Sabian's arm and was secretly grateful for both the physical and emotional support he lended me.

"Yes." King Rubarb stood, placing his mug on a checkered cloth on the table. "Tala, how is your healing coming along?"

I blinked rapidly, responding with hardly a whisper. "Slowly."

"I see. . ." He moved around to the front of his table and leaned back on it almost as if sitting. Crossing his arms across his chest, he studied me. "Kelgare, is she well enough to take on duties?"

"She is still healing, my King," Kelgare responded. "She cannot do anything extensive. But she might be able to do a few simple tasks."

"Very well, I trust your judgment." King Rubarb nodded to himself as if he had come to some kind of conclusion. "Tala, when you heal enough, I am sending you into the Northland Kingdom to spy on the Magicians. Your objective is to find their source of power, and if you are unable to dismantle it, then report back to me. Until then, I will introduce you to the kingdom at the Spring Ball Festival, in six weeks time. You will be known as King's Spy once again, though no one may know your true identity."

He gestured to a bystanding maid, who hurried away and returned with a wooden chest. She set it down in front of me and backed away to where she was standing before.

King Rubarb nodded to me. "Open it."

Sabian quickly crouched and opened the chest for me so I didn't hurt myself. He handed me what was inside: a silver gray wolf face shaped mask with emerald green accent designs that resembled a masquerade mask— covering the top part of the face and only leaving the mouth and lower half of the cheeks and chin exposed— a matching dark emerald tunic with silver lining at the ends of the sleeves, a hood, and a black leather belt. At the bottom of the chest were arrows, a bow, and various daggers. A pair of boots, and thin leather gloves.

"You will wear that to keep your identity secret," the King explained. "And the weapons are yours. You are my Wolf now, Tala."

"Your wolf?"

"My Wolf," he confirmed.

I understood what he meant.

"You trust her to do that without turning on you?" Prince Rayden demanded.

"She cannot turn on me without being killed. Working for me is in her best interest," King Rubarb said, silencing him. "Now, Sabian, show her to her new chambers."

Sabian looked slightly confused. "Weren't you going to–"

Prince Rayden raised his eyebrows and made a stern sound. "Go."

Sabian glared at him, then picked up the wooden chest and led the way out. I nodded to Kelgare on our way, and he gave me a slight smile.

Down the corridor and up three flights of steps, Sabian finally stopped and opened a door to a small chamber with a fireplace, a bed, a table, and an empty bookshelf. A large window overlooking the forest was letting in a slight breeze. Sabian set the chest at the foot of the bed and sighed. "You deserve better than this."

I smiled. "This is more than I've ever had. I've never had my own room before."

"You're a princess, you do realize that?" Sabian pointed out. "One day you could be eligible for the throne! And here you are living in a servant's quarters."

I laughed. "Imagine, me, a princess. Let alone a queen, with a jeweled crown resting upon my head and a scepter in my hand." I shook my head at the idea of it. "I may have royal blood, but I am not a princess." I swallowed hard. "I am the King's Wolf."

I went over to sit on the side of the bed and sighed with contentment. "It's so soft."

Sabian sat next to me. "Tala, how will you keep your hair concealed? It's a dead giveaway. Anyone who knew you will recognize it immediately."

"I'm not sure." I pondered this for a moment. "Maybe I should cut it."

"No," Sabian shook his head. "It's too beautiful and unique to chop off. It's a part of who you are."

"Who I am is the King's Wolf. And I must do what I need to to be who I am, mustn't I?"

"Yes, but don't cut your hair. I can feel the reluctance you have to do it." He looked around, for ideas, perhaps. "Ah!" He stood and went back over to the chest and pulled out the tunic. "The hood!"

"Yes, that should work." I sighed with relief.

"I knew you didn't want to cut your hair."

I smirked at him. "Don't you have some princely duties to attend to?"

"Just to go listen to Rayden complain about me."

"What was it that you were going to say back there, when Rayden silenced you?"

Sabian rubbed his face. "I was going to remind our Grandfather about the incident at the border earlier this morning. I was out on patrol with a few others and we found Rayden speaking to three elves from the Moonland Kingdom. By the time we approached, the elves were gone. I asked Rayden what was going on, and he wouldn't answer me. I mentioned it to Grandfather earlier and he said we would discuss it later. Later came and Rayden wouldn't let me say anything. It's. . .suspicious."

"It is." I thought about it, trying to think of a reasonable answer, but I couldn't think of one. I had a terrible feeling about it.

"What is it?" Sabian asked, sensing my feelings.

"I'm. . .not sure."

Sabian crossed over to the window and shut it, then over to the door. "Well, I'll leave you to get changed. I need to go work on defenses with the royal guard. The attacks are getting closer. I'll see you at dinner tonight."

"At dinner? In my. . .mask?"

He winced. "Yeah. It'll probably take some time for you to get used to it."

I nodded. "I have to hide myself in order to live. What a trade. According to everyone but you and the other royals, I am dead."

Sabian widened his eyes and smiled cheekily. "A ghost! Quickly, before we're haunted!" He spun on his heel and ran comically down the corridor, until he tripped on his own foot and flew face first into the stairwell.

The sound of him rolling down the stairs echoed loudly, thumping mixed with grunts, then, "I'm alright!" he called.

I shook my head. *I really do have a brother now.*

The tunic–dress was comfortable enough, but the mask was a whole other ordeal. It's not that it wasn't comfortable. . .it just felt strange. I'd been hiding for years, doing everything in my power to stay away from my predators. Now, staring at myself in the mirror, I wondered if I'd ever be free– safe– enough to step into the light, without masks, forests, or the shadow of the king to hide under.

But I had to admit– with the large green hood over my head, the tunic and boots and a belt with two sheathed knives at my side once again, and the eerie yet elegant wolf mask covering my face– I felt safer. As if I were cocooned in an elaborate dream that for once I could not be harmed.

It was a foolish daydream, one I shook off immediately. I would never be safe. There would always be someone after me, willing me pain and death because of who I was. If I was to be safe, I had to strike first.

I was a Wolf, after all.

I jumped as the floor creaked under my own weight, my heart thumping wildly. My leg increased in pain, and the memories of my torture snuck up in my mind, tinged red. I pushed it back into the crevice it had crawled out from. It would do me no good to shove down feelings, but I couldn't stand the mere thought of letting myself feel. I could not let that happen if I wanted to survive. Feeling would be too much. . .

But doubt crept in, making the memories brighter like a hot, burning coal. How could I strike first, survive, if I was no more than a puppet in the hand of the King? I was a slave. The little girl who cared for the folk's animals was gone. She died when she was hit by that poison dart.

What had emerged after that? A terrified, wounded, trapped pup.

I tried to gather my spine. I had been working for the King since I could remember, so why were things different now?

Don't be delusional, I scolded myself. *Everything is different*

"I am so confused," I whispered. "So lost." *So afraid.* I refused to utter the rest aloud, even as I stifled a sob. If I said it aloud, then it would reverberate and I would hear the truth of it in my voice. I had to keep going, and if I heard myself say it, then I would crumple and not get back up again.

I desperately grasped for my few, tender memories. Tanny, the little hound with his soft, wet tongue and short, yellow hair, and Kika the rabbit with her little brown, fuzzy babies. Cher, the tomcat, sass as sharp as the sting of frostbite. My only friends. But friends they were, and good ones. The barn was always warm with their furry bodies and the sound of Tanny's excited bark when I would come back to the barn after helping the townsfolk's animals. I would feed them and the old mule who had no name, I called him Jug, because he always burped as if he was constantly downing jugs of beer.

I smiled, my breath steadying. My hazel eyes stared back at me in my reflection. At least with the mask on I couldn't see my scars.

"I am Wolf. I am the King's. I hold no fear."

But even as I said it, I wondered how long I would be able to keep lying to myself.

As I limped into the Royal Dining Hall, I took comfort in the feeling of the two small knives tucked hidden in my sleeves, and the two sheathed at my sides, and a pair at my calves. All except for the ones beneath my sleeves were visible.

The royal family sat at the table, already feasting. The princesses had a surprisingly hearty appetite, but I smiled. Good. They needed more meat on their bones. They did enough "pretty eating" at the frequent banquets and practically starved themselves to fit in the gowns—they deserved to indulge a little.

Sabian was the only one standing, waiting beside the table. I could feel his anxiousness about something that had to do with the war, borders, and of course Rayden. But he hid his anxiety well. He smiled as I walked in, showing no sign of repulsion or awkwardness at my new attire. Before I could join him, King Rubarb gave him a stern look, and he sat down. The princesses thought me to be dead, and the King didn't want that to change. He then turned to me, standing.

"My Wolf."

All eyes turned to me. The queen scowled; apparently she knew my identity. The princesses' eyes were wide and curious. Prince Rayden sat expressionless, his jaw clenched. From the corner of the room, Kelgare emerged from a shadow he'd managed to find despite all the candlelit chandeliers. He met my eyes and gave me a slow nod, his dark eyes like a hawk's.

I stepped forward and forced myself to bow, grinding my teeth in pain. Then the King invited me to the table with a wave of his hand. One seat was still empty, between Prince Rayden and Princess Teyqa. I took it, resisting the urge to sigh as I took the pressure off my leg.

Sabian smiled slightly and I returned it, taking comfort in the gesture. But before either of us could say anything, Kalgare spoke in our minds. *Stop grinning at each other. You look as if you both are in on a secret. Be discreet. Sabian, you know nothing. Tala, eat. They won't do it for you. You need your strength.*

Sabian stifled a laugh and cleared his throat. "Joy, would you pass the squash?"

"Why do we even have servants?" grumbled the princess as she handed over the dish. "You eat more than my horse does, Sabian."

"It's a talent." Sabian winked at her. I couldn't help it—I laughed.

All heads turned to me, everyone but Sabian looking shocked, surprised. At first I felt my ears redden, feeling ashamed. But then I remembered most of my face was covered, so I jutted out my chin. "What? Even the King's Wolf laughs."

Chapter Four

Secrets can be a treasure, or they can be a curse.
Always hidden, for better or for worse
Darkness or light, warmth or cold
Intentions of the mind or of the heart, new or old
Soot or gold
Fools gold can only fool a fool
Secrets can only stay hidden in shadow
Unless the shadow isn't alone

Everyday the following weeks, I worked with Kelgare to refresh my training. Painful as it was with my wounds, it felt good to have the familiar feeling of the weapons in my hands. The stave, the daggers, the sword. And it felt good to take down a man again.

I wasn't an assassin like Kelgare, and I had never killed a man, but I was trained to take care of myself and hold my own in a fight. And I could do it well. Almost as well as I could stay hidden and silent.

Kelgare grunted as he hit the ground again. I offered my hand. "Had enough yet?"

"I'm not as young as I once was," Kelgare admitted as he took my hand and I helped him up.

"Maybe, but you've pinned me just as many times as I have you."

He brushed himself off. "It's nearly dusk. Let's call it a night, shall we?" He led the way over to the edge of the palace's rooftop garden, where we had been training. Spring was in full bloom, turning everything green and colorful with leaves and blossoms.

Kelgare poured us both a tin cup of water from a pitcher that we had brought up with us, and we drank until both the cups and the pitcher were empty.

Over the past few weeks, my wounds had healed into scars. My leg would still ache occasionally, probably for the rest of my life, but I could walk without a limp now. And my other wounds. . .well they didn't hurt much anymore. But the scars would always be there to haunt me.

I stepped up onto the parapet that was supposed to keep people from falling off the rooftop gardens into the rocks far, far down below. I liked the risk; dangling my legs over it, just at any moment able to plummet.

"How are you coming along with getting used to that mask?" Kelgare asked as he set down his cup.

"It is a part of me now," I replied. And it was true. It felt like self betrayal, but at the same time I felt guilty that it gave me the sense of security like how shadow did.

"As are those knives. It is as if you have your natural grown claws back," Kelgare pointed out. I caught him watching me as I danced one of my smaller blades between my fingers. I flipped it back into its sheath at my wrist.

"I must warn you," he continued. "Being the King's is like putting a target on your back."

"I know. Did you forget? I have been his spy before."

"I know. But back then, no one knew. Things are different now. Tomorrow is the Spring Ball. All will know you are King's Wolf. That will draw out enemies for you. And the people, they will assume things. They will not know that you are only a spy."

"Let them assume." I jumped down from the wall. "Besides, you know as well as I do that the King wants more from me than just being his spy."

Two weeks ago, just after Sabian had finally been able to tell our Grandfather about what he had seen at the border, King Rubarb had summoned me to his chamber during the night. Kelgare was the only other person in the room when I entered, not even the King's guards. King Rubarb told me that he had reasons to believe that Prince Rayden was conspiring against him. Of course, after what Sabian had seen, I knew something was going on. But it surprised me when the King said, "Until I know for sure what is going on, I cannot trust even my guards. Kelgare reports that you are a fine fighter, just as I remember you to be. One of the best. I need those skills. You will stay closer to me than ever before, always watching like a wolf in the shadows, ready to spring if need be. And watch Prince Rayden. It saddens me to say, but he has proven to be greedy, and I would not put it past him to try to endanger the Queen and I for the throne."

And so I did just that. What a happy family the royals were.

"Indeed," Kelgare agreed. "That is why he gave you the title Wolf instead of spy."

The breeze felt good. I let my hood drop and my hair spilled around my shoulders, strands whipping my face in the light wind. Kelgare sighed. "That isn't safe to do. You know that."

So I pulled the hood back on and secured it.

Living isn't safe to do. Not for our kind.

And yet we do it anyway, Kelgare shot back. Out loud, "The King is having a tunic embroidered for you for the Ball. Still simple compared to the gowns, but more fitting for the festival."

"Do I get to wear earrings?" I joked. "Ones with little bells, like Princess Joy so fancies?"

Kelgare laughed. "I believe your ears aren't pierced."

"It would be easy enough to do." I sighed. "Embroidery is fine. As long as I don't have to wear heels."

"No, you wouldn't be able to sneak around in those things."

"You think I'll have to sneak around at a ball?"

"It is always a possibility. The Elves will be there."

I snorted. "And so will Rayden. What's the difference?"

Kelgare's eyes glittered. "Just watch your back."

I nodded. "Of course. And what will you wear? Those same old black boots and that gray tunic? Or will you wear a pink gown and dangly, belled earrings?"

He cracked a smile. "You've been spending too much time around your brother."

"Actually, I haven't. He's been too busy doing princely borderline duties and planning attacks, and I've been occupied on following Rayden around."

"Have you caught him doing anything he shouldn't?"

"No. Nothing at all. But I can't follow him *everywhere.*"

"Hmn." Kelgare gazed out across the forest. "Hopefully it stays that way. He wouldn't be smart to do anything without supporters. And right now, the King has all of them."

"Yes," I agreed. "It would be rash for Rayden to pull anything. And yet I–I–" My speech slurred and I began to tremble, my teeth chattering. My legs buckled, and my vision began to fade, but Kelgare caught me and lowered me to the ground as I began to convulse.

"Breathe," he said in an impossibly calm tone. "It will pass."

Another seizure. What would happen if this happened while I was on the mission? It could get me captured or killed.

When I woke up, I was lying on the bed in my room. The door was closed, but there was a fresh basin of water on the table and a meal. A fire was crackling in the fireplace, and my mask was lying on the table.

I took a deep breath and sat up. My heart ached with a longing, and for a moment I wasn't sure why. Then I thought of Spiritwolf, and my eyes stung with tears. I missed her, and I missed my pack.

I missed my home.

The longer I was here in the palace, the more I longed to be back with the pack, with Spiritwolf. I hugged my knees. Once in a while, I could sense her near the palace, but I pushed her away. It wasn't safe for her. But I longed to go out and see her.

I sighed, wiping a tear from my cheek. If I went to go see her, I'd put her in danger.

I got to my feet and took a shaky step to the table, where I sat and ate the meal of warm chicken broth and steamed vegetables. Then I downed the herb tea that accompanied the meal and sighed as the effects of the herbs began to relieve the pain pounding in my head.

It was the morning of the Spring Ball Festival, just past dawn. As I opened the window overlooking the forest, a slight breeze came through, rustling my hair. The new day's sunlight caressed my face. I closed my eyes and took in a deep breath, relishing the feeling.

A blue bird landed on the window sill, looking up at me with its beady eyes.

"Hello little friend," I whispered. Slowly, I held out my hand, reaching with the Keen. *Friend*, it answered as it hopped onto my palm.

"Blue bird, blue bird," I sang what I remembered from the old folk tune. "Feathers light, color bright, sing with me in song / Little wings, stretch wide, dance in the wind all day long."

I startled when a clatter came from down below, on one of the lower floors of the palace. The bird took flight in a panic.

I grabbed my mask and swung out of the window. I climbed down a floor via the roof silently, listening, then moved my way down another floor using the window sills to keep my footing. For a moment, I paused, feeling as if I were being watched. Along with the wind whipping around my legs, I felt someone's eyes on me, but when I looked around, I didn't see anyone.

What sounded like a table being turned over reminded me; something was going on. I leapt onto the next window sill.

Sabian's room.

Through the window, I saw a man flipping tables and searching my brother's chamber. His face was covered with a masquerade mask.

I slipped inside and leapt up onto the man's shoulders, wrapping my legs around his neck. He stumbled backwards, pulling at my legs. I yanked the mask from his face only to realize that he was one of the Royal Guard. I recognized him as one of the guards who frequently guarded Prince Rayden's chambers.

Confusion and surprise made me loosen my grip, and the guard slammed me into the wall. But I reached up and grabbed the man's leg, flipping him onto his back with a loud *thunk*. I straddled him, slipped a dagger from my calf's sheath, and held it to his throat.

"What are you doing in Prince Sabian's chambers?"

Two more of Rayden's guards burst into the room and yanked me off of the man by my arms. They were strong, holding my hands behind my back tightly as I struggled. One of them stuck a needle into the side of my neck, and let me go.

I reached for another one of my knives, but the room spun around me, and I stumbled. As I fell, my vision dimming, the guards left the room, hurrying away down the corridor.

"Tala, Tala wake up!"

I opened my eyes to find Sabian kneeling beside me.

"Hey are you alright? What happened?"

I groaned, feeling groggy. I sat up, steadying myself. "There was a man here, one of Rayden's guards, searching your room. Two others came when I tried to subdue him, and they stuck me with some kind of sedative."

"Rayden's guards?" Sabian helped me to my feet. "For a while I thought I was overthinking things with him, after the incident at the border, since he hasn't made any other moves. But now. . ."

"They were looking for you, Sabian," I murmured, pulling my hood back on. "Watch your back. I won't be far, brother."

I slipped out and into the corridor, keeping to the shadows as I made my way down the line of royal chamber doors, seething with anger. My life in danger was one thing, but my brother's? No. I wouldn't tolerate it.

I tried to force my breathing to calm down, but I couldn't. I turned the corner at the bottom of the stairs and stopped. I took heaving breaths, my fists clenched and stars danced in my vision. I slipped a dagger from its sheath and flipped it, catching it by the tip of the blade.

A hand grabbed my wrist. I whipped around, pressing my attacker against the wall with the dagger against his neck.

"Sabian? What–"

Sabian pushed my dagger away, giving me a very concerned look.

"What? I'm just. . .I'm angry."

"Angry is an understatement." Sabian took the dagger from my hand and sheathed it back at my side. "I can feel you, Tala. You are in a rage."

"Sabian," I growled. "Of course I'm in a rage. These royals have taken everything from me. Everything. They. . .they can't take you from me, too. Not again."

"Okay, come on." Sabian led the way down the next flight of stairs.

"Where are we going, Sabian?" I sighed.

"To let out some steam."

"Some steam?"

A while later, we were standing in the rooftop gardens, my usual training spot with Kelgare.

"Sabian, this isn't–"

"Stop talking," he interrupted, handing me a sword by its hilt. "I'm not going to let you go off and do something you'll regret. Anger is a dangerous thing. You can't be the king's spy without a level head." He took the sparring stance and drew his own sword. "Such a great fighter, and yet you've never proven it to your brother."

"I don't have to prove anything to you." I lunged at him, and he blocked my attack, then countered.

We went at it for almost an hour, and I was surprised to discover that my brother was a fine opponent. Back and forth, we knocked each other down, pinned each other, and dueled just short of actually hurting each other– except for the bruises.

Finally, we clashed swords one last time. "I think if I come at you again, you aren't going to be able to get back up," I teased.

"I don't know, I'm pretty sure you're the one who's having trouble holding up that sword," he countered.

I laughed, sliding the sword into its sheath and handing it to my sweaty brother. "Thank you, Sabian. You were right, I really needed this."

He smiled. "Of course. Usually girls cool off by having tea and biscuits or going to buy a new dress, but I figured that probably wouldn't appeal to you."

"Biscuits don't help let out anger, unless I get to throw them at someone."

He laughed. "As long as it's not me you're throwing it at."

"I make no promises."

I sensed Princess Joy coming up the staircase to the rooftop and quickly put my mask and hood back on.

She burst through the door, her nose scrunching when she saw us. "What are you doing? Sabian you look like you just got dunked in a tub of tar upside down."

Sabian sighed. "Hi Joy. Training. Are you stalking me?"

Joy snorted. "Are you embarrassed I caught you in the garden alone with Grandfather's. . .girl?"

I narrowed my eyes, clearing my throat. "His girl?"

"Spy, assassin, Wolf, girl, same difference," she waved it off. "Do you have a crush, Sabian, on the mysterious masked lady with knives?"

Sabian rolled his eyes. "What do you want, Joy?"

Joy crossed her arms and cocked her head. "Do you find girls with sharp objects attractive? Dangerous women, who can be found creeping through the shadows to your chambers at night?"

"Gross, Joy," Sabian pinched between his eyes. "Training. We were *training*."

"You mean *you* were training," Joy corrected. "She was probably kicking your behind."

I stifled a laugh. "I like her."

"Instead of stalking me and making strange assumptions, don't you have a ball to get ready for?" Sabian prompted our cousin.

"Yes, actually, that's why I'm here." Joy turned to me. "I was looking for you."

I exchanged a glance with Sabian. "Me?"

"Yes. I want your help with picking out which gown I should wear to the ball."

"Y–You want *my* help?" I stuttered, surprised.

"Yep," Joy yipped. "Come on. And Sabian, go bathe. I can smell you from here, and that isn't a good thing." She spun on her heel in a flurry and started down the stairs, calling over her shoulder. "Come on, dangerous sneaky lady that Sabian can't help falling for. All you need is some black leather. . ." Her voice faded down the corridor.

I pointed in her direction. "Is she serious?"

"Probably," Sabian grumbled.

"Do I follow her?"

"Probably."

I shoved him. "Very helpful." I headed after Joy, and caught up to her halfway to her chambers. She was fast for someone in a floor length gown and heels.

"Ah!" she squealed as I came up to her side. "How do you do that?"

"Do what?"

"Just appear out of nowhere."

"Well, I don't–"

She waved it off. "Yes yes, you do it somehow. But anyways, pink, gold, or scarlet?"

"What?"

"Which color best suits my undertone?"

"Your what?"

Joy stopped just outside her doors and gave me a sad look. "So you can fight like a leopard and move without a sound, but you don't know what undertones are?"

When I didn't respond, Joy took my gloved hand and pulled me into her chambers. "Well even so, I still trust your judgment. For some reason."

Her room was. . .colorful. Bright shades of rose, red, violet, and navy decorated everything from her soft, gigantic bed, to the curtains, towels, and even the carpet. She opened her wardrobe to reveal more gowns than I could count of all colors. I stood gaping while she pulled a few of them out and laid them on her bed.

"So, pink or, hmn, maybe this one?" She held a luscious scarlet gown in front of her.

"Why do you want my help? I don't have much experience with balls and gowns."

"Because Princess Teyqa, my aunt, is ridiculously obsessed with making sure the palace has the perfect decorations for tonight, especially since some elves will be attending. She has a crush on one of them, one of the princes." Joy rolled her eyes and sighed. "And I've grown weary of my maid helping me. She's so boring and only says, 'yes miss, of course miss, whatever pleases you miss,' and so I don't have anyone else to help me choose. I just want a good and honest opinion."

I blinked. "Thank you for considering me. I'm honored." I was truly shocked.

"Well," Joy prompted. "Go ahead. Which one do you think would be best?"

I stepped closer to the dress–covered bed, hesitating. No one had ever asked for my opinion on, well, anything other than what food would be best for their animal or what blade would suit which attack best. So I took the kind gesture.

"Uhm, this one." I pointed to the peach colored gown. "I think it may bring out the rose in your cheeks."

"See? Easy peasy. Thank you." Joy put the rest of the gowns away. "Now the jewelry!"

She opened the large wooden jewelry box that sat on one of her dressers and pulled out any and all of the pieces she thought might match with her chosen attire. I forced myself not to drool and not to comment on how the jewels could help people affected by the war.

She decided on a pair of rose gold earrings and had me choose her necklace, which was no easy feat. How could I choose when they all were so beautiful?

Finally, I pointed to a gold chain with an amber teardrop gem dangling from it.

"Good choice," the princess agreed. "I've decided that I like you, Wolf."

I smiled, dipping my head. "I'm honored, my princess."

"What will you wear tonight?"

I felt strange having a casual conversation with the princess. Was this what it was like to be normal? Even though I was a stranger to this type of interaction, I was enjoying it, to my surprise. I blocked out Joy's thoughts and feelings and smiled. "The King is having a tunic embroidered for me to wear to the ball."

Joy wrinkled her nose. "Great gamble, a tunic to wear at a ball? That is quite unfitting, don't you think?"

"I wouldn't know."

"Well, I *do* know. And a tunic is not proper for a ball. Embroidered or not."

"I believe that King Rubarb doesn't wish for me to stand out in a gown."

Joy huffed. "Ridiculous if you ask me."

I stood there, unsure of what to do while the princess arranged her outfit on her bed. Then she turned to me, hands on her hips. "Well, go get that tunic and get ready! Don't just stand there. It's past noon!"

I hurried away, a little baffled. Princess Joy was definitely strong-willed.

On my way down the corridor, I hoped my tunic would be in the royal seamstress' room, otherwise I wasn't sure where I would find it. A clamor startled me, and I pressed back against the wall just as Prince Rayden stormed out of his room, followed by the men who had raided Sabian's room.

"No," he growled, jabbing a finger into one of the men's chests. "I don't care. This is not–"

"But sir–"

"Enough," Rayden hissed. "Enough of this. I am your prince, and you have gone against orders. I do not want to see your faces within the palace grounds again. Understood?"

"Y–Yes sir."

They all stood there for a moment, then Rayden growled, "Get out of my sight. Now!"

They all scrambled away down the corridor, too much in a hurry to notice me. Confusion rattled my mind. I reached out to Rayden's thoughts and feelings as I passed him, but he was seething with anger at the guards. Angry that they had disobeyed him. He couldn't believe they had actually raided Sabian's room.

As I walked past him, he met my eyes and gave a small nod. Respect? I was too stunned to respond.

But, as we passed each other, he stopped me with a raised hand. "Those men didn't hurt you, did they?"

I opened and closed my mouth, confused. "No. Just sedated me."

He shook his head. "They had no right." Then he stormed away.

So. . .if he *wasn't* the one to send those men after Sabian, then who did?

I found my new tunic. It was identical to my usual one, except it was dark red instead of green, and had a leaf–like embroidery that was gold. It was the most beautiful piece of clothing I'd ever had.

I went up to my chamber and got changed, brushed my hair, and braided it into a bun to keep it secure underneath my hood. I went through my daily routine of sharpening all of my knives and sheathed them all at their usual places at my wrists, waist, and calves.

Afterwards, I headed downstairs to my brother's chambers, where he stood in front of a mirror combing his auburn hair, dressed for the ball in accented, expensive clothes.

He jumped when he saw me in the mirror. "You've got to stop sneaking up on me like that."

"How did I sneak up on you?" I laughed. "You can quite literally know when I'm near. Just use your senses, and your mind."

He shook his head with a sigh. He set down his comb and straightened. "Do I look princely enough?"

I crossed my arms across my chest. "Not nearly enough. You need more shiny things sewn to your clothes."

He rolled his eyes with a laugh. "Any more shiny things and I'll be blinded. You look great by the way."

"Thank you. Our cousin wasn't pleased with the idea of me wearing a tunic to the ball, though."

"With the belt and the embroidery, it really doesn't look like a tunic."

"True enough. She made me pick out her gown and jewelry!"

Sabian smiled. "It's a thing girls do together. Pick out clothes for events. Have you never done it, even when you were a royal guard?"

I shook my head. "Never. It felt. . . .strange." I shot to the reason I had come. "Rayden didn't send those men. I watched him yell at them and send them away. I even felt his mind, and he was furious. He even asked if they hurt me and said they didn't have any right."

Sabian furrowed his brows. "Really?" His mind raced, trying to take in all the possible angles.

"Yes." I paced his room. "I need to figure out who sent them, if it wasn't him."

Sabian took my shoulders in his hands. "Hey. Don't worry about it tonight, alright? Take your mind off of this and enjoy the ball. Just worry about what Grandfather wants you to do. Otherwise, enjoy yourself."

I sighed. He was right, I shouldn't worry. But I couldn't help it. I didn't want something to happen to my brother. If I could just get ahead and figure it out. . .

"Okay," I said.

"Good." He let go of me. "Tomorrow I could use your help with some things."

"What kind of things?"

"Strategic things. For the war. At the last council we held, we all agreed we could use your input. We're desperate."

"That desperate, really?"

"Yes." He rubbed his face with his hands. "The attacks are getting outrageous. And closer. So much closer. The past few weeks, I've been helping lead defenses and attacks. It's getting more and more hopeless."

I nodded. "I'll do my best to help. I know how to sneak around, not configure war strategies, but I'll give my input if that's really what you'd like."

"It is, thank you." His thoughts were distracted and worried, going over plans and defenses over and over again. "Well," he said, "I need to head to the Great Hall."

"And I need to go see the King."

King Rubarb was headed to the Great Hall when I found him, flanked by guards and servants. I slipped in beside him silently. "My King."

He jumped a little, startled. "Ah. There you are."

"What are your orders for tonight, my King?"

"I will introduce you before the dinner and the dance. From then on out, I'd like you to keep an eye on the Moonland Kingdom visitors. The elves were invited by the Queen and Prince Rayden, but I am wary of their presence here. We've never been enemies, however, we've never been allies either. I just want to be carefully wary, just in case. Watch them, and if you see or hear anything suspicious, report to me immediately."

I bowed and slipped away into the shadows.

The Great Hall was bustling. Servants carted platters of food to and from the tables. Folk dressed in gowns and expensive suits filled the hall, talking, dancing, eating. The orchestra played from their corner of the Great Hall with violins, a piano, cellos, and flutes. Golden chandeliers hung from the ceiling bedecked with glowing white candles. The King and Queen were arm in arm, greeting guests and making their way to the throne dais. Princess Joy was dancing with a young man, and Princess Tequa was sitting at the long table surrounded by dukes and wealthy men looking to impress her. Sabian was speaking to one of the generals, and I realized just how royal and in charge he looked. With everything he'd been doing with the war, he did it all with such calm and quiet endurance. He would make a fine king.

I stood in the doorway for a moment, taking it all in. It was overwhelming, but beautiful. I blocked out everyone's thoughts and feelings before heading over to the dais. I stood to the back and right of the King's throne and folded my arms back behind me neatly, waiting. It was then that I noticed the Moonland Kingdom elves.

They stood near each other, but not quite in a cluster, near the main entrance as if they'd just come in. There were nine of them; tall, pale skin, ears that came to a point at the ends, dark hair, well dressed but subtly unlike the people whose kingdom they were visiting. Five of them had elegant swords sheathed at their sides, silver and glinting with embedded moonstones. They were quiet and their presence was like that of falling snow; light and cold, only noticeable if you really looked. But even so, they stood out like shards of obsidian amongst rubies and sapphires.

I watched them as they mingled lightly with the other guests. They never started a conversation, but when they were spoken to, they made sure to voice their opinions and thoughts with guarded demeanors. They all seemed to be in their mid thirties, all except one who looked to be around my age. But I didn't have time to study him before the King stepped up onto the dais and gestured to the orchestra, making them go silent.

"My people," he began once everyone had gone quiet, "Despite the war, I am pleased that the annual Spring Ball was able to commence. It has been a ravaging few years. The Spring ball is something many of us have needed to bring some joy back into our lives."

The gathered nodded and murmured their agreement, raising glasses of champagne.

"The war weighs heavy still," King Rubarb continued. "I assure you, I am working to the best of my ability to bring it to an end. But for tonight, let us enjoy the festivities and feast. Welcome to the Highland Kingdom, Moonland elf visitors." He nodded to the elves with a welcoming gesture. "However, before the ball will commence, I have an announcement." He turned to me and gestured me forward. "This is someone who I have taken on. She will henceforth be known as King's Wolf. Her presence in my kingdom, my palace, will go unquestioned from here on out. Her purpose is to serve me for the good of the kingdom and the benefit of the royal family. She also acts as my personal guard."

He met my eyes, but I was busy trying to keep my breathing under control. This was the same place where he had sentenced me to torture and death. Where they had dragged me away to the dungeons and. . .

I clenched my teeth, glad that no one could see my whole face. The man who stood in front of me had put me six feet under. Afterwards, he had resurrected a version of me that was scathed and molded by what I had undergone so that he could use me to serve his purpose. If I wanted to live, I would do so without question. The king I had once served I had respected. But the man that stood in front of me no longer had my respect. The only respect I showed him was out of fear. He always seemed kind, so noble. But he had allowed my torture.

This man would never have my forgiveness.

I steeled myself, hoping those gathered didn't see me sway on my feet. All eyes were on me, and some of the guests whispered and mur- mured things to those around them.

I went down on one knee, a fisted hand on my chest, my head bowed. "My King." Only when he nodded my dismissal did I stand and leave the room.

Once outside in the late afternoon air, I leaned against the side of one of the fountains, feeling as if I couldn't fill my lungs properly. I kept shaking my head and murmuring, "You aren't there anymore. They aren't hurting you. You are. . ." *Safe?* I knew I was never safe.

I lifted my head, spotting the tops of the trees over the walls sur- rounding the palace. I longed to climb those walls and find my pack. I was stuck in a prison– tethered to the man who held the power to let me live, hurt me, or kill me. Locked in the cell of my memories. Pain. I could not get the images and sounds of that night out of my head. They played over and over, chasing me around and around until I was dizzy. It was all still so recent. Still fresh. But it was in the past! It was over! So why couldn't it just be over?

I faded into the shadows along the palace away from the sounds of the ball. I leaned against the outer wall and slid down until I crouched in the grass with my head back against the stony wall.

Watch your back, Kelgare had told me. And yet here I sat, tear stained cheeks and trembling like a leaf in the wind. Part of me was a hurt, frightened little girl, and the other half was a well–trained spy and guard. How was I supposed to move on and balance the different parts of me without tripping?

Stalkingwolf.

I startled. *Spiritwolf?*

It is I.

I let out a soft sob. *I've missed you so much. It has been so hard.*

I sense a storm inside you.

I closed my eyes, allowing her to feel my mind, my feelings. *How do I keep going?*

Freshkill is good. It helps. I do not know these feelings you have. Do not understand. In pain, you limp inside. Singing sad songs like a bird with broken wings, yes?

Yes, friend. I really needed this, thank you. There aren't many I can confide in. But Quinton is dangerous for a wolf. You must get out of here.

I do not wish to leave you. You are trapped in a cage. I wish to set you free.

I do not wish for you to leave me either. I sighed. *I will see you soon. I have a quest, and we will travel together in the forest once again.*

Good. I just barely heard her pacing on the other side of the wall, whining. *You are not alone, Stalkingwolf.* Then, she was gone.

After I pulled myself together, I made my way back inside. I found the King and the Queen talking to two of the elves. The princesses were flirting with a group of young men, and Sabian was being led around by a little girl about nine years of age who blushed every time he smiled at her. Kelgare was nowhere to be seen.

I made a round through the room, keeping along the walls, to make sure all was well. Folks twirled and danced, and I had to be careful to avoid their massive skirts. Then I went over to where a servant held a platter of drinks and took a glass of champagne. I stood to the side of the throne's dais where I had a good view of everything, and sipped the drink. The glass was cold, even through my gloves. But it was refreshing, and I felt like I could really use a drink.

Couples danced in front of me, twirling and stepping to the music like leaves swirling in the wind. It looked so freeing, and their happy thoughts confirmed it. I wondered if that was how birds felt when they flew.

I liked standing here, out of the way, and watching everyone. It was entertaining to see my brother being pulled around by the little girl and the princesses smothering the young men, batting their eyelashes and insisting on dance. The King and Queen looked like they were enjoying themselves, too. The elves looked a bit guarded, but otherwise they seemed to be relaxed and having a good time. I liked watching, and for a blissful moment, the sight distracted me from the toils in my mind.

I recognized a few townsfolk whose animals I had either helped or raised. Some of the royal guards were there too, making rounds around the room and occasionally making conversation with the guests. I had never really known them personally, but a few of them had been like friends to me, and I had enjoyed their company while on patrol or guarding the palace walls or royal chambers. I missed being part of the royal guard and having the company of others while I worked.

I felt eyes on me and scanned the room again to find the younger elf staring at me from nearby. Really close, actually. He stood with his arms folded across his chest leaning back against one of the hall's pillars, watching me with dark eyes. The hair on the nape of my neck stood on end when I realized I hadn't noticed him until he was so close.

He locked eyes with me and slowly approached. I couldn't tell if his hair was black or dark, dark brown. It was slightly curly, and he wore a subtle silver leaf headpiece that was mostly hidden in his hair. It matched the one on his forearm and his silver earring. He wore clean cut black pants, boots, belt, and a black button up dress shirt, sleeves rolled up neatly to his elbows. His eyes were dark, deep brown and sharp like a hawk's. Like myself, he had two sheathed knives at his waist, and judging from the bit of silver peeking out of his boots, he had two tucked away there, too.

"Dance much?" he asked with a slight smile when he was a foot or two away. A light scar bridged his nose, and he had a few silver rings on his fingers.

"No," I answered hesitantly. "I've never danced."

"A shame." He took another step and turned so he stood beside me, matching my stance, hands neatly folded behind him like mine, and surveying the ball. "Seems to me a girl your age would have danced frequently. I'm sure your unique circumstances don't allow it, though."

"Unique circumstances?"

He glanced at me. "I wouldn't think being King's Wolf leaves much room for simple pleasures like dancing."

"Oh. Yes, it really doesn't."

The orchestra switched to a slower ballroom ballad, and the couples slowed to match their dance to the melody. I watched as my brother asked a pretty girl in a violet gown to dance and led her to the dance floor.

The elf turned to me and held out his hand. "Unique circumstances call for unique actions. Come see if you like dancing; I can lead."

I hesitated. "Isn't there a girl whose face isn't masked, hands aren't gloved, you'd rather dance with? I'm sure a prince like you would rather dance with someone in a gown and a pretty face."

The corner of his mouth perked up. "I'm no prince, and the pretty faces here have had plenty of dancing opportunities. You haven't. Give it a chance, and just follow my lead."

After a moment of consideration, I set my empty glass on a table and tentatively placed my hand in his. Silently, he led me to the dance floor. I stiffened when he placed a hand on my waist. "Put your other hand on my shoulder," he instructed. I did so, uncomfortable with the closeness of this. He led me through the dance, gently but surely. I was certain he'd danced like this with many elven maidens, but at the same time I wasn't sure. His demeanor was secretive and quiet, yet at the same time confident and knowing. So I wasn't sure how many girls he'd managed to attract with such a demure and reclusive personality.

At first, I kept stepping on his boots and tripping up. But he didn't seem to notice. His gaze never wavered, and his expression didn't seem to change– he just kept leading me with quiet patience. Eventually, I started getting the hang of it, my light footedness coming in handy. Oftentimes, fighting was a lot like a dance, I realized. It was graceful.

This elf was also graceful, somehow, in the way a hawk or wolf was graceful.

"Kai Stone," he said.

"What?"

"My name."

"Oh! Right."

He didn't seem to smile much, but his eyes sure did. "You go by King's Wolf. Any other aliases?"

I didn't answer. I realized with a start that even when I tried to reach into his mind, I couldn't. I couldn't feel his mind at all. I could see him, feel his hand in mine and on my waist, but to the Keen and my senses, he wasn't there at all. Like a stone.

"You look to be around seventeen," I said.

"I am."

"But you have the air about you that suggests you are. . . canny."

"Why can't I be both?"

I studied his face. "So why did you *really* want to dance with me?"

"Why did you accept my offer to dance?" he countered. Again, I didn't answer. He was difficult.

He let go of my waist as I let go of his shoulder and he twirled me out and away then twirled me back into him, my back to his chest. I was very aware of my racing heart and hoped he couldn't feel my pulse through my gloves. I turned around to face him again and we continued the dance as the music swept on, probably quite the spectacle in our unique attire among the other folks who were dressed for the ball. I realized that Kai was the only elf present who was wearing all black. The others wore dark shades of red, green, and blue. I found it a bit peculiar, but didn't think much of it. Sometimes I paid a little *too* much attention to detail.

"You are the first elf I've ever met," I commented.

"Have I exceeded your expectations?"

"I'm not sure. Although, you are also the first person to ask me to dance."

"I'm not a person. I'm an elf."

"When you speak of your kingdom, do you say your elves, or your people?"

"You make a fine point, Wolf."

I laughed, and he almost smiled. "So she does laugh."

"I'm not a statue. I'm thinking you might be, though."

He narrowed his eyes. "And why is that?"

"You haven't really smiled or laughed."

"You haven't given me a reason to."

I shook my head. "You are something else."

"So are you. Tell me, do your brown eyes match your hair, or is your hair closer to the shade of a flame?"

I furrowed my brow. "What–" But he interrupted me by taking my hand off his shoulder and tilting his head to the doors that led outside. "Would you like to get some air? It is stuffy in here."

I held my ground, not letting him pull me towards the doors. "How did you know what my hair color was?"

At that moment, I noticed Prince Rayden was hastily following one of the elves down a corridor, looking angry and hot headed. I pulled my hand from Kai's and said, "I'll get your answer later." I slipped away and ran after the prince.

I followed them all the way upstairs to the royal family's chambers and watched as the elf entered Rayden's room, with Rayden storming in after him. What was an elf doing up here, and what had he done to anger Rayden so much?

I cut through Sabian's room and out his window to get outside on the roof and climbed over to Rayden's balcony, silently landing on it, crouching down in the shadows. It was evening now, the light of day slowly fading from the sky.

The balcony doors were open, and I could see the elf, just a few feet away from me. He stood looking out at the night sky, his arms folded back behind him. He had shoulder–length black hair but no beard, his skin pale as if he'd never seen the sun. His eyes were shockingly bright green, and he wore tall black boots, a sheathed sword at his side, and a dark blue embroidered dress coat that was long enough to reach his knees.

Rayden came up behind him, his fists clenched. "Prince Oberon."

"Prince Rayden." His voice was raspy and rough.

"Why were my guards ransacking my nephew's chambers earlier today?"

"You tell me."

Rayden took another step towards him, pointing an accusing finger. "You ordered them to."

Prince Oberon turned to Rayden, spreading his arms. "And why does that make you so angry?"

"It wasn't part of the plan, *or* the deal."

The deal? I kept silent and still, keeping my breathing shallow and light, slow. They were close enough that if I moved or made the slightest sound, I would be seen.

The elven prince tilted his head, mocking confusion. "I thought that your nephew was someone you needed off the playing field. I was doing you a favor."

"We had a plan. And I told you not to act of your own accord."

Prince Oberon let out a soft laugh. "The plan." He stepped over to a small table where two glasses and a bottle of wine stood. He filled both glasses and offered one to Prince Rayden. "Have a drink my friend, and we'll talk about the plan."

Rayden shook his head with a sigh. "I knew meddling with elves was a bad idea. They never know how to stick to things unless it's their pride." But he took the glass and drank half of it before he set it down.

Prince Oberon swirled the drink around in his glass but didn't drink. "You see, the thing is, the plan never would have worked for me."

"What?" Rayden said.

"Your plan was to involve me and my elves to help you take the throne and in return you'd give me part of your land."

I resisted the urge to take a sharp breath. So Rayden was plotting something. I didn't anticipate he'd go as far as involving elves, though.

"Yes," Rayden confirmed. "It was. It is. And you agreed."

"I didn't agree to anything. I simply said that I would like to get involved." Prince Oberon set down his full glass. "But I had my own intentions."

"What are you talking about?" Rayden demanded, his voice rising.

Prince Oberon straightened his coat and dusted off a speck of something that wasn't really there. "You had a good plan, Prince Rayden of the Highland Kingdom. But I had a better one. A piece of your land wasn't enough, and I took my opportunity. I am fifth in line to the throne of the Moonland Kingdom, you see, and so I will never be king. But this," he gestured widely, "is a kingdom I *can* rule."

"No," Rayden growled. "It isn't. It will be mine–" He stumbled forward, clutching his stomach with a grunt of pain.

"You may want to sit," Prince Oberon suggested. "This throne is ready for my taking. All I have to do is get rid of Prince Sabian, the King, and you. And I've already taken care of you."

Prince Rayden was on the floor now, groaning and rolling in pain. "W–What have you done?"

"I've poisoned you," Oberon answered calmly. "Sabian and the King will be nothing to worry about in a little while, too. And I've got an assassin hunting the King's Wolf. By morning, this kingdom will be mine. The lovely queen will be, too, as well as the princesses. Or I could sell them to a brothel– I haven't decided yet."

Prince Rayden was convulsing, foaming at the mouth and violently shaking. Oberon crouched down next to him. "Last word of advice; don't take a glass of wine from someone you don't trust. I'm surprised you haven't learned that already, given your family history."

A moment later, Rayden lay still, never to breathe again.

My heart racing and my limbs stiff with shock, I fled. I had to warn King Rubarb before it was too late.

I leaped from window sill to window sill without a sound, my tunic flapping around my thighs. When I reached the King's chamber windows, I opened them and stepped inside, closing them behind me. The chambers were dark and quiet, which didn't surprise me. King Rubarb would still be down at the ball.

I started for the doors to the corridor, but I heard something be-hind me and whipped around, swinging my dagger. A hand caught my wrist and backed me up against the wall roughly, my head slamming against the stone painfully. It was Kai.

I felt a blade against my throat. "So, you're the assassin. It all makes sense now."

He didn't answer, but his breathing was quick and heavy. I kicked his knees and pushed him away, sending him sprawling, and advanced. But Kai recovered quickly, getting to his feet before I reached him, a dagger in each hand. He lunged at me, moving quicker than I thought he could. I ducked to avoid his blade and went for his legs, but had to shift backwards quickly to keep from getting stabbed. I swung my blades, making him take a few steps backwards. I blocked his attacks and slashed my own.

He jumped and kicked me, sending me stumbling back, but I didn't lose my footing. He jabbed and I blocked it with my forearm, immediately slashing back.

While he was busy blocking my attack from one side, I sliced his other arm just above his elbow. He hissed and barreled into me, knocking me off my feet and backwards onto a table, my breath forced from my lungs. He swung his knife for my throat with a reverse grip, but I caught his wrist. With my other hand, I sliced my dagger up towards his neck but he gripped my wrist before my blade could make contact with his skin.

For a moment, we struggled in each other's grips, keeping each other's knives at bay. But with great effort, I turned his wrist and drove it, dagger and all, towards his leg. He hollered in pain as his knife was driven into his leg and loosened his grip on me. I took my chance and leapt off the table and towards the door.

Just as I reached it, Kai garroted me with a steel wire. I struggled and flailed, trying to get air into my lungs as he tightened it around my throat. I kicked against the door, slamming myself back into him, but he didn't even stumble. I kicked and hit and tried to stab, but my weakening attempts failed. Pressure built in my head, and Kai slowly lowered me as my legs gave out. My lungs screamed for air and the wire felt as if it was separating my head from my body. Darkness flooded my vision, and my limbs went limp. Then, I blacked out.

I took a gasping breath. Kelgare was crouched beside me, and I just barely caught a glimpse of Kai as he fled through the window.

"You alright?" Kelgare asked while I lay breathing in gasps of air. "That assassin basically had you."

My lungs ached and my throat felt as if I had swallowed burning coal. "I'm okay," I rasped. "Did you–"

"I was looking for you and heard a scuffle in here. I chased him off. I'm glad I came when I did. You've never dealt with a garrote before, have you?"

"No, I haven't."

"What have you learned?"

"Never to dance with an elf." I got to my feet and blinked away my dizziness. "Prince Rayden is dead."

"What? How?"

I rubbed my throat, wincing. "The elf prince, Oberon, is attempting to take the throne. He poisoned the prince and intends to do the same to King Rubarb and Prince Sabian. That assassin was sent by Oberon to get rid of me."

Kelgare took in the news and stared out the window, his eyes cold. "This isn't what we need right now. The city has been attacked."

"What?"

"The magicians," he explained quickly. "They surprised us. They came close so fast. The King and Prince Sabian are leading the counter attack. Go warn Sabian of the elves, and I'll warn the King before they leave." He flung himself out of the window, leaving me confused and reeling. The city had been attacked? This was getting increasingly overwhelming.

I went out into the corridor, flying down the stairs.

When I got to the Great Hall, I stopped short when I saw what was happening. The elves were gone and the room was in chaos, people running in all directions with shouts and cries of fear. I braced myself as the ground shook. The Queen and the princesses passed me, hurrying up the stairs to their chambers, their eyes red with emotion.

I saw Sabian hurrying out of the armory along with the royal guards, soldiers, and the King himself. I reached him before he went outside.

"Sabian, wait."

He startled. "Tal–"

King Rubarb interrupted. "The magicians have attacked the out-skirts of the city." He sheathed a sword at his side.

"Yes, Kelgare told me. How did they get so close so quickly?"

"They're magicians," he answered. "We don't know."

The ground shook again with an explosion. Soldiers and men rushed past me, armored and bearing weapons. I gripped Sabian's arm. "You're going out there?"

The King answered for him. "We both are. Everyone capable and of fighting age must. I need Sabian to lead alongside me and Prince

Rayden. My people need to see their leaders facing the hopeless with them, otherwise they won't fight. Please tell Rayden to meet us by the south wall."

"Kelgare was going to tell you, but Prince Rayden is dead. He was just murdered by the elf prince, Oberon. They had a plan to take the throne, but Oberon wanted it for himself. He has an assassin and plans to dismantle you and Sabian."

"What?" Sabian exclaimed. "Why does it all have to happen at once?" He mirrored my thoughts exactly.

The King stared at me, unblinking. Finally, he shook his head. "Rayden was meddling with the wrong people. The elves will have to be taken care of, but we must go." He turned and headed outside, calling over his shoulder, "Tala, find the elves and kill them. They couldn't have gotten far. And guard Queen Hersha and the princesses."

He was gone before I could respond.

Sabian's mind was frightened but determined. "I have to go."

I nodded. "Be careful."

Sabian and the King lead the war party through the palace gates and into the city. Fire engulfed the south part of the city, and townsfolk fled in the opposite direction. Screams and the sound of explosions filled the air. I watched them go, hoping that this wouldn't be the last time I saw my brother.

It was shocking how quickly circumstances changed. In just an hour, Prince Rayden was dead and the city was under attack. Just minutes ago, we had all been enjoying ourselves, dancing, drinking and feasting. And now the whole city was in turmoil, just like that.

The ball guests were flooding out from the Great Hall still, their gowns and coats tripping them as they hurried out and to their carriages. The carriages rushed away one by one, horses snorting anxiously, knocking against each other in a hurry out of the palace grounds.

I made sure to watch until they were all gone to make sure that the elves didn't leave with them. That meant that they were still somewhere on the palace grounds, or even within the palace itself.

Kelgare was suddenly beside me. "They left already?"

"Yes, but I made sure to warn them both before they did."

"Good." He turned to me. "I was headed to warn the king but I ran into two of the elves. I put them both in the dungeon for now. Neither of them were the prince or the assassin."

I swallowed hard. "King Rubarb told me to find the elves and kill them, and protect the Queen and princesses."

Kelgare shook his head. "I'll take care of the elves. You just guard the royals."

"O–Okay." I was relieved. I didn't want to kill *anyone,* even if they intended to kill me.

The palace grounds were silent now that everyone had left. Eerily silent, like a graveyard. But inside the palace, the servants and a few guards rushed around, preparing things. It wasn't as loud as the ball was, nor nearly as merry, but it was noisy in the way a busy beehive was noisy. Rations were being prepared, as well as medical supplies, and the Great Hall was being cleared out.

I hurried upstairs to the royal chambers and found a handful or so guards pacing the corridor. They all turned to look at me as I went by, curious and wondering. I wondered if any of them were working for Prince Oberon, and silently made a mental note to be extra wary of them. But they didn't question me as I knocked on the Queen's door.

A moment later, a maid opened the door. She looked puzzled and anxious when she saw me, but she let me in without a word.

"My lady Queen and lady princesses, the King's Wolf is here," she announced.

Queen Hersha and the two princesses were sitting around a small table, sipping tea that a maid had brought to them to help calm them. Joy was teary eyed and sniffling with fear. Princess Teyqa's brows were furrowed and she radiated anxiety. And the Queen was ruffled and apprehensive, breathing hard, her eyes darting around. I was surprised she didn't even give me a bad look.

I bowed and stepped forward. "You all are aware that the city is under siege. There has also been an incident of treason this night. I have been ordered by the King to guard you at all costs."

"Treason?" Hersha asked.

"I am sorry to inform you. Prince Rayden was poisoned. He is dead."

Hersha simply took another sip from her tea, unblinking. But Princess Joy stared at me in shock, a whimper escaping her lips. "H–He's dead?"

"Yes," I said quietly. "I'm sorry." Rayden had been Joy's father.

Joy slowly stood up from her seat and made her way to one of the windows, her breathing shallow and quick. I wanted to comfort her, but I wasn't sure I could.

Princess Teyqa studied me, her eyes brimming with tears. "Who killed Rayden?" Rayden had also been her older brother.

"Prince Oberon of the Moonland Kingdom."

The princess, my aunt, shot to her feet, hands slamming the table. "Why did you have to invite them, mother?" she hissed at the Queen.

Queen Hersha sighed. "It was at Rayden's request. The invite would be more welcome if the Queen gave it instead of just a prince."

Teyqa slumped back into her chair. "First Farley, now Rayden. And the kingdom is about to be lost to the magicians."

"Indeed," the Queen answered quietly.

Little did the princess know that Hersha had killed Farley. But I felt as if I were witnessing something I shouldn't, or as if I were eavesdropping. So I bowed again. "I will be near."

I nodded to the maid— great gamble, bless her dear soul for having to care for these royals— and stepped back into the corridor, shutting the doors behind me. I positioned myself in front of them and stood guard the way I had done so many times as a royal guard.

As I stood there, hours building upon hours, I hoped that Kelgare had found the elves and had locked them up without getting hurt. I wondered why I couldn't feel Kai's mind— I had never experienced that before. And I realized that I hadn't been able to feel Prince Oberon's mind either, nor the other elves'. It sent a shiver down my spine. They had an advantage with that. That's how Kai had been able to sneak up on me. If I'd been able to feel his mind like everyone else's, I would have sensed him before I stepped foot into that room.

They could sneak up on us as long as we didn't hear, smell, or see them. For the first time, I realized Kelgare and I, and all possessing the Keen, *did* have a blind spot if we couldn't feel minds. That realization made me shiver. I didn't like it. I was used to being able to know whenever someone was near, hear their thoughts and feel their feelings.

I also worried about my brother. I'd never actually seen a magician or what they could do, but I had seen the damage they left behind. They were a force to be reckoned with, and they had already taken the

Lowland Kingdom and most of Highland, too. They were in *Quinton*. Already. I knew us humans were no match for them, with our primitive weapons and techniques. They had *magic*. How could we beat that? I anticipated that the King would send me on my mission *very* soon.

I prayed Sabian wouldn't be hurt or worse while he was out there. Or while he was here, if Kelgare didn't catch the elves. Oh why did chaos have to ensue at the wrong moments?

I thought about the dance. I'd had a good time. It had been a wonderful distraction, and dancing turned out to be quite enjoyable. Kai was interesting and peaked my curiosity. He had been fairly kind and good looking, too. But I seethed with anger. Kai had just been trying to get under wraps. And when I thought about when he'd wanted to go outside to 'get some air', he'd probably been trying to get me away to kill me. Kai probably wasn't even his real name.

One night, I thought. Just one, normal, enjoyable night is all I ask for. But I supposed normal and enjoyable nights only happened for normal people living normal lives. I definitely did not fit into that category.

My throat was incredibly sore. I drew one of my daggers and looked at my reflection, examining the purple, bruised line that ran across my neck with a sigh. Hopefully it wouldn't scar.

My breathing began to grow heavy, my limbs trembling, and stars danced in my vision. I felt another seizure trying to come on.

I forced myself to take slow, deep breaths, and leaned against the doors behind me. I couldn't seize. Not while I was on guard, and in front of the other guards. I gripped my wrist with my other hand to keep the others from noticing how badly I was trembling. But I couldn't force away the seizure, no matter how hard I tried.

I managed to ease myself into a crouch without collapsing and leaned my back against the doors. My quickened, shallow breathing made me sound as if I were running a marathon, and my racing heart matched its pace.

A few of the other guards turned their heads, watching me with furrowed brows and judgemental stares. I was trembling so badly now that I couldn't keep my teeth from chattering.

One of the female guards, a slender blonde who went by the name Sari, came over to my side and crouched beside me, her eyes concerned. "Is everything alright? You're quite pale and shaking terribly."

I couldn't answer. I flinched when she reached to put a hand on my shoulder, but her touch was the only thing keeping me conscious.

For a long while, I sat there hugging my knees, shaking and hardly able to breathe. Pain coursed through my veins from the aftermath of the poison, and my head pounded like a sledgehammer. Sari stayed beside me, trying to get me to talk and shaking my shoulder. I hated it, but it did keep me conscious.

Slowly, the pain eased and my trembling faded and stopped. I could take a full breath again. I was exhausted, but it was over, and I had remained conscious.

Finally, I said, "I'm okay now. Just uhm, an episode of something. I'm fine." I got to my feet.

Sari raised a brow. "I've never seen anyone shake like that before. You should be seen by a doctor."

"I will," I lied. I figured I'd humor her.

She nodded, satisfied, and went back over to her position on the other side of the corridor. The guards were minding their own business, but I noticed a few of them glance my way occasionally.

I was shocked that I hadn't blacked out. But I guessed that perhaps the adrenaline of the night's events had had something to do with it. I was relieved that I did, because I wouldn't be very useful if I was unconscious.

While I stood guard, I reached out to Sabian. He was physically exhausted and in pain. But he was alive. *Are you alright?*

He didn't answer, too busy fighting and leading the soldiers, but I could feel his feelings. He wasn't okay, but he would be. I sent him a strong ripple of reassurance and encouragement, then I let him be. I didn't want to be the reason he got distracted and killed.

For hours, I stood in position with the other guards while maids came in and out of the Queen's chambers, bearing trays of tea and food, warm towels, or sweet treats. It all looked delicious, and it reminded me I hadn't eaten since early this morning. I was getting very hungry indeed.

I had almost nodded off when I heard the palace bell ring, long and deep. *Bong. Bong. Bong.*

My heart skipped a beat. That bell was only rung when someone important to the crown died. For a grappling moment, I hastily reached out to Sabian. But I could feel him. He was still alive.

I'm here. I'm okay, he spoke in my mind. *But Tala. . .*

I took in a sharp breath. *What?*

Just then, Kelgare came down the corridor, looking solemn and grim. His eyes looked hollow and worn out which suggested he'd been awake a lot longer than the rest of us, or. . .

He stopped in front of me, not needing to say anything. I knew.

The King was dead.

Kelgare blinked slowly. "I've to tell Queen Hersha and the princesses."

I let him pass and enter the room, but I didn't follow. I stayed where I was, unable to process anything.

A moment later, I heard a sharp wail of grief. No matter how horrible the Queen may be, she had loved Rubarb, her husband and her King. She burst from her chambers, stumbling down the corridor. "No, no, no. I have to see him, I have to see him," she cried. The princesses followed at her heels, leaning on each other and sobbing.

Kelgare was at my side again, his jaw tight. "Our forces have retreated back. They managed to establish a perimeter, but the magicians are too strong. They fell back to regroup, but they'll attack again soon, and there is nothing we can do." He took a deep breath. "King Rubarb was fighting valiantly on the front lines, with his people. A magician drove an arrow made of violet flame through his heart, killing him and dozens of others." Kelgare straightened, forcing perseverance. "I must go. I still haven't been able to find those elves. I need to before yet more havoc wreaks."

He headed away into the shadows.

I hurried after the royals. With the elves still around, they still needed me to guard them.

I found them in the Great Hall, standing around the King's body that lay on a table. His chest was bloody from his wound, and he looked as if he were asleep. But his chest wasn't falling and rising like someone who was still alive. The princesses were sobbing, clutching each other. The Queen had crumpled to her knees, face buried in her dead husband's beard, her body shaking with sobs. Despite the things she'd done to me, I couldn't help but feel sorry for her.

The hall was filled with injured soldiers and townsfolk. The healing rooms had probably run out of room already. Maids and servants and uninjured folk helped the injured, carrying basins of water, bandages, and cleaning wounds.

There were many more dead. Among them, I recognized the King's advisor and a few of the generals as well as some royal guards that I had worked with before.

Sabian was sitting on the step of the throne dais, wincing. He was ghostly pale, breathing hard, and his clothes were stained with sweat and blood, his hair damp and dirty, a mess. One of his arms had a terrible gash that went from his shoulder almost to his wrist, bleeding terribly. It would definitely need stitches. He kept it at his side, but his stiff posture suggested it was causing him a large amount of pain, which I didn't doubt. One of his legs was stretched out in front of him, an arrow–shaped flame sticking out just above his knee.

I hurried to his side. "Sabian!"

He didn't respond, but he nodded to me. I reached out to his mind, pouring calm into him. Slowly, his breathing relaxed a bit.

I tore a piece of my tunic and balled it up, then pressed it into his arm wound. He inhaled sharply, groaning.

"I know, it hurts. Hold the cloth there, you can't bleed out on me."

He did as I instructed, his eyes tightly shut and his jaw clenched. I moved over to his leg, examining the fire arrow. It looked like it didn't have any density to it, no tangible matter like an arrow would have. It was quite literally a violet flame in the shape of an arrow.

One of the servants who had been helping the injured came over and said, "I tried to extinguish it with water, but it wouldn't work."

"We have to get it out," I responded. "Before it keeps burning him." The arrow had burned away the fabric around it, and was searing his flesh. I thought for a moment, then I turned to the servant again. "I have an idea. Bring me a pair of welding gloves."

He did as I asked, and when he brought them to me, I thanked him before he rushed off. I pulled on the gloves over my own and tentatively touched the arrow. I could feel the heat through the gloves, so I acted quickly. I lifted Sabian's leg up enough to pull the arrow out. He cried out in pain, and I put more cloth to the wound as it started to bleed. Sabian was panting. He said, "A little warning next time?"

"Hopefully there won't be a next time." I got him some water and bandages and helped bandage his wounds.

While I did so, the two generals who weren't keeping charge over the perimeter, who had been standing beside the dead king solemnly, came over to us. They bowed to Sabian.

General Calvice spoke. "Prince Sabian, our perimeter is secure. What are our orders?"

"Your orders?" Sabian's eyes were foggy with pain and confusion.

"Yes," General Jrevia answered. "King Rubarb is. . .dead. Prince is Rayden, too. You are next in line to the throne. You are our king now. We need our orders on how to proceed."

Sabian's eyes widened, shock starting to settle in. He opened his mouth and closed it, looking back and forth between me, the generals, and the king's body. Then, taking a deep breath, he steeled himself and seemed to switch from a frightened boy to a trained commander.

"Keep someone on the watchtowers," he said. "Make sure the injured have adequate care, and the soldiers are fed and have fresh clothes and weapons."

"Yes, sir," General Jrevia bowed again. "And what of–"

"We will have King Rubarb's burial in three days' time, in accord with royal tradition," Sabian interrupted her. "For three days we mourn before the King is buried. And before the heir takes his place." His voice trembled a bit with the last few words.

The generals bowed and headed outside to carry out the new orders.

I helped Sabian up per his request, even though he shouldn't be walking around. He leaned on me and limped over to the other royals, standing at the head of the table next to King Rubarb.

After a moment, he insisted he could stand on his own so I let go, but he planted a firm hand on the table to help his stability. "People of Quinton, Highland Kingdom," he spoke, loud and clear for everyone to hear. Everyone in the Great Hall went silent, putting all their attention on him. I would have been uncomfortable being the center of attention, but Sabian didn't seem bothered at all.

"A tragedy has befallen us this night. King Rubarb is dead. We face an enemy too powerful to match, let alone defeat. They killed our king, have taken most of our kingdom, and have taken our capital under siege. We don't know what comes next, or if we will survive. I will not lie; I am unsure of what to do, or how to do it. I have been preparing for this my entire life, but as I am suddenly thrust into this position, I feel utterly unprepared."

The wounded, the servants, the soldiers, and everyone else gathered murmured amongst themselves anxiously.

"But," Sabian continued, "there are people who are older, who have more experience than I who will advise me. Those who have been serving King Rubarb for longer than I have been alive. With their guidance,

I will do everything in my power to ensure the survival and prosperity of this kingdom. King Rubarb died valiantly for you, for us, his people. We will mourn him for three days as we take up swords against our enemies. At the end of the three days, we will hold his burial. We will honor him by meeting the enemy toe to toe, and showing them what happens when they invade our turf, our home. I cannot promise that I will be a good king, but I vow that I will die for this kingdom before I give up on it."

A long silence met his speech. I found myself humbled by his genuine, heartfelt, and equally powerful words. He didn't lie, he didn't give the people delusional hopes. He gave them raw, tangible truth with honor. And with it, he gave them determination and faith.

I eased myself down on one knee in front of my brother and pounded a fisted hand to my chest, my head bowed, just as I had done to the previous king. "King Sabian."

He stared at me, shocked. But slowly, one by one, the others followed my lead, going on their knees, saying, "King Sabian, King Sabian."

My wounded brother blinked, keeping himself together on the outside. But on the inside, he was churning with emotion. He didn't feel worthy. He didn't feel prepared. He felt afraid and overwhelmed.

He smiled slightly, giving me a nod of thanks.

No need to thank me, brother, I spoke in his mind. *I bow to the king, and you most definitely are king.*

He took a deep breath. *I am, but only because the others are dead.*

No. You have been thrust into the position for a reason. You are king because it is your destiny. And if not you, then who else?

After Rubarb's body was taken away to a room of mourning, his wife and the princesses following, I took Sabian away from the people and the smell of blood and the sounds of people in pain, and helped him to one of the map rooms where no one else was.

I had him sit down on a bench while I cleaned and treated his wounds. While I did, he said, "How am I supposed to do this?"

I thought for a moment. "Take it hour by hour, minute by minute. Do everything to the best of your ability, and ask for help and advice when you need it."

He looked ill. "But how do I lead them to their deaths? The magicians are unbeatable. How do we match their power with our primitive weapons and ways? They have *magic.*"

"That isn't true." I pulled the bandage around his leg tight. "Everyone is beatable. You just have to know their weaknesses, their soft spots. And you aren't leading the people to their deaths. You are leading them, yes, but they choose to follow your lead. They choose to risk their lives for the sake of the kingdom, their families. You are giving them the courage to fight by fighting alongside them."

Sabian closed his eyes tight. "I was born out of something terrible. A mistake, my existence. And somehow I am king now. I have the blood of a murderer, rapist, and thief."

"Do not forget, I do too," I said quietly.

His eyes shot open. "Tala, I'm sorry, I didn't—"

"Don't be sorry," I interrupted. "It is true. But we aren't who fathered us. We aren't the blood in our veins or the hair on our heads. We aren't our appearances or the mistakes of people. We are what we've been through, the lessons we learn, the songs that touch our hearts, the books we read. We are the choices we make, the things we say, the things we dream of, the things we do. It doesn't matter what the people before us have or haven't done. What matters is what we do, here and now. What we stand for. That determines who we are. Not the blood in our veins."

I flinched as he put a hand on my shoulder. He noticed me flinch and concern filled his eyes, but he didn't say anything about it. Instead he said, "How did you get all the wisdom? I could use it to rule this kingdom you know."

"That's why I'm here." I took a deep breath. King Rubarb— the man that I had served, then ran away from, who had tortured me and forced my service— was dead. I was free to take off this mask and live with my pack, or live freely with my brother as a princess. I was no longer obliged to anything, really.

But. . .

But.

"That is why," I continued, "I will still be King's Wolf."

Sabian held my gaze, unblinking. "Tala, you don't have to. I can't ask you to–"

"You aren't asking." I took his hand off my shoulder and held it. "I am making this decision. For once, I *can* choose for myself what I will do. And I choose to be at your side. I choose to be what I've trained to be, but for you. I couldn't bear living my life serving a king who. . ." I took another deep breath. "But for you, I offer myself freely. That gives me joy, Sabian."

He smiled, gratitude radiating from him. "Honestly, I'm relieved. I need all the help I can get, and I could use your wisdom. But you are free to do whatever you'd like now, go wherever you want. You do not have to stay within these walls. You are also welcome here, as you, not just as Wolf. You can be heir to the throne, as is your bloodright."

The thought was striking. Tempting, even. But I shook my head. "One day, maybe. But for now, I know what I am to do. And that is enough right now. I am not ready for anything but."

Sabian nodded. "Your choices to make, sister. All yours. And I support every one of them."

My heart felt warm. No one had ever said anything like that to me. "T–Thank you." I sighed. There was so much in my heart and on my mind, I wanted to spill over. "Sabian," I started, "I–"

A knock at the door interrupted me, making me jump. "Come in," Sabian called.

I took a step away from him. We had enough trouble without people making the connection right now. Maybe one day, but not yet.

But it was just Kelgare.

He stepped inside and shut the door behind him. He was bleeding from a cut across his chest, and he was breathing hard.

I started forward, but he held up a hand. "Don't. We don't have time to tend to minor injuries. King Sabian," he added with a bow. "I was unsuccessful. The two elves who I subdued earlier are secure in the dungeon. But the others are still on the loose. I caught Prince Oberon in the corridor on the servant's chamber floor. But he got away. He is a formidable opponent. The royal guard wouldn't be able to take him on their own."

Sabian got to his feet. "How many are still out on the loose?"

"Eight."

"That's enough to cause a lot of mayhem," Sabian sighed. "I'll make sure everyone on the palace grounds is accompanied. Just in case."

Stalkingwolf, Spiritwolf called.

I jerked my gaze to the window. *Why are you so close to the palace again, Spiritwolf?*

"What's the matter, Tala?" Sabian asked.

"It's the wolf," Kelgare answered for me. "I can sense them communicating."

"Is that what that is?" Sabian wondered out loud.

I am always near, Spiritwolf responded. *I found something.*

What did you find?

A long pause. I could sense her own confusion. *I found an empty one. I cannot feel.*

An empty one?

I can see, I can smell. I cannot feel. Like a stone.

I shivered. *Where?*

Where humans used to keep their food. Human shelter, stone walls.

"She found one of the elves," I told them. "I'm going."

"By yourself?" Sabian asked. "Isn't that—"

"Kelgare has to stick around here in case the other elves show themselves. Besides, I think I can handle this one."

Kelgare crossed his arms. "You don't know that. There could be more than one, and last time the assassin almost killed you."

"What?" Sabian exclaimed. "Tala, is that why you have that mark on your neck?"

"Sabian, I've looked death in the eyes more times than you could imagine. And," I added to Kelgare, "I'm prepared this time."

Kelgare gave me a grim nod. "I suppose there isn't any other choice. We need to rid of these elves before they cause more trouble."

But Sabian shook his head. "Tala, this isn't a good idea. What—"

I interrupted him. "I will be okay. This is just part of my job, remember? Besides, Spiritwolf will be with me."

He held my gaze, his jaw tight. "Be careful."

I nodded. "You too, your Majesty."

He cringed. "Please avoid calling me that."

"I make no promises."

I made my way outside and out of the palace gates for the first time in a long time. I followed the road for a while, listening with both my physical senses and the Keen as the moonlight lit my path. The illusion of peace and tranquility that the forest brought made it easy to want to forget about the chaos. As I faded off of the road into the forest, the trees stood tall and close around me, a living shelter. Freedom. Peace. Beauty. But I couldn't let myself enjoy it. There was too much going on, too much happening inside and out of my head, I wouldn't let myself be led away like a fish in a stream. I needed to fight this current. But I relished the crisp night air in my lungs and the sweet taste of pine scent in my mouth. It strengthened me.

I stepped into a clearing and called out to Spiritwolf with the Keen, and a moment later, her weight knocked me off my feet from behind.

I hugged her, my tears coming even though I tried not to cry. "Oh Spiritwolf."

She licked my face, her paws on my shoulders, pinning me to the moist spring earth, her rump wiggling. She had grown so much, but she was still Spiritwolf. My pup. My friend. My family.

Finally, she lay on my chest, her body on top of mine. She lay there, her head tilted, her tongue lolling and her bright blue eyes locked with mine as I ruffled her shiny black fur.

We lay there together, everything better left unsaid. Both of us felt each other's feelings and embraced them through and through. We were together again, and that's all that mattered at that very moment.

After a while, I patted her head. "Show me. The empty one. The stone."

She hopped off of me and let me up. She led me through the forest, both of us solely relying on our senses to navigate through the night. I opened up my mind to hers so that I could pick up her keener wolf senses; her nose, her ears, her eyes. It was easier for her to get around through the forest at night with her wolf senses, and I was thankful I could borrow them as we made our way through the trees together.

We came to a small clearing where an old storage shack stood. It hadn't been used for a long time, evident from the erosion of the window, parts of the roof, and the holes in the walls where some of the stones had crumbled away. New storage buildings for grain and whatnot had been erected closer to the city, so this one had been abandoned.

I didn't sense anything with my Keen, but Spiritwolf's nose told me there was definitely someone inside.

Cautiously, I peeked through the glass—less, unshuttered window. Inside, a tiny light flickered from a candle on the dirt floor next to a bench, where Kai was sleeping under a wool blanket. His breathing was deep and rhythmic, telling me he was definitely asleep. His ankles were crossed and propped up on a small table, where what I assumed was his bag, sat. His leg that I had stabbed earlier was bandaged and swollen. One of his arms rested in his lap, the other lay across his face, covering his eyes. It didn't seem like anyone else was with him. He was alone.

Silently, I walked around to the door and opened it, not caring if it made a sound. It creaked on its rusty hinges, and Kai shifted his position, but stayed asleep. I crept to his side, drawing my knife, and held it to his throat, the cold, sharp point touching the skin right where his jugular vein was.

At its touch, he jerked awake with a start, his hand flying to his knife.

Spiritwolf was at my side, a soft warning growl deep in her throat. "Nuh uh," I said. "I wouldn't try anything if I were you."

His eyes went back and forth between me and the wolf, considering his chances. Evidently, he came to the decision that it wouldn't suit his health to do anything. Wise.

"I suppose you're here to kill me?" he asked. His voice wasn't afraid, but his eyes kept darting to Spiritwolf.

"I'm not an assassin," I replied.

He raised an eyebrow. "The knife against my throat says otherwise. Have you come to coax me into a cage, then? Because I won't go."

"No." I took a deep breath. What was I doing? He had tried to kill me. He probably still intended to. I should do what Kelgare would do— threaten him and demand he tell me where the others are, then knock him out cold and drag him back to the palace dungeons.

But there was the little part of me inside that remembered the things I had done because I had been forced to, against my will. What if he was a slave to his king, too? What if none of this was his choice? I couldn't kill anyone, anyway. I wouldn't. But sending him to the dungeons wasn't killing him, so why didn't I just do that? I knew Sabian would be merciful. But something inside told me to let him go.

"I came to tell you to leave. You and the others. Go, and never return."

He furrowed his brow. "Leave? We have a mission and intend to complete it."

I narrowed my eyes. "I'm the one with a knife at your throat. There needn't be more, pointless death; there's enough of that with the war. Tell the other elves to leave, and you can leave with your lives, your freedom."

"Oberon killed the prince. There is no possible way the other royals are okay with us getting away with it unscathed."

My eyes darted to the floor for a quick second, then back to him. He tilted his head. "Ah. They don't know you're letting us off with a warning."

"King Rubarb is dead," I growled. "He would have been the only one who wanted to punish Oberon. What your prince did was wrong, unforgivable. But I am not the king. I am not a ruler. And the others can't punish me if they think you got away before I found you. Go find your friends and leave."

Kai held my gaze for a long moment. "They aren't my friends. I don't know where they are. Besides, I can't."

"Why not?"

He looked away, his jaw tight. I pulled my knife away from his throat and took a step back. "Whatever they're forcing you to do, you have your chance now. You can leave. You can be free of them."

He turned his dark eyes back to me. "They aren't forcing me to do anything."

"So you wanted to kill me?"

Silence.

"Do you still want to kill me, Kai?"

He held my gaze. "I'll do what I have to do. Yours wouldn't be the first life I've taken."

"You don't *have* to do anything," I chided him. I gestured at Spiritwolf. "You wouldn't lay a hand on me with her here anyway."

Spiritwolf's gaze didn't waver from Kai, her hackles raised and her senses sharp. She would not leave my side, and she would not let her eyes stray from this strange, empty one.

Kai straightened up, setting his feet on the ground, triggering both Spiritwolf and I to tense up. Spiritwolf growled again, stepping protectively in front of me as I gripped my dagger.

"Relax," Kai sighed. "I'm not going to do anything. That wolf would tear out my throat before I could grab my knife."

"She would," I agreed.

Kai bent and picked up the candle and set it on the table, began packing his few things into his satchel. "I'll leave," he said. "But I can't promise I won't come back to finish my job when that wolf isn't around." His dark eyes met mine, the candlelight flickering across his face. "However, I can't kill someone who's already dead."

I understood what he was implying. "Really? I could have sworn that corpses could still be killed," I responded.

His eyes smiled. "You are something else."

"So are you." I crossed my arms. "I still want that answer."

"Answer?"

"My hair. How did you know what color it was?"

He studied my masked face for a long moment, his face unreadable. "Perhaps one day we'll meet again, and I'll have reason to tell you."

I was glad my hood and mask were on and that the room was mostly dark. I could feel my cheeks go pink. I remembered dancing with him, and how much of a good time I'd had. But I managed to keep my voice steady. "I'm a fool for letting you go. It's stupid."

"It really is. Although I do prefer freedom to a dungeon." He slung his satchel over his shoulder. "And I told you. I can't kill someone who's already dead." But his voice was rough, and he wouldn't meet my eyes again. "Can I walk out of here without being torn open?"

I told Spiritwolf to stand down, and nodded. I followed Kai outside, and within moments, he had vanished into the shadows.

I blew out the candle and headed back to the palace.

Chapter Five

*C*ourage is taking the leap even if you don't know if you'll make the landing. Bravery is doing something even as fear courses through your veins.

Hope can be a dangerous thing, a double-edged sword. But weapons can be used for evil, and they can be the reason you survive. As does Hope. It is the little light inside that makes even the most terrible moments and situations somewhat bearable. It does not make those things go away, and does not make them better. But Hope sits with you through it all.

However, it does not make the burden less heavy.

And sometimes, despite the light that Hope may bring, the burden may cause one to crack.

I didn't want to part with Spiritwolf. But she couldn't follow me into the palace and send everyone into a panic. Besides, I didn't want to risk someone hurting her. It was hard to part, but I assured her that we would see each other soon.

I avoided the Great Hall and the chaos, and went in through the servant's door in the kitchen, then I went looking for Sabian and Kelgare. They weren't in the map room, or in any of the meeting rooms or dining halls, so I headed upstairs to the royal chambers.

The Queen and the others weren't there; I assumed they were still downstairs with the dead king, grieving.

It was eerily silent in the corridor, not even a guard or servant in sight. I crept down the corridor warily, my gut telling me something was up. I opened my mind, reaching for Sabian, and stumbled forward, suddenly feeling his pain. His arm and his leg felt as if they were on fire. . . and he couldn't breathe.

Sabian?

He didn't respond. He couldn't. But now I sensed him just around the corner of the corridor at the bottom of the stairs.

I ran down the corridor towards him. Around the corner, I found him on his knees, Prince Oberon behind him with his arm around his neck, strangling him. Sabian's eyes were closed, and his attempts at hitting his attacker were weak and feeble, his face purple. I lunged forward, knocking the elf prince off of Sabian, rolling to the floor with him locked in my grasp. But Kelgare had been right; he was a formidable opponent. Oberon got to his knees and slammed me back into the wall. But before he could reach his sword, I kicked his legs out from under him, sending him sprawling. He hit the ground hard, but recovered quickly. As I reached for my knives, he grabbed my arms and pinned them behind me, and thrust his knee into my abdomen. The breath was forced from my lungs, and I coughed. Behind Oberon, I saw Sabian on his hands and knees, taking gasping breaths.

Oberon forced me back against the wall, but I used it to my advantage. I bent my knees and pushed off from the wall with my feet. He stumbled backwards, letting go of me.

But as I advanced with my knives, Oberon drew his sword and held me at its length. He had an advantage; I couldn't use my knives if he kept me so far with his sword.

"Tala," Sabian croaked. I risked a glance at him, and he tossed me his sword. I caught it by the hilt and parried Oberon's attack with the strength of one whose brother had almost just been killed.

I could tell Oberon was surprised at my skills, and he struggled to keep me at bay. But, he started catching on to my technique, and soon I was the one struggling. He, as all elves were, I realized, were very quick on their feet, and extremely witty. He came in a flurry, and it overwhelmed me. I was used to being able to anticipate things, sense my opponent's thoughts and feelings, but with him, I couldn't.

In two quick slashes, he disarmed me and pulled his sword back, preparing to stab my abdomen. I sidestepped before his sword made contact. But he was too fast. He swung his sword the opposite way as I moved.

Just then, Sabian slammed a bronze candlestick against Oberon's head, and his eyes rolled back into his head and he slumped to the floor, unconscious.

Sabian dropped the candlestick as I came to his side, letting him lean against me.

"What were you doing wandering about the palace without a guard?" I scolded him.

"I can handle an enemy," he argued.

"Evidently." I gave him a look. "You're wounded and exhausted, as well as the new king of the Highland Kingdom. A perfect, easy target."

"Fine, I couldn't handle *this enemy*. At least not wounded as I am."

"Exactly. What were you doing anyway?"

"I was going to grab some clean clothes from my chamber. I can't stand the smell of blood, and I stink."

"That, brother, is true." I helped him to his room and waited outside of his bedroom as he changed. When he was finished, we headed to the map room again. Sabian sent one of the servants to go fetch the generals and Kelgare so we could discuss the plans, and four guards to take the unconscious elf prince to the dungeons.

We sat together on one of the benches in the map room, sipping water. Both of us were quite equally exhausted, and now both of us had sore throats. Water was delicious.

"Did you find them?" Sabian asked. "The elves?"

I didn't say anything, but I let him feel my thoughts.

He made a sound that might have been a laugh. "I trust your decisions."

"I don't," I admitted. "Was it a mistake?"

"I guess we'll find out, won't we?"

I nodded. "I suppose. The assassin didn't know where his companions were. It didn't sound like he would have had much influence on what they did anyway. At least we have the prince locked up now. Hopefully the others will scatter without their leader."

"Most likely they will, if they're at all as wise as elves are known to be."

We stood as the generals and Kelgare entered, each bowing. Sabian shook his head. "No time for formalities."

We all gathered around one of the tables, spreading out the map of Quinton and discussing plans and any ideas that came to mind. Which were down to nothing but chance.

For hours, we grappled for ways we could somehow get the upper hand against the magicians, but to no avail. We had little to no options. And the options we had were high risk. If we went with those options, we'd be gambling the lives of hundreds, maybe thousands.

"They're regrouping. In a few hours, they'll attack again, now that they are so close." General Calvice rubbed his chin with a sigh. "We have perimeters and plenty of soldiers, but they're taking us out like we're nothing more than pieces on a gameboard."

"Compared to their power, we basically are pieces on a gameboard," said General Jrevia. "We are constantly on the defense, and have no way to get the upper hand. They've taken the entire kingdom, and we hardly even realized."

Sabian tapped the map, where we put the perimeter closest to the magicians. "We can defend ourselves a while longer. But we are taking great losses. The King is already dead, and we've lost more soldiers than we can count. That's why we need ideas."

"Ideas?" General Gengal snorted. "We're out of those, Sabian. We are *screwed*. Our best chances of survival are to flee the city. Heck, flee the *kingdom*."

"Then the kingdom would be theirs," Sabian pointed out. "If they take the palace, it'll be over. But as long as we have our city, the palace, we have a chance. Even if it's small. We just need to come up with a clever tactic. We cannot let them have both the Lowland Kingdom and ours."

Kelgare spoke up for the first time, looking at me. "I think we know what this *clever tactic* should be."

"Do tell, assassin, because we're out of plans, out of options. We're all listening." General Gengal spread his arms wide.

Kelgare didn't respond. He just held my gaze.

I took a deep breath. "King Rubarb. . .took me on originally because with my skills, he believed I could penetrate the Northland Kingdom, find their source of power, and report back if I couldn't destroy it myself— all without getting caught or seen. Then we could focus on destroying their source of power. The magicians wouldn't stand a chance without their magic."

"And do you believe you are capable of this impossible feat?" General Jrevia asked.

I met her amber eyes. "The impossible is only impossible if it hasn't been done before."

"No one has ever been able to get through that god–forsaken kingdom and out alive," General Gengal pointed out. "Like you said, it hasn't been done before. I'm all for beating the impossible, but this–"

"It's our only chance," Kelgare interrupted. "Our only somewhat sane option. It's either she succeeds and we defeat these magic monsters, or she dies, and we all die. If she doesn't try, we'll all die anyway. This is our only drop of hope."

Sabian shook his head. "It's too dangerous. I–"

"Sabian," I forced him to meet my eyes. "It is our only chance."

He tilted his head, his eyes watering. I took his hand. "Hey. I'll come back. I promise. And you know me. I won't make promises I can't keep. But I am promising that I will make it."

He shut his eyes tight, taking a deep breath. "Are you sure you're okay with this?"

No. But I kept the thought from him. "Yes."

"You do not have to do this."

"But I do. It's our only chance, Sabian. It was inevitable." I forced my voice to stay steady.

"Okay," he sighed. "What will you need?"

I looked up at the ceiling as if I were pondering his question, when really I was trying to keep myself from crying. But I kept my feelings from Sabian and Kelgare, folding into myself. "I'll need something other than a tunic or dress. Something practical. Some kind of trousers and boots that will withstand a lot of walking. A hooded top of some sort, too. Food that won't perish quickly. And a bow. The rest I have."

"Alright," Sabian nodded. "I'll get everything you need. I'll have the seamstress make something right away."

"Good," Kelgare said. "She needs to leave by early tomorrow morning at the latest."

I clenched my jaw. "I'll go prepare. In the meantime, Sabian, do not be alone ever. You can't defend yourself when you're so wounded." But as I headed away, the trembling started again. The room seemed to tilt, and I collapsed to the ground, convulsing. Pain racked my veins and head and I shook violently. I was vaguely aware of Sabian at my side before everything went black.

When I woke, I was lying on the bench in the map room, everyone gone except for Sabian.

I managed to sit up, taking deep breaths to steady myself. He didn't look at me, his face in his hands, elbows on his lap. I could feel the anxiety and hopelessness coming off him in waves.

"How are you supposed to do this when you have such terrible episodes?" he murmured.

I felt shame burning me like a brand. It made me feel so useless and vulnerable, unreliable. "I–I have to."

He nodded. "Just. . .how, Tala? You can hardly walk out of a room without seizing, going unconscious."

I bit my lip, taking another breath before speaking. *Don't cry, don't cry.* "There is no other way. I'll have to be okay."

I patted his shoulder and slipped away before my feelings spilled over. I climbed the stairs to the servant's chambers floor, my legs shaky and unreliable, and stepped into my room, shutting the door behind me. For a long moment, I just stood there with my back against the door. I knew this was my choice, I knew that I didn't have to go on this mission. But the weight of the responsibility was like a stone tied around my neck, unavoidable and oh so heavy. And these seizures? If there was some sort of god out there, what had I done to make him so angry?

I collapsed, my chest tight and my head pounding. For a moment I stayed there on my knees, unable to breathe, unable to cry. I was choking on my life. It was too much to bear. And for some reason, the weight of all came crashing down on me heavier than ever before.

When I was little, six or seven maybe, I had this fantasy that one day things would get better. As time went on, it would get easier. But the older I got, the more I could see what a lie that was. If I could tell my younger self anything, I'd warn her that I'd take a lot of hits. For a long time, I hoped to one day see the light at the end of the tunnel. Now, I just wanted the tunnel to collapse and bury me. I just wanted it to end.

The seizures, the weight of my mission, fear for my brother, my physical pain. To add to that, the inside of my head was a living hell because of my past. The constant fear, the memories, the ways it had changed me. . .

It was all too heavy. It hurt so much. I was jaded from pain.

I crumpled further until my forehead hit the floor, my arms clutching my sides, and sobbed so hard my stomach hurt. I had to cover my mouth with my hands, afraid that someone might hear.

For a long while, I sobbed there on the cold, stone floor. My physical and mental pain joined and became one large, unbearable burden that weighed me down, keeping me pinned to the floor.

When I had physically run out of tears to cry, I lay there still, my face wet. I felt the miniscule fraction of myself that still had some hope, still had some joy, vanish into the shadows of my heart, leaving me empty. I was hollowed out. Sure, gold was tested in fire. But these fires were too hot, too vigorous. I had been melted down to ash.

I slowly pulled my head up off the floor, then unfolded myself. I sat there, staring at nothing, feeling myself breathe but not feeling alive.

So. . . this was acceptance. I felt it rise in my throat like bile. I would always hurt. I would always feel incomplete. I would always be fighting for my life. I would always be in shadow. I would always be broken.

Hope was a dangerous thing. A good thing while it lasts; keeps one going. But if it's snatched away, over and over again, it tears one apart. A double edged sword that I had wounded myself with. I wouldn't pick up that weapon again, no matter how badly I needed something to help me.

Something in me just let go.

At some point, I had fallen asleep, because I woke up curled in a ball on the cold floor of my room. The chamber was dark and cold, the fire in my fireplace having gone out a long time ago. I could sense it was morning, very, very early– long before the sun would come up from behind the horizon.

I lay there for a moment, not feeling anything inside anymore. Numb. Just like my cold, gloved hands and my booted feet.

I sat up and warmed my hands by breathing on them and rubbing them together. I got to my feet and packed my satchel, secured my knives. Then, I headed out into the corridor, downstairs. I stopped by the kitchen to eat some bread and stew that the cooks had prepared for the soldiers. I ate enough to sustain me and ease my hunger, but I didn't feel like eating much despite the fact that I hadn't eaten for at least 30 hours.

Afterwards, I found Kelgare and Sabian outside the Great Hall. They greeted me with grim nods.

Sabian handed me a bundle, and a bow with a quiver–full of finely crafted arrows. "Everything you requested."

"Thank you, the food too?" I took them and stuffed the bundle into my satchel, slung the bow and quiver over my shoulder.

"Yes."

"And–"

"The clothes are in the seamstress's room."

"Okay, thank you."

"Don't thank me," Sabian said. He wrapped me in a hug. "Just come back."

I squeezed him. *I love you, brother.* Out loud, "Be safe. You'd better be here when I get back."

I love you, too.

I turned to Kelgare. "Keep him safe. And the Queen and princesses."

He nodded. *Keep your wits about you, young one. Don't let the dark stop you from seeing what's in front of you.*

I wasn't sure what that meant, exactly. But before I could change my mind, I forced myself away from my brother without looking back.

Before I left, I stopped by the seamstress. She gave me the clothes, and I changed into them in one of the vacant rooms. The clothes were comfortable and I found that I liked them a lot. A long sleeved, hooded black top with black leather gauntlets, comfortably tight black trousers, black leather belt, and boots– all with plenty of places to strap and tuck my knives. Once I had done so, I put my mask back on, as well as my hood, grabbed my things.

But as I ran through the corridor, the ground shook, making me stumble. I caught my balance as I heard the sound of explosions terribly close to the palace. I wanted to stay and fight alongside my brother, but instead, I ran.

I climbed the palace ground wall, not wanting to risk going out through the gate, and shimmied down until I was close enough to the ground to drop down without hurting myself.

As the sun began to rise above the horizon and the sound of explosions filled the air, I vanished into the forest towards where the corners of the Moonland and Northland Kingdoms met.

The Highland Kingdom was mostly made up of stout oak and birch trees, leafy and bright with spots of sunlight filtering in through the canopy. In comparison, the Moonland Kingdom was dark, with towering pines and climbing vines, minimum sunlight making its way to the forest floor. While on the other hand, the Northland Kingdom was between the two opposites, with spruce and alpine trees.

The leaves and twigs crunched under my boots as the sun rose, warming the chill in my bones. I trekked along the border of the Moonland and Northland Kingdoms, the scent of the morning spring air tasting like rain and greenery. Birds chirped and chased each other overhead, flitting between the branches, arguing.

It wasn't long before Spiritwolf joined me. I had called out to her with my mind after I had scaled the palace ground walls. She matched my pace, both of us relishing each other's silent company. We kept to the trees, far away from any of the roads or trails.

This time, I didn't tune into Spiritwolf's senses. I just wanted to take in what was around me without scenting and hearing every little thing in the forest. And for a while, I was glad I didn't, because I felt that I could actually put my walls down and relax a little now that we were far from other people.

I soon realized that was a colossal mistake.

Just after noon, we stopped to drink from a stream. The water was cool and fresh and tasted like mountain air, a wonderful change from the musty well water at the palace. Compared to this, that water was repulsive.

I knelt, cupping my hands and scooping the water to my lips. Beside me, Spiritwolf lapped from the stream, crystal–like droplets spotting her neck fur. When I had gotten my fill, I straightened, tilting my head back to look up at the clear blue sky. Not a cloud in sight. It seemed too cheerful a day when just miles from here, hundreds were losing their lives fighting against all odds in a war they probably wouldn't win.

I couldn't stop worrying about Sabian, and Kelgare, too. The Kingdom had never really been kind to me, but I cared about it and everyone in it. Even from here, I could sense the anguish of the people. I hoped that somehow, I could succeed and save the kingdom.

Spiritwolf's head jerked up, her body tensing. She heard something nearby, and she could smell something, but she couldn't sense it through her mind, and neither could I with the Keen.

I looked around, scanning the undergrowth, and the canopy. I didn't see anyone. I got to my feet and listened, using Spiritwolf's senses this time. But as I did, my ears caught a sound. I listened, trying to place what it was, and finally I realized it was a flute. Beautiful melody, one I didn't recognize. It was light and soft, the notes blending into each other. For a moment I stood there, trying to pinpoint where it was coming from. But soon, I found myself swaying to its tune, my thoughts and worries scattering like leaves in the wind. I no longer worried about any dangers or threats, my muscles relaxed . . . and all my walls came down.

I was in such fanciful bliss, that I hardly even realized that Spiritwolf was lying on the ground, rolling and thrashing as if in pain. Blood trickled from her jaws, and then she lay still.

It was then that I realized blood was trickling from my own mouth and nose. My eyes dilated so quickly that I could feel it, and my head pounded. I was aware of someone nearby, approaching quickly, but

I was trapped in the trance, unable to do anything but stand there. I couldn't even breathe.

Darkness flooded my vision, and the world lurched under my feet, tilting.

I woke up to the muffled sound of voices around me. I was seated on a chair, my hands tied behind me and my ankles tied to the chair legs. A sackcloth was over my head, and my skull pulsed painfully. I tasted blood in my mouth, and my upper lip was wet with the blood that had trickled from my nose.

I lifted my head, hardly able to, and someone nearby said, "She's awake." His voice was deep and accented.

Seconds later, the sackcloth was taken off of my head. I squinted as my eyes adjusted to the light. I was in the corner of a white wall tent, facing a table where six others sat, drinking from large mugs and eating. Three females and three males, with two male guards by the tent door. All of them were massively muscled, and looked as if they hadn't shaved or bathed in a century. The man that had taken off the sackcloth ambled back over to the table and sat down heavily. He had a peg leg.

None of them paid much attention to me. They were too busy digging into whatever they were eating.

My senses were echoing inside me like an empty cave. It felt as if I was underwater or drunken, my movements slowed, and my thoughts foggy. My eyes were droopy, and my head kept lolling as if my muscles couldn't keep it up. My vision was blurry and everything seemed to blend together. But my captors hadn't taken off my mask or my hood. My mind found it hard to process anything.

I blinked slowly, trying to keep my head up. The man with the peg leg looked up and chuckled, addressing no one. "The King's Wolf. Wouldn't ya know it?"

One of the women, with long gray hair and a nose ring snorted. "Stupid if you ask me. Capturing the King's Wolf. . ." she trailed off grumbling.

"No one asked *you*," one of the other, younger men said. She glared at him and bared her teeth like a cat.

"Why would Cordan want her?" Peg leg asked. "She don't look like much."

"Probably just another one of his *female victims*," a man with a mustache said, rolling his eyes.

"He don't usually tie them up though." Peg leg stared at me. "Not like that. And usually he just, ya know, does what 'e does and discards 'em out in the forest or on one of the trails."

Nose ring woman snorted again. "You're full of questions this day, Davy. You do know smoking first thing ain't the wisest idea?"

Davy pouted. "Don't blame my questions on my bad habits, Jage. You know I'm tryin' to quit."

"Yada yada." Jage motioned her hands over her plate. "Ye say the same thing every morn', Davy. I'll believe it when I see it."

"It ain't as easy as ye think, you old hag–"

A man with a short beard and a wool hat slammed his fist on the table. "Would you two *shut up*?"

"Please," another woman winced. "I've got a headache."

"You always have a headache, Mave," the younger man pointed out.

"Only because you all won't shut up!"

They went on yammering, making the pain in my head sharpen. Finally, Davy pointed at me. "Eh, uh, she ain't lookin to good, fellers."

"Quit calling us fellers," Jage complained. But she got to her feet and marched over to me. She crouched so she was eye level with me, and I struggled to keep my chin up.

"Yer right," she admitted. "She lookin' real ghost–like." I moved my head away as she reached out to touch my cheek with her hand. "Stay still. No reason to be squirmish." Her hand was cold against my skin.

"She's running hot," she remarked. "I wonder why. Maybe–"

"It's the dwam flute," a voice came from the other corner of the tent. I realized then that an elf stood there watching with his arms folded across his chest. He had straight, shiny black hair, and wore dark, hooded robes of crimson and gray. His pointed ears stuck out through his hair, and his expression was that of someone with a large amount of pride.

"The dwam flute I used on her," he explained. "It causes some. . .unpleasant side effects. Some can't even survive an attack from it."

He came over to me, pushing Jage away. He looked down at me with a sigh. "Not sure if she'll survive. I suppose we'll just have to wait and see."

"Why didn't you just, like, *attack her* attack her?" Davy asked.

The elf raised a brow. "Let me ask you this, Stick–leg. Would *you* dare risk taking your chances against the king's spy, and probably assassin, with training even we can't comprehend? And from what I've heard, she possesses the Demise. She may not have sensed *me* approaching, but I had a feeling I shouldn't take my chances. The dwam flute was my best chance. None of you losers wanted to get her, anyway. So don't plague me about my techniques."

Jage snorted. "Dwam flute."

Mave nudged her shoulder with a giggle. "Sounds like–"

"*Shut up*," the elf growled. He rolled up his sleeves and crossed his arms again, studying my face. "Eyes are freakishly dilated. Cordan better hurry the hell up if he thinks he's going to get something out of her."

"What does that flute thing do anyway, Jon?" Mave asked.

"It was fabricated by the elementalist elves," Jon explained. "Some of the most powerful elementalists can even forge things that hold power, like the flute. When played, anyone that hears it, except for the one playing it, will fall into a trace. Really, it causes some things in the brain– and don't ask me what. I only use it and care that it works. I don't care what it does down to the science. All I know is that most don't survive, and those that do have some nasty side effects."

As I half listened, my mind trying to catch up, I realized that they had mentioned Cordan. It couldn't be the Cordan I knew about, Cordan Greyver, the renowned wanted criminal in three different kingdoms— rapist, murderer, thief— and also my father. It couldn't be.

Jon finally gave up staring at me and flounced back to his corner. "One of you dirty rats, go get Cordan. Tell him he'd better get in here."

Everyone at the table began arguing over who should go.

"I went last time!" Davy whined.

"But it's your turn, Jage!" Mave cried.

"No it ain't!" Jage protested. "It's Gregger's!"

Finally, Jon screamed, "SHUT UP! Or I'll use the dwam flute on you *all*!"

They all went silent except for some grumbling. Jon sighed. "Whatever. I'll go." He exited through the tent flap door.

It was quiet for a moment as the others continued their eating, but then one of them spilled a mug of ale and Mave leapt to her feet, throwing the mug at Jage. "Ye made my trousers soaking wet! I look like I wet my pants!"

The mug clunked against Jage's forehead, and she bared her teeth. "I didn't do *nothin*! You little—"

It was easy to drown out the chaos with how murky my mind and senses were. I could feel the heat of my fever, but I shivered profusely.

All went completely silent when Jon returned, followed by a bulky man with a long beard and auburn–red hair like mine. His brows were bushy, and his skin was leathery from weather and sun. He wore thick wool trousers and a stained, off white shirt and a long leather trench coat.

For a moment, he stood there, hands on his hips, glowering down at me. Then he cracked a yellow–toothed smile. "King's Wolf." He bowed dramatically, almost mockingly. "You are in one of the fine establishments of Cordan Greyver." He straightened, pointing a finger at his chest. "I am he."

"Fine establishment," Davy scoffed. Cordan shot him a dark look, and he tucked into himself like a turtle.

My heart was racing faster than I thought possible. It was him. This was my father. Despite the fog in my mind, I thought, *How could Sabian and I possibly be related to this man?*

My chin kept hitting my chest despite my efforts to keep my head up. Cordan seemed to realize the state I was in and bent, reaching to me. I flinched, my senses coming back to life.

I was in danger. I was always in danger.

He pulled back his hand at my flinch and crossed his arms. "No need to be frightened. As long as you cooperate."

I met his eyes and shot daggers at him. It was then that I also realized all my things, including all of my knives, had been taken from me and were sitting in a pile beside the door of the tent.

Cordan tilted his head. "Fierce little one, ain't ya?" He turned to Jon. "Think she'll make it?"

"Probably not."

"I'm fine," I growled. I really wasn't, in fact I was far from fine. But the last thing I needed was them thinking I was weak. Ever since I was born, I couldn't let anyone believe I could be messed with. This was no exception.

"You don't look fine," Cordan said as he went up behind Davy. He grabbed the back of his chair and tilted it, sending Davy toppling to the floor with a thump. The large heap moaned, "Heyyy!"

Everyone else at the table laughed and made jokes while Cordan dragged the chair over and sat down in front of me. He leaned back, stretching his legs out, and crossed his ankles, folding his hands neatly in his lap.

"So, Miss Wolf. Heard you do fine work for that old king."

I didn't answer.

"You just a spy, or are ye an assassin as well?"

When I didn't respond, he chuckled. "Alright. Down to business then?" I still couldn't believe I was sitting, tied, in front of the most wanted criminal on the planet, the man who had sired me through one of his most common crimes.

"I'm sure ye know who I am," he continued. "But what I want from you isn't what I usually intend with my prisoners."

"In order for you to have prisoners, you must have a prison," I hissed. "This is a tent."

He squinted. "So ye do talk." He leaned forward. "Good. Because what I need from you is to tell me the easiest way to get into the Highland Kingdom Palace treasury."

I let out a sharp breath. Wow. "Right to the point."

He grinned. "Ye know, since ye lived there, worked there. Ye know your way around. And besides, it's the opportunity I've been needing. With the war, everyone is distracted."

"I'm not telling you anything."

His smile faded. "I would suggest you cooperate." He swept the side of his coat aside, revealing his dagger. "If you don't talk, I'll make you."

I held my head high, my glare going darker. "Do your worst. Chances are, I've had a lot worse."

He clenched his teeth. Then, he said, "Take off her mask and her hood."

Panic rose inside me. I whipped my head side to side as Jon stepped over and tried to take off my mask. He pulled off my hood, my hair spilling around my shoulders, and he gripped it close to my scalp to keep me from thrashing around. Then, he yanked off the mask, letting it fall to the ground.

He let go of my hair and stepped back. I tried to keep my face down, but Cordan gripped my chin and roughly turned my head, forcing me to meet his gray eyes. When I did, I made sure to make it clear that he had been right— I was fierce.

He studied my face, gripping my chin tightly. "Well I'll be."

Everyone turned to look. Jage's eyes widened. "She's the spittin' image of you, Cord."

"Great gamble," Davy muttered. "Never thought I'd set eyes on one of his offspring."

If I thought my heart had been racing before, now it felt as if it would explode. My breathing quickened, and I felt exposed. Vulnerable. I'd never liked that mask, but it had given me a sense of safety. Now I felt ripped of my protective shell.

All the feelings from the dungeon came rushing back like an avalanche, crashing into me with such a force that it felt as if I had been kicked in the chest, my breath knocked from my lungs. Fear froze me in its cage.

Cordan finally let go of me. "Who was your mother, kid?"

I didn't answer. I knew if I did, I wouldn't be able to speak around my chattering teeth. I couldn't breathe.

"Whatever," he huffed. "It doesn't matter. I just need to know the location of the royal treasury and the easiest, safest way to it."

It didn't matter? I didn't answer.

"Blast," he cursed. "You have some nasty scars there, kid. If you don't start talking, you're going to have a lot more."

I just glared at him with all the hate I could muster. I knew the stories about him, and I knew he was said to possess the Demise. So I wondered if he really did, especially since he didn't use it on me.

He stared at me for a long moment, then he backhanded my face so hard that I was knocked to the ground, chair and all. Stars danced in my vision, and the room spun. The side of my face that he'd struck burned like fire. I knew that sting. It would bruise badly.

I gasped for breath as Cordan crouched beside me, unable to hide the pure panic and fear. It was all too familiar, all too similar.

"Yes," Cordan growled. "Exactly. Start talking, and worse won't come to you." He pulled the chair up, me with it, and stood. "Speak. Now."

I couldn't speak past my panic. Still, I refused. Even if I could speak, I wouldn't have. Things might have gone differently if King Rubarb was still alive. But my brother was king now. He had enough to deal with without all his funds being lost to thieves. I would not betray him.

Cordan was really getting angry. He cracked his knuckles and rolled up his sleeves. "Fine. As you wish." He drew his dagger.

But before he could do anything, Jon said, "Wait. I might have something that could make her talk."

"You're just squeamish," Cordan replied. But he added, "Hurry up."

Jon headed outside, slipping on his hood.

Cordan paced in front of me, his blade glinting in the light while I sat there, panting, but not getting enough air. I was stuck, again. Facing torture, again. Probably facing death again, too. Every hit and kick and the feel of the lash on my back was flooding my mind, drowning me. I didn't have anyone to save me then, I didn't have anyone to save me now. I gasped and gasped, unable to control the panic and fear.

What felt like an eternity later, Jon returned, still hooded. But as he approached me again, I saw who was really under the hood.

Kai.

My eyes widened, and I opened my mouth to say something, but he met my eyes and gave the barest shake of his head. He said, "This should get her to talk," and came up in front of me, keeping his face angled away from Cordan and the others.

I jerked my head away as he reached with both hands, but he gave me a reassuring look. Blocking Cordan's view, he stuck something soft in each of my ears, and stepped back, pulling something from Jon's robes.

Quickly, he held it to his lips. It was the flute. Cordan's eyes widened, but before he could react, Kai blew. I barely heard the sound around the earplugs, but I knew it was the highest note a flute could play.

Everyone in the tent cried out, gripping their ears, grimacing. They all fell to the floor, rolling around in agony. It wasn't long before they all lay still, unconscious and bleeding from their noses.

When all was still, Kai lowered the flute. He tucked it back into Jon's robes and turned to me, drawing one of his knives. I flinched as he came closer, but he only cut loose my ankles, then my wrists. When my hands were free, I took out the earplugs. They were made of some kind of clay.

Kai rolled the unconscious Cordan over with his boot, crouching and holding the knife to his throat. "I could slit it now. He'll never cause any more trouble."

"Don't," I managed. I was still shaking and struggling to get control over my breathing.

"Why?"

"Just don't. It isn't right to kill a man when he's helpless and unarmed."

"We could wake him up."

"No."

"He's killed plenty of helpless and unarmed people."

I didn't respond as I got to my feet and took a few shaky steps. "What are you doing here, Kai? Why did you save me?"

He stood and sheathed his knife, avoiding the question. "You're ill."

"I'm not ill," I said. I hated that he had seen me like this. That *anyone* had seen me like this. I pushed my way outside, grabbing my things on the way out.

Out in the sun, the fresh air, I took five slow, deep breaths. Around me, men lay unconscious. Or dead. I didn't want to know. I shut my eyes tightly, trying to force away the memories, the fear, the panic, and slow my racing heart.

When I thought I had gotten control over myself, I opened my eyes and took a step, but my body had not recovered after all.

The world spun around me, and my legs buckled. But strong hands caught me and helped me lower to the ground. Kai kept an arm around my shoulders, keeping me from tilting sideways. "You're burning up."

I pushed his arm away from me, hunching and holding my sides. "Maybe I am ill."

Kai tossed his own clay earbuds into the undergrowth. "Probably. The dwam flute is quite brutal. It is a wonder you survived."

"So that other elf said." I pulled my knees up to my chest and hugged them, shivering.

Kai scrunched his nose. "These clothes stink. I'm going to change and find you some water." He got to his feet and went back into the tent.

I sat there for a long while, grounding myself. I concentrated on the feel of the grass underneath me, the breeze around me, and the sounds of the forest. The birds chirping, the leaves rustling, and the flapping of the tent doors. Slowly, my breathing calmed down, and my heart rate leveled. I shut out everything except the here and now, shoving all my feelings and memories down, down. There wasn't much I could do about my fever and the effects of the flute except hope it would get better. My senses were getting better, though, and my Keen was sharp once more.

I slid my knives all back into their sheaths, relishing the comfort they brought me.

Kai returned dressed in black pants, boots, and a long sleeve leather black jacket, his knives at his waist and in his boots. Additionally, he had two long daggers, almost like short swords, sheathed at his back. He still had on his silver leaf headpiece, half hidden in his slightly curly dark brown–black hair, and had a gray canvas backpack.

He crouched beside me again and handed me a flask. I took it and opened it, sniffing it.

"Water," he said.

I drank, letting it cool me from the inside out. When I was finished, I closed it and set it aside. "Did you happen to see a wolf somewhere around here?"

He raised a brow. "No."

I sighed, reaching out to Spiritwolf. I hoped with all my heart that she was okay.

She responded, *I am unharmed. But I am tied up nearby.*

I slowly got to my feet and headed in the direction I sensed her. Kai followed without questioning me.

We came to another tent and went inside. It was empty except for Spiritwolf, who lay tied to a pole, her legs bound and her jaws clasped with a muzzle. She thrashed and whined, growling. I rushed to her and cut her loose. Immediately, she gave me a lick of gratitude and nuzzled her face into my chest. I stroked her. *It's alright.*

When she saw Kai, her hackles rose, a soft growl rising in her throat.

"No," I chided her. "He helped us." She relaxed slightly, but I could sense she was on guard. Once outside, she wandered around sniffing, keeping away from the tents and taking in the fresh afternoon air.

"Did you raise her?" Kai asked.

"No, but I've known her since she was born."

"Why does she stick with you? Don't wolves live in packs?"

"They do. She does. But," I explained, "she's had a bond with me forever. And when I'm on my own, she will not leave me. But her pack will be nearby."

We moved away from my father's camp and into the trees, cautious and aware of our surroundings in case of any surprises. Kai seemed more relaxed than I was– with a knife in my hand and tense as a spooked cat.

I had met my father. No, not father. I had met Cordan Greyver, the monster who had sired me. He was not my father, nor ever would be. But it was shocking, still. And the things he'd said. . . It didn't matter who my mother was, he'd said. It didn't matter that I was his offspring, that my mother had been executed because she had been accused of having an affair when really, she was one of Cordan's many victims. It didn't matter that Sabian and I were orphans, deprived of the safety and care that parents brought. That I had been left to fend for myself.

It didn't matter. None of it. To Cordan, I was just a result of one of his criminal habits, nothing more.

That shouldn't have bothered me. I had no love for Cordan Greyver, nor did I wish that he loved me. I didn't need his love. Especially whatever love a criminal could offer, if any.

But the younger version of me, the girl who lived in a stable with animals, grappling for scraps of food, for the mercy and compassion of a stranger, huddled in the hay with her mutt in the dead of winter, teeth chattering, hands blue and frostbitten. The girl who lived in fear that she'd be found out as one who possessed the 'Demise'. The girl who starved when the villagers didn't have any more animals for her to help, and they didn't spare her the scraps she so heavily depended on. The girl who had to defend herself from those bigger, stronger than her. Who had to steal and fight and work hard to survive. The royal outcast. She needed a father, a mother. She needed love.

I was the result of that girl growing up without those vital things. The result of someone who bore those things and so much more. Sometimes I wondered how different things would be if I'd had a mother and a father and a home and love. If I hadn't gone through what I did.

But it was all a part of me now. All a part of this broken girl. And that could never be reversed. I shouldn't dwell on how unfair it was, how painful, because it wouldn't change anything. And it certainly wouldn't change who my father was, or the things I'd been through. My childhood, the dungeons. . .

No, no, no, I chided myself as my past oozed back. No, don't dwell on it. Don't.

But I was so distracted, the next thing I knew, my forehead slammed into a branch with a loud *crack*. I stumbled backwards, grimacing and holding my screaming head in my hands.

Kai's voice was aggravatingly calm. "Don't forget; you have eyes for a reason."

I groaned in pain. "Leave me alone, elf."

He watched me, arms folded across his chest, as I paced back and forth willing the sledgehammer in my head to cease its hammering. When I finally stopped and realized he was watching me, expressionless, I felt my face redden. I'd been humiliated enough; I needn't make it worse. It was then that I remembered; I didn't have my mask. Great gamble, I felt exposed.

I sighed. "I've made quite the impression, haven't I?"

"Quite, though I seem to keep showing up at the wrong time."

"Except for back there."

"What can I say, I like to make an entrance."

I studied him. "You still haven't answered either of my questions; the one from before, and why you saved me."

He turned away, ignoring my questions, and continued through the trees. I chased after him.

"Don't ignore me!" I ran around and in front of him, using my Keen to walk backwards without tripping, and demanded, "How did you know my hair color?"

He kept his eyes on the forest, his expression never changing. "You are as incessant as a mosquito."

I glared at him, clenching my teeth. I was not in the mood for an uptight boy's stubborn attitude. As he strided past me, I struck his face with my gloved fist. He stumbled, then he grabbed my wrist and forced me back against a tree–trunk, pinning my arm above my head, his nose an inch from mine.

But I was quick, too. I had a knife to his throat by the time he pushed me against the tree.

"A dagger?" He raised a brow. "Are you flirting with me?"

"No," I pushed him back. "Tell me. Or I'll show you how a knife works."

He stepped back, looking off into the trees, then the ground. I hated that I couldn't sense his feelings. "Let's just say that the ball wasn't the first time I saw you."

I narrowed my eyes. "It was you. The one whose eyes I felt on me that morning."

Kai nodded. "With the blue bird."

I crossed my arms. "You were spying on me."

"It's part of my job."

"You are an assassin, I was your target."

"Exactly." He shifted.

"So why did you save me, just now?"

He glanced at me, but his dark eyes were distant. "Because you and your mission are noble, necessary. I realized that if things keep going the way they do with the magicians, the world will fall apart."

"So. . ." I thought about it for a moment. "Are you telling me that you're going to help me? With the mission?"

"Yes."

"I don't need help." Certainly not from the assassin who had almost killed me.

"Maybe, but I already did. You sure as hell wouldn't have gotten out of Greyver's hold on your own. Not in the state you were in."

I opened and closed my mouth, but I couldn't find an answer to that. I couldn't argue with the truth. "Thank you."

"For saving you, letting you live, or coming with you?" He raised a brow.

I narrowed my eyes. "For not listening to me when I told you to leave the kingdom."

"I won't leave. I always keep chasing. Like a hunter. It's my instinct."

I cracked a smile. "Quite the hunter you are. Galavanting with and saving your prey from the snares."

For once *he* was the one lost for words. I led the way into the trees, Spiritwolf at my side.

Chapter Six

Kai

*M*y name is Kai Stone.

This isn't my story. This isn't the part where I take over.

This is simply the part where I bring to light a bit of her story from someone else's eyes. Sometimes, one cannot see the full story, the true person, without seeing them from a different perspective.

I had always been a loner. I'd never traveled with anyone before. And certainly never with a human. A human with a wolf.

We tramped through the forest along the borders, making our way slowly along Highland Kingdom territory in silence. The King's Wolf was more tense than I thought was physically possible. She gripped her knives, her eyes scanning our surroundings with impossible speed, her jaw clenched. Now without her mask, I realized just how young she really was. I was seventeen– she seemed a year or so younger. Her features were unlike those of her people. They typically had blonde or brown hair and darker tanned skin. Whereas her waist–long hair was auburn and when the sunlight touched it, it looked like fire. Her skin was on the paler side, and she was wiry and nimble. Her eyes the color of hazelwood.

Her demeanor made me sympathetic. This girl was no ordinary girl, but what had molded her? What had she gone through to make her this way?

It wasn't any of my business. And frankly I wouldn't have cared, except that I saw similar things in my sister. And I knew what had caused it. So I couldn't help but be sympathetic, despite my nature.

When I first saw the King's Wolf, I had been looking for her. I scoured the palace grounds without being seen or caught, trying to get a glimpse of my target. I finally decided my best bet was to find a good vantage point and wait for her to show. I was watching from the palace roofs when a girl on the servant's floor opened her window, inviting a blue bird into her gloved hands. Her flame–like hair danced in the breeze, and though her eyes were tired, she smiled to the bird and sang a tune I didn't recognize, her light voice carrying on the wind. The bird adored her with its beady eyes, chirping.

I was fascinated.

She was unlike any elf or any human I'd ever seen. My curiosity swept over, and I forgot my mission for a long moment. I *never* forgot my missions. I *never* got distracted. My sister's life depended on it. But this girl was the exception.

A crash inside one of the palace chambers frightened the bird away, and the girl disappeared from my view into the back of her chamber. She returned a moment later with a wolf mask on, leaping from her window and pulling up her hood. She headed from window sill to window sill pausing only once, then continued on until she reached a certain chamber window and disappeared inside.

That was when I realized.

That's the King's Wolf. My target.

For a quick moment, dread instilled itself in my soul. But I swept it away with a start. I was an assassin. She wasn't just a girl. She was my target.

Now, as I walked along beside her, I slammed down everything inside and hardened. I was helping her for the sake of the kingdoms, at my sister's risk. At her suffering. This wasn't leisurely. Nor was it something I could allow myself to enjoy.

"Names are a way to understand one another," I murmured.

The girl glanced at me, brushing the white streak of hair behind her ear. "What?"

"A name is part of who you are."

She didn't answer, but she furrowed her brow. I gripped my backpack straps. "So who are you?"

She kept her eyes on the ground, stepping over a log, never letting go of her knives. She opened and closed her mouth a few times, but nothing came out. Finally, she said, "I am King's Wolf. King Sabian's Wolf."

I tilted my head. "King Sabian?"

"King Rubarb is dead."

"I see." So the old king was dead. Interesting. I wondered how things would unfold now that the young prince was king. I wouldn't wish the situation of the war and siege on any new king, let alone a teen boy. "Even so, without that mask and those knives, who are you?"

She pursed her lips. "I have yet to figure that out. But Tala is my name."

"Tala," I tested the name on my tongue. "I've never heard of such a name. It sounds like something from the forest. Something the eagles would sing."

Tala looked thoughtful, pausing to glance my way. "It is from the forest, so to say."

"Stalking wolf," I phrased the meaning to her name. I'd never heard it, but I remembered reading the name once in a book.

"How did you–"

"I'm well read," I explained.

"The Highland Kingdom Assassin is, too," Tala pointed out. I forced myself not to cringe. It wasn't like I *wanted* this job.

"Good for him. Kelgare is remarkable."

Tala studied my face, her eyes never staying focused on mine. "How do you know so much about everything?"

"It's in my job description."

The answer didn't seem to satisfy her. No answer seemed to satisfy her in fact, there were always more questions. She slid her knives into their sheaths at her sides with a distracted look to her face and opted to carry her bow and an arrow instead.

I kept my eyes on what was in front of me. "How does the Keen work?"

She halted for a moment, then continued. "It isn't explainable, really." She side eyed me. "Why do you call it Keen?"

I tilted my head. "Isn't that what it's called? For enhanced senses, connection to beasts and such?" I'd learned about the Keen and knew she had it. It was a fascinating thing, really, but I only knew so much.

"Everyone calls it the Demise," she said. "But in the old transcripts and records, it was called the Keen. I like that better." A long pause, then she went on. "It is enhanced senses, so to say. But it is also knowing, *feeling*, everything around you. Everyone." She kept her eyes ahead of her. "Except for you and the other elves."

"It's how we're raised, trained. From when we're infants, we're taught to block out everyone and everything from our minds. Like stones."

Tala let out a soft laugh. "Stones. Interesting. Because of people like me?"

"Yes, and others." I crouched to avoid a branch. "There are some who use their abilities for evil. Keeping our guard up is a precaution."

"That's understandable," she agreed. "Hypothetically, could you let your mental guard down if you so wished?"

I considered it for a moment. "Perhaps. Are you trying to prod into my mind right now?"

"Earlier at the palace, yes," Tala admitted. "Now, no."

"And what were you looking to find?"

"Answers to my questions."

"You never seem to run out of them."

She half smiled. "The world is full of mysteries."

"You being one of them."

"And you."

We went on in silence, dodging branches and trying to follow rabbit and deer trails to make the going a little easier. The day slowly faded into dusk as we made our way further along the Moonland and Highland Kingdom's borders. The trees began to space out a bit more the further we went, and it seemed as though we wouldn't have to worry about hitting our heads on branches or poking our eyes out. Soon, it was past sunset, and the forest was enveloped in shadow and dark. The only light that remained was from the half moon.

In silence, we stopped to rest for the night. Tala pulled a wool blanket from her satchel, looking slightly surprised but thankful it was there. She lay down in the shelter of a pine, facing me, and closed her eyes, her hands tightly wrapped around her dagger hilts.

I wasn't sure if she ever actually fell asleep, because her breathing stayed the same. Light and quick, unlike the deep steady breathing that indicated someone was asleep. She looked so gentle, despite the knives in her gloved hands. The scars above and under her eyes made her look like a piece of stained glass with history that told a story. She made them look beautiful.

I slid my longer daggers from their sheaths at my back and sat with my back against a tree trunk, pulling my hood up and crossing my ankles. It was a little chilly, especially with the breeze that swept the forest, but I didn't want to draw any attention to us with a fire. I did my best to stay awake, to keep watch and keep away the dreams, concentrating on the daggers in my hand. They caught the light of the moon and glinted, the blade reflecting the slight glow. Most times, these daggers were stained red with my target's blood. People I didn't even know. Lives I was taking for reasons unknown to me, other than to pay off my sister's indenture. All small offerings, small steps to my sister's freedom.

I clenched my jaw and forced away the thought. The life of the girl that lay near me was my sister's ticket to freedom and, instead of killing her, I was *helping* her. I had every right to feel guilty and ashamed. I loved my sister more than anything, so why didn't I just get this job done and free her?

I considered it as I stared at Tala. I had been so close. If that other assassin, Kelgare, hadn't stepped in, Tala would be dead and my sister would be free.

Of all the lives I'd taken, I'd never hesitated. Never once had I considered anything other than that I was working to free my sister. But now. . .

I sighed.

Despite my busy mind, the exhaustion from the day won over. I began to nod off, waking myself each time, but soon I could do nothing but be sucked in by the whirlpool of dreams, of memories. . .

I held onto Aidilane's hand tightly as we splashed through the muddy puddles, following frantically after Pa, the rain heavy on our shoulders. I shrugged my hood on, wiping the cold droplets from my eyes. Why was Pa in such a hurry? Why was he so angry? Why wouldn't he talk to us since Momma fell asleep forever?

Dad looked back at us. "Hurry along. I haven't all day." He ushered us towards the towering building in front of us, up the stone stairs to the front door and inside. He didn't stop to check if we were still following him as he led us down the empty, candle lit corridor. We passed a flight of stairs where about twelve children older and younger than Aidilane and I were heading down, led by an angry elf in long black robes. He held a long stick, hitting the children mercilessly if any of them stepped out of line in the slightest.

Aidilane tightened her grip on my hand as we hurried after Pa. He stopped in front of a door and turned to us, pointing to the chairs that lined either side of the door. "Sit. Don't move."

We obeyed. Aidilane reached a hand out to him. "Pa? W–Where are we? Why–"

He didn't respond as he opened the door and stepped into the room, leaving the door open and us alone in the corridor.

"I–I'm scared, Kai," Aidilane whispered into my ear, a tear tracing her cheek.

"Me too." I squeezed her hand. This place was cold and dark, and the people here were scary.

Momma had been sick for weeks, and then she'd fallen asleep and wouldn't wake up. Her skin grew cold, and Pa began to cry and scream. He had run outside and thrown his carving tools with loud, scary shouts.

I didn't understand why Momma wouldn't wake up. But Aidilane and I watched as Pa and some of Momma's friends dug a hole in the backyard and put Momma inside, then covered her with dirt and sand. Afterwards, Pa wouldn't speak to us or even look at us. We missed Momma, and we longed for some, any comfort, but Pa wouldn't come near us. For three days, it went that way, and then finally, he came home, his black hair and pointed ears dripping wet from rain, and said, "Time to go."

We'd walked in the wet through town, then hired a ride to the countryside. Pa told the driver to stop at a large building in the middle of the Miral Forest that had a sign out front that I couldn't read. I hadn't learned to read yet.

Now we sat, shivering from cold but mostly fear, huddled in our soaked clothes and leaning into each other like we had for the past week.

We listened to the conversation in the room.

Pa's voice. "I can't keep them. Their mother is gone, and it's too much having them around. Both should have elementalist abilities."

"We can take them." An older woman's voice. "How old?"

"Thank the gods. Four and five."

"And when they're older?" the scary old lady behind the desk asked. "Shall I tell them you gave them up or are dead?"

A short pause. Then, "Dead."

My breath caught in my throat. What?

"They will be educated and brought up until they come of age. If they both have elementalist abilities as you say they shall, then they will be put to good use. Sign here, and here."

"Thank you."

A moment later, Pa reappeared and, without a glance at us, started back down the corridor. I leapt to my feet and ran after him. "Pa!" I reached him and wrapped my arms around one of his legs, sobbing. "Pa, please don't leave us!"

He gripped my arms and pulled me off of him as the old lady from the room grabbed my wrist tightly, yanking me back. Pa turned and hurried outside, shutting the door behind him.

Aidilane was at my side again, sinking to her knees and crying, "Pa. . ." her eyes puffy and red, mirroring my own.

"Quit it," the old lady snapped. "Get up and come with me." She dragged us away and up the staircase.

The dream flashed through moments of the following seven years. Aidilane and I in that dreaded classroom with the other orphans, outback learning to fight, and hiding from the mistress and her hired hands. Combat training in the courtyard with many injuries, all treated as "lessons". We might be used in the war, Mistress would say, and we would be prepared if we did. Those of us with elementalist potential would have special classes.

The dream chose a moment, the day I turned twelve, and replayed it.

"Come on," Mistress ushered us into the classroom. "Your turn."

This time, the classroom was empty except for two well dressed men in suits, the Elementalist Commissioners. They had come to test all the kids with potential for abilities.

Mistress shoved me until I stood in front of them. The one with short cut blonde hair and scarlet red clothes looked me up and down, a pen and notepad in hand. "Name?"

"Kai." My voice trembled.

He wrote it down while his companion instructed me to hold my arm out in front of me. He took my wrist, flipped it over, and placed a stone on it. It was warm and was engraved in the shape of a dragon, glowing like an ember, but didn't burn me.

"Breathe," the commissioner said. "Close your eyes. Feel the heat of the stone, accept the dragon's warmth. Let it flow within you."

Warmth spread through my veins in a comforting way, warming me from the inside out. I opened my eyes.

The first commissioner set down his notepad and held out his hand. A droplet of water began to form above it, growing larger and larger until it was the size of my head. The other commissioner waved his hand, sending a ripple of wind to the water, causing it to fly towards the wall and splash to the floor.

"Now," he said, "your turn."

I looked at the dragon stone balancing on my wrist, tilting my head. I remembered the legends we'd learned in class about when dragons were still alive, still living side by side with the elves.

I remembered all the painful moments in my short life. The fear, the abandonment, and the anger, all things I had pushed down to survive. But now, I let them ignite me. Like a. . .flame.

A tongue of fire began to form just above my palm, growing brighter and larger as I willed it, fueled by my anger, my pain. I didn't smile, I never really did, but I encouraged the flame to dance, swirling and sparking.

The commissioner with the water element rained droplets on my fire, extinguishing it with a puff of steam.

"Good," he said. He nodded to Mistress. "He will be of good use to us. Fire elementalists are quite rare indeed."

"Thank the gods, I was getting tired of him. He's like a shadow, dark and quiet but always there." She shivered. "Next one is his sister."

Aidilane was rushed inside. Her curly raven hair braided and her blue eyes frightened. When she met my eyes, she smiled. She always did that, no matter how terrible things got.

"A year younger. Girl, what's your name?"

"Aidilane," she said quietly.

The commissioners placed the dragon stone on her wrist, their anticipation very clearly growing with the prospects of two fire elementalists.

But even after they instructed and encouraged her, wide–eyed Aidilane didn't turn out to have powers at all.

She didn't seem too fazed, until the disappointed commissioners dismissed her and the mistress dragged her to another room. Despite the commissioners' stern commands to stay put, I followed.

I found my sister and the mistress in a room with three men, all dressed roughly and looked as if they hadn't bathed in days. The mistress was growling, "Yes, yes, she has good prospects for a brothel. She'll bring you good business with her fair skin, fine shape, and sky blue eyes."

I ran to my sister's side, taking her hand. She was crying.

The men gave the mistress a bag of coin, and roughly grabbed Aidilane by her arms. "No!" I screamed.

I ignited my flames. I was young, sure, but I knew what a brothel was. I would not let them trap my sister in a situation like that.

But in the end, there was nothing I could do. The commissioners from the classroom held on to me as the rugged men hauled away my sister.

That night in the commissioner's wagon, I ran away to follow the tracks of the men that had taken Aidilane. For three days, I tracked them, and finally came to a city, where the brothel was.

I summoned all of my courage and stepped inside, pushing my way through the many people until I found an important looking room, where an important looking man sat behind a desk.

"Aidilane," I said. "Where is she?"

"Hey, this ain't no place for a kid–"

"*She* is a kid."

The man shrugged. "Well that's different. She's a slave here now. I bought her and I own her."

"Where *is she*?" I demanded again.

The man laughed as if it was all a humorous joke. "Upstairs. Doing her job."

My stomach twisted. I felt sick. Oh Aidilane. . .

Another man entered the room, looking urgent. "Sir, have you hired an assassin yet? Things are gonna keep getting bad."

"No," the man sighed. "I haven't."

"Well that's not convenient. How are we supposed to keep everything in line with our competitors breathing down our necks?"

"I don't know, George! How about–"

"I'll be your assassin," I said.

Both men stared at me for a moment, then began to laugh. I glared at them, refusing to be intimidated. I added, "I'll pay off Aidilane's indenture through my work."

The man behind the desk laughed a moment longer, then sighed. "Ah, you're just a kid. You can't possibly have the guts, or the skills, to kill someone."

"Let me prove it to you."

He peered at me, then spread his hands. "Fine. *Prove* it. And if you do, then we have a deal."

And that was the night I took a man's life for the first time. My dream flashed to every time I had taken a life, the blood on my hands, the scars from the fights, the struggle of my targets, the bodies at my feet. Many. Too many.

Every time I took a life, I lost a piece of me. But I knew the same thing happened to Aidilane with every man that touched her, every night spent in that brothel. So I did anyway, in the hopes that one day, she would be free. It was all for her.

Nevertheless, I was a killer. No matter my reasons. I was guilty and ashamed and angry with myself. Every time I took a life, I cut a notch on my arm to remind myself that it was wrong. It was all wrong.

I punished myself for it.

And in a way, each cut brought a little comfort. For a moment. It was my penance.

Then it was replaced with shame just as quickly.

The dream cut to the day I saw Aidilane for the first time in years. I had snuck into her room after a man left, and nearly frightened her to death. But when she realized it was me, we embraced and sank to the floor in a crying heap.

"It's s–so horrible, Kai," she sobbed. "They. . ."

She told me the things they did to her, and it fueled my drive, filling me with rage. "I'll get you out of here, one way or another. I promise."

"Don't make promises you can't keep, brother."

"Aidilane–"

"Stop," she said quietly. "Please. Don't give me hope. It'll only hurt more when it's ripped away."

The bruises on her skin, the tremor in her voice, the way her eyes darted around, the way she was always tense. . .

My dream drifted again. I was now standing over a curled up Tala.

My anger boiled, my breathing growing heavy. My sister, or this girl. The choice should've been easy to make. Why was I hesitating? Sure, she was the only chance at beating the magicians, but. . .

Aidilane.

I tightened my fists. Enough of this. I would get this over with and free my sister. She was more important to me than anything, especially some bickering old kingdom with crazy magician enemies. Those magicians had been my kingdom's, the Moonland Kingdom's, enemies. But still. I didn't care anymore. All I cared about was my sister. And I would do what I had to in order to save her.

I crouched down beside Tala, drawing my dagger with a shaking hand. I never trembled.

I knelt there, my breath coming in gasps. All the times I'd taken a life came back to me. I never forgot their faces. Never.

The woman with the green eyes and blonde hair who worked at a saloon, one of my boss's competitors. I used a knife.

The young man with umber hair and blue eyes, who hadn't paid off his debt to my boss. I used my daggers.

And all the others.

I remembered trying my hardest to make their deaths as quick and painless as I could possibly manage. But every time, I knelt beside them, saying, "I'm sorry. I'm so sorry." A monster, a killer. That's who I was and I couldn't deny it.

My heart raced, remembering everything. I felt the feeling of my targets, almost as if they were here, gripping me, tearing me apart. My dagger clanged to the ground.

I gasped, falling back and scrambling away from the sleeping girl in front of me. I felt my other dagger in my hand now, and I tried to fight away my targets' ghosts, who tore at me and called my name.

I couldn't breathe.

And then hands, human and very much alive, reached through them to me, and touched my temples, gently but firmly. "Calm," a soft voice said. And I did. It felt as if whoever was there was breathing peace into my mind, forcing away the nightmare, the memories like a wave washing away shells on a sea shore.

I opened my eyes.

Tala was there, kneeling, bent over me with her gloved fingers on my temples, her eyes closed. I stared at her, my breathing slowly calming down, my memories fading like fog back into the far corners of my mind.

Her hair spilled over her shoulders and into my face, frizzy from sleep, and her brows were scrunched in concentration. No matter what I had just felt moments ago in that dream, I couldn't reach those feelings anymore as if she had taken them and hidden the fear and the pain from me.

Then it struck me.

My walls had come down.

My breath caught. My walls had come down while I slept. She had been able to get into my mind.

But. . .strangely, I didn't get angry. And even more strangely, it didn't scare me like it should have. Instead, I was thankful. So utterly thankful.

Tala opened her eyes, looking tired, worried. But when she saw that I was awake, staring back at her, she quickly pulled her hands back to herself. "Uhm, you were thrashing around. Almost hurt yourself with your own dagger. And. . .I could feel your mind. You were. . .really distressed. I had to help you. I'm sorry, I–"

"No," I said, my voice a little shaky. "Don't be sorry."

She blinked. "I thought you'd be—"

I shook my head, sat up. I glanced at the gorges I'd made with my dagger in the ground beside me, and the tree roots were cut. I was surprised I wasn't, too. "Thank you, Tala. Thank you."

She scooted back a little when I sat up, looking surprised, overwhelmed, and confused. "Y–You're welcome. Can I. . .May I say something? About what you were feeling?"

I hesitated. I was uncomfortable knowing that she knew what I felt, what I'd done, what I'd been through. She saw me for who I was. No one had ever, but now . . . Odly, I was comforted that someone knew now. It was hard to wrap my head around it, though. I felt raw, exposed. Like a wound being ripped open again. "Go ahead."

She took a deep breath. "Y–Your sister. . .If it takes my life to save her . . . then do it." She shook her head, her brows furrowed in deep thought. "I always wondered what purpose I had, but now I see. Maybe this is why I'm here. To be sacrifice, so that another's life would be better. Would be saved."

I was shocked. She seemed so. . .genuine. Unafraid. Unconcerned about herself.

"No," I said softly.

She looked at me, confused. "But—"

"Your purpose is way beyond being a sacrifice. That's why I haven't gone through with my job, despite Aidilane. She. . .I will save her. But," I paused, locking eyes with Tala, "I'll do it another way."

Tala held my gaze for the first time, not looking away. "And I'll help you. I see that our destinies are intertwined, for better or worse. And if I'm not meant to give my life for Aidilane's, then I will make sure I fight for her instead."

"You don't even know her. You hardly know me. And we're from different kingdoms. Enemies. A completely different species, in fact."

"Why does that matter?" There were flames behind her eyes. "She is a kindred soul, Kai. And so are you. I will not abandon those like. . .like me. I wish that–" her voice caught. "I wish that someone would've fought for me. I cannot abandon anyone the way I have been abandoned."

We gazed at each other, both near strangers, both having just learned a million things in a single moment. And suddenly, we didn't feel like strangers any longer.

Tala tore her gaze from mine, looking flustered. She got to her feet and gathered her things in silence, moving slowly and stiffly. I noticed then that the back of her shirt was damp, as well as her hair, and she quivered like a quaking leaf in the wind.

"You still have a fever," I said as I slid my daggers back into their sheaths.

"It really isn't that bad," she replied. "I'm alright."

I narrowed my eyes. "The way you're sweating and shivering simultaneously seems to make me disagree."

"It's rude to comment on how a girl sweats."

As she reached to pick up her bow, I grabbed her wrist. She tensed, her eyes wide and her jaw clenched. I locked eyes with her, keeping silent but speaking through my gaze. After a moment, she blinked, and let loose the breath she'd been holding. Slowly and gently, as if I were handling a newborn kitten, I pulled her hand closer to me while keeping my eyes on hers. I unbuttoned her leather glove and slid it off. Her skin was hot to the touch, clammy, and her pulse raced.

"Fever."

She pulled her hand back to herself. "I'm fine, Kai."

"The problem is, if you journey in this state, you aren't going to make it far, Tala. Then what would be the use of going at all? Your kingdom wouldn't be any better off."

". . .I suppose you're right."

"I suppose I am."

She was so much like my sister, I couldn't help but care. Perhaps that was another reason why I couldn't go through with killing her. It'd be like hurting Aidilane, and I couldn't do that. "We'll wander a bit until we find a creek or some source of water, and then we'll make camp there. You'll benefit from the cool water and I can use the herbs that grow near it to make a remedy."

Tala eyed me. "You know herbs?"

"Last I checked, although I'm better at poisons."

"Who taught you?"

"Who taught you to fend for yourself?"

"Fair point." She swayed on her feet, growing pale. I took her arm and held her up, keeping her from falling.

"Are you going to be able to make it to water?"

"Yes."

"I'm not so sure about that."

"Neither am I, but when are we ever sure of anything?"

So we started off again, Tala's wolf in the lead, looking as if she was on a mission. She scouted ahead until she was out of sight, then circled back. Over and over again, and whenever she came back to us, she'd huff as if she was growing impatient with our slow gait. After a while, Tala explained, "She's leading us to water."

"How does she know that's where we need to go?"

"I tell her."

"Like how you and I are talking now?"

"In a way, yes."

"But through your mind. And she knows where the water is?"

She nodded. "You're just as full of questions as I am."

"Perhaps."

Tala's fever grew by the minute. I could feel the heat radiating from her like a bonfire in a heatwave. As time went on, her hair became damper and damper with sweat. She leaned heavily on my arm, and almost collapsed a few times from all the shivering she was doing. At some point I took her satchel and bow and carried it along with my own things, and she probably would've protested if she had the energy. But she hardly registered that I had taken them.

When the sun was just barely near its peak, I started to hear the faint sound of rushing water. Still a ways off, but there. "We're almost there," I said.

"O–Okay," she panted.

But the next step had her collapsing. I caught her, and she shook her head. "Kai, I–I'm about to have a seizure."

"What?"

She squeezed her eyes tight in frustration, and maybe even pain. "Just down. . .I need to. . .lay down."

I was confused, but I helped ease her to the ground. I realized then that her shivering had turned into shaking. Her teeth chattered.

"Tala, a seizure?" I stammered. "You've had them before?"

"Y–Yes."

"Alright, okay, just breathe." I had no idea what to do. Did I help her somehow? Keep her from shaking? Or–

Tala's eyes rolled up into her head, and she started to convulse, her limbs flailing. Great gamble, what was I supposed to do?

I held down her legs with my knee and her arms with my hands to keep her from injuring herself, and hoped I was doing the right thing.

So she'd had seizures before? Was it a condition, or…I tried to piece together what little I knew about her, but none of it gave me any hint to what may be causing her to have seizures. Perhaps the fever? But if she'd experienced it before then it couldn't be because of the dwam flute.

She was unconscious now, and her head jerked from side to side. It wasn't like me to panic, but I could feel it rising inside me. She'd saved me from those dreams, and here I was unable to help her.

Her wolf paced around us, a high pitch whine in her throat. She made me nervous, but she seemed to understand that I was trying to help, not hurt, Tala. A moment later, though, she started to growl.

I felt my breath quicken. "Woah, hey it's okay. I'm trying to help."

She bared her teeth at me, her hackles rising. I let go of Tala's arms and held my hands up in a placating gesture. "Easy." It was then that I realized her eyes weren't on me, but on something behind me.

In a quick move, I stood and whipped around, drawing my daggers. Before I could take in what was there, my daggers were knocked from my hands by an invisible force, landing several feet away from me. Four magicians were emerging from the trees, surrounding us, their wands held at the ready. They were dressed in long, colorfully embroidered military wool coats and tall leather boots. Two females, two males, their pale hair pulled back tightly into many thin braids and their beards shaved.

With my daggers taken away, I took a protective fighter's stance over Tala, turning continuously to keep an eye on each of the magicians. I summoned my power and brought my flames to life, keeping the magicians at bay with the heat.

One of the magicians, a tall pale man, narrowed his sky blue eyes. "An elven fire elementalist and a. . .sick human. Interesting. What might you be doing this close to the Northland Kingdom?"

"And a wolf pet," one of the females growled.

They circled us slowly, looking me up and down and eyeing Tala, who had stopped convulsing and lay still, unconscious. Her wolf growled profusely and wouldn't leave her side. I wouldn't answer the magician's question. Whenever they drew a step closer, I warded them back again with my fire, making the flames hotter and angrier.

The man who had spoken before spoke again. "From what I can gather, you two are either runaways, or are on a mission. I consider the likelihood of both of those possibilities, and I seem to be certain that you are on a mission. Runaways do not dress ready for sneaking around or carry weapons used in close combat. Besides, if you *were* runaways, intending to elope perhaps, you wouldn't be headed towards the Northland Kingdom territory. We are too much of an enemy to both the Moonland and Highland kingdoms." He paused, adjusting his grip on his wand. "So you are on a mission. And clearly," he added with another glance at Tala, "something has gone quite wrong."

I kept my usual, neutral expression, calm but ready, watching. "Congratulations. You have eyeballs and a brain."

The man narrowed his eyes, a tight smile forming on his lips. "I can piece together what you are intending to do here. But I never foresaw a human and an elf working together."

"We've never been enemies."

"And yet you've never been allies, either. You elves have always found the ways of humans primitive, selfish, and dirty. Humans have always seen you elves as mysterious and untrustworthy. So you must be desperate, then." The smile grew, and his eyes darkened. "Good."

"I find it interesting that you think your efforts to destroy the world have made us desperate. I won't argue, but I won't confirm it either. You seem pretty confident that you're winning. I find that slightly amusing."

The magician narrowed his eyes. "And why is that?"

I kept my gaze steady. "I'm sure you'll find out sooner or later."

The other magicians exchanged glances. The man, who seemed to be in charge of the group, was unblinking. "You, elf, are outnumbered. Stand down and answer my questions. If I were you, I'd choose my next words carefully."

I didn't move, didn't put out my fire. "Take one more step and I'll burn you all to ash."

The magician held my gaze for a moment longer, then he said, "Take him."

The others started closing in around me. Tala's wolf snarled and leapt for one of them, but they stopped her in midair with their magic and tossed her aside. She hit a tree trunk and fell to the ground in a furry heap, suddenly very still.

I bursted my flames and blazed them around me at the magicians, scorching the ground and setting the undergrowth on fire. The magicians moved back to avoid the flames as I kept going, letting loose my fury.

One of them lifted her wand and a long rope–like glowing strand shot from its tip and wrapped around one of my wrists. She maneuvered until she was behind me, pulling my arm behind my back. I moved to face her again and free my hand, but one of her companions did the same, and they criss–crossed their strands so that both of my arms were tightly pulled behind me. I was forced to extinguish my flames to keep from burning myself.

The others put out the fire and the other female knocked me to my knees and gripped my hair, yanking my head back, leaving my throat exposed and forcing me to meet the eyes of their leader, who was standing over me now.

I struggled in my captor's grips as he nudged Tala with his boot. "It's a shame, really. We could have gone about this much more peacefully. Although," he added, "maybe not."

I glared at him. "Magicians are something."

"Magicians?" he scoffed. "Hardly. Magicians do magic tricks, sleight of hand and children's games to trick the eye. We are mages. We deal with the forces of– well that isn't your concern. Drastic difference."

"As drastic a difference as a mule from a donkey."

He gripped my shoulders and kneed me in the ribs hard, knocking the breath from my lungs. I would have doubled over if it weren't for the other magicians holding me.

I looked up at him and grinned. "So you *do* have muscle. I thought you magicians just hid behind your magic."

His face grew red with rage. He lifted his wand again and murmured something. Suddenly, a sharp pain erupted in my chest, making it difficult to breathe. I kept my poker face on for as long as I could muster, but as the pain grew, I couldn't. I gasped for air and my heart raced. It felt as if a hole had been stabbed into my lung.

"What you are feeling now, elf, is a pulmonary embolism. Caused by my magic, of course. It is just a taste of what us mages are capable of. I suggest you wise up before you get yourself killed."

He tucked his wand into his sleeve and the pain ceased. I took in gasps of air, sweat beading my face.

They pulled me to my feet and the leader picked up Tala, carrying her like a sack of potatoes. A sharp pang of protectiveness seized me and I growled, "If you hurt a hair on her head there isn't a place in the world I wouldn't find you."

"Are you threatening me, or telling me that if she dies I'd be your next romantic choice?" he said. "Too bad you aren't my type, or the right gender."

They left Tala's wolf and dragged us through the forest, taking our gear with them. They kept up a quick pace considering their fancy garb and stingy behinds. I made sure it wasn't easy for them, though.

It wasn't long before a camp came into view. Large, white wall tents that were strikingly similar to Cordan Greyver's tents were scattered around a clearing. Campfires dotted the clearing and magicians swarmed it like a busy hive, all dressed in their colorful uniforms.

My captors brought us over to one of the tents, and the group's leader laid Tala on the ground and stepped inside. He returned a moment later led by another magician; a tall woman with light caramel hair and gray eyes.

"Put up quite a fight, this one," the man said.

She looked me up and down, then scanned over unconscious Tala and our weapons and gear. "Speak, kid."

I kept my expression neutral as always, but didn't say a word.

She narrowed her eyes. "I said, speak, kid."

"What am I supposed to 'speak' about?" I asked. "About the weather? Perhaps the seasonal change? Or maybe how much I dislike magicians? Because I'm not going to tell you what you really want to hear, and you're quite daft if you haven't realized it already."

She licked her lips and shaded her pale face from the sunlight that poked through the canopy above. "Pointy ears, sarcasm, a way with words, and an even better way with weapons. I'd say we have ourselves an elf, gentlemen."

The group chuckled.

She stepped into the shade of a nearby tree and crossed her arms. "From what my lieutenant here has reported," she paused to point at Tala, "she is important to you, is she not?"

"She is not."

"Then why the whole 'if you hurt a hair on her head there isn't a place in the world I wouldn't find you'?"

"Partners protect each other."

"Right. But there are all kinds of partners out there. The real question is, what kind are you?"

"I'll leave that up to your grand imagination."

She paced in front of me. "I'm going to list off my assumptions, and I'd like you to correct me if I get something wrong." She stopped and stood in front of me, her hands folded neatly behind her. "The humans of the Highland and Lowland kingdoms have become so desperate that they've asked for the help of their neighbors, the elves. You are both here on a mission–"

"Wrong."

"-to spy on us and to gather information–"

"Wrong."

"-on our strategies and war plans–"

"Wrong."

"-and to report back to your kingdoms to gain an upper hand."

"Correction– wrong."

"Then enlighten me, elf," she hissed. "What I want is a full explanation of why you *are* here."

"We don't always get what we want, do we?"

She held my gaze for a long moment. Then, she turned her back. "I am General Jenia. Just thought you should know who I was before I begin issuing commands and punishments." She looked over her shoulder. "You are a fire elementalist, yes? Good thing. I have a very eager scientist who would love to run some tests on you, for research purposes of course, while you decide between giving me an explanation on why you are here or have your 'partner' here inflicted with some very harsh treatment. It is entirely your decision. We don't always get what we want, after all."

An icy claw made its way down my spine as the general nodded to her soldiers. They hauled Tala and dragged me through their large camp and to one of the tents. It was clearly either a medical tent or a lab, and from what the general had said, I assumed it was the latter.

A metal table the size of a single mattress, with what looked to be wrist and ankle cuffs, was in the center of the tent. Around it were longer but skinnier tables with cabinets and a messy array of documents, syringes, and all sorts of things I didn't know the names for.

The magicians dumped Tala on the floor beside the tent wall, where they cuffed her to a support beam. Then they hauled me onto the table, or tried at least. I fought hard. At some point, they almost managed to cuff one of my wrists, but I kicked one of them in the face, punched another, and was almost free when three more magicians came in along with a short, portly man with glasses and a blonde beard. One of them readied to cast a spell on me with his wand, but the short man exclaimed, "No magic! It will ruin my efforts! Use this instead."

They managed to keep me down long enough to jab a needle into the side of my neck. A moment later, my surroundings tilted and everything went black.

I slowly came to, and for the first few minutes, my vision was blurry and I couldn't think straight.

Finally, my eyes cleared and I realized I was on the metal table, my wrists and ankles cuffed to it. They had taken off my shirt and jacket, too. A moment of panic seized me, and I struggled against my bonds. I was not about to be an experiment.

"Not very wise," a comical voice warned. I turned my head and saw the same short, bearded man with glasses from before, standing with his back to me, hunched over something on the table. "Things will go smoother if you lie still." He turned to me and came over, a syringe and several glass vials in his hand.

"Don't touch me," I growled.

"Now now, General Jenia gave you a generous chance to tell her what you were doing here, but it was your choice to be stubborn, wasn't it? Now you are a prisoner of war, as well as your friend here. We are free to do whatever we wish with you. So while you contemplate the decision the general has given you to make, I'm just going to run some tests now, ya?"

"No, not 'ya'. I'm not–"

"Not an experiment?" he finished. "No. Quite the contrary. Your gifts are beyond perception, and gifts should be shared for the greater good. I am not experimenting on you, young elf. I am simply trying to find answers to my questions about the marvel of elementalists, and how you do the things you can do, and where your power comes from. But most of all, how to manifest it."

"Manifest it? Don't you mean harvest it for yourself?"

"That is what I'm trying to find out. If that is possible."

"You magicians are lunatics, in case you weren't aware."

He smiled. "Lunatics, maybe. But also determined and willing to do what we have to to get what we want."

"Like killing innocent people? Destroying entire kingdoms? For what? To rule the world?"

"If we take the world, no one else can. Which means no one worse will take or destroy it."

"Right. Like you haven't destroyed it already, right? You're saving it."

"Precisely."

"You really are daft."

He shook his head, smiling to himself. Incredible.

"My name is Dr. Lantsof. I need your name to put on your subject records."

"No."

He shrugged. "We'll get it eventually." He uncapped the syringe and felt my arm for my vein. I struggled, but I could do nothing but watch as he slid the needle into my arm. Within seconds, my blood started filling the glass vials.

I clenched my jaw. Never in my wildest dreams had I expected to be a lab rat. May as well try to get some information out of the guy.

"So what is a scientist doing traipsing with an army?"

"I run tests on our captives, but most importantly take care of anyone who is ill or wounded."

"Do you make remedies, or medicines, to treat your patients, or do you use magic instead?"

He gave me a look. "Medicines, remedies. Magic only for crisis situations."

"Why?"

"Magic is. . ." he stopped. "Never mind."

I resisted the urge to wince as he adjusted the position of the needle in my arm, pushing it in further. I clenched my teeth. "Do you have any waterside herbal remedies?"

Dr. Lanstof bit his lip as he concentrated on the blood that filled the next vial "Yes, they are most useful." His eyes strayed suddenly to Tala. "The General mentioned the patrol found you while she was having a seizure. She looks ill. Is she–"

"She's fine."

He narrowed his eyes. "Sure."

I avoided his gaze. "Do you store your remedies like we elves do, in cool temperatures?"

"Depends on the medicine. But most of the waterside remedies I keep in a cool place, yes, in my medicine cellar." He nodded towards a wood flap door on the ground, covering what I guessed was an underground storage place. "You seem to know a lot about herbs, young elf."

This time I stayed quiet. The scientist slipped the needle out of the vein and tossed it into a bin, setting the blood–filled vials on his countertop. He adjusted his glasses, examining my blood. He took one and placed a drop of it under a microscope and studied it for a moment. A few seconds passed, then he straightened quickly. "It isn't possible!"

While he was focused on his project, I wriggled my wrists, trying to slip free, but as much as I struggled and pulled, it was no use. The bonds were so tight, my fingers and toes tingled from lack of circulation. I supposed it was smart of them, but I was frustrated and angry. This was ridiculous.

My teachers at the orphanage had told us that our abilities shouldn't be taken for granted. They also warned us that since we were exceptional, there were those in the world who wanted our abilities and hunted elementalists. A memory long pushed down came to my mind, suddenly. One of my sessions of Pre–Element, my teacher received a request via correspondence. She had stopped to read the letter, and told us to leave class.

Later, while outside with my sister, a black carriage pulled into the orphanage front yard, where three men in long dark capes stepped out and went inside. Hours later at dinner, I slipped away to eavesdrop.

Mistress and the mysterious men conversed in hushed voices in her office.

"I told you, you aren't supposed to be here," the Mistress growled.

"We'll get out of your hair as soon as you give the child to us." A deep voice.

A moment of silence. "And if I don't?"

"We already told you what would happen."

"But he hasn't even developed his abilities yet!"

"Good. We can see the process for ourselves."

"You scientific squabble–"

A loud crash made me jump and back away from the door.

"Do you understand now?" The same deep voice.

"Yes," Mistress answered quietly.

"Very good. Where is the child?"

"In the courtyard."

The sound of coins in a bag, and then, "For your troubles, Mistress. Good doing business with you."

I had barely enough time to hide before the door opened and the three caped men swept out. I followed them.

Once outside, they walked straight up to Cal, one of the other orphans around my age. He was playing hopscotch with my sister.

The men scooped him up without a word, carrying him to their carriage. Cal kicked and screamed, to no avail.

I ran after them, yelling, "Hey! Stop! Where are you taking him?"

Two of them got into the carriage with screaming Cal, but the last one turned to me before getting in. I couldn't make out his face from under his hood. "Elementalists have power others don't. For now. They deserve to share it." And then they were gone, bumping along the dirt road, leaving me in a cloud of dust.

Now I understood what had happened that day. It made a lot more sense. Elementalists were being experimented on like lab rats. Why hadn't I realized it this clearly earlier? I felt dumb for not putting it together sooner.

But elementalists' powers were gifts. Passed down by blood and fate for a reason. The powers weren't meant to be tested and isolated, or used by someone who they weren't given to. Chaos would ensue the second the powers were in the wrong hands.

I began to panic again. The magicians had more power than we could comprehend already. And if they had elementalist abilities too. . .I felt sick.

Dr. Lanstov was murmuring excitedly to himself as he slid the blood from the microscope and began running tests on it. With each test, he grew more and more excited.

"What?" I said, forcing my voice to stay calm.

"You have it!" he exclaimed, as if it were the most important thing in the world.

"Have what?"

He scribbled on a piece of paper, folded it, and called a guard into the tent. He handed her the note and said, "Give this to the general, quickly."

The guard obeyed, heading back outside. Dr. Lanstov turned to me, awe and wonder in his eyes, his chubby face flushed with excitement. But before he could say anything, General Jenia swept inside. "What do you want, doctor? It better be important. I have an army to oversee and do not have time for any more of your absurd ideas."

Dr. Lanstov nodded so hard I was concerned he might lose his head. "It is *very* important, general. Once you hear what I have to say, you'll want to send a message to the magistrate immediately, and perhaps even the royal court and king and queen."

The general scoffed. "We'll see about that."

The doctor was trembling with excitement. "Remember *Project E?*"

Her eyes darted to me immediately, widening. "Are you serious?"

"Yes. It is fortunate we found him. His blood. . .his cells are the first I've seen that could allow us to isolate and manifest his abilities. He is the one we've been needing. General, it's possible. We can use elements as well as magic now. We'll be unstoppable."

A grin spread across the general's face as she continued to stare at me. "I will be highly rewarded for his capture. The magistrate will be through the clouds with this news. How long will it take?"

"Well, I need to collect a *lot* more of his blood so that I can isolate the cells and use them to create an injectable serum for us to take. Should take a day or two."

"Excellent."

"What about our deal?" I growled. "You said if I told you what my partner and I were doing here, you'd let us go."

"I said no such thing," she replied. "I simply said that you'd better give me the answer unless you wanted your *partner* to be inflicted with harsh treatment. But I changed my mind. She'll just be a prisoner of war, and I'll have her taken to the city to have her processed and they'll decide on what to do with her. You, however, are an anomaly that we have been looking for. For so long, every one of the elementalists that we've caught didn't have the cells that allowed us to take their power. But you were sent from above, my boy. Sent from above." She turned to the doctor. "Begin the process. Do what you have to. I will send someone to mark him, and to collect a sample of his flames."

"Yes, general."

General Jenia looked me over one last time, a look in her eyes that reminded me of someone who had just hunted the largest deer. "You're sick," I spat. She simply smiled and swept away.

My mind went wild. Panic. Fear. I hated fear.

Dr. Lanstov put another needle into my arm, and another in my other arm. Clear tubes ran from the needles to clear bags, which began to fill with my blood. "Hmn, too slow," he murmured. The doctor pulled a wand from his pocket and tapped each bag. Suddenly, they started filling a lot faster. So fast that Dr. Lantsov had to replace the bags within a few minutes.

I started feeling faint and weak, like life was being drained from me. I ground my teeth, determined to stay awake. I had to get out of here. I was Aidilane's only hope. If I was a lab rat, or died, she didn't have a chance at freedom.

That thought kept me conscious, even though my head lolled and my eyes drooped.

To my left, Tala stirred. She opened her eyes wearily, taking in her surroundings. She looked like she was on the edge of life. Dark under eyes, splotchy, flushed skin, and weak breathing. Clearly, the fever hadn't gone anywhere, and the seizure had made it worse.

She met my eyes, and her brows furrowed in confusion.

Where are we? What happened? What are they doing to you?

I was startled when I heard her voice in my head. I hadn't let my guard down . . . she shouldn't have been able to get in.

You're weak, Kai. And I suppose the connection I made with your mind earlier, when I woke you, is still there. I think that a part of you is unguarded towards me. I can feel it.

I avoided her gaze, confused. I didn't understand what she meant. Maybe she was delusional from her fever.

I opened my mouth to answer her earlier questions when two other magicians came into the tent. One was a tall and slender male with a pointy nose and sharp eyes, holding a large, round glass bottle. The other was a burly female clad in a long, leather blacksmith apron. Ash was smeared on her face and her bare, muscular arms bulged as she carried a white–hot brand shaped as an *E*.

I stiffened, panic seizing me once more.

Dr. Lanstov sighed loudly. "Can't you save that for later? He's already weak and I need him to keep up the strength he has left so I can get as much blood out of him as I can."

"General's orders, Lanstov," the tall elf said.

"*Doctor* Lanstov to you, Malgen."

"We need to mark him in case he finds some way to escape later in the future. That way we can easily identify him. And we need a sample." He unscrewed the bottle and held it beside my hand, meeting my eyes. "Go ahead. Ignite your power, elf."

I stared at him, keeping my straight face.

He narrowed his eyes. "Now."

Tala was quiet, but I could feel her at the corners of my mind. She didn't know I was an elementalist. Hardly anyone knew. And I had intended to keep it that way. But now she was beginning to piece it together.

"I said *now*," the magician growled. When I didn't do anything, he nodded to the burly female who moved over to Tala and held the brand close to her face. "Do it now or she burns."

I ground my teeth in frustration. Idiot, me.

I felt the familiar tug in my gut as I summoned my flames and brought them to life. I heard Tala suck in a breath. Once the bottle was full of the flames, which I wasn't sure could be possible, the tall magician closed it and set it on the counter nearest to me.

The female came back over to me, and my breath quickened when she brought the brand close. Time seemed to slow as she brought it nearer, nearer, my body stiffening and going rigid as the heat grew hotter as it came close, at the left side of my exposed chest.

"Stop!" Tala protested, pulling at her bonds with what strength she had.

The second it hit my skin, I felt her wrap her mind around mine, pulling my consciousness into hers. Darkness enveloped me, and so did peace.

I slowly came to my senses, numb at first. Tala's voice in my mind warned, *I don't have the strength to keep the pain away any longer. Brace yourself.*

Her mind let go of mine, and simultaneously, the burning crashed into me. The pain knocked the breath from my lungs like a kick to the gut. My chest felt like it was on fire, the large E shaped burn still steaming. I blinked, fighting the terrible nausea. Beads of sweat made their way down my face, and I squeezed my fists, the scent of burning flesh tainting the air.

I tried to keep you out for as long as possible. I'm sorry. I wish I could do more.

"You did enough," I managed, panting.

"What, elf?" The tall magician was still there with the doctor. He came to my side and glared down at me. "What are you babbling about?"

I turned my head to look over at Tala. She leaned her head back against the support beam, her face ghostly and her breath shallow, her eyes closed. She looked like hell.

Thank you, Kai.

I turned back to Dr. Lanstov. "She's ill. And she's getting worse. You need to help her."

He was busy replacing the blood bags. "No, elf. I must concentrate on you and getting this. . ." his voice faded into his quiet rambling.

Nearby, Tala slumped over completely. I felt the tingle of her mind in mine disappear.

"She needs help now," I insisted loudly.

Dr. Lanstov ignored me while the magician studied the fire in the bottle. "How interesting," he murmured. "It almost looks alive."

I set my jaw. I needed to get us out of here. And now I knew how.

Subtly, I managed to twist my hand around so that my palm faced me. Then, I allowed the tiniest bit of flame to kindle in my hand and willed it onto my bonds. Within a few moments, I had burned through.

I did the same on my other wrist, then before anyone could notice, I sat up and knocked the bottle of fire from the magician's hand. It shattered on the ground, and I willed the escaping flames to spread and consume the tent.

The magician yelled and cursed as he tried to hold me down, but I grabbed his arm and burned it, then shoved him to the ground. I burned through my ankle bonds and leapt over to Tala's side.

Dr. Lanstov was frantically trying to save as many bags of my blood as he could before they were consumed by the fire, which was quickly consuming the tent. I heard shouts coming from outside as the tall magician ran out, coughing from the smoke.

I melted Tala's cuffs and pulled her to me, her head lolling against my chest. I ignored the pain it caused my burn. She was almost quite literally burning up. I knew the fire wasn't helping.

I looked around again, surrounded by flames and smoke, and couldn't see the doctor anywhere. Good riddance.

I got to my feet, picking up Tala, and searched for a way out. But I didn't need to.

The fire was suddenly distinguished, vanishing with a warm gust of air. Fragments of the remains of the burned tent lay scattered around me, ashes falling like fresh snow.

Dr. Lanstov sat a few feet away, coughing and yelling something about, "Save it! All of it!"

Magicians surrounded me, aiming their wands. Tala lay limp in my arms, boiling.

General Jenia stood in front of me, fury bright in her eyes. "Kill the girl, get him."

They moved towards me, but something inside me burst. I went down on one knee while at the same time letting go the loudest cry I could manage. The ground shook beneath me as a ring of fire rippled from me and exploded like a shot.

When it was over, I looked up. The camp was flattened. As if an explosion had gone off right where I was standing and had blasted everything down. Everything was scorched. All the magicians were knocked out cold, all scattered on the charred earth. All breathing, all unhurt for the most part. I was shocked. How had I done that? How was that possible?

I checked Tala to make sure she was alright. Or as alright as she was before my. . . outburst? Explosion? Fire ripple?

I let out the breath I'd been holding. "Okay," I panted. "Okay."

I laid Tala on the ground, checked her pulse. Weak. Hardly there. "Okay," I repeated, my voice trembling.

I gathered my strength and began what I'd planned to do while that scientist. . .did what he did.

I found mine and Tala's things, slipped on my shirt and jacket, and searched the ruins of the lab tent. I found the hatch to the waterside herbal remedies and pulled it open. I searched through them and gathered the herbs I needed. I wasn't really sure if what I intended to make would actually work or not, but it was worth a shot. What other chance did Tala have?

I ground up the herbs and added some water to the mixture. Then, I ignited a tiny spark and let it fall into the remedy, causing it to sizzle and boil for less than a second. It was as ready as it could ever be.

I brought it over to Tala, who had started to convulse again weakly, and it looked like she was struggling to breathe.

I pulled her up into my lap, supporting her shoulders with my arm, her head falling back over my arm limply. I poured the mixture into her mouth and helped her swallow by gently rubbing her throat.

A minute went by. Two. Three.

Five.

Ten.

I was blinking rapidly then, my hopes falling. I didn't understand why I was so disappointed. . .but I was. Part of me sunk deep, like I was going down with her.

Her voice rang clear in my mind, *I didn't make you out to be a sentimental type.*

Tala sucked in a breath, her eyes fluttering open. I sighed. "I'm not. You just seem to bring it out in me. Which is pretty irritating, by the way, human."

She laughed. Great gamble, I liked that laugh. Why?

"What happened?" she asked. "You were on the table, and then. . .I don't remember."

"I'm not sure what happened myself," I said honestly.

She sat up, scooting away from me as she surveyed our surroundings. Her mouth went slack. "Kai. . .how?"

"I don't know."

"Are fire elementalists capable of this?"

"Not that I've ever heard of."

Tala hugged her knees, her eyes going wide. She touched a finger to her temples "Kai. . ."

"What's wrong?" Had the remedy done something worse?

Her hand dropped to her side, and she slowly turned to meet my eyes. Her hazel eyes were alight with disbelief. "The seizures. . .the poison. . .it's gone."

"Poison?"

She nodded. "Years ago, I was blamed for treason and murder of one of our princes. So I ran. But the crown assassin caught me and poisoned me. Somehow I got away. A pack of wolves found me and took care of me, and I lived with them for a while. But the poison had racked my body and made me have seizures all the time. The constant feel of burning in my veins, the pain in my head, and the seizures. . .it's all gone now." She held my gaze, excitement pouring over. "Not only did you cure the effects of the dwam flute– you cured me of my seizures."

My head spun. I was trying to piece together the information she'd just given me. But I didn't say anything about it. She trusted me enough, somehow, to tell me those things. I wouldn't pry.

"Yes, I trust you, Kai," she murmured, her voice soft and shaky. "And I don't trust many people." *Thank you for saving my life, and ridding me of that curse.*

I helped her to her feet. "I trust you, too." Unspoken words passed between us, and I knew she understood. She would tune out my thoughts and feelings from then on out.

Tala crouched to pick up her things and then we fled from the wrecked camp before the magicians woke up, and got as far away from there as quickly as we could. I led her to where we'd first been captured, and found her wolf. Unconscious and bleeding from a deep gash on her flank where she hit the tree.

Tala knelt beside her and stroked her fur, a tear running down her cheek. I got the feeling that she was sending mental messages to the raven black beast. She furrowed her brows, her eyes tightly shut. Then she tensed, her breath catching. She doubled over, gripping her side. She was taking on the wolf's pain.

I crouched beside her, keeping silent. Two minutes went by, then three. I was about to finish counting the fourth when the wolf opened her eyes with a comical huff and sat up, gave a little shake of her head. Tala released the breath she was holding and relaxed, wrapping her arms around her friend. "Spiritwolf." She met my eyes. "Her name is Spiritwolf. She was born into the pack that took me in. We've had a special connection, bond, since then."

I felt my eyes smile. "It's good you had her."

She took a deep breath. "Yes." She held my gaze as she tentatively took my hand and held it out to Spiritwolf. "He is good," she murmured.

But I wasn't. I was the farthest thing from *good*.

Spiritwolf sniffed my hand, then allowed me to stroke her head. It was a little unnerving, with all the stories I'd heard about vicious, bloodthirsty wolves. But those stories weren't true. This was no vicious, bloodthirsty beast. Merely a beautiful, wild creature with stamina and strength beyond comprehension, and apparently more loyal than people.

I couldn't help but ask, "Tala, when I blacked out back at the tent, when they branded me, did you take the pain onto yourself like you just did with Spiritwolf?"

She nodded.

"Why?"

"I couldn't just sit by and watch."

"So. . .you felt it?"

"Yes," she responded quietly.

"Why would you do that for me?"

She shrugged. "You're human. Alive. I won't let anyone suffer if there's something I can do about it."

"Actually, I'm an elf."

She laughed. "You know what I mean."

The rest of the day and into the night we spent hiking far away from the magician camp. Tala was an impressive hunter, and I was thankful for her skills. As dawn started to bring gray light to the sky, we stopped near a river to eat the rabbit she'd hunted with her bow. I got the fire going while she skinned the rabbit, then I cooked it over the fire on a spit. It was fairly tasty, though a little gamey. But the food was welcome in my painfully hungry stomach.

It felt good to rest. I was still weak from blood loss, and the burn on my chest hurt a lot more than I'd admit. I didn't want to find out what it looked like. I cursed myself for not saving any of the herbs from the magician's camp to ease the pain.

After eating, I rested back against a tree trunk as the stars began to flicker into sight. The scars on Tala's face caught the firelight, and I fought the urge to ask her about them. Instead I asked, "So. Your plan?"

She was sitting beside me and looked up from cleaning Spiritwolf's wound. "I don't know. I'm supposed to find the source of the magician's power and either figure out how to destroy it, or destroy it myself. I don't know where it is, or what it is. I am going in blind. I'm just hoping I'll find something that helps give me an idea of what I'm looking for."

"And you were sent by the king, and the king before?"

"Yes."

"And they thought you could do that single handedly because. . .?"

"Well, I'm the kingdom's best spy. King's Wolf. And I possess the Keen. But mostly, we're desperate."

I studied her face for a long moment. "You're a mystery, Tala. I can't seem to figure you out. And I figure *everyone* out."

Her gaze fell to the fire, the flames dancing in her eyes. "Some mysteries are better left unsolved." She shifted, letting out a soft sigh. "Most have answers that are better left unknown."

I knew her name and her occupation. I knew that she'd been framed for murdering the prince and had been poisoned. I knew she was involved deeply with the royals, but how? How did she come about working for royalty? Why? And what had she been through to make her so much like Aidilane?

"Tell me Kai," she said softly, "Do I have you figured out?"

I held her gaze. She'd seen, felt, and heard everything in my dreams the night before. And that. . .well that all was pretty much my life. My father abandoning Aidilane and I. The orphanage. Finding my abilities. Aidilane taken away. Becoming an assassin and working, no, killing for the sake of my sister's freedom. "I think so."

She hugged her sides, shooting me a small smile. "And is that a good or bad thing?"

"You tell me."

She reached over and put her hand on my knee. "You are a good person, Kai."

I avoided her gaze. "Don't make me delusional."

"You are. The things you've had to do aren't good. But I felt you. I *saw* you. You are good."

I tilted my head. "What makes you so sure of that?"

"I just am."

"Why? I'm a murderer."

She was quiet for a moment. Then she whispered, "You are a boy who is just as enslaved as his sister."

The words pierced my heart. I turned away, blinking rapidly. I didn't deserve sentimental excuses for my actions. Tala slid her hand from my knee to my hand and squeezed it gently.

"Kai. Kai look at me."

I met her eyes, and she smiled. I shook my head. "How can you smile during all this?"

"There's nothing else to do," she laughed. "Besides, why not? It keeps me hoping when I've run out of reasons. You should try it sometime."

I stared at her, feeling the corners of my mouth twitching despite myself. "There you go!" she exclaimed. "You look sort of like you've just caught a skunk's scent, but–"

I couldn't help it. I laughed. A real, genuine laugh. For the first time in. . .well, years. Tala joined me.

When we stopped, I realized she was still holding my hand. I smiled down at it, then back at her. It took her a moment to realize, and then she pinked and pulled her hand away, tucking a loose strand of her flame hair behind her ear. She cleared her throat. "We should rest. I'll take first watch."

"No." I put another stick on the fire. "I will."

"But you need your rest after the magician's experiments. I'll–"

"Sleep isn't really my thing," I interrupted. "My mind tends to remember things I'd rather forget. It's pretty dark and deranged."

She studied my face. "Are you afraid of your dreams?"

"Yes," I answered quietly.

"I'm afraid of my dreams, too," she said, tilting her head back to gaze at the moon until the ends of her hair brushed the ground. "The things behind me chase me like a hunter after prey. We can just stay awake then. Watch the stars sparkle and the firelight dance, and let the moon bathe us with her light."

Relief flooded me. I was exhausted. But reliving my past over and over again wasn't worth getting rest. It was like she said– the past chases me like a hunter after prey.

But instead of watching the stars or the moon, I watched her.

Chapter Seven

Tala

*T*wo people, two broken souls scarred with the wounds from their pasts and their demons, playing a dangerous game of trust. A dangerous game that usually had regrettable outcomes.

Yet, trust was starting to become easier, somehow.

I slowly woke with the dawn, finding Kai awake and stroking Spiritwolf's head. I watched them for a moment, amazed how quickly Spiritwolf had taken to him. She could probably sense what I did in Kai. She rested her head on his lap, eyes closed, snoring lightly and enjoying his gentle touch.

I realized then that I'd fallen asleep when I'd told him we'd stay up together. Guilt tugged at my heart, especially since I'd gotten good rest without a single nightmare for the first time in a very long time.

I sat up, Kai's jacket sliding off my shoulders. I felt my face redden. He'd covered me with his jacket.

"The fire went out after a while," Kai explained. "You fell asleep and looked a little cold."

"T–Thanks," I stammered, embarrassed. "I'm sorry, I–"

He waved aside my apology. "Don't be. You needed to rest."

"Did you get any sleep?" I asked.

"A little," he lied. I wished I'd stayed up with him, but I couldn't help but notice how well rested I was. I hadn't slept so well in a long time. I felt refreshed for once. Renewed. Which made me feel guilty all over again.

"She likes you." I nodded towards the snoring Spiritwolf. "She never sleeps past dawn."

He chuckled. "Oh she was up. But then she came over to me and curled up. I wasn't sure if she'd be alright with it, but I started to pet her, and she seemed to tolerate it."

"She loves it." I busied myself with braiding my hair back. Then, I sharpened my daggers.

"You never sit still, do you?" Kai observed.

"I don't?" I laughed.

"Not that I can tell."

I shrugged, not thinking much of it. I finished with my knives and put them all back into their sheaths. Then I poked the fading embers in front of me. A sound nearby made me snap my attention that way, tensing and reaching for my dagger. But it was only a bird.

Kai was silent as he gently eased Spiritwolf off of him, who leaped up and prowled away into the undergrowth, hunting for her breakfast. Kai stepped over to me and crouched down beside me, put his hand on my shoulder, making me flinch. "Tala, hey, take a breath."

I met his eyes, confused. His eyes smiled, and he pointed to the sunrise. "Look at the sunrise. Isn't it beautiful? How many colors do you see?"

I stared at him for a long moment, then forced myself to pull my gaze from his to look at the sky. "It is breathtaking. Uhm, blue, rose, amber, gold, purple." I realized my heart rate was gradually slowing down a bit.

"I think I see a little green."

"Green?" I squinted at the sky. "Where?"

He pointed. "See? Right under that cloud, between the blue and gold?"

"Oh!" I breathed. "Wow."

He gently squeezed my shoulder with a smile. I felt more relaxed. "Smiling does wonders for you."

He raised an eyebrow. "Oh?"

"Massively."

"Noted."

I stood up, brushing the leaves and dirt from my clothes, and pulled the food from my satchel, handing some to Kai. We ate in silence as the sky's wondrous colors faded into its usual blue and the sun climbed up over the trees. Spiritwolf was quick to return with a large rabbit, which she finished even more quickly.

We cleaned up our little camp, making sure to cover up the ashes from our fire and ridding of any evidence that we'd been there. Then, we made our way through the woodline and over to the river.

I took in a sharp breath when I saw it. It was incredibly wide, and very swift. I couldn't tell how deep it was, but I really didn't care to find out. But I had the sinking feeling that I would have to soon.

"How are we supposed to cross it?" I wondered aloud.

Kai paced the bank, eyeing the water like it was some sort of complicated equation. "I don't know. We should probably just keep going along the bank until we find a spot that's safer."

Spiritwolf was already padding away up river, her instincts taking over. We followed her. She led along, zig zagging to sniff at scents she found and to lap at the water occasionally.

Kai and I trekked side by side, keeping a few feet of distance between us and the river. I noticed he was still weak from the magician's experiments. He stumbled frequently, and was breathing as though walking took a lot of effort. It pained me to remember the sight of him on that shiny metal table, chained down, shirtless, and eyes drooping. He'd been so pale and weak. And then the brand. . .I shivered. That had been painful. But at least I didn't have to deal with the aftermath of it. He did. I had no doubts that it caused him a lot more pain than he admitted. I could tell by the way he moved his upper body very stiffly.

It was past noon when Kai stumbled again, and I caught his arm. "Sit down. Let's rest for a moment."

He shook his head. "I'm fine."

"No," I insisted, "You are not fine." I tugged on his arm. "Sit down."

He sighed, relenting. "Just until I catch my breath."

Spiritwolf retraced her steps back to us with an impatient huff. *Why stop?* She complained.

He is unwell, Spiritwolf. Recovering from what the mad men did to him.

She understood, plodding over to me and flopped down, rolling in the wet sand and stones to cool herself off. I was utterly relieved that I didn't have to worry about having seizures any longer. My heart still throbbed with gratitude and my head tingled with excitement. The seizures had become such a huge part of my life. . .now that they were gone, I felt free.

Clouds started to cover the sun, putting us in shadow. I shivered, it felt a little colder, suddenly.

Kai felt it, too. He looked up, narrowing his eyes, his pointed ears twitching. "Strange."

"Mhn." I got back to my feet, rubbing my arms. The temperature really was dropping. Moments later, I could see my breath in the air. "Uh, Kai–"

Spiritwolf leaped up then, her hackles standing on end and a growl rising in her throat. She was staring at something in the woodline.

Kai slowly stood as I reached for my daggers. Five magicians stepped into view, their ivory wands glowing icy blue. I vaguely recognized them from the camp.

"Don't move," one of them growled. Ice started forming beneath our feet, and I looked up to find snowflakes falling. The temperature was dropping fast.

As they moved towards us, Kai's hands lit with flames. "Stay back!" he shouted.

They didn't.

He shot flames at them, but they deflected them with ease, being prepared. One of them, a tall and skinny man, lifted his wand high above his head, and then swept it downward in a quick motion.

I gasped as the air grew intensely, bitter cold. I almost dropped my knives in surprise.

Kai clenched his jaw, determined, taking a defensive stance in front of me and blasting his fire at the magicians. Snow gathered on the ground impossibly fast. The magicians fanned out around us, shooting painful blasts from their wands at us. One hit Spiritwolf and sent her tumbling into the rushing river with a frightened yelp.

"No!" I cried, trying to go after her, but a magician shot me with a purple streak of light, sending me crashing backwards into Kai with a painful *thunk*. We both crashed to the ground in a sprawling heap of flailing arms and legs.

A magician grabbed me by my arms and pulled me up roughly. I kicked and thrashed, but I couldn't dislodge him. But Kai was quick. He burned my captor, freeing me. At the same time, a magician wrapped a magic strand of rope from his wand around Kai's neck. Kai choked, his flames going out, falling to his knees and gripping at his throat.

I threw one of my knives at the magician, hitting him square in the gut. His magic vanished like vapor, and Kai fell on all fours, gasping for air.

I retrieved my knife as Kai summoned his strength. I yelled, "Do whatever you did back at the camp!"

"I don't know how!"

I jabbed at the magician that tried to grab me. But I was slowing down, the cold making me stiff. Kai wasn't doing any better. I knew we didn't stand much of a chance.

So, I took a run for it. I dodged two magicians and grasped Kai's wrist, pulling him towards the river.

"Are you serious?" he exclaimed as he stumbled after me.

"We don't have any other choice!"

At the river's edge, he stopped and turned to face the magicians, raising his hands and closing his eyes. Fire bursted from his hands, and he dragged it in a sweeping motion, making the magicians fall back to keep from getting burnt long enough for us to leap into the river.

It was freezing. It shocked me, knocking the breath from my lungs and making my limbs lock up. Immediately, we were swept away.

I lost sight of Kai, and I struggled to keep my head above the water. I couldn't reach the bottom with my feet, and I kept getting slammed into rocks. I tried to swim, but the current was too strong. I kept getting pulled under, and was inhaling painful amounts of ice water. I wasn't sure how much time passed– it could have been two minutes or two hours– when I knew I wasn't going to make it. I was drowning.

An arm wrapped around me, pulled me up. My head broke the surface and I spluttered, taking in gasping breaths.

Kai dragged me through the water until I felt my boots hit rock. Then I managed to half crawl half wade onto the frozen, snow–covered bank. Once I coughed up all the water I could, I realized that Kai was still struggling to get on solid ground, hardly able to keep himself from being swept away.

I stumbled back over to him and pulled his arm over my shoulders. "Come on, elf," I groaned. "You're much h–heavier than you look."

We both collapsed on the ground, shivering so badly our teeth chattered. Kai's lips were blue, and I was certain mine weren't much better. Kai coughed up the river water, an amount that could have watered four horses. Slowly, he sat up, his usually sharp eyes, droopy. "A–are you o–okay?" he asked.

"C–Cold," I managed.

Snow was still falling, and it was as cold as mid–winter, but as I scanned our surroundings, I couldn't see any sign of the magicians.

I tried to get to my feet, but I was quaking too hard. I collapsed again, amazed that I'd managed to hold onto all my things, including my bow. But, it was broken, snapped in two.

"F–F–Fire," I nudged Kai.

He nodded, unable to respond, and crawled over to the undergrowth beside me. I gathered up what twigs and dry leaves I could find underneath the snow and piled them in front of him. He held his shaking hands over the pile and sparked a fire. We both leaned in over it, desperately trying to soak up what little heat it put off.

Finally, we forced ourselves to our feet and gathered more fuel for the fire, feeding it until it was much larger. The heat was the best thing I'd ever felt in my life. But my soaked clothes clung to my skin, and the winter cold still gripped me.

"H–Hypertherm–mia," I said, my breath still coming in short gasps.

Kai met my eyes, looking about as miserable as I felt. "C–Clothes. O–Off."

"E–Excuse m–me?"

He rubbed the bridge of his nose, frustrated. "We'll die o–of hyperthermia, like y–you said. Our clothes. . .t–trapping the c–cold." He stood and turned around, started peeling off his jacket and shirt.

After a second of realization, I turned around. This wasn't happening. I let out a frustrated growl and began to do the same as him. I kept looking over my shoulder to make sure he stayed turned around, and when I was finished, I frantically wrapped myself in my wool blanket. It may be wet, and I'd smell like wet sheep, but wool would keep me warm even if it was wet. I squeezed my wet braid until most of the water was out, then I unbraided it so it could dry. Or freeze, from the looks of it.

"Tala," Kai whispered behind me, making me jump. He was also wrapped in a wool blanket, his wet hair dripping into his face. His brows knit with concern as he brushed my hair aside, looking at my exposed shoulders.

Then I realized.

My scars.

I turned away, my breath catching. Now I wasn't shaking from the cold, but from the memories. I stood there with my back to him, opened and closed my mouth, but nothing came out. My heart raced, and my eyes darted around wildly. I couldn't breathe.

Kai ran a gentle finger along one of my scars, making me tense up and take a shaky, gasping breath. "Who did this to you?" he half whispered half growled. Then, he slowly wrapped an arm around my shoulders and eased me down beside the fire as I stared at it, numb, a tear running down my cold cheek.

For the longest time, I couldn't speak.

Kai held me as I shook and gasped like a child waking from a nightmare. The lash, the kicking, the shouting. . .

My chest spasmed with the pure panic that rose in my throat, and I gripped the sides of my head, pulling at my hair, unable to take in air. Kai wrapped another wool blanket around my shoulders and pulled me in closer, murmuring, "It's okay. You're safe." His calm voice and gentle rocking back and forth dragged me back to the present.

Slowly, gradually, I started to calm down. "Deep breaths, Tala," Kai murmured. "In through your nose, out through your mouth. That's it." He breathed the same way, helping me to slow down and match his breathing.

I leaned my head on his chest, relaxing. Tentatively, he stroked my wet hair. I closed my eyes, and I wasn't sure when, but eventually my exhaustion won over and I fell asleep.

Evening sunlight woke me, shining into my eyes through the canopy of trees above. Kai was still holding me as he drowsed, my head still rested on his chest and his arm draped over my shoulders. I stirred, sitting up, and he opened his eyes with a small smile.

"I–I'm sorry," I said. "I don't know what I–"

He stopped me. "No apologies." His eyes softened. "I knew there was a reason you reminded me so much of my sister."

I took in a deep breath, then let out a soft sigh. "I do?"

He nodded, his gaze never wavering. "You don't have to tell me anything, Tala. I'm sorry I rubbed that wound raw. But I'm here. And I'm not going anywhere unless you want me to."

I took another deep breath, pulling the blanket tighter around my shoulders. "I'm King Sabian's sister. And Cordan Greyver is my father."

Kai raised his eyebrows, sucking in a breath, but didn't say anything. So I continued, letting myself shiver as I remembered. But in Kai's company, his arm around my shoulders, I felt safe. For the first time, I felt safe to say out loud the things I'd been through.

I started from the beginning. My mother and how she had begotten us and died because of it. Separated at three from my twin and sent to fend for myself in the stables, working and scraping to survive. Then my life as a royal guard and King's spy. The prince's poisoning. My fleeing and being poisoned myself. Living with the wolves.

"One day, Spiritwolf and I were separated. I sensed she was in danger, so I kept looking for her, following where I felt she would be. Turned out it was Kelgare, the Royal Assassin, putting those feelings in my mind to draw me into a trap. He somehow knew I was alive, and had the idea that I was the one who could save the kingdom.

"My brother found me and helped me. But we were caught by Prince Rayden. He brought me in, and King Rubarb put me on trial for the murder of the prince and for possessing the Keen." I took a deep breath, my next words shaky. "They decided I was guilty. Penalty was death, and King Rubarb let the queen see to it however she saw fit. In the end, Kelgare stuck his neck out for me. Convinced the king that my skills were too valuable to be wasted– that I could be the key to stopping the magicians. He is the only reason I survived."

Kai shook his head. "How could it be so easy for the king to send you off to torture and death after all you did for him?"

"His wife was the one who killed the prince, her own son," I said quietly. "Tell me, would you believe the words of your wife and queen or some stable girl turned spy?"

He sighed, meeting my gaze. "The world is cruelest to those who least deserve it."

"I just. . .I wish I could get over it. But I feel stuck there, in that dungeon. I should be grateful that they didn't kill me. Instead. . ."

"You don't just get over things like that, Tala." Kai shook his head. "People can do worse things than kill you."

I nodded, my lip trembling. Then I continued, "Now that my brother is king, I don't feel so trapped in my duties. But I still feel that it is my duty. I'm doing it not for my king, but for my brother and the innocent lives at stake. With my brother on the throne, the world will be a better place. But not if the kingdom falls under the magicians before he gets a chance to bring change."

Kai looked determined. "Then we'll figure it out."

"And we're going to save your sister," I added with a meaningful look. He pursed his lips, staring at the fire.

I stood up and dragged my sopping wet clothes to the fire, where I spread them out to dry. Then I did the same with Kai's. The temperature was finally back to normal, the magician's spell wearing off.

Now that he'd seen my scars, I felt raw, exposed. I hated the feeling.

But maybe, just maybe, it wasn't such a bad thing after all.

Kai had seen my scars and instead of being disgusted or repelled by them, he held me. He knew my story now, saw me for me, and he didn't seem to dislike it.

"Tala," Kai said. "Have you ever wondered why they did that to you? Other than they thought you murdered the prince?"

"I possess the Keen, the Demise."

"Yes. They were afraid of you."

"What?" I stopped what I was doing and turned to him.

"They were afraid of the power you held," Kai said as if it were obvious, "of what you were capable of. So they tried to kill you, and when they couldn't do that, they tried to control you like light on a torch. But you are a wildfire, Tala. You can not be controlled. Your flame cannot be smothered."

I considered that. "Perhaps. Me, my abilities. . ." I sighed. "I would either be a monster or a weapon in their eyes."

"But, you were just a child."

We locked eyes. "So were you. I suppose we were both forced to grow up fast." I smiled. "Thank you, Kai. For being there for me earlier. For grounding me. I. . .I didn't realize you could be so comforting, uh, I mean—"

Kai stopped me with a raised hand and a charming smile. "I've been called a lot of things, but comforting isn't one of them." He chuckled, shrugging. "I just did what I thought you needed at the moment." His eyes went distant for a moment, his smile fading.

"What's wrong?" I asked.

"Nothing." He shook his head. "I just worry about Aidilane."

I crouched down, scrunching my brows as I thought. "We could find her before we keep going. The Moonland Kingdom border isn't far from here. And I can't allow myself to continue knowing Aidilane is still there. We can't let her suffer any longer. Besides," I added, "We don't know where to go, really. We don't even know what we're trying to find. Maybe we'll figure something out while we rescue your sister."

Kai studied my face. "You're being serious."

"Of course."

He nodded. "But how are we supposed to get her out?"

"I'm not sure. But we'll get her out, Kai. Whatever it takes."

He didn't look so sure, but he agreed. "Then let's get dressed."

And find Spiritwolf, I added to myself. I could feel her still, so I knew she was alive. But I worried that she was injured, and I needed her at my side if anything was going to work.

We packed our things, and before we headed for the border, I tried to mend my bow. But whatever I tried wouldn't work. I didn't have the right supplies. I sighed, frustrated. "How am I supposed to hunt without my bow? Hunting without it is massively difficult."

Kai shrugged. "We'll get something to eat once we get to Eclipse."

"Eclipse?"

"The nearest Moonland Kingdom town."

I nodded. "Maybe we'll find some berries on the way, too." I stood up. "Ready? Let's go."

"Hold on." He reached towards me suddenly, making me flinch and sending my heart racing. His dark eyes softened. "It's okay. Just a pinecone in your hair." He picked it out of my hair and tossed it aside.

I relaxed, feeling my face redden. "Sorry."

"When you've been in the dark so long, the sunlight hurts your eyes," he murmured.

The Moonland border was truly mystical. The name suited it well, especially under the moonlight. I hadn't seen anything like it before.

The trees were tall willows, the hanging leaves reflecting the glow of the moon. Bluebells spotted the bushes, putting off the light that they'd soaked up during the day. The moss and lichen was also glowing. Owls hooted overhead, the sound of their wings beating in the air sent shivers down my spine. My senses felt so alive here. . .like my Keen had been dipped in cool water and come out renewed.

Kai and I had just crossed the border as nightfall arrived. I turned to him now, marveling at the forest. "Wow. . .Kai you never mentioned how beautiful your kingdom was. It's. . . .magical."

"*This* part of Moonland is. The kingdom was named after this forest– Moonwood. But the other parts of the kingdom are more like the dark side of the moon." Kai took my hand suddenly, and used it to point at a towering oak. It was much larger than any oak I'd ever seen.

"It's huge!"

"Yes, but look at the hollow."

I tilted my head, concentrating on the hollow in the tree that was probably twice my size. A large bird emerged, and my heart nearly stopped as it took flight and soared over our heads, its tail nearly brushing my hair.

"A Phoenix!" I gasped.

"A *Moon* Phoenix," Kai corrected.

Its feathers were pale blue, iridescent and glowing like the stars, eyes indigo blue like the night sky. Its flight was almost silent, simply a whisper, with only a soft breeze left behind. I could feel it. . .her. She was magnificent.

I let go of the breath I was holding as she disappeared into the canopy. "Wow," I whispered.

"Wow's right. We're fortunate to have seen one. They're even rarer than fire Phoenixes." Kai's eyes reflected the glow around us as he stared at me.

"What?" I sighed. "Is there a pinecone in my hair again? Those little things keep–"

"No no, just your eyes. . ." He peered closer.

"I was thinking the same about yours," I laughed. "They're reflecting the light."

"No, it's not that." Taking special care to be slow and gentle, he took my chin in his hand, tilting my head so he could study my eyes. Why did he have to be that tall? "Tala, your eyes are hazel. Now they're blue! Glowing pale *blue.*"

I felt nervous with his face so close to mine, his breath on my cheek. "T–They are?"

"Yes, it's strange. Are you feeling alright?" He raised a brow.

"I feel fine." Was the temperature getting warmer? "Uh, heh, I didn't notice those little green flecks in *your* eyes before."

He smirked. "Are you not concerned that your eyes are glowing blue?"

I shrugged. "There isn't anything I can do about it, and I feel fine." I took his wrist in my hand and pushed his hand away from my chin. But I didn't let go. Instead I held his hand in my palm and stared at it. "How did you go from about to kill me, to holding me during a breakdown, Kai?"

He gazed at our hands. "Faith. Hope, maybe."

"How is it that your hands are scarred from murder and yet I trust them anyway?" And it was true. I did trust them. Trust him. Somehow. And the moment he'd held me, so gently, bringing me back to the present, I'd known it. I trusted him.

"You shouldn't trust me, Tala."

"Why not?"

"You don't deserve to be let down again."

"What do you mean?"

He let go of my hand and kept going through the trees. "Kai!" I called after him. "What are you talking about?" I caught up with him.

"I'm not the trustworthy type, Tala. It's not in my nature."

I laughed. "And neither is comforting someone while they break down. Come on, Kai, don't say things like that."

He glanced at me but didn't say anything. I didn't understand what had gotten into him. A little while later, I suggested, "We should probably stop to rest for the night."

"No, look," Kai said. "Up ahead."

A little ways away, a valley sat just beyond Moonwood with a town nestled within it. When we finally reached it, it was like stepping into an entirely different world.

Eclipse was dark. Not just because it was nighttime, but the whole place had an aura about it that sent shivers down my spine. It was a very clean town, almost as clean as the palace back home. But it was eerily quiet and cold, as if the whole town were anticipating something wretched. Shadows followed us as we wove through the tightly organized shops, bars, homes, and other buildings. Round street lights lit our way, dim and blue just like the forest, but instead of being beautiful, they were ghostly. Elves in long cloaks moved through the shadows like phantoms, rushing as if being chased, and didn't pay much attention to us. But I felt eyes on me the entire way.

"Is this the town Aidilane is in?" I whispered, afraid to speak any louder.

"Yes, she'll be at the Nightingale," Kai whispered back. "Eclipse is more lively during the day," he added. "Nighttime here is for those who don't know what's good for them."

I wasn't sure what he meant by that, but it didn't reassure me. I'd been in all the kingdoms on missions for King Rubarb, all except for Moonland. It was new and unpredictable, and that was something I didn't like.

Kai led the way with a confident but silent stride. He didn't pause even once, and obviously knew the way around the town very well. I glanced at him, noticing his furrowed brows and clenched jaw. I almost slammed into him when he stopped suddenly, something having caught his eye in the dark alley to our left.

"Wait here," he said, disappearing into the shadows. I stood there, my senses and Keen hyperattentive, even more so than usual. I hated not sensing other minds. I felt blind and deaf only relying on my physical senses instead of my mind.

I nearly screamed when a hand touched my shoulder, but it was just Kai. "This way." He led the way into the same alley he'd just come out of. He stopped halfway through the alley and turned to me. "Do we have any more water?"

"Yes." I rummaged through my satchel and handed him one of the flasks. He took a long sip, and I realized just then how thirsty I was. And hungry. Very, very hungry. I turned in the direction the scent of food was coming from, lighting up my hunger. My stomach clenched painfully. When I turned back to Kai again, he handed me the flask and I took a good, long drink.

I sighed with contentment when I was finished. "I'm so glad we filled up the flask at the river. Otherwise, o–otherwise. . ." I started feeling lightheaded, stars dancing in my vision. I swayed, sleepiness crashing into me like a wave. I looked down into the flask, then at Kai. "W–What did you–" My legs buckled.

Kai caught me and lowered me to the ground gently. "I'm sorry," he murmured.

His face blurred from my sight, and I weakly tried for my knife. But my limbs wouldn't obey me, and then everything faded away into darkness.

Chapter Eight

Kai

*M*istakes, curses, shadows. All of one. All of me.

When we had been walking past the alley, a small light had caught my eye. It was a normal flame, yellow, not blue, which was unusual for Eclipse. They only used moon blossoms encased in glass for light during the night, rarely ever fire. So the little lit candle at the back of the alley could only be one thing. A message for me.

I told Tala to wait where she was and padded to the candle, picked it up. A folded piece of paper was stuck to the side with melted wax. I opened it.

Here's to second chances. If you want your sister, bring the King's Wolf. An exchange. Or I'll tell the king you're working with her.

A nightingale was stamped under the handwritten note. I shivered. Aidilane's owner, Wyne, had found out I was here with Tala. Those cursed spies– they must have recognized me coming into town and told Wyne. A small paper pouch was also with the candle, filled with a powder that if poured into water, would be tasteless but would make one sleep.

A plan raced through my mind. Pretend I was agreeing to the exchange, bring Tala in, then escape with both her *and* Aidilane. I knew my way around the Nightingale, and I'd have the advantage with my fire.

But. . .it would probably be more convincing if Tala didn't know the plan. If she believed I really was betraying her and giving her over for my sister.

I glanced back at Tala's silhouette, waiting for me. Guilt pricked my heart, but I pushed it away with a frustrated growl. This was a *perfect plan* that didn't involve me killing her, and involved us all escaping with Aidilane. Besides, Tala would understand when it was all over, wouldn't she?

Now I held her limp, unconscious form in my arms, and I couldn't help but wonder if I had made a mistake.

Again, I pushed the guilt and doubt away. It would work. Everything would be fine. Tala and Aidilane would be safe and free, and I would be free of my assassin work for Wyne. And Tala would understand. Why did I care if she understood or not anyway? This was my sister who was on the line.

But. . .everything inside me wanted Tala's understanding, and I couldn't deny it.

I carried her and our things as I headed to the Nightingale. My heart raced with anticipation and excitement– I was about to free Aidilane! And I hadn't seen her in almost four months.

I found the place with practiced ease. I stepped inside, setting my jaw. This *had* to work.

Girls in low back silk dresses moved like trained dancers around the Nightingale, catering drinks and finger food with the gracefulness of swans. But their eyes were filled with pain, misery. I avoided their gazes as I wove through the patrons who enjoyed their food and drinks and music. I found Wyne's office and stopped in the doorway.

He sat at his desk, peering at some correspondence and signing papers. He jumped with surprise when he saw me. "Didn't hear you come in, friend!" He scooted his chair back and walked around his desk to pat me on the shoulder as if we were good pals. "I see you found my message. Is this really the King's Wolf?" He reached to touch Tala's face but I took a step back.

"Yes. Where is Aidilane?"

"She'll be down in a moment, friend."

"Don't call me that."

He smiled. "No need to be a prick, son. Set her on the chair here." He gestured towards a cushioned couch beside his desk. I moved to it and laid Tala down as gently as I could. She stirred, the powder beginning to wear off. Good. I needed her awake if what I was planning was going to work.

Everything is going to be alright, I said in my mind in case she was awake enough to hear with her Keen. She opened her eyes a miniscule crack and murmured something I couldn't understand.

I turned to Wyne. "Let's get this over with. Where is the prince?"

He scrunched his eyebrows. "The prince? Prince Oberon? Ha!" he laughed. "You think I'll turn her in for a prize, don't you? No, my friend. This human will join my other girls here at the Nightingale."

"What?" I exclaimed. "But–"

"A girl for a girl is how it works here, son," Wyne said as he patted Tala's head. She groaned, shifting again, and opened her eyes fully, then made an attempt to swat his hand away but couldn't move very well. She met my eyes, glaring.

Tala I promise this isn't what it looks like, I said in my mind. But she didn't respond in any way that suggested she heard me. She really was staying true to keeping out of my head.

"Where is *Aidilane*," I demanded. "I agree to the exchange, but I–"

"George!" Wyne called, interrupting me. "Bring her in."

George entered a moment later with Aidilane. I sucked in a breath when I noticed how skinny and malnourished she was. She wore a lavender silk dress that revealed too much just like the other elven girls, her wavy raven hair pinned half up, and her blue eyes frightened and tired. When she saw me, she lit up. "Kai!"

I felt tears prick my eyes as I embraced her, the scent of the perfume strong but not able to mask her familiar scent completely. "Aidilane," I whispered. "I missed you so much."

She pulled away when she saw Tala. "Kai, what are you doing?"

Wyne answered her before I could. "Well dear, your brother has decided to ditch his usual work for me in order to pay off your indenture, so he's agreed to an exchange. This particular human girl for you."

"What?" Aidilane exclaimed. "Kai, no!"

"What do you mean? Don't you want out of here?"

"Of course I do. But not like this." She scrunched her brows.

"Would you rather I keep taking lives instead?" I asked.

"No!" she cried, bringing her hands to her temples, frustrated. "Kai, I don't want another girl to. . . be here. Especially not in *my* place."

"But–" I stopped. "Aidilane, please *trust me*." I hoped she understood what I was trying to say, but I couldn't be sure.

"Enough," Wyne growled, slamming a fist on his desk. "That's alright darling. You don't have to worry, okay? Because the human will not be *replacing* you. She will simply join you."

I whipped my head around. "Wyne, what–"

"Oh son," he interrupted. "I wish it was different. But I'm afraid that you've become the object of interest."

I clenched my fists. "Wyne–"

"I suggest you corporate," he said, crossing his arms. Then he called, "Evian, come on in."

A tall elf clad in navy robes entered the office. He had frosty blue eyes, stubble for hair, and a short beard. He looked me up and down, eagerness clear on his face.

"Wyne," I growled. "What is this?"

He grinned. "I found the best deal, my friend. One where I come out on top, financially. I get *both* girls, elf and human, *and* I sell you to a very interested, high paying customer. The profit I gain!"

My stomach clenched. "This wasn't the deal–"

"It is now. You know how it works here in Eclipse, friend. It's just business. Nothing personal. No hurt feelings."

On the couch, Tala was trying to pull herself up into a seated position, which wasn't working very well for her. Her droopy eyes darted around the room, settling on each of us for short moments, always returning back to me.

Evian handed Wyne a very large, heavy pouch. "The gold." Then he turned to me and spread his hands. "Young fire elementalist, let's do this the easy way, shall we? So as to not burn the whole place down? Besides, I do not intend to harm you."

I ignited my flames. "I'd love nothing more than to burn this place down."

Wyne backed up towards the door, grabbing Tala by the arm and yanking her to her feet, where she collapsed. He caught her and dragged her out. She didn't say anything, but the glare she shot me was enough to kill a man. They were followed by George who took Aidilane. "Kai!" she sobbed.

I blasted my fire at George, but he was already out of the office. Evian sighed, blocking the doorway. "Kai, be reasonable–"

I shot my flames at him, but he blocked them with his hands, where a bubble of water surrounded them and distinguished the fire in a cloud of steam. He was a water elementalist. Just perfect.

"Really?" I scoffed. "What do you want with me–"

He blasted me with water so hard that the force slammed me backwards into Wyne's desk. I felt at least three of my ribs snap, and the breath was knocked from my lungs. I slid to the floor, gripping my side in agony and holding up my other hand with fire to keep Evian at bay. I clenched my teeth and glared at him.

He shook his head. "Do the right thing, Kai. Stand down. For the sake of you and everyone in this building."

I curled my lip, refusing to show how badly my side hurt, and pushed myself to my feet. "No, Aidilane, Tala—"

"I'm sorry," Evian said. "It isn't my business what goes on here except that you're coming with me. Please, I don't want to hurt you."

I was finding it hard to breathe, each breath feeling as though I were being pierced with a lance. I gritted my teeth and concentrated my fury and pain into my power, growing the flames and aimed at Evian.

"Don't—" he warned, but I willed the flames at him before he could finish. But as he distinguished the fire, unharmed, something rolled from the doorway to my feet. Before I could react, it exploded into a cloud of dust, making me cough and struggle to see.

A strong, muscular arm wrapped around my neck, knocked me to the floor roughly, pinning me down and clasping my wrists with some kind of cuffs. The dust cleared as I struggled, and when I could finally see, I saw two other elves standing over me beside Evian. One of them, a short blonde elf with round glasses cringed as his partner, the muscular one, lifted a bat and swung.

Pounding pain in my head brought me back to consciousness. I slowly opened my eyes, squinting through the stars that danced in my vision. I was upright in a cave pool, up to above my waist in blue water. Glowing, colorful koi fish swam around my legs, and stalactites hung low from the cave ceiling, lunar bugs crawling the rocks and putting the cave in a soft glow. My wrists were chained up over either side of me, and when I tried to ignite my flames, I found I couldn't.

I felt more panic rise in me. But as I struggled against the chains, my broken ribs almost made me cry out in pain. I bit my tongue and let out a frustrated growl that echoed around the cave. They'd taken off my jacket and shirt, too, leaving my brand exposed. My side was horribly bruised. What was it with people taking off my shirt?

I slumped, clenching my teeth. Ridiculous. First the magicians and the experiments, now my own species had me chained up. Blood dripped down into my eye from where they had hit me with a bat. The rippling water around me and the feel of the koi swimming around my legs nauseated me. I didn't like being wet at all. Never had. And now that I realized it was probably because–

"Strange, isn't it?" Evian's voice echoed around the cave. He came to stand at the edge of the pool, crossed his arms. "How you can't use your powers here."

I kept a neutral expression but made sure my eyes shot daggers.

Evian tilted his head. "As a fire elementalist, water is your opposite. Therefore you cannot use your ability when you're in water."

"Ah so that's why you've got me chained up in here. You're scared of what I'm capable of."

"Ha, perhaps, though scared isn't the terminology I'd use. It's more of a precaution," he responded smoothly. "What you're capable of is actually exactly why I bought you. See, I–"

"I really don't care what you want from me," I interrupted. "Because I'm not doing *anything* for you. Especially not until my sister and partner are free and safe."

Evian studied my face. "I don't appreciate interruptions. As I was saying, your powers are exactly what I need to make my plans possible.

I'm hoping I can talk you into it *civilly*, though that is entirely up to you."

"And if I don't *want* to 'talk civilly'?"

"That would be quite unfortunate, now wouldn't it?"

I opened my mouth to make a snarky remark, but more voices echoing around the cave stopped me. My ears pricked as three girls entered the cavern. Aidilane, Tala, and a third elf with shoulder length silvery hair and ivy green eyes.

"Mira, what is this?" Evian growled between clenched teeth. "Why did you bring them here?"

Mira crossed her arms, standing her ground. "Aidilane is his sister, and Tala his partner. They deserve to see him."

"How dare you! You know I specifically told you all to stay outside while I talked to him!"

"I know what you said. But surely you understand?"

"No, I–"

"Kai!" Aidilane ran to the edge of the pool, knelt beside it, her features concerned. Meanwhile, Tala slowly came to her side, her expression unreadable as she avoided my gaze. I noticed she was missing all her knives.

"Tala," I began. "I–"

"Enough," Evian sighed, pinching the bridge of his nose. "Listen, girls. I have him chained up so he can't use his powers. Otherwise he'd burn everything down."

"How would I burn down a cave?" I pointed out, irritated.

"Even so," Evian growled. "I need to talk to him about my terms–"

"We agree to your terms," Tala said.

"*What*?" I exclaimed. "Tala, what are you doing?"

She wouldn't meet my gaze. Instead, she planted a firm stance in front of Evian. "I speak for my partner in this. We agree to your terms."

Chapter Nine

Jala

*B*etrayal stings like a burn. When someone you care about lets you down or betrays you, it pierces deeply. Wounds heal. But when you believe someone has hurt you, the wound is unimaginably hard to seal.

I lay there on the couch, watching the scene before me and unable to do anything about it.

Kai ignited his flames, and even though I wouldn't pry into his mind, I could feel the panic radiating from him like the heat from his fire. The pudgy elf was selling him. And keeping me. I was utterly hurt and angry with Kai. He'd betrayed me and now whatever plan he'd had clearly wasn't unfolding the way he'd intended.

"I'd love to burn this place down," he growled.

The pudgy elf, Wyne, yanked me up by my arms, but my legs were still asleep. He caught me before I fell and carried me away, his employee dragging Aidilane behind us, who cried, "Kai!"

We were dragged around a corner and Wyne shoved us both into a pair of seats outside his office, crossed his arms, and stared down at me with contempt on his features. "I'll fetch your new clothing, dear, while you recover from the powder." He stationed George to stand guard over us and disappeared down a corridor.

I struggled to wake myself up more. My limbs were coming back to life slowly but surely. But my mind was still in a sedated fog. Aidilane, with her gorgeous raven hair and blue eyes sobbed beside me, tearing at her dress with clenched fists.

We both stiffened when a loud crash sounded from inside Wyne's office, followed a moment later by a *pop*. Then, Evian and two other elves came out, dragging an unconscious Kai between them, bleeding from a nasty hit to the head.

Aidilane jumped to her feet, yelling, "No! Where are you taking him?! Kai!"

George held her back as the elves dragged him away and outside. Aidilane slumped back into the chair and dropped her face into her hands. Finally, I managed to speak.

"Aidilane?"

She turned to look at me, dried tears streaking down her face. I managed to sit upright and hugged my shivering sides. "My name is Tala. Kai and I were coming to get you out of here, but. . ." My voice faded. "He double crossed me. I don't understand why, but. . ."

Aidilane reached over and put a hand on mine. "Thank you for trying."

"Whatever plan Kai had," I continued, "didn't work. But Aidilane," I added, careful that no one else heard, "I'm still going to get you out of here."

Her sad eyes lit up for a quick moment, but then the excitement faded. "Don't give me false hopes, Tala. And with Kai gone. . .nothing will work." I didn't listen in to her mind, but I could feel her despair like a gaping pit.

I didn't answer. I would simply stick to my word instead. And I didn't need Kai to get us out of here. Besides, they didn't know who they were messing with. With my Keen, I *would* get us out of here.

Wyne returned a moment later with a dress similar to Aidilane's and handed it to me, then he and George took Aidilane and I by the arms and pulled us up a staircase and shoved us into a room, slamming the door behind him.

Aidilane sank to the floor, letting go a whimper. I turned in a slow circle, noticing every detail of the room from the flourished bed and drapery to the candlelight and strong perfume scent. I set my jaw and threw down the dress, trying to ignore the way my heart was racing and the doubt turning my stomach.

"We're never getting out of here, Tala," Aidilane whispered.

"Yes, we are." I searched the room for anything that might be useful to me but came up with nothing but a bottle of perfume. I'd realized a long time ago that my knives had been taken away, but I reached to my sheaths anyway, out of habit.

I pulled myself together, pushing all my anxiety, fear, and hurt down. I didn't have time to deal with those feelings at the moment. I steadied my shaking hands and crouched down beside Aidilane, giving her an encouraging smile.

"Aidilane, I'm here now. We *are* getting out of here. But you need to work with me here. Okay?"

She met my eyes. "I—I don't believe you."

"I don't blame you. And you don't have to until we're out and I've proven it to you. But please, I need you to be willing to try."

Aidilane's gaze dropped to the floor, but she nodded silently.

"Okay." I stood up, taking in a deep breath. "Does Wyne lock you in this room often?"

Aidilane nodded again.

"When does he return?"

"When he finds another client."

I shivered. "Alright. I think I may have a plan." I told Aidilane what I'd conjured up, and though the doubt in her eyes didn't fade, I was hopeful about it. And the thought of the joy Aidilane would have when she was finally free kept me going. After we were both on the same page, we waited.

An hour went by, and half of another one before finally, we heard Wyne unlocking the door. I positioned myself so that I would be behind the door when it opened, quickly, while Aidilane stood just a few feet away, perfume bottle in hand.

Wyne swung open the door and stepped inside, followed by another man, lanky and somewhat short, smelling of beer and wine. I could feel the lust radiating from the client's mind, disgusting me. Absolutely sick. Anger boiled up in me, and I channeled it to fuel me.

"Where is the King's Wolf?" Wyne demanded. But he hardly completed his sentence before I emerged from behind the door and wrapped the dress he'd given me around his neck and latched my legs around his waist to keep hold of him as he stumbled backwards and struggled. I just needed him to pass out from lack of oxygen.

The client watched in stunned horror for a moment before he lunged towards Aidilane.

"Do it!" I prompted her.

She backed away from the man, eyes wide, and sprayed his face with perfume, getting it directly in his eyes. He screamed in agony and clutched his face, stumbling around and hollering for help.

Finally, Wyne slumped to the floor, unconscious beneath me. I was thankful that whatever Kai had drugged me with had worn off in time for this plan to work. I grabbed Aidilane's hand and pulled her with me, heading down the hall and down the stairs. "Hurry," I ushered her, hoping the other patrons hadn't heard all the commotion we had caused.

Once downstairs, I pulled Aidilane along behind me, trying to look inconspicuous among the patrons, but doubting I was in my untraditional black attire. We wove through the elves and the tables, but it wasn't long before we drew attention.

"Hey! Where do you think you're going?" George was on our tail.

I let go of Aidilane's hand and pushed her in front of me. "Go," I said. "I'm right behind you."

She gave me a wide eyed look but didn't hesitate any further and headed for the door.

George reached me and swung a heavy blow, but I easily dodged it. His momentum sent his fist crashing into a table, making the patrons there leap up and yell. I stepped up on a chair to swing up unto George's shoulders, wrapping my legs around his thick neck, and pummeled a point on his head with my elbow. By then, the place was a hurricane of chaos.

George gripped my ankles and flipped me down into a table, knocking the breath from my lungs painfully. He pinned me down by my arms before I could recover, but I kicked his chin up with my knee, then slammed my heel into his nose.

I heard a horrible crunch, and then George let go of me, stumbling backwards and hollering in pain as blood dripped down onto his shirt.

I ran for it, dodging other elves who tried to grab me, and streamed out the door along with some of the patrons. Out in the crisp twilight, I found Aidilane hiding behind a pile of barrels.

We ran down an alleyway, and down another. We kept going until I was certain we weren't being followed, then stopped. Aidilane bent over, hands on her knees, to catch her breath, while I turned in a slow circle, taking in our surroundings. We looked to be in a more rundown part of town.

I was startled when Aidilane tackled me in a hug. "Thank you!" she cried. "Thank you. We really did it. I'm free," she whispered the last few words, as if in disbelief.

I smiled. "Of *course*, Aidilane. I wouldn't have left without you."

"Are you okay?" she asked. "George really slammed you into that table pretty hard."

"I'm fine," I said, though where my back had made contact with the edge of the table really hurt. I was certain I'd at least bruised something pretty badly. "Are you alright? All this–"

"I'm better than I've been in a really, really long time," Aidilane reassured me. "But. . .Kai."

My stomach turned, and my heart skipped a beat. Kai. I felt tears prick my eyes, the betrayal stinging more than my injury. I was confused beyond anything else. If we had worked together, it would have worked. We would have gotten Aidilane out. But. . .

And yet, now he was in danger. Who knew what those elves were doing to him and why. Idiot.

I sighed. "We'll find him."

Aidilane studied my face. "After what he did to you, I'm sure you don't–"

"He hurt me. He messed up, bad. But I won't let him suffer at the hands of whoever took him away. I. . ." *Still care?*

Aidilane smiled sadly. "Thank you. He is lucky to have you, despite what he did. *Especially* after what he did."

"Lucky to have me?"

"You said you were working together? Partners, right? Well, he betrayed you. . .and you still want to go rescue him."

I wanted to say that of course I did. But why?

I sniffed, wiping the tear from my cheek and hoping Aidilane didn't notice it. "Right. He's done a lot for me. I have to believe that. . .that there's a good reason for what he did."

"But it all went wrong," Aidilane sighed. "My brother usually isn't like this. But then again. . .I never thought he'd become an assassin for my sake. It makes me ill just to think about it. My own brother. . ."

I put a gentle hand on her shoulder. "We go to extensive measures for those we love."

She shook her head, denial radiating from her. It was then that I realized that I could sense her emotions, her thoughts, as well as a few others while I had been back at the Nightingale. I thought my Keen couldn't sense elves' minds?

I brushed the thought aside for later. I needed to focus on finding somewhere to spend the night safely.

We wandered the part of town for a while, keeping our heads down and trying not to draw attention to ourselves until we found an old building. The letter R was burned on the door just barely noticeable beside the handle. We slipped inside, finding it empty, but I still led the way just in case.

It was musty and dark, cobwebs hanging low, the dust in the air making Aidilane sneeze behind me. I couldn't really tell what the building had been used for except storage. A few crates stood piled in the corners and a couple in the middle of the room, but everything looked untouched for a long time.

I reached out with my Keen, and too late, realized we weren't alone.

Someone dropped from the ceiling beams, knocking me to the floor hard in the process. Aidilane screamed. I got to my feet quick enough to block a kick to my neck, and advanced to try and get the upper hand.

It was a girl about my age. Short, dirty blonde hair and ivy green eyes, dressed in a tunic that brought out her eyes.

I aimed a thrust for her stomach, but she blocked it easily and returned it with a jab to my jaw, which I dodged. I swept her ankles, sending her sprawling, but she kicked me hard in the gut when I went to pin her down, pushing me back with a grunt. She tackled me before I recovered and pinned my hands to my sides, but I flipped her back and over me.

Move for move, and it wasn't long before both of us realized we were equally matched in this fight.

At some point, I found a sharp piece of metal, and it was then that she drew a knife. Jab after jab, neither of us were cut, both of us blocking each other's attacks and dodging them as if we'd trained together forever.

We rolled on the floor, our wrists locked, and finally came to a stop, both breathless. "Truce?" she suggested.

"Truce," I agreed.

We backed away from each other, and I tossed the metal aside, brushing the dust from my clothes. Aidilane came over to my side and stood so that I was between her and the other girl. "Are you okay?" she asked me.

"Fine," I said, keeping my eyes on the girl.

She sheathed her knife and nodded to me. "I haven't had a worthy opponent in a long time," she admitted. "So what are you doing on my turf?"

I glanced around. "We didn't realize this was anyone's turf."

"Good. Then I've done my job well."

I exchanged a glance with Aidilane. She shrugged. "We were just looking for somewhere safe to sleep tonight."

The girl crossed her arms over her chest. "You two look like you've been through a lot this night. And every night before that, now that I really look at you."

Aidilane suddenly became very interested in her feet, and I sighed. "It has been challenging." I clutched my stomach, trying not to cringe. My hunger was really lighting me up from the inside in a painful fashion, and I felt as if my stomach would start gnawing on my spine soon, if it hadn't already.

The girl's gaze softened. "I can make sure you both have a safe place to stay tonight. But first, you both need to eat. You–" She pointed at Aidilane– "are undernourished. And you, worthy opponent, are clearly starving. Follow me." She led the way outside.

I hesitated, unsure of whether or not to trust her. But she was right, and she also seemed to know her way around this town. We needed a guide. Besides, when I prodded her mind, she felt genuine and authentic, with good intentions. So, we followed her.

As she led the way along the streets, she said, "We'll make sure to steer well clear of the Nightingale." Clearly she could tell from Aidilane's clothes where we had come from.

"Thank you," Aidilane whispered, though she was so quiet I doubted the girl heard her, so I repeated the thanks, but a little louder.

"Of course. That place is a madhouse anyway. I pity anyone who's enslaved there." She shivered, then glanced at me. "So what is a human doing in the Moonland Kingdom? And in Eclipse of all places?"

"It's a long story."

"Mmhn." She didn't seem satisfied by my answer. "Better question– how is a *human* such a good opponent? Most elves can't even hold their own against me, but you? We could have kept going and going until we both died of exhaustion."

"I'm well trained."

"Mmhn."

"What?"

"That isn't an answer."

"I don't go about telling my life story to strangers who just happened to fall on me out of the ceiling."

The girl laughed. "Fair enough. My name is Mira."

"I'm Tala. And this is Aidilane."

Mira stopped in her tracks. "Did you just say Tala? And Aidilane?"

"Yes?"

She shook her head. "This is utterly ridiculous."

"What?"

"I'll explain. But first, food." She led the way into a nearby tavern. It sort of reminded me of the Nightingale, except less noise, more candlelight, and not as many people.

Mira chose a table and gestured for us to sit down. "Don't be shy," she said.

I sat across from her while Aidilane scooted in beside me. I fidgeted with my sheaths, uneasy about being anywhere without my knives. I felt naked without them, and my hood and mask.

After Mira ordered our food, I said, "We don't have Moonland currency."

"Don't worry about it. I'll take care of it." She eyed Aidilane with compassion. "You both need to eat."

"Thank you."

When our food arrived, we dug in. Mira ordered seconds and extra bread to go with it. I'd never had food like that before, but it reminded me of stew, just more flavorful and had spices and vegetables that I'd never seen or heard of before.

"Why did our names concern you?" I finally asked once I'd finished eating.

"Well," Mira said around a mouthful of bread, "I'm part of a group called the Renegades. Our main goal is to stop the mages from the North. But one of us has some questionable morals. He made a deal with the elf that runs the Nightingale. Used most of our gold to buy a fire elementalist from him. He's convinced that this elf is what we need to get the upper hand with the mages, but no matter what I told him, he wouldn't be convinced otherwise. The fire elementalist was unconscious while I helped transport him to our base, and he kept mumbling 'Tala, Aidilane'. And now I know why."

I sucked in a sharp breath as Aidilane gasped, "You have Kai? That's my brother!"

Mira's eyes studied me. "And what's he to you?"

I took a lot longer to reply than I would have liked. "He was my partner. We were on a mission together."

"Was?" She raised an eyebrow.

"He. . .double crossed me. Sort of. I don't understand why. But he did. Then, whatever he had planned didn't work. It would have if he had just. . ." I sighed. "Your boss has him?"

"Pff," Mira scoffed. "Evian is *not* my boss, though he likes to think he is. But yes. We have. . .Kai? Yeah. Evian had him chained up in our cavern last I checked. Keep his powers in check while he tries to 'convince' him to work with us."

"You don't think Evian will hurt him, do you?" Aidilane asked, her voice thick with fear.

"More than he already has? Who knows. You never know with that old elf."

I pinched the bridge of my nose. "I'm sorry you've been dragged into this, Mira. But I'm glad we happened to run into each other."

Mira cracked a smile. "You mean you're glad I jumped you from the ceiling beams in Oli's old lab?"

Despite myself, I couldn't help but laugh. Mira had an aura about her that made me relax in her presence. "Yes. Oli?"

Her cheeks pinked. "Friend of mine. Also a Renegade. He's a sciency type— too smart for his own good. We use his old lab for storage now, but every once in a while he asks me to go back and find something for him. This time though, he just left me a note." She reddened even more. "Cheeky, that one."

I chuckled. Love and affection was pouring from Mira as she thought about a blonde, messy-haired elf with round glasses that sat up on his head. I quickly shut my mind away from hers, feeling as if I were intruding on something she'd wring my neck for spying on.

"Anyway," she said, "I'll take you guys to Kai. Evian will just have to adapt and understand. He'll get over it. Eventually."

"Why are you doing this for us?"

Mira shrugged. "You two have clearly been through a lot. I'm not going to let *Evian* stand in your way."

"Thank you." I meant it.

"Of course." Mira sipped from her mug, then glanced at me. "What are the human kingdoms like?"

I sighed. Broken. Cold. Bittersweet. But that was just my perspective, from my experiences. I wondered if people saw the world through a brighter lens than I did, and if so, what was it like? "It's not as clean as here. But not as dark either. Probably less advanced, too."

"Interesting, but you're beating around the bush," Mira said. The look in her eyes suggested she somehow knew more than she let on. About what, I didn't know.

I felt Aidilane's eyes boring into me as I stuttered, "Uhm, what do you mean?"

Mira's eyes strayed to the mug in her hand. She set it down with a thunk. "Never mind. Sorry. I–" She stopped, then flashed me a smile. "Let's go find Kai, shall we?"

"We agree to your terms," I said.

"*What*?" Kai exclaimed. "Tala, what are you doing?"

I avoided his gaze and held my ground. "I speak for my partner in this. We agree to your terms."

Evian studied me for a long moment. "And how can I know you're genuine? And. . how do you know my terms?"

Mira had brought us to the Renegade's camp. Everyone else was asleep anyway, but she led us straight into a cavern near their camp, where a pool was and Kai in the center of it, chained up. His side was a mess of dark bruises, and he was bleeding from a gash above his eye where they had knocked him unconscious. I couldn't meet his gaze, let alone open my mind to his. I just couldn't.

But I did search Evian's mind enough to understand his motives for buying Kai. He thought that Kai's abilities would further aid him and the Renegades when it came to the magicians. He wanted to raid magician camps and stop groups of them who were trying to get through the kingdom. His terms were that Kai could have his freedom as long as he goes along with Evian and the Renegades' plans.

I took a deep breath and hoped Mira would go along with what I was about to say. "Mira told me your terms. And I'd like to help your cause. I'm from the Highland Kingdom. I was sent to find the source of the magician's power and either extinguish it, or report back to forces who can. Kai here was. . .helping me. We had to find his sister, but. . ." I glanced up. Kai was staring at me, his eyes confused. "We're on your side," I continued. "We'll help you, since by doing so, you'll also be helping us."

Evian spread his hands with a wide grin. "Well! What a pleasant surprise! Thank you. . ."

"Tala," I introduced myself. "And this is Kai's sister, Aidilane."

"Nice to make your acquaintance." Evian turned back to Kai. "Do you agree with Tala here?"

I felt Kai's eyes on me for a long moment, but I couldn't meet his gaze. I was afraid I'd break down, and I couldn't afford to do that.

Finally, he responded quietly, "Yes."

"Seems to me we all have an accord then," Evian exclaimed. "Mira, why don't you free our new friend."

"I'm not your friend," Kai growled.

"You strung him up though!" Mira protested. "Why should I–" Evian cut her off with a dark look before turning and heading outside. "Fine," Mira said softly.

"I'll help you," I volunteered.

We waded out into the cool pool. It only went up about waist high, and the koi fish swimming around our legs and their lazy thoughts reminded me suddenly of Spiritwolf. Again, I hoped she was alright, and that we would be reunited soon. The ache in my heart left by her absence was becoming nearly unbearable.

Mira handed me a key and I unlocked one of Kai's cuffs while she did the other. I worked the key for a moment, the rusty cuff giving me trouble. Finally, it came loose, and Kai stumbled forward. He held his side, clearly in pain, and struggled to stay upright in the water. I reached out not only with my hands to support him, but also with my mind, just enough to find that he had four broken ribs. It startled me– I didn't realize I was capable of finding exact injuries in someone. I could also sense that the water weakened him.

I pulled his arm around my shoulders and helped him out of the pool with Mira's assistance.

We all stumbled to the Renegade's camp in silence, and Mira disappeared into a very large, dark green wall tent that sat just outside the cavern to prepare somewhere to sleep. For whatever reason, she asked Aidilane to help her. So, it was just Kai and I. I let him lean most of his weight on me, but it was hard. . . being so close again.

"Tala," he began. "I–"

"Please don't," I interrupted him softly.

"No, I need to explain–"

"There's nothing to explain, Kai." I squeezed my eyes shut tightly to keep the tears from coming. "Nothing at all."

He was silent for a few heartbeats. "Please," he whispered. "Use your gift and feel my mind. So that–"

"No." I kept my eyes on the grass at my feet. "I–I can't, Kai. I can't."

"Why?"

"Because I can't look at you and not feel. . .scared," I admitted, shaking my head. "I trusted you. I told you. . .everything. *Everything*, Kai. For the first time in my life, I felt safe. I–I trusted. . .you. But. . ." I didn't look at him as I let go. "Can you stand on your own?"

His voice shook as he said softly, "Yes."

I stepped away and ducked into the tent, where the sound of light snoring greeted me. Cots were lined along either wall, most of which were occupied by who I assumed were Renegades. Mira and Aidilane were just finishing setting up three other cots– one in the empty spot nearest the door, and the other two on the opposite side.

Mira saw me. "Take whichever cot you prefer. Where's Kai?"

"Thank you. He's just outside." I took the cot nearest the door and sat down on its edge, keeping my boots on in case I needed to escape quickly. Surrounded by the warmth in the air of warm, sleeping people that I didn't know made my skin crawl. I wanted nothing more than to sleep outside far from the camp underneath a tree, where the cool night air was, and where people I didn't trust, weren't.

Aidilane slipped outside, and I could just barely hear her and Kai having a proper reunion.

I fidgeted with the corner of the blanket as I scolded myself for not finding my knives before escaping, but then again, I wasn't sure how I would have gotten out of there with them *and* my freedom– or even my life. But I wasn't sure how I was going to get them back. It was part of my training to get in and out of a place undetected, but. . .I didn't *want* to go back.

I rubbed my face in my hands. *Coward.*

"Look," Mira said, taking a seat beside me. "I know I've just met you. But I did bring you here. I did help you. So I can't help but ask, things are pretty complicated between you and Kai, aren't they? More than just him betraying you."

I studied her face through the shadows. "What do you mean?"

She shrugged. "He betrayed you, and you are torn apart by that. But it wasn't a simple betrayal, was it? Because you love him, and his betraying you hurts more than just a betrayal."

I reeled back. "I don't *love* him. I care about him– he's my partner. And he's done a lot for me. I *trusted* him. And I thought. . ." I shook my head. "I just. . .I thought I could trust him. And it isn't easy for me to trust *anyone*. There are very few people I trust. But . . .now I'm just confused. And my instincts were right all along– I was deranged to trust."

Mira reached over to put her hand on mine, but I flinched, so she just held up her hands in a placating gesture. "Sorry. Tala, trust is a good thing. However much you've been conditioned otherwise, it is. And I couldn't help but overhear part of your conversation, and I hope I'm not stepping out of place here, but maybe you should try to hear him out. Boys are idiots, and sometimes, they mess up– even though they mean well."

I sighed. "I don't think I can. Trust. And hear him out. I'm not ready."

Mira shrugged. "And that's okay, too. You don't have to right away. And that's completely understandable. But please, don't give up on trust."

I met her eyes. "Trust has always been a fragile thing for me. Once broken, I'm not sure I can fix it."

"You don't have to. He broke it— it's up to him to fix it."

My gaze fell to the floor, the dust around my boots glittering in the air. "It's easy to break something. But healing it? That isn't."

"I never said it needed to be easy. Just possible."

"I don't think it's possible."

"It is. But it takes time."

I jumped as Aidilane returned to the tent with Kai a step behind her. He locked eyes with me, but I quickly turned back to Mira. "Thank you. I'll try to see the truth of your words."

"You will." She winked. "This team wouldn't survive without my wise guidance and leadership– even though they'd never admit it."

"I'm sure," I chuckled. "And thank you for taking us in."

"Of course. Welcome to the Renegades. You can meet everyone else tomorrow morning. I envision an exciting and interesting future now that you've arrived." She set a bundle of clothes on my cot and stood up, headed over to a cot near the back of the tent. "Here's a change of clothes, sleep well."

I ignored the feeling of Kai's eyes on me as I lay back on my cot, and considered what Mira had told me, confused. It was too warm in here to cover up with the blanket, but I did anyway. It felt safe, secure– a beautiful hallucination.

I took a deep breath and closed my eyes.

But sleep never really came.

When dawn was just short of arriving, I crawled out of bed and slipped outside. I transmitted to Spiritwolf again, but she still didn't respond. So I decided to change into the gray tunic, pants, and cloak Mira had given me. Then I wandered around the camp as the sun rose. There was nothing very special about it, except for the fire pits. There were two in total, outside two of the tents. I studied one of them, circling it. It was a silver, braided ring a few feet around and about knee high tall. The ground, the grass, inside and underneath it wasn't even scorched, and there were tiny fragments of rose crystal littering the circle, making the grass sparkle.

I paced beside it, running my fingers through my hair to detangle and smooth it. Then I braided it down over my shoulder as Kai ducked out of the tent. He locked eyes with me, and started forward, but I turned away to fold my other clothes– but not before I noticed how stiffly he moved. I sensed his broken ribs had done just about no healing overnight, which was expected, and the bruise–cut above his eye wasn't much better either, but I kept quiet. I still didn't understand how I could sense such things.

I sensed him stop just behind me and take a deep breath, but before he could say anything, Mira emerged from the tent and waved to me with a quiet, "Good morning,", followed slowly by Evian and the other Renegades. Lastly, Aidilane came out and embraced Kai. He wrapped his arms around her, glancing towards me, but I focused on everyone else, keeping my guard up.

They all settled in the grass around the fire pit, and Kai, Aidilane and I did the same– but I sat across from Kai, and a little ways back, a safe bubble of distance between me and anyone else.

Mira stretched her arms above her head with a wide yawn. "Everyone, this is Tala, Aidilane, and Kai. Kai is our new resident fire elementalist. And the other two are also our new members."

A few of the Renegades murmured amongst themselves at her words, staring at Kai, then turning their attention to me. One of them– a beautiful elf with coily, bushy hair and dark skin, her eyes a stunning shade of gold– narrowed her eyes at me.

"And what talents do you have to offer? We aren't running a charity."

I hesitated, but Mira jumped in for me. "She and I had quite the scuffle, and neither of us could win."

The Renegades exchanged glances, and the messy–haired blonde elf beside her widened his eyes, looking back and forth between Mira and I. "No way. Mira, you win every time."

She shrugged. "Point is, she's an intense fighter with skills I didn't realize we were lacking. We need her." She winked at me, to which I returned with a small smile.

The blonde elf tilted his head, shooting me a charming smile and pushed his round glasses up a bit. "Kudos to you, Tala. She *never* admits defeat."

Mira nudged his shoulder. "Hey, not true!"

He raised a knowing eyebrow, and she pinked, then admitted, "Fine, yes." I didn't even have to open my mind to theirs to feel the affection and love between them.

"Anyway, this is Oliver," Mira introduced the blonde elf. "And you know Evian."

Evian nodded while Kai rolled his eyes, but Evian was focusing his gaze on me, making my skin crawl.

"I'm Val," the elf with the gold eyes said. She wrapped her arm around a younger boy who looked to be around the age of ten or eleven with the same skin tone and coily, but less busy hair. "This is my little brother, Navy." He waved, flashing a bright smile.

The last Renegade was even taller than Kai, and was very muscular. He had long, light brown hair that was pulled back in a ponytail. He introduced himself as Felix. They were an interesting little group, but my senses told me they were good people– for the most part anyway. It took a lot of mental effort to keep out of their heads– which confused me. I wasn't supposed to be able to use my Keen on elves, even when I was first walking through Eclipse, I hadn't been able to sense anyone. But now. . .

I thought about the feeling I'd had when I'd first stepped foot in Moonwood– as if my Keen had been dipped in cool water and come out renewed. It was as if being in the Moonland Kingdom had strengthened– or even added to– my abilities. Being able to feel the elves' minds just as easily as humans now, and being able to sense injuries. Could I sense illnesses too?

I felt guilty about it, but I reached out my mind to Navy's. I was shocked to find he had a mild case of asthma. He confirmed it with a small wheeze, which turned into a cough. Val rubbed his back in small circles.

I considered telling them about my Keen, but decided against it for now.

Everyone began to disperse, finding things to eat. But Mira wandered over to me, Val at her side. They told me about each of the Renegades abilities; Oliver was a chemist and a scientist, but they didn't really elaborate on that; Felix was their muscle and brawn, and was also an earth elementalist; Val was an air elementalist; Evian– water elementalist; Mira was an ex–royal guard for the elven king; and Navy was pretty much a highly skilled thief.

Val demonstrated her air bending skills while we ate breakfast, and I was genuinely astonished. I'd only seen a few elementalists perform their skills, but every time left me amazed. Kai was impressive with his fire, but Val looked so elegant and graceful when she bended and shifted the aircurrents and bursted gusts of powerful wind.

I explained about my hunting skills and asked if they had any bows and arrows I could use. They showed me to their supply tent and they worked on arrows while I crafted a bow. Then we emerged with my new set to find Navy in the clearing alone, just outside the cavern chasing a frog through the grass.

"Where is everyone?" I asked.

Navy shrugged, too focused on catching the frog to give me a proper answer. Val answered for him. "Felix is posted sentry either outside camp or at our lookout. Evian is probably in town, and–"

"Oliver is working on the chemical bomb idea he had," Mira filled in.

I raised my brows. "Chemical bomb?"

She shrugged. "Who knows. But I won't argue– he gets cute when he has a new idea. Goes all sciencey. It must be hard to be that way in a world with magic. He still hasn't given me a reasonable scientific explanation for magic."

That piqued my interest. "Does he have any idea what the explanation, or source, of the magic is?"

Mira looked to the sky, thinking. "Well, he has *theories.* He's said that in order for the mages to be so powerful, their source of magic must be extremely potent. And either the mages must contain a piece of the source in their wands, or. . ." She held up her hands. "Oliver has speculated about the source being alive. . ."

"Alive? Like, a person or a beast?"

She nodded.

"How is that possible?"

Val moved an air current, lifting fallen blue bells that were scattered beneath their stems and made them dance like periwinkle jewels. "How is elementalism possible?"

"It's possible through your connection to nature, to the elements of the world." How I knew that, I wasn't sure. But I was certain of it.

"Right." Val dropped her hand. "So what connects the mages to their source? I think that's the question we should all be asking."

"There's that word again," I pointed out. "Mages. Why do you call them that? In the Highland Kingdom we call them Magicians. Humans corrupted by magic."

Val snorted. "Magicians perform slight of hand and plays to trick the eye. Mages really have a source of magic. Real magic. No trick of the light or slight of hand." Her eyes darkened. "Magicians make children smile. Mages destroy. Mages *kill.*"

I shivered as I recalled the damage that had been done in Quinton; the wounded, my brother among them, the fires, the screams. . .the death. I couldn't understand why someone would desire something as vain as power at the cost of lives. Many lives.

I shook my head. "There are too many things we don't understand. Too many things that we can't explain. But the magci– mages," I corrected myself, "the mages' morals aren't one thing we have to question. They're ruthless. But so are humans. And elves. It makes me wonder if the mage's power is a drop of mercy for the other kingdoms. Because if the humans or the elves possessed such a power. . .who knows? Maybe the damage in the world would be even worse."

The whip of the lash. The kicks. The shouts. The pain.

I felt myself draw out from the present again. What would they have done to me if they had magic?

Mira nudged my shoulder. "Tala? Are you alright?"

I jerked back to myself. "Yes." Smiled. "What was I saying?"

"Quite some wise things," Val said. "You are a fascinating creature, Tala. I haven't ever heard anyone put things that way. As if the terrible things in our world might have an ounce of good to them. Still," she added. "It isn't that easy to convince me of such." She turned and headed towards her brother.

"I'm going to go check on Oli," Mira said. "Last time he was working on chemical bombs, he almost blew the camp to hell with fertilizer." She padded away towards one of the smaller tents, where gray smoke was drifting out from the door.

Despite myself, I decided to go find Kai. It made me uneasy that he'd just slipped away without anyone noticing, but I supposed it was in his nature, just like it was in mine.

I searched around camp, assuming he wouldn't have gone far with his wounds, but he wasn't anywhere to be found.

So I began to head towards town on one of the trails, but I sensed him approaching, so I waited just inside camp so as to not give the impression that I had been looking for him.

He stumbled into camp a moment later, carrying none other than a bundle containing my daggers.

I stood there, keeping myself from gaping. "How did you. . .?"

He handed them to me, our eyes locking, his fingers brushing mine as he handed me the finely crafted weapons. "Your knives."

"Thank you," I breathed, relishing the familiar feeling of the blades in my hands, my perpetual inner panic relaxing a little.

It was then that I noticed how pale he was, his pupils dilated, and his breath shallow. When he'd handed me the knives, his hand brushed mine, and his skin was burning.

"Kai, you're running a fever," I pointed out. "You shouldn't be going into a risky place and stealing things. You should be resting." I set down my daggers on a nearby tree stump, just in time to catch him as he collapsed.

I grunted as I helped ease him to the ground, his eyes rolling back into his head. "Help!" I cried. "Someone, bring cold water!"

I wasn't sure what I was doing, but I let my instincts take over. I opened up his shirt to reveal the patchwork of horrific bruises covering his side. Kai groaned as I placed a gentle hand on where I sensed his broken ribs were, and felt a few of the bone edges pressing up against his skin, threatening to break through. He grabbed my wrist and pushed it away, but I whacked his hand.

"Excuse me. This is a result of your own mistake. Don't push me away, Kai."

I held his gaze for a moment, my words sinking in. I was reminded of that night by the fire, under the copse of trees and twilight. I'm not going anywhere unless you want me to, he'd said. And then I'd told him about everything.

I clenched my jaw, snapping my focus back to his side. I wondered if his pain was as bad as the ache in my heart.

Aidilane rushed over, her hair still dripping, and set a bucket of water from the cavern pool beside me. "Kai," she said. "I told you it wasn't a good idea. You needed to rest! Now look at you. It was too much for you."

Kai groaned in response.

I tore the hem of my tunic and ripped the cloth into strips and dipped them in the cold water, then placed them on his forehead, neck, and chest. Then I breathed deeply, placing my hands on his side and closing my eyes.

I allowed myself to connect deeper, not only with his mind, but with his nervous system, and I could feel them–each bone, each vein, each muscle and tissue– down to the shards from the broken bones. I felt a tug in my mind and my gut, pulling from my very being, and pushed out, channeling it into Kai, pulling the damage together molecule by molecule. Beneath my fingers, I felt the bones shift together, back into place and mending the fractures.

Finally, I opened my eyes, unsure of how long I'd been kneeling there.

The bruises were gone, and so was the fever. Kai stared at me wide-eyed, unblinking, his color returning.

"Woah," Mira breathed over my shoulder. I looked up and realized nearly everyone was gathered around us. I felt my face heat up.

"How did you do that?" Kai said as he sat up, touching his side. "Tala–"

"I don't know," I whispered. Truthfully. I was as astonished as they were.

"And your eyes!" Oliver marveled. "They're glowing blue now!"

"Again," Kai said for only me to hear.

I looked down at my shaky hands. "I–I don't understand how I did that. . ." I pulled myself to my feet, but immediately regretted it. My legs buckled, unable to hold me up. Mira and Kai caught me and helped me to tree stump.

"However you did it, it took a lot out of you," Mira noticed.

I felt very, very hungry suddenly, and as if I couldn't possibly ever get enough air, and I was shakier than a quaking leaf in the wind. Aidilane handed me a cup of water, but I couldn't hardly bring it to my lips, so she helped me, the cold water dripping down my chin.

But my vision began to dim, and everything felt miles away, everyone's voices fading.

A voice, calling out to me. Not in words or language, but true and strong, a voice pleading a melody.

Her voice.

I knew it was a female, but of what, I didn't know. I couldn't see anything– it was too dark.

I called out, "Hello? Tell me where you are!"

The call sounded again, quieter this time, fading away.

"No! Don't leave!"

Her presence was similar to the moon phoenix's. Powerful, majestic, but it also filled me with a strong sense of urgency. It was gone as quickly as it had come, leaving me in darkness.

The next thing I knew, I was slowly waking up in my cot, the last light of day fading away, casting a soft glow inside the tent. I sat up and waited for my head to stop spinning.

How had I healed Kai? How was that even possible?

I stared at my hands. Had it been the power of my mind? It sure had felt like it. As if I had drawn from my mental and physical strength and used it to. . .to what? Mend *broken bones*? Heal the damaged tissue? Or had I reversed the injury entirely?

I couldn't wrap my mind around it. But even though it had drained me, it hadn't felt *wrong*. It had been instinctual, like what drives the geese down south before the cold hits. I just. . .*knew.*

My chest tightened. They *all* had witnessed it.

I pushed myself to my feet, taking slow, shaky steps towards the tent door, my heart racing, roaring in my ears and thumping in my wrists. They knew now that I was capable of more than just fighting– but that wasn't necessarily a good thing. They would surely prod me with questions, unless they'd already figured out that I possessed the Keen. Was my healing a Keen ability? And had Kai told them?

Either way, I feared what their reactions would be. Kai had made it sound like the elves saw the Keen differently than humans did. But was that true?

I needed them on my side. I needed them to trust me. They were well motivated in defeating the magicians, and would be valuable assets. But. . .

In the Highland Kingdom, the penalty for being one of the Keen was death. I nearly fell under that fate, but was tortured and brought back to life only to serve the king who had sentenced me.

How would the elves react?

What was the penalty in Moonland for. . .existing?

I ducked outside to face the consequences of my rash, dramatic demonstration of my new found abilities.

After I collected my knives, I found the Renegades outside the supply tent, seated on log stumps around one of the fire pits. Evian looked disgruntled, standing to the side, his arms crossed across his chest, a frown etching his face. Mira, Oliver, Val, Felix, and Navy were discussing plans and issues to be solved. They talked about ambushing a patrol of mages that they got word were going to pass by near Eclipse. Navy also brought up the mages undercover he'd spotted a few days ago when he'd been quick–handing things in town. I was surprised at how mature he sounded when just earlier he'd looked so. . .childlike. It made me wonder– what had he been through? Maturity at a young age didn't sprout from easy things.

Hardships force one to grow up too fast.

"Tala," Kai noticed me. He had been forming fire orbs above the round fire pit, the pieces of crystal as drawn to the flames as magnets to metal. It was fascinating how they encased the flames and kept them alive and floating just above the fire pit, even as Kai dropped his hands to his sides. "You're awake."

All eyes turned to me. I swallowed the dread and fear rising like bile in my throat and clasped my hands together so everyone wouldn't notice they were shaking.

Mira patted the empty stump nearest her. "Come, sit."

I hesitated, and I hated that I knew Kai noticed. I could sense he could tell I was afraid. But he didn't step forward, he didn't make any move to me, so just as I did when King Rubarb had sentenced me, I held my head high as I took the seat beside Mira and squeezed the hilt of one of my daggers.

"Why didn't you tell us you could *heal*?" Val exclaimed.

"It's incredible!" Mira agreed.

Confusion and surprise made me reel back. "What?"

Oliver shook his head in amazement. "I've never seen anything like that before. Tell me, is it through some kind of magic or through–"

Mira nudged him, silencing him with a look. "Like Val said, why didn't you tell us? It's amazing, Tala!"

"I didn't know I could," I admitted. I met Kai's eyes. He smiled sadly, wrenching my heart.

"Thank you," he said. In his usually dark but now softened voice, I heard the hidden words, *I know you risked it all.*

I did.

I realized then that I'd actually heard his thoughts just then, and had projected a reply, just like Sabian and I would do, or Spiritwolf and I would do. I sucked in a breath. Why was my subconscious feeling his mind even though I was purposefully shutting him out?

I held his gaze. *This hurts, Kai. I can't let myself hear you now, I'm not ready to listen.*

He searched my gaze, a single thought surging through his mind along with desperation. *Please.*

I turned away, shoving his thoughts out as much as I could until they were just a light hum in the back of my head. I flipped my dagger once, twice, then asked Mira, "You really think it's. . .amazing?"

She nodded, her ivy green eyes bright. "You didn't know you could do it?"

I shook my head.

"Fascinating," Oliver breathed.

"But," I added, my whole body tensing. "There is something I haven't mentioned." My whole body screamed *Don't!* But as I searched each of the Renegade's minds, I found them all trustworthy– except for Evian. But he was someone I could deal with if I had to. Despite my fear, I knew what I needed to do.

I needed to take a leap of faith. A leap of trust. Again. Over and over again, my trust had been broken. But I needed these elves to trust me in order for what I had planned to work, and in order for them to truly trust me, I needed to show them a part of me.

I took a deep breath and faced their expectant faces. For a short moment, Kai and I locked eyes. I kept far out of his head, but he knew what this meant for me. He knew what it took for me to say the next words. And despite what he'd done, his gaze gave me the courage to tell them.

"I have the Demise, the Keen."

Evian raised his eyebrows, his eyes darkening. But the other's eyes widened.

"Woah, really?" Felix asked.

"Are you serious?" Val exclaimed. "I've never met anyone with the Keen!"

Mira just smiled, nodded encouragingly at me. I stuttered, "W–What? Aren't you all. . .angry? Afraid?"

"Are we supposed to be?" Oliver grinned. "Can I take measures of your brain waves while you do. . .whatever it is you do exactly. I want to see if—"

Mira interrupted him with a look, then she put a hand on my shoulder, making me flinch. "No one's taking measurements of your brain waves. But Tala, don't look so pale. Your abilities are amazing–I've read about the Keen. That is something to be proud of."

It took all I had not to gape at her. My heart kept skipping beats. I glanced at Kai again, and he was searching my face, his brow creased with not so well hidden worry, and I hated that it made my chest feel warm. "B—But, don't you all think the Keen is evil?"

"Why would it be?" Mira shrugged. "After all, a knife isn't evil unless it's used for evil. It could also be used for something beautiful, too, like providing food, safety or carving elegant shapes or patterns, among many other good things."

I looked down at my hands. "So. . .you aren't freaked out at all? Aren't afraid that I'll—"

"No," Mira, Val, and the others said while at the same time Evian said, "Yes. Do I have no say in anything anymore?"

Oliver grumbled under his breath while Val rolled her eyes. But no one answered, so he got up in a huff and stomped off into the tent. Navy burst out laughing, then giggled, "Why can't I tell him, 'No, you don't, grandpa'?"

Val shoved him playfully. "I already told you. He may be a stuck up, rude, and sometimes a pretty nasty old elf, but he is our elder. He must be paid some respect, at least. We keep him around for his experience. We don't want him to wander off too quickly."

Navy sighed. "Okayy." Aidilane giggled.

The tension in my stomach began to ease, and I forced myself to unclench my jaw. I could imagine how I looked right now, like a stunned deer under the light of an unexpected lantern. But I couldn't help it. I was *shocked*. A little terrified that they were all playing some sort of twisted game. That it was all just a ruse, and they'd drag me off to be slaughtered as soon as I fell asleep.

But their minds were genuine. I kept repeating that over and over again in my head.

They're genuine. They are speaking the truth. Genuine, genuine, genuine.

Still, my fist kept tight around my dagger.

Mira seemed to notice and faced everyone. "While we're on the subject of confessing truths, I have one of my own." I looked back up at her as she went on. "Ever since I can remember, I've had dreams–"

"Oh, this," Oliver interrupted, his eyes widening. Of course she had already told him. I suppressed a giggle.

"Yes," Mira continued. "I told Oliver and Oliver alone– I've always been afraid no one would believe me. But here goes nothing." She took a deep breath and let it out sharply. "I've always had dreams. Of things that have already happened, and of future events. When I was young, I thought that they were just dreams, but. . ." She squeezed her eyes shut tight for a moment, and I could sense the pain in her. "One afternoon, my brother and I had been playing by the creek near our home. He and I laid in the warm sunshine afterwards to dry ourselves before we went home, and I dozed off. I dreamt that we had a house fire, a terrible one. I could hear screams coming from inside. My brother woke me, crying, and pointed to where a wall of black smoke was billowing up from the trees in the direction of home." Her voice caught. "We ran home, only to find it up in flames. . .mother and father were both inside."

My heart clenched, and I put a comforting hand on hers. She smiled sadly and squeezed my hand, a tear slipping down her cheek, landing like a cold stone on my hand. She went on, "After that. . .I took my dreams seriously. Sometimes I can avoid future events, but sometimes they've already happened. But the point is, I've been having dreams recently, about Tala."

"About me?"

"I've had dreams about you before," she admitted, a sad, knowing look crossing her face, "But these were different. These *haven't* happened yet."

Haven't happened yet? Was she implying she knew things about my past, too? My heart sank. I'd ask her later.

"What do you mean?" Kai asked. "How do you know they haven't happened yet?"

"I just. . .know." Mira shrugged. "Like how a mother knows when her child cries, even though her senses don't. The dreams have been persistent, recurring. I see you," she turned her gaze to mine, "walking into some sort of cavern, or prison– I can't really tell which. You slowly approach this massive, reptile like creature, with shimmering scales and glowing eyes, and wings. It was. . .female, I'm not sure how I knew that, but I did. Her presence was strong, *powerful,* and overwhelmingly pleading. Like she was calling out, asking for help."

"A dragon," I breathed. I knew right away, it was *her.* "When I passed out, I dreamt about her too. Calling out. Pleading me to come to her. Rescue her." I shivered. "You described exactly what her presence felt like."

Mira's arms rose with goose bumps. Everyone else exchanged looks. Aidilane put her chin in her hands with a deep sigh. "I have a feeling this is connected, in more ways than you two having similar dreams."

"Maybe. . ." Kai murmured, his expression thoughtful.

"Maybe?" I pressed.

"What if it's connected to the magicians?" he suggested.

"Mages," Mira, Val and I corrected him. He looked confused but he went on, "*Mages*. It could be possible."

"But how could a dragon be connected to the mages?" Navy asked.

Kai shrugged, spun his long knives before shoving them back into their sheaths at his back. "I'm not sure. Just a thought."

I nodded. "It's worth looking into, especially since we have no other leads." I took the opportunity to tell them that I had been sent by the King of the Highland Kingdom to find the source of the mage's magic and report back, maybe even potentially destroy it if I could, but I left out the part about the king being my brother.

"This may not be a good excuse for a lead," Val grumbled. "But it's *something*. And that's more than what we had before. Now we just need to connect the dots, if there even is a connection between this dragon and the mages."

We all agreed, then we ate a dinner of potatoes and blue vegetables that looked almost exactly like radish, but tasted more like blueberries. Strangely, it went well with the potatoes.

Val took first watch just outside camp while the rest of us scattered in the twilight to get ready for bed. I wasn't really tired, having just woken up and energized by the idea of these potentially new friends that I'd somehow managed to conjure up despite. . .despite *me*.

Friends.

I smiled as I leaned back against the trunk of a glowing willow. They not only accepted me, they. . .they actually thought I was *amazing*. I didn't even realize that was something I'd ever be lucky enough to hear– let alone believe about myself. But they truly thought I was. . .and that was something I struggled to wrap my head around.

Me, amazing? My abilities, amazing?

I'd almost been *killed, executed,* for being who I was. What would my life have looked like if *everyone*, even the humans, thought the Keen could be good? If. . .

I didn't let myself finish that thought. It was no use thinking about the what ifs. Besides, not all elves thought like the Renegades did. Evian clearly hadn't been pleased with my confession.

I sensed Mira approaching, and I saw the light of her lantern flickering closer. She came up beside me and settled down under the willow with me and patted the grass. I joined her, folding my legs beneath me.

"I know you're wondering," she started. "And I want to be honest with you, Tala. I know, I've *seen* what you've been through."

Our eyes locked, and behind hers was a mixture of deep sorrow and overwhelming, condescending compassion. My heart swelled with warmth, with a raw exposure, but I wasn't scared of the vulnerability, not this time. This time, I felt like someone *saw* me, the real me, the good and bad, the pain included. Kai knew, but he hadn't *seen* it.

I knew it then that Mira and I would blossom into an unbreakable friendship. I wasn't sure how I knew, but I did. And the certainty that came with it was stronger than finely forged steel.

"I'm sorry about your parents," I said quietly. I wasn't sure if it was appropriate or just weird, but I added, "I can feel your pain, Mira. It may have happened years ago, but that kind of pain doesn't just fade away."

Mira closed her eyes for a brief heartbeat. "Exactly. Sometimes I wish more people understood that."

"Well, I do. Deep pain– it cuts deep. It leaves valleys carved behind, vast scars in our hearts, our minds. It's easy to get lost in them."

Mira nodded. "Thank you. Strangely enough, I really needed to hear that. I beat myself up inside when I let myself feel that pain. I always think that I need to just move on. To get over it already. But some days. . .some days I just can't."

"And that's okay," I reassured her. "It's alright to not be okay sometimes, no matter how far behind you it happened. Is your brother still around?"

Her eyes dropped to the ground. "He's alive. But he's made some questionable decisions. I've kept my distance from him for some time."

"I'm sorry."

She shrugged. "Sometimes people grow apart. I hope that one day he'll change, but I cannot be around him until then. Oliver has helped a lot, though."

I smiled, nudged her playfully. "I don't need to have the Keen to see and feel the love between you two. The sparks are *flying*."

Mira blushed. "He's a goof, but a smart one, and even more so sweet. Speaking of sparks flying, I've seen the way Kai looks at you when you don't see."

My face grew hot, and my heart felt fluttery. "What?"

She raised her brows with a nod. "There's no mistaking his care for you, Tala."

"The care that made him betray me?"

"Have you talked to him yet? Heard his side of the story?"

I shook my head. "I'm too afraid of what I'll hear. What I'll find."

"But what if it's something good?"

I blinked rapidly. "I still need time."

"That's okay. Just don't be too late."

I sighed. "Yeah."

"He cares for you, and I can see the way you look at each other. Like the world around you ceases to exist."

I denied it. "You're mistaken then. He's the first friend I've ever really had, but that's all. No sparks flying. Mira, he was an assassin– sent to assassinate *me!* And almost did. The only reason we're friends now is because of our shared purpose– defeating the mages. He was kind while we traveled together, and we had some close shared, vulnerable moments together. But really, *nothing* more. Besides, after what he did. . .I'm not sure we can stay friends. At least for now."

Mira nodded. "I don't blame you. But I won't back down– I can see the chemistry between you two– the tension of not just from his betrayal. One day you'll tell me, 'You were right, Mira!'"

I laughed. "We'll see about *that*. Well, I can foresee little elf babies with blonde hair and teenie round glasses running around camp and a golden band around this finger." I tapped her ring finger with a wink.

She reddened. "Actually, I prefer silver– and Oli better remember that."

The next day, Val, Mira and I hunted together, and then we cooked a large breakfast for everyone. Then, while Oliver, Navy, and Felix played a game that involved a flying orb– and kept begging Kai to join them– the girls and I trained.

I showed Aidilane some self defense maneuvers and helped her practice until she had them perfected. After her experiences at Nightingale, I knew it would be reassuring for her to have some more ways to defend herself. I could sense her confidence rise a little bit with every move she perfected.

Val and Mira did a mock duel with swords which was impressive to watch. Of course, Mira won, to which Oliver cheered and whooped, which left him distracted and caused him to have a flying orb slam into his abdomen. He bent over double with an animated groan while we all laughed.

Kai joined us with his knives, and he and Val and Mira did a three–some mock fight. At some point, Mira took over training Aidi-lane while Val and Kai continued with a duel, so I worked on my precision with throwing my knives. I used an old oak as my target, but after a few throws, Kai stopped to come over and watch from a few yards away. Of course, of all times, my throw faltered.

"Your aim is a little off. Here, let me help you–"

But before he could take a step towards me, I threw my knife dead center at his head. Even before he did, I knew he would catch it– I would never hurt him, though it was satisfying to see the surprise in his eyes as he caught it inches before it hit his face.

"My aim is just fine," I retorted.

He tossed me my knife, and I caught it by the hilt. "Tala, not every person that enters your life is a villain you can't trust."

Everyone's eyes were on us, but I didn't care. "I know, Kai. But please, give me time."

He stepped closer to me. "Tala–"

I stopped him with a raised hand. "I need time." I slid my knives back into their sheaths and buttoned on a gray cloak that Mira had given me, one with a hood, and started out of camp. "I'm going to town for a while."

"You shouldn't go alone," Kai protested. "It's dangerous for an outsider and–"

"I'm going *alone*. And don't try to stop me." I needed to get away for a while, be alone for a time. Everything that was going on was leaving me crazed, and I needed my solitude.

Eclipse *was* brighter and more lively during the day. Elven children skipped about with their friends, people on horseback rode by, carting goods and finery, and the shops had colorful displays of their abundant specialties. Tavern and bakeries' food scents drifted on the breeze. It almost seemed like a regular town, like the humans had. Except for the unique elven characteristics, you might have assumed it was a human town at first glance.

But attention to detail made it obvious that this was an elven town– like the blue street lights that had seemed so eerie before now looked like midday moons. And the passerby in their long cloaks seemed less like phantoms now, and more like dancers. I had to admit, elves had a natural grace and elegance about them, graceful as if they were all trained dancers.

The thought led me to think of my first dance, with Kai. But I pushed the memory away, along with the warmth that came with it.

I wandered around, peeking through the shop windows as I passed, and taking note of all the things that could be significant later on. As I padded past an apothecary, I noticed the shimmery liquids of all colors, all labeled for different ailments. But as I read the sign on the window, Spiritwolf called to me.

Stallkingwolf, I am awake now.

My heart leapt. *Spiritwolf! Are you alright? Do you hurt?*

I do. But an empty one has helped me.

An empty one? That was what she had called Kai, since his mental barriers had kept her from feeling his mind. *An elf?*

Yes. I fell into the rushing water, and then I woke here, the empty one cleaning and caring for my wounds.

I'm so glad you're alive! Where are you?

Nearby. Use your mind, you know, the one in your head?

I laughed at her sarcasm. *Yes, yes. I'm coming.*

I sensed her yelp in pain, and her fear rise, boiling up quicker than a volcano. She stopped projecting to me, and that was when I knew. She was in danger. The elf had to be hurting her for her to suddenly be so afraid, and in so much pain.

I took a moment to feel her, and the direction she was at, and then I headed that way, weaving through the passerby and zig—zagging through town faster than I would have thought possible.

Finally, on the edge of town, I came upon an old barn near an old homestead. I knew Spiritwolf was inside, I could feel her just inside the doors, her fear and pain choking me.

I drew two of my knives and crept inside the musty old building without a sound, the strong scent of rat scat and soiled hay stuffing my nose. It was dim, but I could see her in the far corner of the barn, whimpering in pain, an elf hunched over her, his hands at work doing. . .whatever it was that was hurting her so.

I slithered up behind him, and quick as a snake, I had him up against the wall, my daggers against his throat.

"Woah! Geez!" he exclaimed. "Seriously, what– great gamble! Those are sharp!"

"They are," I agreed.

He had frosty blonde hair, almost white, and a very well put together style that suggested his wealth and his status. He looked around my age, maybe a year or two older, and had a very pronounced jawline, and a smooth accent that made me want to listen to his voice forever. It sort of reminded me of Mira's subtle accent.

"Could you, maybe, let me go?" he suggested. "I don't have any weapons–"

"No." I pointed at Spiritwolf with my chin. "Why were you hurting her?"

"It's a her?"

I pushed the blades a little harder against his skin, and he paled. "I wasn't hurting her! I've been taking care of her! I found her washed up on the river back, bleeding and unconscious but alive, so I took her here and helped her."

I narrowed my eyes. "How do I know you're not–"

Tala, he speaks the truth. The pain and fear I just had were instinctual, but he was merely tending my wound.

I relaxed my hold on the elf. "What's your name?"

"Rowan," he replied.

"Thank you," I said as I let go of him and sheathed my knives. "For caring for her."

I knelt down beside Spiritwolf and stroked her head in greeting, then took note of her injuries. One of her shoulder blades had a deep gash the length of my forearm, and the flash of bone was visible beneath the blood. One of her front legs was clearly broken, and she had a head wound that made one side of her head so swollen that I could hardly see her eye.

"What exactly have you done to help her?" I asked Rowan. There were soiled bandages strewn about the floor, but other than that, I saw no evidence of further intercession.

"I've mostly been trying to keep the wounds clean," he explained. "And I figured I should stop the bleeding before I did anything else, since that was most important. But, that has proven to take longer than I expected."

I glanced at him. "If you would have stitched these up, the bleeding would have stopped faster."

"I thought of that, but I don't have the skills for that. I didn't want to make things worse. You seem to know her well?"

"I do." I stood and looked around the barn. "Do you have some sort of tarp or blanket?"

"Sure, here." He unrolled a wool blanket and we spread it out flat beside Spiritwolf. "On three, we'll roll her on here. *Gently.*" I got my arms underneath Spiritwolf's head and shoulders, while Rowan did the same with her haunches. "One, two, three." We grunted with the effort– she had grown so much, I realized.

"So what are you doing, tending to injured wildlife in a smelly old barn?" I asked.

He shrugged, understanding that I was referring to the way he was dressed– he wasn't supposed to be here. He belonged somewhere more. . .clean. Important. Some might even say fancy. "I won't let someone suffer if there's something I can do about it."

I studied him. "Do you have somewhere to be, or do you mind helping me carry her to my camp?"

"I don't mind. Lead the way, human."

We each took two corners of the blanket and managed to lift up Spiritwolf. I made sure to go through the more quiet parts of town with fewer eyes, but as much as we could manage, we went through the woodline along the town to avoid drawing attention.

I didn't like the idea of bringing a complete stranger into the Renegade's camp, and frankly neither would they. But I needed to get somewhere safe where I could heal Spiritwolf, and the camp was the only place I could go to.

Oliver was stationed sentry just outside camp and jumped up when he saw us approaching, his eyes wide. "Uh, Tala, what's this?"

"Help us carry her in," I panted. He took another corner of the blanket, eyeing Rowan, and helped us carry her to the cavern. Kai was sharpening his knives in the shade of the cavern's entrance, Aidilane beside him, chattering, and as we passed, his eyes narrowed then brightened when he realized it was Spiritwolf.

"You found her!" he exclaimed, and I was surprised to sense his relief. He took Oliver's place and sent him to fetch bandages.

Once inside the cavern, we laid Spiritwolf down gently on the moss that lined the edges of the stone floor. Kai lit several lanterns and placed them around us so we could see better in the dim cave light. I gathered up water from the pool and rinsed Spiritwolf's wounds with it. Oliver returned with a bundle of pristine white bandages and placed them within my reach, then left, calling for Mira.

"What now?" Rowan asked. "Don't you need a needle and thread?"

Before I could answer, Kai said, "She knows what she's doing," and gave me a knowing look, a slight nod. Encouragement. A silent, *you can do this.*

Rowan crossed his arms, his brow creased with confusion, but remained silent. Nearby, Aidilane watched, her eyes wide. There was still a lot she didn't know about me– including this wolf sister of mine.

I closed my eyes as I placed my shaky hands on Spiritwolf's flank, feeling her injuries and the infection that came with them. Slowly, cell by cell, I knit her back together– her broken bones, her bruises, her cuts. I could feel her relax as the pain gradually faded with my healing, and finally disappeared. When I was finished, I opened my eyes, and she licked my face.

How? Thank you.

I don't know. But of course, dear friend. Thank you for staying alive long enough.

She nuzzled my neck with her muzzle, and I wrapped my arms around her shoulders, pushing back happy tears, and took in her familiar scent– pine needles and fresh rain, moist earth, and of course her warm puppy scent that I was certain would never fade.

Rowan broke the silence. "That was. . . unexpected. But impressive. I've never seen anything like that before. You must be some sort of angel."

I felt my face warm, but I pointed a threatening finger at him. "Don't speak of this to anyone."

He raised his hands in a placating gesture. "Never. But are you alright? You're getting really pale."

I felt myself tilt, the cavern spinning around me, my strength drained. Kai reached out to steady me, but I managed to push his hands away. "Don't touch me, Kai. I don't need your help. . ." My vision began to dim.

Even as I struggled and fought against him, Kai held me up. But I didn't want his help. I didn't want him near. "Let go of me. . ." But he was silent and patient while he held me against his chest as my struggles diminished and weakened. "I'm not going anywhere," he murmured somewhere far away, but I was sure that it was probably just a fragment of my memory resurfacing, just to make the ache in my heart throb harder.

Chapter Ten

Kai

Guilt and regret grow like poison without forgiveness
Shadows reach with eagerness
Ghosts haunt with restless pursuit
And all the while
The trapped cry out like an endless dispute.

I stroked Tala's auburn hair, running my fingers through the fiery strands as she slept. Her anger, her hurt, her pushing me away– it was fair. I shouldn't have expected anything less. She had every right to be angry. I didn't blame her.

But I couldn't deny the burn in my soul that was left behind every time she avoided my gaze or pushed me away. She had been the first person to see me– my mistakes, my pain, my past– and not only accept me, but care for me.

I see that our destinies are intertwined– she'd said that day, after saving me from my memories, my nightmares, pushing them back with calm and peace. *For better or for worse.*

Worse, it turned out. I'd hurt her, and I hated myself for it. She didn't deserve more hurt, more pain. She'd been through enough.

I cursed under my breath. I had hurt and chased away the one person who had helped me ease the darkness inside, quiet the ghosts that haunted my every step. She had been the only one willing and capable, but I had created a vast canyon between us that she wasn't ready to cross yet– if she ever would be.

Her expression was soft, peaceful as she slept, and I knew that the only reason she wasn't tossing and turning in her sleep from memories and nightmares was because of how the healing had drained her. Every night, I could hear her murmur things. *No, please. . .It hurts. . .Help me.* She was always restless, day and night. So I found a little comfort knowing that the exhaustion that these healings brought allowed her some real rest.

She'd healed *me.* After all I'd done.

I didn't deserve it– her heart was too kind, too beautiful, too pure for me. Part of me was glad she was pushing me away– so I'd never ruin or hurt her again. And I deserved the lonely, empty feeling that came with her distance. It was all too familiar, a feeling I'd lived with since the day my father had abandoned my sister and I. Tala was the only one that cleared those feelings away like vapor in the wind. So without her, it was better I didn't feel anything at all– the strategy I'd reverted to for years. It was the only way I survived. To feel nothing.

What burned worse was that Tala had also been the one to make me feel. To ease my numb soul and let me feel again– but not just pain, fear, anger, guilt, and all the rest– but the good things too. Happiness. Companionship. Loyalty. A sense of fullness.

But I didn't deserve those either.

In the cavern, I saw how pale she had become after the healing even before Rowan pointed it out. She had begun to tilt, her eyes drooping and pupils dilating, and I caught her before she could hit her head on the rocks. I held her even as she fought against me– she didn't have the strength to keep herself upright. But her angry growls tore me apart. *Don't touch me, Kai. I don't need your help.*

Quietly, I murmured, "I won't give up, Tala. I can't reverse my mistakes, but I will do everything in my power to make it up to you. Above all, I won't let anyone hurt you again." *The way I have.*

I stood and covered her with a blanket, then ducked outside.

Mira and Rowan were arguing, and I emerged just as Mira stomped away.

"What's going on?" I asked Oliver, who had been watching them, his brow creased.

"Rowan's her brother."

"Oh." *Great gamble.* Weren't things complicated enough? "What were they arguing about?"

"Mira doesn't trust him," Oliver explained. "Their history is rocky, but she won't elaborate." He jogged after Mira.

I studied Rowan, who rubbed his face with his hands and let out a sigh. There was something eerily familiar about him, but I couldn't quite put my finger on it. I knew I'd figure it out eventually, I always did. There was a reason he felt familiar, and I was going to find it.

Spiritwolf came to my side, nuzzling my thigh with her snout. I stroked her head, still unable to comprehend how Tala had done it. She was definitely more than she seemed. I wondered if her abilities consisted of more than just the Keen. Or if maybe her Keen consisted of more than. . .than what it usually did. She was. . .

I took in a sharp breath. I wasn't going to finish that thought. There were too many ways I could finish it. None of them were quite right.

She was more.

Spiritwolf let out a faint sigh. "Go on," I told her. "Get yourself something to eat." She prowled away into the trees without a sound, bouncing like a puppy. "Bring something back for me, will you?" I added with a smile. She was a majestic creature with a heart like a sparrow– playful and free, wild. Capable of dangerous things, but not in the vicious way wolves had been told of. Like Tala.

"I never would have thought a wolf would take to you," Aidilane said. She'd sidled up beside me. "Tell me, Kai."

I wrapped my arm around her shoulders. "Tell you what?"

She bit her lip, her nervous habit, and was silent for a moment. "Tell me why you did those things."

My mind flashed the moments, the ugly, dark parts of me. The things I regretted. The things I would never be redeemed for. The reasons I hated myself.

Aidilane's eyes softened. "Please, brother. Don't keep those things from me. I'm the reason you did them. It's my fault. I deserve to know."

I clenched my jaw, letting go of her. "None of it was your fault. None. Of. It. My actions are my own. And I'm sorry for what I said back at the Nightingale. Those words meant nothing. I did them to free you, yes, but it wasn't your fault. Aidilane, I'm not who I used to be. And you don't deserve to know anything. You're free now, and that's what matters." My words were rushed.

She blinked. "Kai–"

I interrupted her with a quick shake of my head, and took her shoulders in my hands gently. "None of it matters." I smiled reassuringly. "The only thing that matters is you, Aidilane. You." I pulled her close and held her.

"Thank you," she whispered, her voice shaking. "T–Thank you for not forgetting me."

"Never. I would never forget you." I didn't let my voice break. I didn't let the emotions show. Just as I would never forget her, I would never let her know what those years had done to me. She'd suffered enough. She knew that I had become an assassin, but she didn't need to know it all. She didn't deserve the guilt. I did.

She stepped back and wiped a tear from her cheek, letting out a shuddering breath. "I don't know if I'll ever recover from. . .that place. But I have hope now. Something that I couldn't indulge in the Nightingale."

"No one will touch you ever again, sister," I vowed. "Not while I'm still breathing. You're safe now."

She smiled. "I know. You've always protected me."

"I should have protected you sooner," I growled quietly.

She took my face in her hands. Soft, like they'd always been. "You were a child."

"As were you."

She squeezed her eyes shut tight. "We both were."

We all sat around the fire orb that I had formed after dinner, when Evian had summoned us after finally emerging from whatever hole he'd come from. Something important, he claimed.

Tala sat across from me, watching the flames. The light danced in her eyes, making them glow. They reminded me of drops of honey. Very different from when they'd glowed blue in the forest, and when she healed me and Spiritwolf.

She watched Evian as he jabbered about his learning days. Scrolls. Rowan sat to the side of our group, awkwardly twitching his fingers against his leg. I studied him again, trying to remember.

"Do you have a point to all this?" Val asked Evian, interrupting him.

"Right," Oliver agreed. "No offense, but you've already told us all about the things you learned when you were still under training."

Evian glared at them. "Despite your impatience, there is a reason I repeat things. You young ones don't listen most of the time."

Mira rolled her eyes. "Yes, but please get to the point. Soon," she pleaded.

He sighed. "My point is this. In my training, I learned about amplifiers. Objects that enhance one's abilities. One of these amplifiers is the Sea Gem. There are only three in the world, and the closest one is in an underwater cave system in the Mirage Sea. I believe it would assist our efforts."

"In the Mirage Sea?" Felix wondered. "Isn't that on the coast?"

"Precisely."

Tala spun one of her knives. "You really think that this Sea Gem would help us?"

"It would give us a better chance, at least," Evian confirmed. "And if you and Mira are having vision dreams about a dragon that, by the way, is our only current lead, then perhaps this amplifier will help narrow things down by enhancing those visions. At least we'll get more information, and therefore a better lead. It'll confirm if our suspicions are correct or not, and either or, will also amplify anyone of our abilities. Elemental or otherwise." He glanced at Tala.

"What's the catch?" I asked.

"Catch?" Evian scrunched his brows dramatically. "No catch, really. Just one problem."

"And what might that be?"

"We'll need a ship."

We all went silent for a long moment, everyone exchanging glances. Finally, Val prompted, "Anyone have any connections that could get us a ship to sail into the Mirage Sea?"

"I do."

We all turned to Rowan, who had stood up. "I know a guy. I can get us a ship."

I narrowed my eyes. "We're weighing our lives on 'I know a guy'?"

He shrugged. "It doesn't look like you guys have any other choice unless you want to ditch this old elf's epiphany of an idea."

Evian crossed his arms, his eyes darkening. "What–"

"We can trust him," Tala pipped up. "He saved Spiritwolf. And I can feel his mind– it's genuine."

"Alright then," Val sighed. "Looks like we're going for a little ride on the ocean."

"Hold on." I stood, pointing one of my blades at Rowan. "We're just going to let him in? Follow him?"

Tala met my gaze, her eyes distant but boring into mine at the same time. "It's a chance I'm willing to take, if the Sea Gem can really help us. And don't you trust *me*? I can *feel* him, Kai. Do you doubt me?"

An awkward silence filled the space between us, and everyone busied themselves with looking everywhere but at us.

"Of course I trust you, Tala." *More than anyone else.* "But I can't help but–"

She stopped me and turned to everyone else. "It's settled then. And I have a plan."

I pulled the straps of my blade sheaths tight and adjusted my boot laces. We'd gone over Tala's plan and decided that Mira, Aidilane, Val, Navy, Tala and I would go, along with Evian– who insisted on going since he was the only one who knew what the Sea Gem looked like– and last but not least, Rowan, who'd be getting us a ship. Felix would stay behind with Oliver to guard camp while we were away.

"On the other side of the trail, Navy," Val guided her little brother. "Hurry. They'll be here soon."

We were taking our positions in the undergrowth along the trail that we knew mages were going to come by on. They were going to be traveling in a stagecoach, headed towards Tala's kingdom, making deliveries. We were going to ambush them and steal their ride to get to the Mirage Sea. It would be quicker than going on foot.

Mira took Oliver's hand, then pointed to me. "Oli, Aidilane and I will take watch down the trail. You and Tala wait here for our signal. Rowan and Evian–"

He silenced her with a dark look. "You don't have to repeat my part." He stomped off across the trail and called, "I'm the adult here. The one who captured and brought down that fire elf." Rowan shot Tala a look and then hurried after him.

Oliver rolled his eyes. "Right." He hefted his sack of explosives. "See you in a bit." He and Mira and Aidilane headed away into the trees.

Tala turned her attention to the trail, her form tight and rigid, her knuckles probably white under her gloves around the hilts of her daggers. "I think they put us together on purpose," I mused.

She swallowed. "Actually, I put us together. The plan would go smoother if we were teamed up."

"How would it go smoother?"

Her brows pinched, as if she wasn't quite sure herself. "Our skills are better combined."

I wished she'd just. . .look at me. But then I wanted to kick myself. I deserved her anger.

I made sure to keep space between us as I crouched down beside her, behind the bush and the boulder that kept us hidden from view. "I wanted you to know, I don't think you have to worry about your brother."

Her gaze snapped to mine. "What makes you think that?"

I scraped my finger along a grove in the boulder. "Well, if the mages are at all wise, they'd wait until the opportune moment— which seems like they have. But with the way magic works, they have to regroup at some point. And with all the magic they've spent up, it'll be a while until they can keep at it."

Tala sighed. "But from what I've seen, their power, their magic, doesn't expire."

"Maybe," I said. "But everyone has a weakness. And even mages need to rest. Every time they have to regroup, your brother will also. And every time, he'll come back stronger than before."

Tala's eyes softened, her focus on the trail wavering. "He's human, Kai. He doesn't have powers, or magic, or nature's forces on his side. He can't bend fire, or water, or air, or earth to his will. And neither can the rest of his kingdom. Just human."

"Like you, and yet here you are, taking on a near impossible mission," I pointed out. "Tala, just like you, your brother is capable of incredible things. You have to have faith in him. And he has the Keen. Besides," I added, "The mages are human, too. Corrupted by magic. Just like your brother and his kingdom, they'll need rest."

Tala nodded. "I do have faith in him. It's a lot easier than having faith in myself."

"You don't have to have faith in yourself." I kept my eyes on the trail. "Because I do. And that will never change. In spite of the things you've been through, including my mistakes, you will rise, Tala. Like a Phoenix. And the Kingdoms will never forget it."

Tala let out a soft breath. "It's hard to believe that when I'm still suffocating in the ashes."

I squeezed my eyes shut, hating myself. She had been through so much, was going through so much, and I. . .

I unsheathed my blades with a metallic *siing*. "Those that burned you into ashes will one day regret they ever lit the match." *And I already do.*

The ground shook as a loud *bang* filled the air, and dust came spilling around the corner of the trail. Tala and I glanced at each other and nodded. Despite my unforgivable, unresolvable mistakes, we'd still have each other's backs– it was all I could offer her. She pulled her hood over her head and set her jaw. "I never thought I'd miss my mask."

"That reminds me," I said, and quickly pulled something from one of my pockets. "Here. I tucked it away, thinking you might need it again in the near future."

She took it with a small gasp. "My mask?" She looked up at me as she put it on, her eyes shining through. "Thank you."

The stagecoach came rumbling around the bend, in a cloud of dust and ash, missing one of its wheels. The four horses' eyes were wild with fear from the explosion, and despite the missing wheel, they were crashing along at full speed.

"Great gamble," I growled. "They were supposed to slow it down!" I leapt out into the trail, Tala close at my heels. The mage driver was frantically trying to further speed up the team to escape the danger.

I ran as fast as my legs would go, and grabbed hold of the side of the coach and leapt up next to the driver. I kicked the wand from his hand before he could cast a spell, and wrestled him for the reins to the team. Another mage heard our struggle and stepped through the curtain onto the driver's seat and slammed into me, nearly knocking me from the coach. But I used the momentum to swing around to the other side and yank the reins from the driver's hands. I pulled on them, calling out, "Woah! Woah!"

The driver slid a long dagger from his belt and lunged at me, but I blocked his blade with one of mine. Tala was up beside me now, her blades flashing. Between us, the two mages were on the ground within a few seconds. The stagecoach came to a stop as the doors flew open, five mages pouring out, aiming wands.

But before any of them could use their magic, Val emerged from the trees and brought her hands up above her head, then pushed the air current around the wands down, knocking them from the mages' hands.

Tala and I leapt down and joined Val, Mira, and Rowan, and soon, all the mages were unconscious on the ground, scattered bodies. We bound them with rope and dumped them in the trees where Felix and Oliver would carry them back to camp, one by one.

"Stage one of the plan is complete." Rowan grinned at Tala, who smiled back.

"Nice job everyone," Navy piped. "But next time, I want to do something."

"Noted," said Val. "But no."

"Come on," he whined, pulling at her tunic. "I steal things in town for us all the time. Where would the Renegades be without me?"

Val crossed her arms and raised her brows at her little brother, and he glared back at her, but said "Fine."

"Well," Oliver sighed. "Looks like its farewell from here."

Mira took his hand and squeezed it. "We'll be back in a few days. You'd better miss me."

Oliver stared at her for a second, taking a slow, deep breath, and I couldn't help but notice how nervous he looked. Then he closed the space between them and kissed her.

Her face turned the color of ripe strawberries, and after a moment of stunned shock, she closed her eyes and took his face in her hands, kissing him back. I kicked the dirt, feeling awkward, and turned to give them some privacy. The others followed my lead.

"It's about time," Val whispered to Tala and Aidilane, who giggled in turn.

"Yuck," whined Navy. Evian just grumbled something about "kids."

I noticed Tala glance at Rowan, her ears pinking. I swallowed, looking away, and was shocked with myself when I realized that jealousy was rising in my chest. I pushed away how the way she looked at him made me feel. It wasn't fair of me.

However, my distrust of Rowan was real, and I couldn't deny that. I needed to figure out why he felt so familiar, for Tala's sake.

Finally, Mira jogged over to us while Oliver called, "Be safe!"

Val, Aidilane and Tala all gave her knowing looks, bumped her with their elbows, while she rolled her eyes, but they were shining, and she was glowing, her grin wide. "Everyone ready?" she asked.

We all loaded our gear into the stagecoach, fixed the wheel, and I offered to drive. Everyone loaded up inside, and since there wasn't enough room, Val and Navy sat up front with me.

After an hour or so, I showed Navy how to drive the team and let him take the reins. He looked bored, but brightened up with the notion of being in full control of our voyage for the time being.

I watched the sun rise, dawn tucking the earth in a warm glow, and the haze from the rain from the night before filled the air with humidity, bringing the bugs. So Val and I busied ourselves with swatting the little vampires away in silence. I wasn't sure what to talk about anyway.

I knew where the Mirage Sea was, but I'd never been there, or in Mirage Harbor. It was a long trip there, and it was sunset before we would reach it. I found myself disappointed that Tala wouldn't be by my side for the ride, but I didn't see any reason why she'd want to.

Still, ever since that night beside the fire, when she cried and shook and recounted her past, I longed to hold her again. Tell her how sorry I was and just hold her. Hold her for my mistakes, hold her for everything she'd been through, and as selfish as it was, hold her for *me*.

Her trust and care and rawness with me felt more real than anything, and having her in my life felt right. Felt like maybe, just maybe, I could be complete. I could be... different. New. And from the moment I held her, I knew that I would be different for her. I was dark, and my morals twisted, and I. . . I had my demons, my ghosts pulling at me. But she was worth fighting for. Maybe the darkness could recede.

But again, my stupid mistake. And she would probably never let me hold her again.

Good, I scolded myself. *She better not let you hold her again. Not after what you did.*

And besides, I was too broken, too far gone. She deserved more. She deserved better. Better than me.

"She cares about you, you know." Val broke the silence. "That's why she's taking what you did so hard. If she didn't care, then this wouldn't be so difficult for her."

I didn't answer for a moment, letting the sound of the creaking wheels and crunching rocks beneath them fill the space around us. Finally, I said, "I don't deserve her care."

"Maybe not." Val shrugged. "But it doesn't change the fact that she does. I can see it. And you care for her. You both will pull through with time."

"Her friendship was everything to me," I admitted. "But I ruined it. I hope you're right, but I won't ever forgive myself. And if she never does, I'll be glad. Because her forgiveness isn't something I'm worthy of."

If I had had possession of the reins, we would have lurched to a stop. The memory resurfaced then.

It was the day Prince Oberon sought me out with a job. He had intercepted me on the way to the Nightingale and sat me down at a nearby tavern.

"I've heard your skills, boy, and I am in dire need of them. The King's Wolf of the Highland Kingdom would be your target— I need her out of the way. Your payment— anything you desire."

I didn't even need to consider it. The risks were worth it. "Finish buying my sister's indenture at the Nightingale for me, and I'll do it."

We shook on it, deciding that once the job was done, he'd fulfill his end of the deal. Meanwhile, his lieutenant stood beside the table, witnessing the exchange between us, one of a few guards who'd accompanied the prince.

Rowan.

Rowan was the prince's lieutenant.

Chapter Eleven

Jala

When I look back on these moments, I sometimes wonder how things would have gone if I had trusted myself more. Had more faith in me. But the past is a haunting thing. And sometimes, the darkness drowns out things like hope, faith, and trust.

But I know now– those things were never absent, never drowned in the dark. They were always there, but like a flower, they needed a little light to make them bloom.

With every bump of the stagecoach, my shoulder bumped Rowan's. He sat next to me. Mira and Evian sat across from us.

I fidgeted with my knives, but I couldn't help but glance at Rowan every once in a while. Especially when I felt him looking at me. He was unrealistically attractive.

Evian had his eyes closed and his head leaned back, but Mira, however, was glaring at Rowan.

"So," I started, breaking the awkward silence. "Rowan. What do you do?"

He shrugged, glancing at his sister. "I'm a journalist. I travel, mostly, and dabble with opportunities."

Mira snorted. "Go ahead, *brother*." She shook her head, looking out the window. "I just don't understand you."

His brows pinched, and he stared down at his lap. "Sorry," he mumbled to me. "I'm not the best brother. But I'm trying."

Mira crossed her arms across her chest. "All you do is lie."

"I'm not lying, Mira," he said quietly. "Why won't you just listen to me?"

"I made that mistake a long time ago," she sighed. She leaned her head against the side of the coach and closed her eyes, and after a while, she started to snore softly.

"What happened between you two?" I whispered. "If you don't mind me asking."

Rowan folded his hands. "A few years after our parents died, I told her that I found a job in town, but really, it wasn't in town. And she went looking for me one day, but I wasn't there, and she thought I'd left. For good. That I'd abandoned her. When I came back a week later, she broke down at first, but then she was just angry. Rightfully so. I shouldn't have lied. But I was young, an idiot little boy. Still, I was her only family. And I had lied and just left. Since then, she hasn't trusted me. I don't blame her. But I'm different now, and I wish she'd see that."

I could hear the pain in his voice. His regret. I felt guilty when I remembered I was making Kai feel that way, too.

"I'm sorry," I said. "I'm no expert in family things, but I can imagine how hard that must be. But betrayal isn't something that's easy to brush off."

He nodded. "I know. That's why I gave her space. But that seemed to make her even angrier."

I did my best to conceal my disbelief as I stared at him. "If I may– of course it made her angrier! Your leaving was what hurt her in the first place!" I sucked in a deep breath, jerked my gaze back to my boots, and shook my head. "I'm sorry, I shouldn't lash out like that." I gripped the hilt of one of my daggers, fear gnawing at me. He'd be angry.

"It's okay, you're right," he said quietly. "I'm an utter fool. Thank you for helping me realize that. And," he added, putting a hand on my knee, "You needn't be afraid. I won't hurt you."

He'd noticed how I was feeling. I let go of the breath I hadn't realized I was holding and met his eyes, unsure of what to say. I felt heat rising in my face at his endearing gaze, and I stuttered for words. "It's commonplace for men to be fools."

He threw his head back and laughed. "Mira wouldn't dare allow me the pleasure of being called a 'man', though I'm fully aware that I'm not deserving of that title."

He pulled his hand away from my knee and smiled. "But I want you to know you can trust me, Tala. Search my mind if you don't believe me."

I pulled back. "How did you–"

"I overheard Mira and Oliver last night," he explained. "They were talking about the dreams she'd had and how your Keen may be influenced by them, too."

"Oh," I mumbled. "And you aren't frightened of me?"

He flashed a smile. "No. I'm just honored to have crossed paths with the savior of the Kingdoms."

I laughed, shaking my head. "I'm no savior."

"You shouldn't doubt yourself– you will be. I'm certain of it, and so are the prophecies. You needn't doubt your potential. It's your past that holds you back."

"Prophecies?" I asked. "What prophecies?"

He tilted his head. "I thought you must have heard of them. But I'll let my friend tell you and the others. It will be better that way– I'm not good with reciting transcriptions and verses of old. I've never been good with words."

"I thought you said you were a journalist."

"I've been good with others' words," he corrected. "My own are a whole other universe– one I can wrangle."

I reached my hands out. "Are you sure you want me to do this? This will reveal everything about you to me– your past, your present, your mistakes, your greatest joys– everything. I'll know you fully and completely, Rowan, and I can't take it back once it's over. I vowed to myself that I would never search a mind without good reason. It's an invasion of oneself. I only feel the things I can't block out, like strong emotions."

He nodded. "I'm sure. I want you to know me, Tala. Fully and completely. I will have no regrets. Since I found your wolf, I knew I was getting into something bigger than myself for once, and I want you to know I am on your side."

I studied his gaze for a long moment, feeling unsure. But the emotion radiating off him was strong– genuine. Other emotions crashed into me, too– eagerness to be part of something more, regret, fierce determination, loyalty, and strong attraction– but I ignored the last one.

"Okay." I placed my fingers on his temples and dove into his mind.

Memories laced each other; days by the river with his sister as children before their parents died, grief, then careless days of wandering– doing anything to escape the pain of the past. Hard working days in fields, and then in factories. Then finally something he actually enjoyed– journaling for the elven scholars. Leaving his sister for the opportunity of something greater, only to return to her shaking with fear, sadness, and anger. Loneliness when he left again, thinking he was doing the right thing, and the short visit he had with Mira, who left before he could say a word. Writing, writing, writing. . .then the wolf. Then me.

I saw his memories of me– when I'd healed Spiritwolf and the awe he'd had, even as I passed out in Kai's arms. His worry for me as I lay unconscious by myself when no one– not even Kai– had come to see me, he'd been surprised and shocked. So he'd come into the tent and sat with me, making sure I was okay. Making sure the savior of the kingdoms would live. He'd left when he saw me stirring so as not to frighten me. He was only a stranger after all. But just as he'd cared for Spiritwolf, he cared for me. And the attraction was more so care, a different kind of care. One that both frightened me and made my stomach flutter with butterflies at the same time.

All the memories, all the past versions of himself, all the regrets, the joys, the sorrows, and the emotions that came with everything– I knew his mind now, inside out. My gut tingled with doubt, for what reason I didn't know. But he'd said it himself– I shouldn't doubt myself.

Finally, I let go of his temples and breathed deeply, opening my eyes and letting everything sink in.

"Well?" His violet eyes searched my gaze.

I hoped the heat in my face wasn't showing. "Uhm, all good."

He sighed with relief. "My loyalty is yours, Tala. I will see you through to your victory."

Tentatively, I put my hand on his shoulder. "Thank you for trusting me. I trust you. And just so you know. . ." I cleared my throat. "Uhm, well–"

He reddened. "I hope it isn't weird. A cute girl is a cute girl."

I knew I was blushing then. "It's not weird."

He smiled. "I'm glad."

"Oh would you two *shut up*?" Evian moaned. "This is outrageous. If you would have warned me, I would have opted to sit with our fire elf driver."

"Sorry," I apologized. "I–"

He waved it aside. "Yes, yes." But to my astonishment, he smiled at us. "Young ones. Always jumping to see the beauty in life despite all odds. I remember those days– treasure them. They aren't always going to be there." Then he closed his eyes again and leaned his head on Mira's shoulder, but she shoved him off absentmindedly with a sleepy, irritated groan.

Rowan and I laughed.

It was sunset before we arrived. The stagecoach rolled to a stop, and Kai banged on the side, calling, "We're here."

Evian stepped out first gasping, "Finally, fresh air! It's—" he glared back at Rowan and I— "stuffy in there."

Mira yawned and stretched as she hopped down from the coach, murmuring incomprehensible words, still half asleep. Rowan followed, then turned and offered his hand. I gladly took it— it was quite a step down.

Mirage Harbor looked orange under the setting sun. It was small, but it looked like a smaller version of Eclipse, but older. Much older.

We paid a stablehand to care for and house our horses. We paid for two days' time, and if we were gone longer then we'd finish paying the rest when we returned. Finally, we got some food at a local tavern, then as twilight unfolded over us, we headed for the docks.

Rowan took the lead, with everyone following, and I trailed behind, taking the rear. We didn't need any more trouble right now, and when you least expected it was always when it happened. So I expected it. Always.

I scanned the alleys and watched the passerby closely, the hooded elves that swept through the shadows now and again. I relished the comfort my mask brought— no one saw my face, and few knew who or what the King's Wolf was, so I was just a masked, hooded stranger. And anyone who would come too close would learn very quickly who the King's Wolf was.

Kai slowed until we were side by side, our paces matched.

"Thank you," I said.

"What for?"

"My mask. It's. . .grown on me."

"Your stride is more confident when you wear it and your hood," he observed.

"It's like playing a character, I suppose," I mused. "The real me is hidden, nonexistent. And while I'm wearing it, sometimes it's almost like the real me, and everything I've been through, isn't real either. Like for a little while, I'm someone else. I'm not Tala– Stalkingwolf–the tortured one of the Keen. I'm just the King's Wolf. Just completing a mission."

"You're so much more than that, Tala," Kai murmured. "One day you'll see that."

We walked in silence together, then finally I reminded him, "Was there something you wanted to tell me?"

There's a lot of things I want to tell you, Tala, he thought. I hadn't realized my mind had subconsciously opened up to his. I quickly pulled back.

"Yes," he answered. "It's about Rowan."

I tensed. "What about him?"

"We can't trust him," he declared.

"What?" I scoffed. "Kai–"

"He isn't who he says he is, Tala. I know him. He–"

I stopped him. "I searched his mind, Kai. He *let* me. And he's genuine. I trust him. Don't take that away from me."

Kai's expression was confused. "What? How? He–"

"Just, stop, Kai," I hissed. "I don't need this. Not from you. Not right now." I sped up my pace until I was walking alongside Aidilane and Mira.

It wasn't long until Rowan stopped in front of a fancy, embellished building right beside the docks with a large purple sign that said *Sea-Farers*. He stepped inside, telling us to wait a moment. A few minutes later, he emerged with a tall elf in a long trench coat. He smoked a pipe.

"Quite the little group you've got here, Rowan," he observed, his eyes landing on me the longest. "Alright. I'll take you. But don't expect a freebee," he added with a look at Rowan, then he introduced himself. "I'm Captain Glenn."

We took turns introducing ourselves, and when it came to me, I just said, "Wolf."

"Interesting name," mused the Captain, "but I respect it. Now, my usual crew is currently at sea with another captain, so you all will be manning the ship. Can you manage that? She isn't a very large vessel."

We all nodded, but I was unsure. I'd never been on a ship before, let alone manned it. I would have to look to the others for guidance.

"Alrighty, we leave at dawn. Get your rest– you'll need it." He turned to go back inside.

"Wait, no," Mira interjected before he could leave. "We need to leave now. What we're looking for is urgent."

Captain Glenn narrowed his eyes with a sigh. "So I've been told. Really so urgent that we must leave now?"

"Yes," Mira, Kai, Rowan and I said simultaneously. The captain grumbled, "Fine. But this'll cost more. Rowan, you know where the ship is. I'll meet you all there. I want her ready to go once I get there. And you better have enough food– I'm only packing for myself."

He went back inside and Rowan led us through the docks until we reached a smaller vessel with two large sails. We climbed aboard, and everyone started to prepare her. But Kai stood to the side, glaring at Rowan. "We can't trust him," he insisted.

"Stop it, Kai," I growled.

He shook his head. "I don't know how he did it, Tala, but what you saw in his mind isn't true. He's a liar, and conniving, and who knows what his motives are."

"What?" Rowan said, looking hurt. "Why would I lie?"

"You've lied before," Mira grumbled.

"Enough!" I cried. "All of you. Just get the ship ready." Everyone set back to their tasks, and Kai slipped into the shadows.

Rowan seemed to notice that I wasn't sure what to do, so he took my hand and guided me to one of the masts. "Tie this double," he instructed. "Then this one triple."

"Thanks," I sighed with relief. "I'm sorry about Kai."

He shrugged it off. "It's okay. He doesn't know me, I'm sure he has his reasons for the way he is."

"He does," I agreed. "But it's no excuse to throw accusations around.

Soon, the ship was ready, and Captain Glenn came aboard, shouting orders that I didn't understand. Finally, the sails caught the wind and we were off, the waves carrying us.

Even though it was dark, the moon was bright enough to illuminate the water, the ripples, and I watched the fold of the water as the ship sped over it, leaving behind a trail of foam and bubbles. Occasionally, I caught a glimpse of a fish beneath the surface, tiny, colorful and glowing. I was filled with awe at the sights and the salty ocean air, along with the sound of the rush of the waves and the feeling of the ship rocking beneath my feet.

"Beautiful, isn't it?" Rowan came up beside me and leaned on the rail, his hands dirty and raw from the ropes.

"Truly," I breathed. "I wish I could have been more of a help. I've never been on a ship before."

"You were plenty of help."

My eyes strayed to where I knew the horizon was. The night sky seemed to merge with it, becoming one, the reflection of the moon shimmering on its surface. "What do you think lies beyond these waters?" I asked, musing mostly to myself. "Do you think there are more kingdoms, somewhere out there?"

Rowan shrugged. "Who knows. Legend says the only creatures to have crossed the oceans were the dragons."

"Do you believe those legends?"

He turned to me. "Are you asking if I believe in the existence of dragons?"

"Perhaps."

"Do you?"

I thought for a moment. "Before, it was hard even to believe in another tomorrow, another sunrise. And some days I wished there wouldn't be. But after my and Mira's dream. . .I'm certain of it. At least of the existence of a dragon. And I'm going to find her. Whatever it takes. For her, the kingdoms, and my brother's sakes."

"Do you think she really is connected to the mage's magic? The others told me a bit about that."

I swallowed, my brows scrunching. "I'm not sure. In my dream, she was pleading for help. She seemed like she was trapped or in pain. Maybe both. She felt like she was being. . .drained."

Rowan considered this. "Well, whatever it is, we'll figure it out. Hopefully, the Sea Gem will help."

"It will." Evian had come up behind us. I'd known he was there, but Rowan jumped, startled. "I know what I'm talking about. It will boost your or anyone's abilities. It gives us a better chance."

"Thank you for the suggestion, Evian," I said. "It was wise. And I hope you're right."

He nodded. "Just make sure you concentrate on the task at hand." He glanced at Rowan and then wandered off.

"ALRIGHTY," boomed the Captain. "I've got the rest steady for now. Get your rest."

"Goodnight." I smiled at Rowan, and as I walked away, I felt his eyes on me. I felt my cheeks heat up.

Down in the hull, I chose one of the hammocks next to Mira and settled down, trying to get comfortable. Mira was sitting up in her hammock, rocking gently. "I heard something earlier," she whispered.

"What?"

"Down here, just before you came down. I heard someone in the back, somewhere behind those crates." She pointed to a shadowy part of the hull, towards the back, where a large stack of crates and barrels were.

"Stowaway?"

"Maybe. I'll check it out."

"Ok, I'll go with. It'll be a good distraction from the feel of the ship. Making me nauseous."

"Weren't you just rocking in your hammock?"

"Trying to counteract the rocking of the ship."

We snuck through the shadows, our blades at the ready as we circled around the crates. Behind it, we found a rusty holding cell. Inside was an elderly, crumpled woman– so old, in fact, that I couldn't tell if she was elf or human or otherwise. I held up a lantern and set it down on the ground.

Mira and I exchanged looks. "Is she alive?" We both whispered at the same time.

"Yes," the old woman creaked. "Alive. Otherwise I'd be a pile of rotting bones." She turned to look at us, squinting her cloudy eyes. She was blind. "Finally. You've arrived." She pointed a shaky, bony finger at me. "Savior."

Mira and I exchanged another glance. "Me?" I asked. "I'm no savior."

"Ah," she laughed, spluttering with a coughing fit afterwards. "But you are, dear. I am unaware of the seasons anymore, but you are. That I am certain of. You will cleanse this world of the evil it's been tainted with."

I shook my head. "Ma'am, why are you locked up down here? Are you alright?"

She cackled again, then let out a long, wheezy sigh, and began to recite a poem.

"Her's is the face of a wolf
Heart of Truth
By pain made pure
A child she never was
In fire gold is made ready

For she will be for a better cause

Brought up in the stables, the barracks, the halls of sword and stone

Separated from her blood

She will be the eyes and ears of the King alone

But one day death will come

and for which she will be shunned

Hunted, with the pack she will become one

But the one who bears the King's blade

Will be the one to call her home

There she will be tarnished with blood and pain

But mercy of the King's blade will disdain

Any thought of execution

So long as the King's wish be made

But hence the war of magic will darken

And the king's voice she must harken

To more

For the fate of the kingdoms and the land

She must offer her hand

Blood shall be shed

Hence, her blood will take command

King's wolf she will be

Of her choice she will see

Savior of the Kingdoms wide

The King's Wolf will face a divide

Savior she may be

But much cost she will pay

Darkness, pain, and past

She'll lose her way

Unless she airs on the side of caution

The way she walks will lead to destruction

Savior she will be

But she must be careful not to lose herself in the process, see

She will save the kingdoms

With the one that makes her complete

And when the darkness threatens to over take

The trance of darkness he will break

Lost in the murk of pain undone

He will bring back the One

The savior of the kingdoms

In no time there will be

King's Wolf will come

And bring the world to peace."

I sucked in a sharp breath, hardly able to breathe. "W–Where did you. . .hear that?"

"I read it dear, in the scrolls of the ancient ones. The ones from before," she explained. "The Prophecy of the Savior. The King's Wolf. I transcribed it to many of my students."

I was shaking, and for a moment my mind panicked. A seizure? But no, I was just startled? Scared? Shocked?

Mira gripped my arms. "You should sit down. You're getting pale."

"I–I'm fine," I whispered. I held onto the bars of the cell to keep my legs from crumpling beneath me and demanded from the old woman, "Who wrote that prophecy? And when?"

"An ancient prophet and visionary, Elisabetta Starlof. Centuries ago."

I struggled to regulate my breathing– she had just described my life in a poem– and it was an ancient prophecy? I had been foreseen centuries ago by some visionary? I appreciated Mira's silent support, her comforting presence. "You're the one Rowan mentioned to me," I finally managed.

The woman's eyes darkened. "I don't know a Rowan. But take the prophecy to heart, girl. You are the One. You have been on a difficult path, but the road only gets steeper from here. Be cautious. Be wise. And don't forget a word I've said. Don't forget a word of the prophecy. It just might save your life."

Slowly, the woman crumpled back up, hunching and laying down, curling back up underneath her damp excuse for a cloak. She closed her cloudy eyes and her breathing fell into a deep rhythm. She was asleep.

The floorboards behind us creaked, and I sensed Rowan coming.

I picked up and swung the lantern in his direction just as he stepped into view. "Who is this?" I demanded.

He licked his lips, his eyes darting from Mira, to the old woman, to me, his eyelids fluttering confusingly. "I don't know who this is," he said. "It seems like you think I do. But I don't."

I prodded his mind. He was telling the truth. "Okay," I said. "But we need to find out. She's frail and probably ill, and who knows how long she's been down here without food or water."

Rowan nodded. "I'll ask Captain Glenn." He tilted his head, offering his hand. "Tala, are you okay?"

"I. . ." I took his hand. "She just told me. A prophecy. She told me what you said– that I was the savior of the kingdoms, that's why I thought this was the person you mentioned."

He shook his head. "No, this isn't her. The elf I was talking about was one of Glenn's crew members. What did the prophecy say?"

I recited the prophecy, having memorized every word. When I was finished, I leaned against Rowan, taking slow, deep breaths. "Every word of it. . ." I said softly. "Every word of it is true. It all happened. Except for the last few verses."

He held me and kept me from collapsing. "Breathe. Come on, let me get you to your hammock. Mira?"

She took my other arm and they supported me while I walked back over to my hammock. Mira didn't say a word, but I sensed her uneasiness. I asked her and Rowan not to say anything to anyone else about it. I wanted to be the one to tell them.

Mira laid back down in her hammock beside me, and after giving me a drink of water and making sure I was okay, Rowan chose a hammock for himself and lay down.

"Don't tell me you told me so," I murmured quietly.

"Me?" Rowan laughed, but there was an edge to his chuckle, like maybe he was happy that someone had proved I was going to be a savior after all. "Well, I told you so. Do you believe me now?"

I sighed. "I wish I didn't. I wish–" I stopped. "I just hope there's been some kind of mistake. Because I cannot be the One. I'm just. . .me. King's Wolf. Nothing more."

"Just the King's Wolf who was prophesied by an ancient visionary prophet."

I turned on my side, supporting my head on the crook of my arm. "I'm still just me. And I don't think I have what it takes. Not that I have a choice. I *wish* I had a choice. But I won't let my brother and his kingdom die at the hands of mages. Not while there's anything I can do about it."

"Exactly. You *chose* it. And that is exactly what saviors do."

"Have you ever met a savior before?" I asked, jesting. "Do I surpass your expectations?"

Rowan gazed into my eyes. "You surpass every expectation or dream I could ever have."

I gazed back at him, letting the rock of the ship lull me. Soon, I was deep asleep.

The voice. Her voice.

She pleaded to me through the dark, calling. Her soft whimpers echoed around me, and I felt smooth scales beneath my fingers. I ran my hand along her side, even though I couldn't see her. I felt her emotions, her soul. She was tired, ill, and she was growing weaker. Much weaker.

"Hang on," I told her. "We're coming."

She whimpered, letting out a soft growl. I heard her message clearly. Hurry.

My dream shifted. I now stood in front of King Rubarb and Queen Hersha once again.

"Guilty," the king said.

Then I was in the dungeons again, curled in a ball on the floor. They were there, kicking me, taunting me, shouting and yelling at me. The lash, the chains keeping me to the rough support beam. The pain. My racing heart. My struggle to breathe. My struggle to stay alive.

Then I gave up. I didn't need to struggle anymore. I didn't need to fight anymore.

Kelgare's hand gripped my chin. "Keep going. Don't give up."
Sabian replaced him, looking urgent. "Stay with me."
But the pain was too much.

I gasped, sitting up in my hammock. I nearly fell out. I was shaking and gasping for air, and all my scars felt as if they'd been torn open again, fresh and bleeding. I yanked off my cloak, trying to cool off, but I still couldn't stop sweating. I rocked back and forth, trying to keep the tears back, but I wasn't completely successful. *Calm. Calm. You're safe.* But my body didn't believe me.

I concentrated on the things around me. The creaking of the ship, the *swoosh* of the waves, the breathing of my comrades, the rough fabric of the hammock.

Rowan, Mira, Aidilane and the others snored softly around me, but Kai was missing. Desperate for a distraction, I opened up my mind. He was on the deck. I sensed him there, unable to sleep, his mind in turmoil.

He was afraid, terrified, like I was. His memories flooded his mind, haunting him– just like mine. But most of all, shame and regret and self hatred boiled him from the inside out.

My heart skipped a beat.

I got up from my hammock, leaving my cloak behind, and crept up the ladder to the deck.

Kai was sitting with his back to me, leaning back against the main mast of the ship with his knees to his chest. He ran his fingers through his hair, rubbed his face, and his foot tapped the floor in a random, panicked rhythm. His hands shook. Something inside me shifted, settling. Seeing him there like that, like *me. . .*It was a strange sort of comfort. Like the eye of the storm. The calm in the midst of chaos and hopelessness.

Silently, I padded over to him. "You can't sleep either?"

He startled, his tapping ceasing. "Tala." Then his expression changed from its usual neutral and his eyes softened. "You had nightmares again."

I folded my legs beneath me, settling beside him. "And you did, too."

He was silent for a heartbeat. Then he asked, "Are you okay?"

"Not really," I admitted, looking up at the moon, letting the cool night air and ocean breeze cool me. "But I'm better than you."

He laughed. "Maybe, maybe not."

I took a deep breath. "I'm ready to listen now," I said softly as I turned my gaze to his.

His earring glinted in the moonlight and he let out the breath he'd been holding. "Are you sure? I don't want–"

"I'm sure," I confirmed, and took his hand. His pulse raced beneath my finger. "I can't keep going about like this. Your friendship means too much for me to keep putting this off."

"Okay." He relaxed. "That night in Eclipse, I got a note from the Nightingale. They knew you were there. That the King's Wolf was in Eclipse. Wyne threatened to tell the crown of Moonland that I was working with you unless I brought you in. So I came up with a plan, a trick. That I would bring you in, pretending to go along with the deal. But after, I would leave with Aidilane, and return that same hour for you. Clearly, what I intended to do didn't go as planned."

"Why didn't you just. . .tell me your plan?"

He swallowed. "Honestly? I don't know. I. . .panicked. When it came to Aidilane, I–" He stopped, and I could sense how difficult it had been for him to admit those things. "But I screwed up. Massively. And anything I can say to apologize isn't enough, doesn't amount to how much I hurt you." His gaze never wavered from mine. "So all I can say is I'm sorry. I'm. . .*so* sorry, Tala." A tear traced his cheek, and all the self hatred and guilt and regret that was tearing him up from the inside overwhelmed my emotions.

I wiped a tear from my own face, then embraced him. "It's okay. Shh, it's okay. I forgive you. It's forgotten, now. Stop hating yourself, please. It's too much. And you don't deserve that."

He pulled back from me, struggling to regain his composure. "I will never stop hating myself, Tala. For what I did to you, and the things I've done. . .I do deserve it. And it's the least of the penance I can offer. That I will never truly forgive myself. For anything."

"That isn't penance," I chided him. "It's destruction." I placed my fingers on his temples and transmitted peace into his mind, using it to envelope his other feelings and muffle them, softening them. I concentrated, closing my eyes, and breathed deeply, calming his heart and breathing. Everything that was twisting him like a noose I drowned it out with more powerful serenity.

When I was finished, I opened my eyes, pulling my hands back. Calming him had calmed me a little, too.

Kai searched my gaze and wiped a damp strand of hair from my face. "Was there never anyone to take away your pain? To calm your storm within, like you just did for me? To push away the memories?"

I had my brother, and I had Kelgare. I loved them deeply, but they were just reminders of the things I'd been through. And neither of them had been able to stop it. They were powerless.

"No," I answered softly.

But I remembered the night Kai had held me, and the times he'd pulled me from the memories when I was drowning in them, drawing my concentration to the sky, or the forest. I leaned into him, resting my head on his chest, and he wrapped his arm around my shoulders, warming the chill that had crept up on me. "But," I whispered. "You calm my storms, Kai. You make it a little more bearable. You are my best friend, and that will never change."

"And you mine," he murmured. "I won't hurt you, again, Tala. I vow that on my life. And I won't leave. I'm not going anywhere."

I listened to his heartbeat. Strong, and finally relaxed. I realized then that our heartbeats were synchronized, beating as one.

Thump.

Thump.

Thump.

"So, they know I'm here," I said. "The elven royals."

Kai took a deep breath. "They'll be on to us in no time. No doubt they still want you dead, and they'll want my head for disregarding their deal. Rowan was sent on their behalf for certain—"

"Kai," I argued.

"I'm not trying to upset you, Tala," he assured me gently. "I just don't want our mission jeopardized because of Rowan. He's lying. He is up to something, and it isn't good. I'm certain that he's here because the royals sent him."

I sighed. "Kai, I know you're certain. And I understand why you would distrust him. But it doesn't change the fact that you're wrong about this. Please, believe me. I've seen inside his mind, it's of pure intention. He just wants to help me. Help us. He was there when I was unconscious in the tent, after healing Spiritwolf. You weren't. *He* was."

"I was there," he objected. "Tala, I was there. Can you just search my memories?" Kai suggested. "You'll see. He was at the meeting I was hired for your. . .hired by Prince Oberon. Just look."

I shook my head. "Kai–"

"Please."

I pulled away from him. "No. I'm taking a chance, a risk, I know. But I trust him, Kai. Just like I trust you. And I'm not going to break that trust by–" I paused. "By listening to you. Because. . ."

"You don't believe me."

"I think that you've mistaken him for someone else."

He sighed. "Fine. But don't say I didn't warn you."

We sat in silence for a while longer in each other's quiet company and the light of the moon, the gentle rock of the ship. Then, I recited the prophecy out loud while Kai listened without a word. When I finished, I explained, "There's an old woman down in the hull. She's blind, and probably ill. She called me a savior and recited that prophecy."

Kai rubbed his face, then put his hand on mine and squeezed it. "Your life in a prophecy. . .it's unnerving. But I don't doubt the truth in her words. And I don't doubt you. You are quite the savior in my experience."

I let out a shuddering breath, a slight laugh, and stared at the damp wood of the floor. "It's daunting. *Unless she airs on the side of caution, the way she walks will lead to destruction.* What if I'm destined to mess up?"

"What you're destined to do is save the kingdoms." Kai took my chin in his hand and turned my gaze to his. "Tala, you aren't alone in this. You won't ever be as long as I'm alive. You don't have to carry this alone. And the others have your back, too."

I pushed his hand from my chin and held it, tilting my head. "I know. But I can't help but be. . .afraid. I'm always afraid, Kai. Since the moment I was pinned as the prince's murderer, I was afraid. And since the night in that dungeon. . ." I took a shaky breath and tucked a strand of my hair behind my ear. "That night, my fear morphed into terror. After that, I didn't try to stay hidden just because I was a spy. I stayed hidden because I was always terrified. If I wasn't seen, then I couldn't be hurt." I pressed my hand to his chest, where his burn from the brand was hidden beneath his clothes. "You were branded with fire. I was branded with fear."

Kai didn't say anything. Instead, he pulled me close and held me, just as he did that night in the forest. I leaned into him willingly, feeling the things he didn't say, beating like a sure drum.

You're safe now.

You aren't alone anymore.

"Ay, get up you two!"

Captain Glenn startled us awake with a kick to Kai's boot and then mine. "Up! Up! I'm pretty certain you don't want the others to see you like this."

Like this...? I rubbed my eyes groggily, and realized I was still laying on the deck with Kai, my head on his chest and his arms wrapped around me. I unfolded from him and sat up, stretching my arms above my head while he rubbed his face and yawned.

Captain Glenn stared at us with his hands on his hips, his head tilted. "Well good morning, sleepy sweethearts. GET UP!"

He stomped away, and I felt my face burn, especially when I felt the warm emotions radiating from Kai, confusing me.

Dawn was just lighting the horizon, turning the sky gray. A few clouds specked the sky, but a few darker gray ones were in the distance. The winds kept us at a steady pace towards a collection of black specks in the distance.

Mira burst out from the hull, yawning. Her sharp eyes saw me next to Kai immediately, and a grin spread across her face. She crossed her arms. "Well, good morning."

I cleared my throat and got to my feet as everyone else emerged from downstairs and the Captain had us gather. First, he sent Kai up to the helm with a disgruntled, pointed look at me.

When Kai was gone, Captain Glenn stared at us all for a good minute. Then he said, "Evian, we're still on course in the direction you pointed out to me. The craigs you described are in view, it'll just be a few hours before we reach them. Now, I'd like to know what to expect once we're there."

Val raised her hand. "I would too, actually."

I rubbed my arms in the morning chill, and Rowan seemed to notice. He moved over to my side and wrapped his arm around me. "Isn't the Sea Gem underwater?"

"Right," Evian confirmed. "In an underwater cavern to be precise."

"An underwater *cavern*?" Captain Glenn shouted, making me jump. "And how exactly are you supposed to get a gem out of an underwater cavern in the middle of the sea?"

"We haven't exactly figured that out," I said, staring Evian down.

He held his palms up. "Hey, I didn't tell you to go get it. I just told you about it."

"You could have mentioned how we're supposed to get this thing *before* we came all the way out here!" Kai called from up at the helm.

Captain Glenn scrunched his brows, turning his head to look up at him. "How can you hear from all the way up there? Doesn't matter– did I tell you to listen in or did I tell you to man the helm?"

Silence.

"That's what I thought." The Captain turned to us again, crossing his well-muscled, dark arms across his chest. "Oh wise old elf, please tell me I didn't waste an entire night and day– possibly two days– on a tour to see rocks."

Evian licked his lips, looking uncomfortable. I spoke up. "We'll come up with something. Right guys?"

Everyone murmured their agreement, and the Captain growled, "You'd better." He stormed away, leaving us to come up with the impossible. We debated any possibilities that could work, but as the sun rose and we drew closer to the craigs, we couldn't think of anything reasonable or safe in any way.

Soon, we were right beside the craigs. As the Captain headed back down to talk to us with Kai a few steps behind him, I asked Rowan, "Did you tell Captain Glenn about the old woman?"

He nodded. "He said it wasn't any of my business and that we shouldn't press the matter. He said we should stay away from her, even after I told him about her condition. But he did say he'd make sure she was taken care of."

I considered this. "But–"

He interrupted me by taking my hand. "We're lucky he even took us out here. Let's trust he'll stick to his word."

"Okay."

"Hey," he said, and embraced me. "She'll be okay."

I hugged him back, appreciating the comfort, but I couldn't deny the butterflies flitting around inside.

"Well?" demanded the Captain.

Rowan and I pulled away from each other, and I turned to see Kai glaring at Rowan. I exchanged looks with Mira and the others. "Well," I explained. "We haven't figured anything out."

Captain Glenn stared at me for a long moment. "Alright," he sighed. "Then let's get back to the harbor."

He turned to leave, but Navy piped up. "Wait. I have an idea."

Val jabbed him with her elbow. "What?"

"Tell us boy," the captain commanded.

Navy looked back and forth between his sister and the rest of us. "Well. . .Val, remember when I used to go to that well, the super deep one with all the coins, and dive down to get the money?"

Val shook her head. "I know where this is going. Navy, you are not–"

"Let him," said Captain Glenn. "Unless you have any other ideas?"

"Fine," she grumbled.

Navy grinned. "Well, I could dive down and find the Sea Gem. I could do my deep breathing for a while, and then go under."

"No," Val stated. "Not in the ocean. Not by yourself."

"I'll go with him," I volunteered. "He can show me the deep breathing and I'll practice holding my breath."

"But you don't know how to swim, do you?" Kai protested.

"I'll be fine. I know how. Remember? I was the one that dragged you out of the river."

Beside me, Mira and Aidilane giggled.

Evian shrugged. "It's our best chance."

I nodded. "Yes. So. . .?"

Everyone exchanged glances. Val glared at me. "You better not let my brother drown."

"*He* better not let *Tala* drown," muttered Kai. Val shot him a look, and he held up his hands. "Hey, Navy's the one with diving experience."

"In a *well!*"

"Stop!" Navy cried. "We're doing this. And neither of us will have to save the other. We'll be fine. Besides, Evian can control the water currents to keep us moving. It'll be faster than if we just swam."

Evian agreed. "I can do that."

"Good job, kid. Smarter than the rest of these." Captain Glenn patted Navy's shoulder. "Get to it. I don't want to be here all day."

Navy led me to the starboard side of the ship and had me sit down while Val shooed away everyone else, saying, "Scat. They need to concentrate. Go help with the ship, or scrub the deck for all I care. Rowan, with me."

She came over to us and settled down beside her little brother, telling Rowan to do the same with me. "We need to keep track of their pulses. They need to be slow enough so that they can hold their breath for a long time." She took Navy's wrist and felt for his pulse.

I smiled at Rowan and felt myself blush as he took my hand and held my wrist. Navy instructed me to take the deepest, slowest, breaths I could manage, and demonstrated. In... and out. In... and out. I found it more difficult to control my breathing than I thought it would be. After a good long few minutes, he told me to start holding my breath, each time longer. Soon, we were holding our breath for five minutes.

I felt euphoric, hyperoxygenated, like never before. I felt ready to take on the world.

Val and Rowan confirmed that our pulses were slow enough. We were ready.

Everyone gathered again, and Rowan helped me up. I asked Evian, "What does it look like?"

"It could be purple, blue or green," he described. "It'll be smooth, oval, and have a sort of iridescent sheen. Like a moonstone. It'll be at the base of the craig."

I nodded. "Okay. Evian?"

"Ready."

"Are you sure about this?" Kai asked me.

"She's sure," Rowan said for me, still holding my hand. Kai set his jaw, looking close to hurting someone.

"I'll be fine," I assured him.

Navy and I sat on the rail of the ship. "You have to go in backwards," he explained. Evian stood beside us, and when we were ready, we dove in. The last thing I heard was Aidilane saying, "Please don't die."

The water was cold, but not unbearable. I held on tight to Navy's hand as Evian surged the water current around us and sent us deeper and deeper into the water. It was hard to see, and my eyes burned, but the things I saw through the bubbles were fascinating.

Colorful, glowing fish, some the size of my eye others the size of the ship. Other creatures lurked, scaly ones, gray ones, some long and skinny like snakes, others more mammal–like.

The water current pulled us down next to the base of the craig and stopped, swirling around Navy and I, keeping us in place beside it. I looked around the base of craig, but I couldn't see anything. I reached out, feeling for the gem, scraping around the rocks with my free hand, trying to find it as I kept track of the minutes that went by. Three, four.

. .

Suddenly, I felt Navy squeeze my hand harder. I faced him, and he pointed at something further down. I saw it, then, something shiny half covered by a very large rock. But it was out of our reach unless one of us moved out of the funnel of surging water.

I transmitted into Navy's mind. *Five minutes are up. This is much deeper than a well. We need to hurry. You are going to go back up, and I'll get the gem.*

His eyes widened briefly before I let go of his hand and he shot up with the funnel, leaving me behind. I swam forward, deeper, pumping my legs and pulling the water back with my arms.

Six minutes.

I reached the large rock and grabbed hold of it with both hands. I was getting dizzy, and I was beginning to panic.

Calm.

I yanked the rock free, releasing the gem. It was the size of my palm. As I held it in my hand I felt a tingle go up my arm, and suddenly I was aware of every living creature around me from the fish to the people on the ship to the algae around me. If I wanted to, I could have put my thoughts into their minds, could have controlled each one of them, and could heal anyone. Maybe even bring them back to life.

I countered the feeling of power, trying to keep a level head. I started upwards, kicking with my legs.

Seven minutes.

I felt myself growing weaker with every movement, but I kept going. Halfway to the ship, I couldn't go any further. I transmitted to Evian, *I'm here. Here.*

Then I let go of the breath I was holding, the bubbles floating up, up to the surface. I resisted the intense urge to take a breath. But I couldn't for very much longer. I thrashed, panicking, nearly dropping the gem.

Then I felt the water around me funnel and surge again, and then I was laying on deck, gasping for air, the Sea Gem clutched in my wet hand.

"Great gamble!" exclaimed Mira. "You were down there for nine minutes!"

Rowan and Kai were on either side of me as I coughed and spluttered. Rowan cradled my head in his hand and Kai held my hand.

"I'm fine," I insisted when I finally caught my breath. "Is Navy. . ."

"I'm good," he said nearby. "Did you get it?"

I held up the gem. "Is this it?"

Evian sucked in a sharp breath. "It is."

"Impressive," Captain Glenn admitted. "You all make quite the team."

"We do," Val agreed. "Thank you for sending up my little brother."

"Of course."

"I'm not little!"

"You're little to me. But now you've done something very important," she congratulated him.

"Are you okay?" Rowan asked me.

"Obviously not," Kai growled. "She just held her breath under the ocean for nine minutes, and look at her hands."

It was true, my hands were a bloody mess from scraping and digging around the rocks. But I shook my head. "Kai, they're just scrapes. Really, I'm fine."

"You just need to rest," Rowan suggested. "Come on, I'll help you downstairs."

I felt Kai's eyes on our backs as we headed for the hull, but I was too tired and too annoyed with his obsession with Rowan to care.

Chapter Twelve

Kai

Some things you learn to expect. Like grief, fear, anger, regret, sadness. But some things take you by surprise. Joy, peace, happiness. And love. You either see it coming from a mile away– or you don't see it coming at all.

I watched Rowan and Tala disappear into the hull. I wanted to rush after her and make sure she was really okay, bandage her hands. But I also wanted to hit Rowan and throw him off the ship to the sharks.

So I watched them go instead, not trusting myself. I would deal with Rowan myself if I had to, but not in front of Tala. Clearly. . .she cared for him. Differently. Which made me even angrier. He was taking advantage of her.

I assisted the captain with getting the ship turned around up at the helm, then he said he needed a nap, so I took over steering the ship. He'd shown me how the day before, but it still made me nervous. I wondered why he put me up to this task and never one of the others. I depended heavily on the compass he let me borrow.

I tried not to think of what was going on down in the hull. Aidilane kept me company and helped me stay on course for the harbor, but my thoughts were elsewhere.

For years, I numbed myself to my feelings. They were dangerous. And I couldn't deal with them, couldn't function with them. Without feelings, pain didn't matter. Regret didn't matter. Anger didn't matter. Fear didn't matter– because I couldn't feel them. So I shoved them down for so long I forgot what it felt like to feel anything at all.

But when I looked at Tala. . .it was like a clump of ice inside me melted. Last night felt right. And I. . .I was beginning to wonder if maybe what I was feeling was more than just care.

I knew I loved Aidilane. But it was a sibling sort of love. I'd do anything for her, it was in my blood. But this new feeling for Tala was foreign to me. Foreign and frightening. And now that Rowan was around, I wasn't sure what to do. I wouldn't let him hurt her, but I also didn't want to hurt her. She denied everything I said about him, and I could see the way she looked at him. She was smitten. But he would betray us if I didn't step up and do something soon. So what was I supposed to do? I was confused. I was jealous. I was angry. I was feeling things, and I hated it. It was a lot easier to be numb.

"You should eat something." Aidilane offered me a sailor's biscuit.

"I'm not hungry. Besides, you need it more than I do."

She didn't argue, but she said, "Do you think it'll work?"

"The gem?" I had thought about it. But I wasn't sure how a shiny rock would help us. "I don't know. We'll have to see."

Mira came up a little while later. "How long until we reach the harbor?"

"A few hours. Sunset, maybe," I responded.

"Alright." She settled down beside Aidilane, then remarked, "Kai, you're gripping that wheel as if you're trying to strangle it."

"I'm imagining it's your brother."

She laughed. "I understand that, then."

The girls spoke together, conversing about different types of swords, daggers, and whatever else girls talked about. I concentrated on the horizon and the compass. Clouds started rolling in, and the wind started to pick up fairly quickly. The sea began to be bumpier, the waves grew.

Evian came up to the hull, his face creased with worry. "It's getting stormy. I'll try to control the water around us to keep us steady, but there's only so much I can do."

"Thanks," I responded around clenched teeth. The wheel was getting harder to keep control over.

Evian ran back down to the deck, shouting things, and the captain emerged from the hull, yelling orders over the shrieking Evian. Over the commotion, I heard a cry come from the hull. I turned to my sister, "Can you take over here?"

"Sure." Mira helped her as I ran downstairs, then climbed down the ladder to the hull.

I found Tala in her hammock, muttering, groaning, crying, in her sleep, her bloody hands bandaged. Rowan was standing over her, trying to wake her. I shoved him aside. "What happened?"

"Nothing! She fell asleep just fine, but then she started crying out and sobbing and turning."

I felt Tala's pulse– it was racing at a dangerous pace. She clutched the Sea Gem in her hand, and I realized it was glowing.

I turned and slammed Rowan up against a beam, and demanded, "What the hell did you do to her?"

"I didn't do anything!"

"You lying bastard! You told her I wasn't there for her, back at camp. And I remember you from the meeting with the prince. I know what your motives are."

A sly smile spread across his face. "Maybe I'm a liar. But not about this. Maybe it's the stone. I don't know."

I struggled to keep control over myself. "This isn't over."

I pulled back and knelt beside Tala's hammock and tried to pry the gem from her hand, but she wouldn't let go of it. I couldn't pull it from her grasp. She twisted and turned, and gasped for air as tears streamed down her cheeks.

She was probably having another nightmare. I guessed the gem was enhancing it. Great gamble– was she reliving her past? Everytime she cried out, it felt like my heart was being ripped in two.

"Tala!" I shook her, calling her name, trying to get her to wake up.

The gem then glowed brighter, the light pulsing like a heart. Then it went out, and Tala went still. Too still.

"Tala?" Rowan came to her other side, taking her hand. "Tala, I'm here."

She was turned facing his direction, so she didn't see me when she opened her eyes. I stood and stepped back, clenching my jaw. "Rowan? What. . ." She sat up, wiping the tears from her face.

I opened my mouth to say something, but Rowan interrupted. "Another nightmare? Are you okay?"

I shot him a lethal glare.

Tala swallowed, regaining her composure, and answered in a shaky voice. "Y–Yes. The worst one yet. It felt so completely real that I. . ." she turned and met my eyes. "But at the end, the dragon came to me again. But this time, she spoke to me. Through my Keen. Just like Spiritwolf and I do. And we were right. She is the source of the mages' power."

I ran my fingers through my hair. "Wow. Ok, what did she say?"

"She said that. . .that she's dying. The magic that the mages are draining from her is her primal source of life. It is her essence. They've almost drained her body completely, but her mind. . ." She took a shaky breath, staring into the shadows. "She left her consciousness in me."

"What?" Rowan and I both exclaimed.

"How?" he asked.

"My Keen," she explained, "and the power of this gem allowed us to have a strong enough connection to each other, and for her to. . .transfer her consciousness into me."

"How does that even work?" I wondered. "And why?"

"It was the only way for her to stay alive."

"But. . .if she died, wouldn't the problem be solved? No dragon, then the mages have no source of power."

Tala shook her head. "It doesn't work that way with dragons. When they die, their bodies become conduits of more energy, pure magic, and any part of their body can be used for power. The mages have been making their wands from her scales and drops of her blood. But if she dies, they have a nearly unending supply. They'll be unstoppable."

"Wait so. . ." Rowan thought about this. "Is this you we're talking to or the dragon?"

"Me." Tala sniffed, and dangled her legs off the side of the hammock. "I'm sort of like a host. Her consciousness is bonded with mine to keep her alive, but I'm still me."

I wasn't so sure of that. Her eyes looked distant, in a different way than before, and she looked completely drained, completely numb.

"What's happening?" she asked, noticing the powerful rocking of the ship and the creaking of the wood from the rain that was now pouring.

"It's a storm," I explained. "We need all hands on deck. Tala are you–"

She shot me a deathly look, shaking her head as she got up and headed up to the deck. I went to follow her, but Rowan stopped me with an outstretched arm.

"She won't believe you until it's too late," he murmured. "And there's nothing you can do to stop me."

"There's plenty I could do," I hissed as I drew one of my blades.

He clicked his tongue. "Ah, but you won't. Because of her. Because you can see she's in love with me."

I bared my teeth, quaking with the effort of not driving my blade through his chest. "You don't care a rat's tail about her."

"As if you would know anything about care." Rowan let go of me and climbed up the ladder, leaving me in the shadows. Why didn't I just end his life? Why didn't I–

I knew why. He was right. Because of her.

Up on deck, the ship's bow dipped up and down, making it difficult to keep our footing on the slippery wet wood. Captain Glenn was up at the helm, shouting orders, while the others scrambled to obey them and keep the ship floating. I ran upstairs to the helm, taking the stairs two at a time, and asked the captain, "How can I help?"

"Help me keep the wheel steady," he replied, grunting with effort. I gripped the other side of the wheel, straining against how much it jerked around and wanted to spin out of control. It was hard with how slippery it was.

Evian stood at the ship's bow with Val, struggling to control the waters around the ship, and Val was straining to get the air currents around us under control and in our favor, while Rowan, Mira, Aidilane, Tala and Navy did their best to keep the sails up and from tearing.

I was drenched to the skin in a matter of seconds, and the wheel kept slipping through our fingers. The waves crashed into the ship, tossing us about like wet ragdolls. Captain Glenn shouted over the noise and chaos, "We're going to capsize!"

I pushed down my panic and thought hard, squinting through the pelting rain. "I have an idea," I yelled loud enough that the others would hopefully hear. "But I don't know if it'll work."

"On with it then!"

"I'm either going to keep us from capsizing or burn us all to hell," I called over my shoulder on my way down to the deck.

"WHAT?" cried the captain.

I took my position next to the other elementalists. "Keep doing what you're doing, Evian. Val, I'm going to create a bubble around us with my fire, and you need to keep it up around us. If my theory is correct, it should balance the atmosphere around us to get us to the harbor without keeling over."

She shot me a grim nod, and then I held my hands up, palms facing each other but not touching, and began to form a hollow orb of fire. The heat from it dried me enough to use my abilities. I guided the orb up over my head, making it larger and larger.

At the last second I took a deep breath. I couldn't fail.

I threw the orb up, using all my concentration and strength to enlarge it and spread it over our ship like a dome. There was a moment of adrenaline, live or die, until I was certain I wasn't burning the ship, and then the rain wasn't pelting us anymore. Val controlled the air currents to help me keep it there and around us, but it was up to me to keep the flames alive.

No more rain, no more crazy winds, the ship wasn't being thrashed around anymore– and neither were we– and the heat from my fire dome kept the sails going, along with Evian's control of the water. It was an eerie sort of calm, like being in the middle of a hurricane– which we may as well have been.

Sweat and water dripped from the three of us elementalists with the effort of the feat we were attempting, and I found I was thankful to be on a team. I'd always been a loner, but I found it wasn't as hard as I thought it would be to work with other people. In fact, it made things a little less hard, unless it came to quarrels.

My hands shook, my legs threatened to give out– I felt as if I were holding up the ship itself.

"No," Tala said, suddenly beside me. "Just an entire storm." She supported me, keeping me from collapsing, while Aidilane, Rowan, and Mira did the same for Val and Evian.

The next three hours felt like an eternity. Reaching the harbor was truly the light at the end of the tunnel.

I dissipated the flames, careful not to burn anything in the process, and then collapsed along with Val and Evian. We all lay on the deck, panting, while the others got the ship secured at the docks. Then they brought us water and food, and we all ate in silence together on the deck.

"Here's to our three elementalists." Aidilane raised her tin cup with a tired smile.

"Indeed," the captain agreed. "Thank you all for keeping her afloat."

"For keeping *us* afloat," Mira corrected. "Who knew fire would be the answer in a storm?"

I leaned back against the main mast with a sigh, having finished my food. "I'm just glad it's over and we got what we were looking for." I couldn't help but feel a rush of pride, though. *My* fire had saved us. I had done something good for once. Saving instead of destruction. Life instead of death. And they recognized it.

Tala smiled at me. She sensed what I was feeling. I smiled back. But her eyes. . . she hardly seemed present, like she was somewhere else in her mind entirely. While everyone talked and laughed and discussed things, she stared off into the sunset, expressionless. I knew the look too well. She was numb.

I stood to go to her, but Rowan scooted over to her and took her hand, turning her gaze to his, murmuring things I couldn't hear. I blinked, trying to keep my typical neutral expression, but it was hard.

Because I was feeling things.

I set down my tin cup and padded over to the railing. I could hear Val paying the captain for our venture, and the others telling each other stories. The sun dipped below the horizon, darkening the sky and lighting up the stars, letting the moon take its place. Balance.

But something caught my eye. A group of men, no— Moonland soldiers— were heading towards us through the harbor, carrying crossbows. At least thirty elves, all dressed in the classic Moonland warrior attire– dark like assassins. My stomach clenched.

"We have company," I warned the others.

They gathered at the rail to see, and then scrambled back. "More of your *friends*?" I questioned Rowan pointedly.

"What are we supposed to do?" Tala asked, pulling her hood over her head, her eyes like hunted prey.

"They knew you were here," I said. "It was only a matter of time." I glared at Rowan.

He narrowed his eyes. "I'll take care of this."

"What?"

"How?"

Everyone began berating him with demands, but he said, "Just trust me. I'll explain later."

He headed down the ramp to the docks, meeting the soldiers before they reached the ship. We couldn't hear the exchange, but after a few minutes, they turned and left without a sound.

Everyone relaxed except Tala and I. We both still held our blades in our hands when Rowan came back aboard. I glared daggers at him.

"I'm Prince Oberon's lieutenant," he explained. "I dissuaded their attention, said I just needed a short cruise to get away for a while, and you all are my friends."

I blew out a breath. "*Friends.* See? I told you all—"

"Thank you," Tala interrupted, embracing Rowan affectionately. The pit in my chest dropped. "What?" I stuttered.

She turned to me. "The lieutenant of the Moonland Kingdom crown has risked his life to save us, twice now. Instead of hunting you and I like his superiors are, he chose to help us. See, Kai? So please, stop obsessing over your distrust."

It wasn't like her at all. She really was smitten.

Beside me, Mira huffed. "Tala, I don't know about all this. I'm not necessarily taking sides in this matter, but my brother isn't someone you can trust."

It amazed me how genuinely hurt Rowan made himself look. He sighed. "Look, if you all don't want me on this team, then just tell me. I'll leave. Without a word to the crown."

"You two are ridiculous," Val chided Mira and I. "Stay, Rowan. We need you."

Navy, Evian, Aidilane, and Tala piped their agreements. I opened and closed my mouth, then said, "We need to get back to camp, don't we?"

"We do," agreed Mira.

"I'll get the horses," I muttered, volunteering myself. "Hurry up, all of you. I'll see you at the edge of town."

I headed down the ramp without looking back.

I was in the middle of tacking up the horses when Rowan came around the side of one of them, buckling a strap that I missed.

"What do you want?" I growled.

"I'm just helping you," he said cheerfully. "Do you have a problem with that?"

I felt Tala's eyes on me from up in the driver's seat. "No," I replied.

"Good."

We finished up and I took the reins, but Rowan snatched them from my hands. "I'll drive this time. You should get some rest."

I narrowed my eyes, my brow twitching. Then I stepped up into the stagecoach with the others. I was squashed between Evian and Navy. They snored and drooled over me the entire trip, and every bump sent my head knocking back against the coach. I didn't get an ounce of sleep.

It felt like centuries before the coach finally came to a stop. I crawled out before anyone else did, desperate for fresh air. Oliver and Felix were outside, and when everyone got out, there was a happy exchange of greetings.

I stood to the side and untacked the horses, dumping the gear in a pile. Then I guided them to a patch of grass to let them graze. I mounted one of them bareback and lay on my back, looking up through the canopy of trees and I matched the rhythm of my breathing with the horse's, finding it oddly calming.

"She's pregnant."

Tala came up beside the horse, running her hand along her flank. "Twins."

"She's the quiet one." I patted the horse's right side. "Hardly ever kicks. The one on the left, though," I patted the other side, "keeps mama up all night."

Tala smiled up at me. "How did *you* know?"

I shrugged. "I know my way around horses." I turned to look at her. "What happened during that dream?"

"I–"

"Other than the fact that a dragon's consciousness is now stuck inside you."

Her distant gaze concentrated on the horse's hooves. "That's all."

"I know it isn't. That was no ordinary nightmare."

"I told you," she murmured. "It was just more realistic than the others."

I stared at her, hoping she'd look at me, hoping she'd tell me the truth. But she didn't. Finally, she asked, "Do you think you're going to be okay eventually? With Rowan helping us."

"He isn't helping us," I insisted. I took in a deep breath and stifled a sigh. "Please. I don't want to keep arguing about this, Tala. I just wish you'd listen to me, or at least look inside my mind, but you won't. So, no. I'm not okay with Rowan "helping us.""

I sat up and turned so I was facing the horse's neck and took hold of her mane, clicked my tongue. I led the other horse behind me and headed to camp.

We all sat around the crystal–fire orb that I'd created, munching on our dinner and taking turns telling Oliver and Felix about our little trip.

"And I thought we were all gonna burn!" Navy cried. "But Kai was all *whoosh*, and serious face, and *swoosh!*" He demonstrated the movements with his hands.

"And I've never seen an air elementalist help hold up fire before," I added. "Especially not to keep a ship from capsizing."

"And there were no issues with retrieving the gem?" Oliver asked.

"Nope," Rowan said, squeezing Tala's hand. "Tala had us worried for about four extra minutes, but all was well."

"Wow," Felix sighed, leaning back. "Next time I'm going."

"Hopefully there won't be a next time," Val chided with a pointed look at her brother, who stuck his tongue out at her.

"At least we didn't have to deal with the soldiers," Tala pointed out.

Mira and Oliver sat side by side, hands clasped. The fire reflected in Oliver's glasses, and Mira's eyes looked happy, but confused, too. "It's strange. I haven't had any dreams with the dragon for a few days."

Tala and I exchanged a look, then she retold them what happened on the ship. Everyone was quiet for a long moment, then Mira whispered, "We were right."

Beside me, Aidilane asked quietly, "She's dying?"

Tala nodded. "I'm keeping her alive as best as I can. But they're draining her. We need to find her, rescue her before she's completely gone."

"Especially since the mages will be unstoppable if she dies," Val murmured.

"Right."

"At least we know the Sea gem worked."

Spiritwolf slinked into camp then and settled down beside Tala, who stroked her fur and murmured greetings. It pierced my heart to see her so empty looking. So drained. I hoped that she wasn't being drained along with the dragon.

The next morning, Oliver asked Rowan and I to help him with a project in his tent. It was quite an extraordinary lab– tubes, bubbling concoctions, and piles upon piles of tools and unfinished inventions.

Mira had a pair of goggles on and was monitoring a bottle of sizzling blue liquid while Oliver led Rowan and I to one of the piles of unfinished projects. He set a round, spiky object in my hand. "This is a simple spike grenade. When set off, all those spikes shoot out, hitting anything within five yards. Don't worry, this one isn't set. But do you think you guys can replicate the design for me? Make a few more? It's simple mechanics, really."

"Sure," I said with a glare at Rowan, who shrugged.

"Great! Feel free to look over the grenade and take it apart if you need to. I'll be right over here with Mira if you have any questions." He stepped over to the table where Mira stood and got to work with another concoction.

I turned the grenade over in my hands, careful not to poke myself with the sharp spikes. "Wouldn't want to get shot with one of these."

Rowan raised a brow as he went through the pile of grenade pieces. "Is that a threat?"

"Could be."

"Right. Let me see it." I handed it to him and satisfaction surged through me when one of the spikes poked his palm, making him wince.

I searched the pile for any parts that looked like ones on the grenade and began assembling one, my jaw clenched. I was working with the enemy. I couldn't stand seeing him holding hands with Tala, hugging her, feeding his lie. She would be so utterly torn when he betrayed her, and here I stood making grenades with him instead of doing something about it.

After about fifteen long minutes, I had assembled six more grenades, all identical to the one Oliver built, while Rowan only made four and a half.

"Not your specialty, is it?" I remarked.

"Making Tala happy is," he retorted, then whispered, "Or at least making her believe she is."

I struggled to remain calm. "Hand me that screwdriver, will you?"

He grabbed it and held it out to me, but dropped it before I took it. He smirked. "My bad."

It was the last straw— I lost my cool. I balled my fist and slammed it into his face, knocking him backwards through the tent flaps and outside, where he fell on his backside in the grass, holding his hand to his eye. But I surged forward and pinned him, delivering another punch to his face.

"Woah! Stop it!" cried Oliver, and Mira yelled, "No, let them finish hashing it out."

"Finish killing each other?!"

Rowan kicked me in the stomach, knocking me off, and punched me in the jaw, but I came at him again with another fist to his nose, and he stumbled back, blood dripping down from his nose and shock forming in his eyes. "My bad," I growled.

I lunged forward again, but then Tala was there between us. She shoved me back. "*What* are you *doing*?" she cried. "What is wrong with you!" She turned to Rowan and examined him gently, her face creased with worry, anger, and affection. Then she turned to me again, quaking with anger. "How *dare* you! Kai–" she stopped short, pressing her fingers to her temples. "Go away. Go anywhere. I just don't want to see you here right now."

I took a step back, stuttering, "Tala–I–"

"Leave!" she yelled, tears escaping her eyes.

So I did.

Chapter Thirteen

Tala

S ome things you expect, some things you choose not to. Denial is a dangerous thing– life saving as it may be at times, it always comes around to sting you eventually.

"Are you okay?" I asked Rowan as I cleaned his black eye and bloody nose.

"I'm fine," he sighed. "I'm sorry."

"You have no reason to apologize," I chided him. "Whatever got into him?"

"I was handing him something and accidentally dropped it," Rowan explained. "Then he just came at me. I didn't want to hurt him, but I had to defend myself."

"Don't worry about him," I growled. "He'll have to deal with the consequences of his own actions. You however, I will heal." I gently put my hand to his eye and nose, closing my eyes and did my new found specialty. When I was finished, I pulled back. The bruises were gone, and so was the swelling and blood. "Good news is, your nose wasn't broken." I held up a little mirror for him to see.

"Thank you," he said. "You work wonders."

"What can I say, you look better without a black eye and bloody nose."

He laughed. "Who knew getting punched by someone with rings on would be so much worse then without?"

I shook my head with a sigh. "I cannot believe him."

He took my hand with a gentle squeeze. "It's ok. Take it easy on him. I think he's just jealous."

I laughed. "Jealous? Of what?"

"Of, well, us."

I frowned. "Us?"

"I think he cares more about you than you realize," Rowan explained. "He's just having a hard time showing it. And now that you and I. . .well, he doesn't like it. That's probably why he's so against me, too. He's jealous."

I struggled with that information, trying to let it sink in. "But. . ." I sighed. "Why is life so hard?"

"Because it's our first time living."

I laughed. "That's true."

We all headed to bed, but Kai didn't show. I was glad. I was too angry at him to see his face. I settled in my blankets, tucking in. Rowan was already snoring across from my cot, and so were the others. Nearby,

I thought she was already asleep too, but Mira whispered, startling me. "What are you doing, Tala?"

I sat up to peer at her through the darkness. "What?"

"With my brother. And Kai."

I tilted my head. "What do you mean?"

I heard her sigh. "Tala, I'm not going to step into this. But I just want you to know that you are hurting Kai. And you're making a mistake with Rowan. Do what you think is best, but please. Really listen to your heart, to your instincts."

"I am." I knew exactly what my heart was telling me. It was drawing me to Rowan.

"Okay," Mira relented.

"Are you upset with me?" I asked, my voice shaky.

"No. Just. . .taking in all possible angles."

I lay awake for hours in the dark silence after that, listening to my companions' soft breathing, cradling the dragon's consciousness within me. It felt like I was carrying her inside my mind, like she would come awake and begin talking to me again. But she didn't. She drew on my strength, the same strength that allowed me to heal, and I let her. I fed her consciousness with mine, willingly keeping her alive. Her bond with me was now like steel, unbreakable. Like Spiritwolf and me. Except the dragon was an actual part of me now, part of my mind until she was reunited with her body.

I wondered if the prophecy about me was leaving out a part about sacrifice. Because I was beginning to think that sacrifice was inevitable. A sacrifice that would change everything. But I denied it. I denied it and pushed away the feeling, the premonition. There had to be a way around that.

I couldn't shake the dream I'd had in the ship, with the gem, before the dragon had come to me. I'd had nightmares every night for years, but that one was. . .so real. I was there again, in the dungeon. Except I didn't know it was a dream. I relived the chase, the trial, and the night in the dungeon, everything up to when I woke up in Kelgare's room. When I woke, my body was on fire and I expected every scar and place where I'd been hit, kicked, or hit with the lash to be bleeding, bruised, and fresh. When I'd realized it had just been a dream, and Rowan and Kai were there, I went numb. Again. Like the day it happened. I couldn't bear to feel. . .all that again. It was too much.

So fear of my dreams kept me from falling asleep until the first light of dawn, and then I was finally able to sleep for an hour or so, then I got up with everyone else.

First, Mira told me about the dream she'd had that night. It had told her exactly where the mages were keeping the dragon. Oliver and Rowan helped us map it out, and then all of us practiced our combat skills.

Afterwards, I played a game with Navy, Aidilane, Val, Mira, Oliver and Rowan that involved hiding and seeking each other out while Kai, Felix, and Evian discussed different options for a plan to rescue the dragon. I kept sensing Kai's eyes on me, but I ignored him.

The Renegades were really growing on me. I was thankful for their friendship and help, especially Mira. She was like the sister I'd always wanted, likewise with Aidilane and Val. And Navy was like a little brother to me. I missed Sabian, hoping Kai was right about him. He had to hang on until we stopped the mages.

We were finished with the game when sunset faded in, laughing and panting after chasing each other. Navy suggested a bonfire, one without the crystal fire pits. "We could roast chocolate truffles!" he exclaimed excitedly.

We all agreed to it– our last fun thing before we set out on our impossible mission. Navy ran over to Kai, pulling him by the hand to a spot in the clearing where we were gathering wood for the fire. "Can you light it? We're going to have a bonfire! With chocolate truffles!"

He laughed. "Sure. But only if I get a truffle." His jaw was bruised from the scuffle. He held out his hands over the pile of wood and formed a flame, then lit the pile, making the flames grow until all the wood was burning.

"Thank you!" Navy squealed.

"Of course." Kai ruffled his hair playfully. It made me happy to see him like that. But I felt a twinge inside my chest as I stared at the flames. I remembered the torches in the dungeon, flickering over me and igniting the shadows of my torturers. . .

"I'll go get the truffles," I volunteered, and headed into the supply tent. I felt Kai's eyes on my back all the way there.

I rummaged through the supplies and food, wondering what chocolate truffles looked like– I'd never had one before.

"Need some help?" Rowan entered the tent, setting a lantern on a table. "It's dark in here."

I smiled back at him. "Thanks." We dug through the crates and sacks, and finally, we found a round, flat tin and opened it, overwhelmed by the strong scent of cocoa. "They look delicious," I moaned.

"How do we roast them without them melting?" Rowan wondered aloud.

"I'm not sure." I popped one into my mouth, then threw my head back with a gleeful, "Yumm."

I gave one to him, and his eyes widened. "Mmm. Wow."

"A taste of heaven," I said with a dramatic flourish of my hand, making Rowan laugh. Then his expression turned serious, but gentle. "Are you okay?"

My smile faded. "Why?"

"You stared at the fire back there," he observed. "Your eyes. . .it was like you weren't there at all. Then you used the truffles as an excuse to get away."

"It wasn't an excuse," I lied.

"Yes, it was." He took a step closer until our chest's were touching, and he took my shoulders in his hands, his breath warm on my face. He whispered, "I'm here."

I gazed into his beautiful violet eyes, the light from the lantern illuminating them like stars. His presence filled me with warmth and the butterflies that fluttered inside me every time he was near came alive once again. "How is it that you always seem to know what I'm feeling?" I asked softly.

His gaze danced in mine, then strayed to my lips. "I'm an empath," he whispered. Then he closed the little space between us and his lips met mine. I wrapped my arms around his neck, leaning into the kiss, the butterflies replaced with warmth all over like the growing orb of fire inside me had burst and spread through my veins. His hands ventured to the small of my back and the back of my neck, pulling me closer into him. The kiss took my breath away, but I couldn't get enough.

A *thunk* startled both of us out of the kiss, and we turned to see Kai standing in the entrance of the tent, his arms full of firewood, having dropped a piece. My face heated, and his paled. I sensed his dismay clear as crystal, like a rush of cold winter wind. He swallowed hard and set his jaw.

I pulled back from Rowan, starting, "Kai—"

But he turned and left, storming away before I could finish. I said to Rowan, "I'm sorry. I should to go talk to him." He nodded with a smile, reassuring me. "You should."

I rushed after Kai, who was heading towards the cavern. "Kai!" I called after him. "Wait! Please."

He stopped just outside the cavern and turned to me, blank of any emotion, his face expressionless. I caught up to him, panting. "Kai. You're upset. Why? I really, really like Rowan. You need to get over your feelings about this."

He searched my gaze as if he couldn't believe what I'd just said. "Tala," he said in an impossibly calm tone that pierced my heart, "My feelings are a problem, yes. But they don't matter. What matters is you just kissed the enemy. You may love him. But he is going to hurt you. He doesn't really care about you. He is taking advantage of you, *using* you. He's like a scorpion– ready to sting you the moment you turn." He sucked in a sharp breath, his voice cracking. "I'd give you my heart if yours stopped beating. I'd take an arrow for you. I'd pull you out of every nightmare as long as I lived. But he–" His lip trembled, tearing my heart in two. "He is going to rip you open like prey. And by then, it'll be too late. And I will have regretted holding back yesterday."

I opened my mouth to say something and reached out to take his hand, but he stepped back. "No," he hissed. "Don't. Do not keep telling me the same things. I know. But I will not just sit by and watch as he makes the same mistake I did."

I blinked, taking a step back, shock and emotion surging through me. Kai turned and stormed off to sentry for the night, just outside camp at the lookout oak without looking back, calling over his shoulder to the others, "I'll take watch for night."

I stood there for a moment, letting everything sink in. Then I swallowed, let the others know I was headed to bed, and went into the sleeping tent to crawl into my cot and sob.

The tears wouldn't stop coming.

When everyone else filtered into the tent and got into bed, I held my breath to keep from letting them know I was awake. When I sensed they were all asleep, I let out the breath and cried silently, my tears soaking my pillow.

After a while, Rowan got out of his cot and crept over to me, kneeling beside my cot and brushed a strand of hair out of my face. "Hey. The talk with Kai didn't go so well, did it?"

I shook my head, then sat up and leaned into him, sobbing into his shoulder, wondering where it all went wrong. He rubbed my back until I stopped crying. Then I whispered, "He's my best friend, Rowan. I can't lose him over this."

"You won't," he assured me. "He just needs time."

I wiped the tears from my cheeks, nodding and sniffling. "I can't sleep."

He gazed at me for a moment through the dark, then he took my hand and helped me up. "Come on. Let me get you away from here for a little while."

He led me outside and through camp, twilight shining over us through the canopy. The trees rustled lightly in the breeze, but the night chill was chased away by Rowan's warmth. I sensed Kai on lookout outside camp beside the oak, dozing lightly. He never did fall asleep completely. But I turned my attention to Rowan, letting myself be drawn away from all that was hurting me inside.

He led me down a wooded trail, and we stopped to pick small, diamond shaped berries that tasted like honey and looked like they glowed in the moonlight. We talked and laughed over stories. He told me about the times he'd had with his sister, and I told him about the good moments Sabian and I had shared. Soon, I forgot all about my troubles.

We kept going a little deeper into the forest, following a creek that was illuminated by the stars and moon like a glowing, shimmering vein. It tasted like fresh winter air.

Finally, we came to a clearing, and Rowan stopped and whispered in my ear, making me tingle and smile. "Listen very carefully."

I did. And that was when I sensed them. My smile faded.

Mages emerged into the clearing, surrounding us. I drew my knives, taking a defensive stance, but Rowan just stood there, looking at me. My stomach dropped. "No."

He smiled a charming smile. "Don't make a sound to alert the others." The mages closed in, greeting Rowan like teammates while I did my best to keep an eye on all of them, my knives ready, my grip around them tight.

"Rowan..." I wouldn't accept it. "Rowan please tell me this isn't–"

"What it looks like?" he finished for me. "I'm afraid it is."

My heart raced. "So–"

"Yes," he answered. "Kai was right."

Everything inside me crumbled. I shook my head, taking a step back, trying to control my breathing. "H—How? I looked into your mind. I saw you were telling the truth! Rowan—"

He held up his hand, stopping me. "It's a skill I've developed as an empath. Now, not another word." One of the mages handed him two objects. Remotes. "Tala, King's Wolf, do you know what these are?"

I didn't answer. He held them up. "They're detonators. For two highly lethal bombs." He paused, his gaze piercing mine. "One of which is buried just inside your friends' tent, where they all sleep peacefully at this very moment. The other," he nodded towards the edge of camp. "Is in the tree where Kai is keeping sentry for the night."

My mouth went dry. I shook my head and hissed, "You're lying. Like you have been all along."

"No," he smiled. "About this, I'm not lying. Now, you have two options. You can leave peacefully with us, without alerting the others, and your friends stay safe and alive. Or, you can cause a struggle and I blow your friends to bits. Since you don't take my word that there really are bombs," he added. "Let me demonstrate."

He pressed the red button on one of the remotes and, a second later, an ear-piercing explosion cut through the air, and a gust of hot wind and splinters blew through the trees, nearly knocking us all over. It came from the direction where Kai was.

Everything inside me ripped. Just like Kai said it would.

"No," I whimpered, shock verberating through my bones. "No."

Rowan brushed the splinters from his sleeves. "Yes. Kai is probably back there bleeding out if he isn't dead already."

I frantically reached out to him, transmitted to him, calling his name over and over. But I couldn't feel him. He was gone.

"Now," Rowan growled. "Will you go the easy way or does everyone else have to die, too?"

I didn't say a word as I stared into oblivion and my hands fell to my sides, my weapons dropping to the ground. Two mages rushed forward and grabbed hold of my arms, keeping me in place even though I didn't move, didn't struggle. Another came in front of me and slammed a fist into my face, knocking my head back, then kneed me in the ribs so hard I buckled over and fell to my knees, my breath knocked from my lungs.

Kai was dead. And it was all my fault.

Rowan gripped my hair and yanked my head back so I was looking up at him. "Be careful who you trust," he murmured.

Chapter Fourteen

Tala

There are many things I regret as I look back on my life. Things I've done, and things I didn't do. Many of those things would have been avoided if I'd just listened to the people who cared for me the most.

I knelt on the cold stone floor, my hands tied behind me and around a beam. I was a prisoner, again. In the dungeons, again. They hadn't even done anything to me yet, but being there was torture enough. It was just like that night.

But even more so was the gaping hole inside me. I couldn't even cry. I felt empty. Kai had warned me, and I didn't listen. He'd tried to help me, tried to keep this from happening, and instead of listening to him, I let myself be led away and tricked by a handsome face and words I wanted to hear.

I'd give you my heart if yours stopped beating. I'd take an arrow for you. I'd pull you out of every nightmare as long as I lived.

I killed him. But not before I hurt him and pushed him away. I'd been angry at him, even. But now he was dead. Just. . .gone. And I didn't even have the chance to tell him how sorry I was.

Every breath was an effort, an effort I didn't want to make. Every beat of my heart rang with the thought, *He can't be dead. He can't be dead.* But I knew it. As much as every fiber in my being screamed that it couldn't be, I knew it was true. That explosion . . . there was no possible way he could have survived that.

He had been right along. Right about everything.

And I. Didn't. Listen.

It was all my fault.

I killed him.

My mind berated me over and over with those thoughts, drowning me in remorse and horror.

Kai is dead. I killed him.

My head was filled with images of him, lying lifeless and bleeding, his body in a million pieces. His words echoed within, shattering whatever else was left in me.

I'd give you my heart if yours stopped beating. I'd take an arrow for you. I'd pull you out of every nightmare as long as I lived.

I'm here. And I'm not going anywhere.

His strong arms around me. His rare smile like a precious gem. His soft murmurs. The way his eyes softened when he looked at me, like I was the one good thing in his life.

The door to my cell opened, creaking on its hinges, letting flickering light from the torches in the corridor pour in. A tall elf with long dark hair tied up in a ponytail and dressed in a floor–length cloak that covered anything else she was wearing stepped in front of me, tilting her head as she looked down on me. "Hello."

I glared up at her through my lashes. Her mental barriers were too strong for me to penetrate them.

"You can't get inside my head," the woman said. "I'm a Mind Muse. I was sent down here because I owe someone a favor. Rowan is irritating, at times. But I side with the winning team. So," she explained. "I am going to bring forward your memories, the ones that hurt the most. This isn't personal, really. Rowan has a plan, and this is my end of it."

She reached out her hands and pressed her icy fingers to my temples as I thrashed my head from side to side, hissing, "Don't touch me!" She did her best to hold on to me, but I wouldn't let her. "Hold still!" she growled, but I bit her wrist instead. She screamed, letting go of me and buckling over her hand, muttering and groaning in pain. Rowan burst through the door, demanding, "What is going on?"

"SHE BIT ME!" the woman screamed. "I'm not doing this unless you get control over her! Look at me, I'm bleeding!"

Rowan stared down at me, his eyes wild with fury. Then he slammed his hand over my head into the beam, his nose an inch from mine. "Tala, I'm not going to say this twice. Hold still, and let Fey do what I've asked her to do. I need to enlighten you."

"Don't say my name," I spat, even as my body quaked with fear. But I wouldn't show them I was afraid.

Rowan's eye twitched, and I felt the rage pouring out of him. He straightened and stepped out into the corridor, then returned with a blunt iron mace. He hefted it, then slammed it into my left leg, snapping my femur. I cried out in agony, buckling over, and my vision blackened at the edges. Stars clouded my sight, the pain threatening to take me under, and I opened and closed my mouth, unable to take in air.

Rowan dropped the mace and knelt in front of me, gripping my chin in his hands and squeezing my cheeks, his nails digging in, turning my head so I was forced to look him in the eye. "I'm sorry. But I need you to understand. Enlightenment is what you need."

He let go of me roughly and stood, taking his place in the corner. "She won't give you any more trouble, Fey."

I trembled, grimacing in pain, and if it weren't for the chains keeping me bound to the beam, I would have fallen to the floor completely. I'd had a lot of pain before, but the pain from my broken bone was the most intense agony I'd ever experienced, leaving me unable to breathe.

Fey crouched and placed her fingers on my temples once more, and this time, I was in too much pain to fight. A moment later, I felt a surge in my mind, and I was whisked from one agony to another.

Chapter Fifteen

Kai

L ove is like a beating heart, and even when yours stops, when death comes knocking at the door, Love keeps you fighting. Because when you love someone, you're fighting for more than just you.

My ears rang, and I couldn't hear anything except the high pitched frequency in my head. I blinked ash and grime from my eyes, my uneven breaths wheezy and painful, making me feel as if I were being rubbed raw with sand paper from the inside. My vision was black at the edges, and I could hardly see through the red tinge. *Blood?*

I lifted my hand, flexing my fingers and touched my forehead, then my chest. Both stained my hand scarlet. I dropped my hand to my side, my energy spent from the small movement.

I tried to swallow, to cry out, but I couldn't. Blood trickled from my mouth. I drifted between life and death, my consciousness like a draining balloon, and I couldn't tell whether or not I was unconscious or awake. But I must have woken again because when I opened my eyes again, I could hear Mira's voice somewhere far, far away.

"Great Gamble! Guys! Over here! It's Kai." Then, *"Kai! Kai, can you hear me?"*

I was certain it was a hallucination or a dream, because I couldn't see her, and her voice sounded so echoey and distant, like she was calling out to me from deep inside a cave or a tunnel.

"Kai. Kai, come on. Fight. If not for yourself, then for Tala and Aidilane."

Tala. Something had happened. . .I couldn't think.

Then I heard Aidilane's wail. *"Oh Kai. . .KAI!"* My body suddenly racked with pain.

Mira. *"No, Aidilane, don't. Let go of him. It won't wake him, you'll only do more damage. Oliver! Felix! Over here! Hurry!"*

Everything faded again.

I choked, coughing painful gasps. "Easy, you need to drink, it'll ease the pain." Aidilane sat beside my bed on a stool, supporting my head in her hand and lifting a cup to my lips with her other.

I pushed her hand away, wincing as pain came from a million different places. The sleep tent walls spun around me, making me unable to focus my eyes on anything, and I couldn't keep my head up. "W–What–" I broke into a fit of coughs, wheezing and gasping as the pain became profusely worse.

"Don't try to speak or move," Aidilane said, her voice tight with worry. "I'll tell you what happened. Just lie back and try to breathe."

I closed my eyes, grimacing. Aidilane was silent for so long that I opened my eyes again to look at her. Tears streaked her cheeks as her wavering gaze held mine. Then she stood abruptly and spun so that her back was to me. Her shoulders shuddered.

"I'll tell him," Mira volunteered quietly from the entrance to the tent. "Go and get something to eat, Aidilane. You've been in here all night."

Aidilane shook her head. "But–"

"Go. It's okay. I'll take care of him. Wash up and eat, then you can come back."

"Okay," Aidilane whimpered. Then she slowly padded outside.

Mira came to my bedside, sat down on the stool while I fought the nausea rising in me. "It's difficult for her. Seeing you like this." She paused. "I had a dream, and it told me that there was a bomb underneath our tent. This tent. And then the explosion woke me. For a horrifying moment, I thought that I was dead. That our tent had blown up and we all were gone. But when I came to my senses, I sat up and woke Oliver. Told him about the dream. We found the bomb and he diffused it. And that was when we heard the explosion, from the tree where you were keeping watch for the night."

I squeezed my eyes shut and open again. "I. . .I–" I wheezed in a breath. "I d–don't. . . remember."

"That's probably a good thing," Mira murmured. "The damage is pretty bad, Kai. And I'm not talking about the tree."

"T–Tala," I said.

Mira was silent for a long moment. I managed to turn my head to look at her, and she held my gaze. "She's gone. So is Rowan. They were gone when I woke up."

I turned away, clenching my teeth, hardly able to form a thought.

"We both knew it would happen, and she wouldn't listen," Mira said. "They took her. I don't know where."

I tried to sit up. "I–I need to g–go. . .find her."

"No, do not, Kai." Mira kept me from sitting up. "It's going to be okay. Lie back down. You need to heal. You wouldn't last five minutes on your feet. You've got burns all over you, and shrapnel from the explosion. . ."

I looked down, then. Pieces of metal were sticking up out of my chest, blood trickling from around them. Burns, first and second degree, were a patchwork mess on my body. From the pain on my neck and shoulders, I guessed it wasn't much different. Stars danced in my vision, and then I swirled into the darkness.

"No, Aidilane. We can't remove them." Oliver's voice.

"He's going to die of infection if we don't!" Aidilane cried.

"And he'll bleed out if we do." Mira's voice. "He can fight an infection, but he can't fight death."

I groaned. "Did y–you. . . find Tala?"

They all looked at me. Aidilane's eyes softened. "You're awake."

"D–Did you–"

"No," Mira answered me. "We have no way of knowing where she is. We don't know where to start looking. We're focusing on helping you heal, but–"

"N–No," I interrupted. "Not me. . .find her."

Oliver, Mira, Aidilane, and Val all looked down on me, exchanging glances, their faces canvases of worry and anxiety. Oliver tilted his head, adjusting his glasses. "Look man, you're finally somewhat stable, you need to focus on breathing. I think the shrapnel is penetrating your lungs."

"You should drink something, Kai," Aidilane held a cup to my lips. "You need hydration. And herbs to help the pain."

I pushed her hand away. "No, I need to find Tala. They could be h–hurting her."

"Kai, please, you need to rest. You need to heal. Please *heal*," Aidilane sobbed. "I can't lose you!"

I searched everyone's eyes frantically, wildly trying to get an ally. But they all just stared at me as if I were on my deathbed. But I refused to be. I couldn't die until Tala was safe. Until I knew she was okay. Until then, I was just fine.

I sat up, turned, and set my feet on the ground, my jaw clenched and my vision filled with stars from the pain. But I didn't care. Oliver and Aidilane took hold of my shoulders, trying to ease me back into the bed, but I wouldn't let them. "I'm warning you," I threatened. "L–Let go of me."

Wisely, they let go of me, but they didn't move away. Mira's gaze was sympathetic as she placed a hand on my knee. "Listen, Kai. Its–"

"Don't," I growled, interrupting her. "Don't t–tell me that it's going to be okay. Because right now, it isn't. And it isn't going to be until Tala is safe." I had already made up my mind. I wasn't going to lie here and do nothing while Tala was in the hands of Rowan.

I stood, swaying, but managed to stay upright. "Don't try to stop me. I'm going. With you or without you."

They didn't move. Aidilane's watery red eyes were a mixture of worry and fear. "Kai, please don't. You'll die. And you can't help Tala if you're dead."

I wasn't going to die. Not until *Tala was safe.* I wouldn't let myself die until then. I took a step forward, letting the thought of Tala drown out the pain. Oliver shook his head, warning, "Kai, you're a smart elf, you know you need to lie down. If you don't," he paused, swallowing hard, his brow sweaty with nervousness, "Then I'll make you. So that you live past this."

I held his gaze, satisfied when my dark look made him take a step back. Val held out her hands to me. "Kai, we *will* force you if you don't lie down. It's for your own good."

When I didn't do as they told, Mira and Val came closer and reached out to take hold of me, but I already had the dwam flute in my shaky hands. I played the lowest note, not wanting to hurt them. They stopped, swayed, and then slowly dropped to the ground one by one, their eyes rolling back in their heads, their breaths deep with sleep.

"I'm sorry," I rasped. "But I have to go find her."

Outside, Evian, Navy, and Felix were all unconscious, too, lying on the wet grass. I stumbled past them and out of camp, where Spiritwolf emerged from the undergrowth, looking anxious and whining urgently. "Where d—did they take her?" I asked. "Show me."

She hurried off into the trees, weaving a path for me to follow.

I'm coming, Tala. I'm coming.

Chapter Sixteen

Jala

*T*here are many things that make us who we are. Some things we're proud of... Others, not so much.

And when we're in the midst of despair, hope seems far off. Maybe even impossible, and answers are unreachable. Darkness closes in, and it's so much easier to just let go. To give in to which plagues us. To let it consume us. To let yourself fade.

But hope, and answers, they may be just out of reach. Like a rope over water to hold on to, to keep you from drowning. Sometimes, you just need someone to throw it to you.

Still, you must be willing to grab it.

I gasped, coming back to the present as Fey let go of me. The pain of my broken leg took over again, but it was next to nothing compared to the terror the past had just brought me. I opened and closed my mouth, willing the tears back into my head, but they wouldn't listen. My heart raced.

"Please," I begged, my voice hardly a whisper. "Stop."

Rowan uncrossed his arms, letting his hands fall to his sides. "Thank you, Fey."

"Yep," she replied pleasantly. "Is that all I can do for you?"

"I think I've gotten the results I needed. But," he added, "Wait a moment. There might just be one more thing." My head lolled against my chest, and my damp hair stuck to my sweaty face. He crouched down in front of me. "Tala, that was. . .horrible."

The tone of his voice surprised me. Compassionate, sympathetic, caring. I slowly met his gaze as he went on. "Tala, I'm sorry. I'm sorry I had to put you through that again. But I needed it fresh. So that you would understand why I'm doing this."

"Understand?" I cried. "How could you possibly expect me to *understand?*"

He brushed the side of my face with the back of his hand. "You carry the weight of all of that. It has changed you into someone who is always afraid. Always on edge. Always hiding. You flinch at the slightest sound or touch. You grip the hilts of your daggers until your knuckles turn white. Nightmares plague you, stealing your rest. Anger boils beneath your skin, even if you won't admit it. You feel unworthy of love because of all those years as a child by yourself, fending for yourself in the bitter cold, starving, lonely. You can't trust anyone, because the second you turn, you're certain they'll plunge a knife into your back. The feelings you bottle inside are too much to bear, so you let yourself go numb. The only thing that keeps you going is the need to move. Anything but to sit still with your memories, thoughts, and pain. You always have to be ready. Always be prepared for the worst." He paused, his eyes soft like lavender. "I know I betrayed you. I killed Kai. I know you want to slit my throat– you'd have every right to. But Tala, I didn't do all this to hurt you. It was inevitable, but I regretted every step of the way. I did it because I can help you. Don't you want the pain to stop?"

I was silent for a long moment, but even before I said it, I knew the truth. I was more sure of that than anything. I just wanted it all to end. "Yes," I whispered as a tear traced my cheek.

Rowan wiped it from my face gently. "I can make it stop. Fey can erase your memories. You'll never remember anything that happened. You'll never have another nightmare or flashback. You'll never be afraid again. You'll have a fresh start. You'll have your innocence again. You can be happy, truly happy, without the pain of the past and the fear. You'll be a new person. A *better* person."

The tears came heavy, then. I sobbed, the too good to be true fantasy that Rowan was lying before me drawing me in. Pulling me, calling me, like the dragon nestled inside me. I felt her consciousness stir a little, almost like a warning. But I clung to the realization that all this could be over. I could just let go. I could be *free.*

The prophecy repeated once more in my head.

Savior of the Kingdoms wide

The King's Wolf will face a divide

Savior she may be

But much cost she will pay

Darkness, pain, and past

She'll lose her way

Unless she airs on the side of caution

The way she walks will lead to destruction

Savior she will be

But she must be careful not to lose herself in the process, see

And a small voice inside me said, *Sabian, what about Sabian? And Kai?* But I didn't care. And Kai was dead. I didn't care if I lost myself anymore. What *was* there to lose? This broken, messy, hollow excuse for a girl? An outcast princess born of a criminal with the Demise? I had always fought for someone, always had missions to complete for the King, always had a duty. But for once, I didn't care about my duty to anyone. I was just so tired. So utterly tired of fighting.

I was holding onto a branch over water, holding on with strength I didn't have anymore. Holding on was doing more harm than good, making my hands raw and bloody.

"Just say the word," Rowan said softly.

"Do it," I rasped, pleading, "*Please.*"

He smiled. "Fey." She took his place in front of me again, placing her fingers on my temples, and I let go of the branch, plunging into the calm water beneath.

Chapter Seventeen

Kai

Can't give up. Can't give up. Cannot. Give. Up.

For her.

I staggered through the forest behind Spiritwolf. She had slowed down enough for me to keep up, but we were moving at a swift pace despite my injuries and the metal shrapnel in my chest. The adrenaline kept most of the pain at bay, making me near delusional. But I wasn't so delusional that I didn't realize that, so I figured that was a good sign.

The trees whirred past me and time didn't exist. I felt like I was moving through water. It could have been four days or four hours, but before I knew it, we were standing outside a fortress. It was the old summer palace for the elven royal family. It was five stories high, and

I assumed there was a basement with a holding cell for just—in—case situations.

Spiritwolf stopped just inside the woodline and turned to me, her eyes pleading. I understood her message.

Rescue my girl.

I slipped through the shadows, being sure not to be seen by any of the guards that were posted by every door. They didn't think they'd have any trouble out in the middle of the forest, I presumed, because the amount of security was pathetic. I found an open window on the first floor and pushed it open far enough for me to crawl inside. It was a dark office with no occupants. I stepped into the corridor and headed down the hall without a sound.

Finally, I found the door that led to the holding cells downstairs. Two guards dozed in front of it, and I knocked them unconscious before they even woke up, gently setting them on the floor so as to not make a sound.

Then I went downstairs, and cautiously turned a corner into the cold corridor. No one was there. It was suspiciously quiet, eerily unguarded. Still, I drew one of my blades. Each holding cell that I passed was empty, but as I turned another corner, I felt drawn to a certain cell. I followed the instinct to the last cell and found the door unlocked. I pushed inside.

A beam was in the center of the cell, with chains and cuffs lying on the floor near it. A small candle flickered in one corner, illuminating the room just enough for me to see Tala lying in the farthest corner, her leg at a gruesomely awkward ankle. She lay on her side, facing me and shivering, grimacing in pain. Her face was pale, and her eyes were almost. . .lifeless.

"Tala?" I stumbled toward her, kneeling beside her. "Tala, I'm here."

She stared at me, confused and hollowed out. "I–Is that my name? Who are you? You seem kind. You look hurt, there's metal–" she paused to wince, "-in your chest."

My stomach dropped. I pulled her up into my lap gently, cradling her head and shoulders, careful not to move her leg. "Tala, what's the matter? What did he do to you?"

Her eyes went unfocused. "I don't remember."

My heart skipped a beat. "What do you mean?"

She smiled, eerily relaxed. "I don't remember anything. Why do you look so afraid?"

Panic rose in my throat, making the edges of my vision dance with stars. "Great gamble. . .they wiped your memory." I pulled her closer, my breath catching, and I struggled to stifle a sob. "Tala, you *have* to remember!"

She thought about it for a moment, then whispered, "I'm not sure I want to. I. . .I think I wanted this."

I stared at her, realization hitting me. "Oh Tala. . ." I realized then how calm she seemed. Her eyes concentrated solely on me instead of darting around. She didn't fidget, didn't flinch at my touch, and her body was completely relaxed apart from the pain from her broken leg. She was so. . .peaceful.

However, her eyes were empty of the glow they usually contained, and they reminded me of a newborn's freshly opened eyes– untouched, unscarred– her innocence completely restored. Blissfully ignorant.

But however much my heart ached for her, I knew it wasn't good. "Tala," I said gently, "Listen, *really* listen. The past. . .hurts. It's like a thorn bush, and every time you reach in to deal with it, to cut it out, it cuts you and pierces you, making you bleed. So you pull back. You push it down, forcing it away, but it always comes back to bite like a venomous adder. You think you've escaped it, but the thorns just keep growing thicker, keep wrapping tighter. There are things you wish you could forget, and things you regret–" I choked on my words and paused to swallow, then continued. "And as much it hurts, without your past, you aren't you. You're just a hollow shell. You don't have your experiences– the good and bad– to make up your personality, your skills, your quirks, your knowledge. . .*you*. Your memories, experiences. . .those are what create your soul. They are what make *you*. And there is strength, Tala, in the pain you've endured. What didn't kill you did *not* make you stronger– you became stronger by fighting in spite of the pain. You developed your strength, your heart, by pulling yourself up. By saving yourself."

I brushed a strand of her hair out of her damp face. "You made it, Tala. You raised that little orphan into a beautiful, capable, strong young woman. You fought through the starvation, the loneliness, the fear, the pain– for her. For the girl in my arms. You protected her, fed her, cared for her when there was no one else. You made her into the woman she is today. The pain, the past. . .it didn't break her. Because she– you– kept going. You cracked over and over again, but you always got back up. And I–" I sucked in a deep breath, letting a tear slide from my eye. "I thank you for that. Because I wouldn't have my best friend if you didn't." I held her as if she was my whole world. I gently touched her cheek, and she leaned into my touch instead of flinching away. I smiled down at her sadly. "You're tired now. You've been fighting so long, and taking another step seems impossible. But you brought that girl to me. You do not have to fight this on your own anymore. You *can* take care of yourself. But I've simply joined in."

She gazed up at me, her pupils wide. "You *have* to remember," I urged. "I've got demons, you've got scars. You might think your story is dark, hopeless. . .but it's yours to tell. The past and your experiences may have shaped you, but you are in control of your story now. It's yours to tell. Stay in the light, Tala. Don't let the shadows sweep you away like I have." A deep breath. "I will be with you– I'll be here. I'm fighting for you, Tala. I won't let go." I set my jaw, determined. "I may not be able to ease your pain. But," I added, holding out my palm and forming a tongue of fire, "I can light up the dark for you."

The flames danced in her eyes, turning her eyes into flickering honey.

"So come back," I commanded. "Come back to me, Stalkingwolf. The world still needs you."

Her eyes went blurry, and her focus on me shifted to something I couldn't see. She winced, squeezing her eyes shut with a whimper. Six long, shaky breaths later, she whispered, "What. . ." She opened her eyes and for a moment, she didn't comprehend what was going on. Then her gaze focused and her breath sped up. "Kai? Kai!" She surged into me, making me grunt in pain, wrapping her arms around my neck, sobbing into my shoulder. "You're alive! I thought you were. . ." She pulled back, registering my injuries, and her face dropped. "Great gamble– Kai, how in the world did you survive? Better yet, how did you get in here?"

She examined my burns and the shrapnel, her face a mixture of horror and guilt. "I–I'm so sorry–" she gasped. "I didn't listen to you. . .I denied it. All of it. But you were right, a–and now–"

"It's okay," I stopped her. "It's *okay*. Love can blind us. But I'm fine. Spiritwolf guided me here. There weren't many guards."

"I thought I killed you," she whispered, her eyelids heavy. "And you're so hurt. With wounds like these. . .that explosion–"

I put a finger to her lips. "Shh. Mistakes are part of life. What matters is that you're okay. That lickspittle broke your leg." Hatred filled me.

Tala swallowed hard. "I was fighting the Mind Muse. He. . ." she swallowed, wincing. "He wanted me to stop fighting. After the Mind Muse resurfaced my past, I. . . didn't see a point in fighting anymore. I asked them to erase my memory. . .I begged them. I begged them, Kai. I'm a coward."

"No, you're just tired." I looked at her leg, letting the sight fuel me for my next confrontation with Rowan. "Can you heal it?"

Tala's jaw was clenched in pain. "I won't be able to until you set it."

"Set it?" I asked. "I've put dislocated joints back in place before, but I've never set a broken bone."

"There's a first time for everything, right?" Tala grimaced. "Besides, we can't get out of here with me like this. And you can't either. You may not realize it because of the adrenaline, but your body can't handle those injuries much longer. I need to heal you, but I can't do that until *I'm* healed, so yes. Set my bone, Kai."

I positioned myself, my heart racing. "If you make a sound, they'll come running."

She squeezed her eyes shut tight. "I won't."

She did.

As soon as I snapped the bones into place, she cried out in agony. I leapt to cover her mouth and held her tight until she stopped. She was shaking, but her color was returning to her complexion rapidly as she started to gradually mend the bones. I felt flushed with relief. But my rush of adrenaline started to fade, replaced by utter exhaustion and pain. I slumped forward, buckling over the shards in my chest, stifling a cry of my own. Tala supported me enough to lean back against the beam, my breath coming in shallow rasps.

Now with a clearer head, Tala examined the shrapnel once more, biting the inside of her cheek. "If I pull these out you'll–"

"Bleed to death," I forced out between clenched teeth. "And if they stay in, I'll die of infection– I know. The others told me. They tried to keep me from going after you, but I still went. I couldn't–" I paused to wheeze in a breath, "-couldn't abandon you."

"Great gamble," Tala hissed, her voice panicky. "Foolish. You shouldn't have–"

I took her hand. "I am right where I need to be."

She took a deep breath, nodding mostly to herself. "Okay. Okay. . .I'll take them out one by one and heal each before you lose any more blood." She experimentally, gingerly, touched one of the shards, the smallest one. Then, after counting to three, she yanked it free.

I doubled over, feeling close to vomiting as she closed the wound before much blood was spilled. But the last three pieces wouldn't budge, as much as she pulled and wiggled them. I nearly passed out from the pain, so she stopped. "They're too deep."

"I'll be fine. We need to get out of here." We managed to get to our feet, but we leaned heavily on each other like half–chopped trees as we headed out of the cell and into the corridor. We limped past the cells and then struggled up the steps. Stumbling down the hall of the first floor, we neared the exit.

"Damn you, Kai."

Rowan stepped out from around the corner in front of us, his face twisted with hardly controlled rage. "You're supposed to be dead."

"Sorry to disappoint," I rasped.

His eyes darkened. "See, I was hoping that Tala would walk up those steps unaccompanied– on my side of this charade. But here you are." Guards surrounded us as he continued. "You are like an incessant *flea*. You just won't die. But I have news for you– she chose *me!*"

"No," Tala hissed. "I was blinded by your charm. Mesmerized by something that was too good to be true, and I knew it. But instead of listening to Kai, I–" She stopped, her jaw clenching. "I never should have trusted you."

"That's right, you shouldn't have," Rowan spat. "But you did. And now Kai has three highly explosive pieces of a bomb in his chest." He held up a remote, a detonator, and tilted his head. "This look familiar?" he asked Tala.

Her face went pale, and she whispered, "What?"

Rowan smiled. "Yes. That bomb that went off was made of multiple smaller ones. Only a few went off in the tree. The others. . ." He nodded at me. "Well, you see where they ended up."

My blood went cold, and I felt Tala go unsteady against me. "That's right," Rowan noticed. "I am in control here. Tala, step away from him. And Kai, kneel. Don't you think about using your fire element– it'll make the explosives go off."

"No," Tala growled. "*No.*"

"Yes!" Rowan shouted, making Tala flinch. I held her tighter. "*Yes,* you *will.* Because if you *don't,*" he swore icily, "that metal in Kai's chest will explode. And this time, he'll *really* be dead."

We stood there, frozen against each other, both as helpless as hatchlings. Rowan shook with rage and yelled, "NOW!"

Tala held my gaze as she let go of me, stumbling back. Two guards took hold of her arms, yanking her back as Rowan stepped closer to me, holding out the remote threateningly. As he did, the pain in my chest sharpened, making me double over and cry out. Tala pleaded, "Stop!"

"On. Your. Knees," Rowan hissed.

I fell to my knees, clutching at my chest. Guards roughly gagged me and pulled me back to my feet after taking my weapons and tying my hands behind my back. Rowan's breath was hot on my face as he declared, "Back to the mage scientists with you. I'm sure you will be a good donation to their cause."

"You were working with the mages this whole time?" Tala asked. "What about those soldiers at the harbor? Was that just a mirage to make us trust you?"

Rowan grinned. "Actually, I'm sort of the middle man for both. But I pick and choose depending on the situation and what each party has to offer me. I have resources, so do they. It's mutually beneficial, and in the end, we all get what we want."

"And what's that?"

Rowan stared at Tala for a long moment. "The world is a puppet. Its fate lies in the hands of the one holding the strings."

"Power," Tala translated. "This is all about power? What about all the lives that have been taken, all the lives who have been destroyed? All for a hand in power?"

"Sacrifices must be made," Rowan chided her. "You of all people should understand that."

Tala blinked, her breath catching. Of course he was referring to the prophecy, but why was she so taken aback by his words?

Rowan stepped close to her, taking her face in his hands as she glared up at him. I fought against the guards holding me. "Dear Tala," Rowan said with icy calm. "I had such big plans for you. For *us*. But now you will simply be what you were in the beginning– a pest in the grand scheme of things, in need of extermination. Kai will measure his stakes with the mages, and you will be turned in to the crown like he was supposed to do in the first place. They can decide what to do with you, the mages get their experiments, and I get paid. A win win, really."

He signaled to the guards and they started dragging me away down the hall, while I grunted and thrashed. Tala cried, "No! Rowan, please!"

The last words I heard him say were, "You would have been a valuable asset, Tala, being an heir to the throne of the kingdom my employers are trying to overtake. You could have made things easier for both your people and mine. Less blood would have been shed. Instead, you chase after something you have no hope of finding. Now the Moonland Kingdom royal family has a prisoner of war– Princess Tala of Highland. Now they could use you as leverage, or they could kill you. Choice is theirs."

Then they were out of earshot, and the guards hauled me up a flight of stairs and into a cold room. It was frigid and sterile, with a metal table in the center. The guards forced me onto it and cuffed my wrists and ankles to it, keeping me in place and vulnerable. Then they took off my gag, and left the room.

I lay there, trying to fight my bonds and my mind going feral. Rowan would pay for this. He would pay for his betrayal, for breaking Tala's heart and her leg, for blowing me to hell, and for *this*. All of *this*.

Eventually, I gave up trying to get free. It was useless, and I was in pain. So much pain. If I fought against the cuffs any longer, I'd lose consciousness from the agony. Every breath felt like I was being ripped open from the inside out. I lay my head back, trying desperately to think of a way out of this. I couldn't use my fire, at least not until I knew for certain that Rowan was lying about that, too. Until then, I couldn't take any chances. I didn't want to blow up the whole building with Tala in it. I was beginning to regret using the flute on the Renegades. Sure I'd gotten here, but now what? In my feverish haze and blind desperation to rescue Tala, I hadn't exactly thought of what to do if things went wrong. Foolish was right. But I couldn't regret coming here, as much as things had gone off the rails. Because at least I was here with her. She wasn't suffering alone.

Tala, I thought, hoping she'd be listening.

A moment later, I heard her in my mind. *They're taking me to the palace in the morning, but I think I have a plan. Hang in there, Kai.*

Are you okay?

A moment of silence, then, *Are any of us? You're the one with bombs in your chest.*

And you're the one with a broken leg.

It's almost healed. I've been doing it slowly so I don't pass out. But it's nearly mended. Where are you?

Second floor, third door on the left.

Okay. Are they. . .?

I'm fine. No one else is in here yet.

I'm sorry, Kai. I should have listened–

Stop saying you're sorry, I scolded her. *How could I hold this against you after what I did at the Nightingale? You forgave me. I forgive you.*

I sensed her relief. *Thank you. I can't imagine a future without your friendship. So don't die, please.*

I don't plan on it.

Good.

A mage opened the door and stepped inside, shutting the door behind him. It was the same mage from the camp, the one that had done experiments on me before. Dr. Lanstov.

He slapped on latex gloves and smiled at me. "Hello again. I really didn't appreciate that you burned down my tent and all my lab supplies. But lucky for us, I was able to save that blood I took from you and concentrate it. With you, it really is possible to give another your abilities. It is truly incredible. Now, I still need some more data before it is proven, including more of your fire to test, but I can't do anything before I remove those from your chest."

He opened a cabinet and rifled through it. I growled, "Don't touch me."

"I can't do that, I apologize. If I don't, then I'll get fired, and then I'll be homeless because this is basically the only thing I'm good at. Besides, if I don't take those out, you'll die." He found what he was looking for– a syringe and a little bottle of something. He held the bottle upside down and stuck the needle into it, filling the syringe with the liquid. Then he moved to my side and slid the needle into my arm.

"Anesthesia," he explained. "So the pain doesn't kill you."

Immediately, my vision began to blur and my head lolled.

I wasn't sure when I fell asleep, but when I came to, the drowsiness was so strong that I was unable to move.

"Yeah, you're going to be out of it for a while," Dr. Lanstov said. "Be grateful I used the anesthesia. Those pieces were lodged in your lung. But I was able to remove them and repair the damage. I also treated your burns. You'll be of no use to me sick with infection or dead."

I groaned. The pain had faded into an intense soreness, but it wasn't so bad. Three large incisions were where the shrapnel had been, and thick black stitches neatly kept them closed. The skin around them was swollen and red, but other than my burns, I wasn't in too bad a shape, except for the fact that my head felt like it was in the clouds.

"You've only been out for about three or so hours," Dr. Lanstov told me. "I see the brand has healed fairly well." He began muttering to himself about ridiculous mandatories and rules.

I blinked the fog in my brain away, trying to return to my senses. As much as I hated being here, I was relieved that I didn't have to worry about having explosives in my chest, controlled by Rowan. Now, he had a little less leverage.

I flexed my hands and my feet to get the feeling back in my extremities and hoped that whatever Tala's plan was, it would happen soon. I also prayed to whatever god might hear me that Rowan wouldn't lay a hand on her. That she would get out of this alive and unharmed.

"Don't make me burn through these cuffs again," I warned.

Dr. Lanstov looked up from the syringe he was meddling with with an amused smile. "Right. There is no burning through those cuffs."

I attempted it nonetheless, but he was right. The material wouldn't melt, wouldn't burn. It didn't even singe or char. I let out a frustrated growl. "Do you have no ounce of guilt, strapping a living being to a metal table and doing who—knows—what to him for the sake of your evil plans?"

"Why should I be guilty?" he asked innocently. "I just saved your life."

"Only so you could use me."

He wrestled with the packaging of another syringe. "The supplies here are unbelievable. Who do they think I am? An intern?" He made a frustrated screeching sound and then ripped the packaging open. "Ah. Finally. Absolutely unbelievable," he muttered.

He placed an IV in my arm and began pumping something into me. He explained, "This isn't evil. This is development. Doing this will enhance our world."

"You mean to enhance your power."

He shrugged. "Depends."

I glared at the tube in my arm. "So what are you pumping into me?"

"A chemical. I'll get some data depending on how your body reacts to it."

"Chemicals," I repeated. Great.

"Indeed. But don't worry, the reaction will be molecular. You shouldn't feel anything." He drew some blood and brought it over to the counter and began testing it. After, he made a little gasp sound and then rushed out into the corridor. He returned a moment later with another mage and showed her the vial of blood that was now the color of lavender– a chemical reaction? The other mage grinned and squealed excitedly. "The general will be so pleased!"

"Yes," Dr. Lanstov replied proudly. "In order for me to run more necessary tests and get things finalized, I need more resources. We need to get back to the palace. But first, help me with something, will you?"

"Sure."

They discussed another test and then both took position on either side of me. Dr. Lanstov held a cup of orange liquid to my lips. "Drink this."

"No."

He nodded to the other mage and gripped my head to keep me still and held my jaw to keep my mouth open while I tried to thrash and break free of her grasp. Dr. Lanstov started pouring the bitter rancid liquid into my mouth.

Tala's voice in my head startled me. *Kai!*

Tala, are you okay?

I am. The Renegades are here.

What?

Yes, are you ready? Can you get away?

I tried to keep myself from swallowing the liquid but Dr. Lanstov forced it down, making me gag and nearly choke. *Not exactly.*

A pause. *Kai, you have to. This won't work unless you get away.*

They're pretty set on keeping me here, Tala. Everything in here is fireproof. I can't get away.

The Renegades don't have a way to get you out from there. I've been transmitting to them, but–

Tala, it's okay. I coughed as the two mages stepped away from me and stared, looking for some kind of reaction. My eyes watered and I felt near vomiting. *I'll be fine. I also have a plan. Just get away from here. Go back to camp and I'll meet you there.*

But—

Just trust me. Please.

Another pause. *Okay.*

I coughed and spluttered, fighting the nausea and burn in my stomach. When I coughed, tiny pink droplets came up. Dr. Lanstov collected them and placed them under a microscope while I tried to recover. He and the other mage excitedly discussed their findings.

A moment later, I heard a slight rumble downstairs. Then came the shouting and the sounds of panic and fighting.

The mages exchanged concerned glances, their brows creased with anxiety. Tala's connection to my mind rippled, feeling different, but in a good way. As if something inside her had clicked, like a solved puzzle.

It wasn't long before the noise faded and disappeared completely. Dr. Lanstov and the other mage continued with their experiments, apparently not concerned enough to check and see what had happened.

Rowan burst into the room, looking as if he'd just seen a ghost, and leapt at me, dagger in hand.

"Hey!" Dr. Lanstov yelled, keeping the maniac from getting to me. "We still need him!"

"Yeah, yeah," Rowan grumbled. His murderous glare held mine. "She's a monster. A beast. And those Renegades blew up my cellar. Then she escaped with them after exploding a smoke bomb."

I barely managed to stifle a laugh. Whatever did he mean by 'she's a monster'? A beast? "You'll get what's coming for you in due time," I responded. "Don't be too disappointed that they didn't kill you."

"Sir," Dr. Lanstov interrupted our glaring match. "I need to move him to the palace. I need better resources, ones you don't have here."

Rowan sheathed his dagger. "Right. I'll escort you personally. Your general owes me payment anyway, and I'd personally like to make sure this particular elf gets where he needs to be without causing you any further trouble."

"Thank you, sir. When can we proceed–"

"Right now," Rowan declared. "We leave now, before those Renegades return for him and cause more hindrances. I'll go get the stagecoach prepared."

He left the room, and Dr. Lanstov rolled his eyes. "Elves are such self absorbed creatures."

"Indeed," the other mage agreed.

About an hour later, both mages were packed and ready to go, and the guards unlocked my cuffs and led me downstairs, then outside to the stagecoach. I could have easily taken them, but I forced myself to be patient. That was an assassin's main quality– his patience. I would wait for the opportune moment to strike, and not a moment sooner.

The anesthesia had long worn off by now, but I pretended I was still out of it. I let my head loll whenever I could, let my eyes stay droopy, and made my steps clumsy and unsteady. I needed them to think I wasn't much of a threat, so that they would treat me like I wasn't.

They shoved me up into the stagecoach by my arms. Rowan, Dr. Lanstov and his assistant sat inside the coach with me, along with the two guards that sat on either side of me. There were three other guards who sat out on the driver's seat. In total, there were eight of them.

As the coach swayed and bounced, I let myself move with it as if I couldn't keep my core stable. After a few minutes, I slowly leaned forward, my eyes closed.

"Great gamble, what exactly did you do to him, doctor?" Rowan asked, his voice thick with uncomfortable disgust.

"Between his injuries, the operation, and the experiments, his body is weak. The anesthesia and physical trauma. . .it takes a toll. But he won't cause any trouble like this."

"Well deserved. But, he won't vomit on us will he? He looks, well, sick."

Dr. Lanstov laughed. "I don't believe so. Even with the sun serum he didn't so I doubt he will now."

I groaned, fueling Rowan's anxiety. He scooted back as far as he could. "Are you sure?"

"Yes, sir."

"Stop calling me that. It makes me sound old."

"Yes, sir." A moment later. "Opps, sorry, sir–" A cough. "Sorry."

I let a few more minutes go by, and then I made myself go completely limp, falling forward onto the others. Then I started to shake uncontrollably, mimicking what Tala did when she used to have her seizures.

"He's seizing!" Dr. Lanstov exclaimed. "Stop the coach! Now! I need him alive!"

The coach rolled to a stop, and the guards carried me outside and laid me on the ground per the doctor's request. He began rummaging through his bag, no doubt searching for some kind of quick fix.

After a moment more of my violent shaking, I leapt up, simultaneously sliding one of the guard's swords from its sheath at his side. Dr. Lanstov stumbled back before he came into harm's way while I drove the sword into one of the guard's abdomen. Two others lunged at me, but I sidestepped and swept their feet from underneath them. A kick to one of their heads sent him unconscious, the other's leg I sliced.

I ran after Dr. Lanstov and knocked him to the ground, where he hit his head on a stump and slumped unconscious, bleeding. His assistant pulled out her wand, but I kicked it from her hand before she used the magic.

The last two guards lunged at me, nearly overwhelming me. But I sent one of their swords flying, and then blasted them with fire. I turned to find Rowan, the last one standing.

He twirled his sword. "Not so helpless after all. If you hadn't done it already I would have knocked that idiot scientist into a tree stump myself."

I charged first, and our swords clashed with a metallic *clang*. I went at it for a few moments, giving myself the satisfaction of fighting with this elf. But I had to get back to Tala.

I ended with an uppercut and sent his sword clattering to the ground, far out of his reach. Then I kicked him backwards, crashing him into the stagecoach, stunning him long enough for me to collect my personal blades from the coach and slice one of the horse's harness and reins free. I mounted him, pulled his mane back and jammed my heels into his flank, making him rear.

His front hooves came down on Rowan's left leg, and I heard the snap of his femur. He shrieked and doubled over into a ball on his side.

"Break her leg, I break yours." And then I shot the stagecoach with my fire and brought it up in flames before I galloped away.

The sun was low in the sky when I neared the Renegade's camp. I was exhausted and utterly drained, fueled only by the thought of Tala. I swayed on the horse, keeping firm hold of his mane to keep myself from falling off. But in all consideration, I was in good shape. Better tired than dying.

The first thing I saw was the tree. Or at least, what was left of it.

A black, charred hole in the ground lay where the lookout tree had stood. A few blackened branches lay scattered here and there, but otherwise, the tree was completely gone. The surrounding trees had charred trunks from the blast, and many of them had branches burned off as well as the undergrowth.

I was truly fortunate to be alive.

I entered camp and found everyone gathered around a fire, eating. They all had minor injuries– cuts and bruises– from the stunt they pulled. They all looked up when I rode in, and Tala leapt to her feet. "Kai!"

I got down from the horse as Tala ran to me, her leg healed. She threw her arms around me with relieved tears, nearly knocking me over. I buried my face into her shoulder and hair, breathing in her scent, and held her tight, afraid to ever let go.

I will never let you slip through my fingers ever again.

I know.

Chapter Eighteen

Tala

*P*ain creates monsters. It also creates poets, writers, and knights. Artists, musicians, dreamers, fighters. People who see the beauty in little things. Who find magic in sunsets, ripples, birdsong, and the gentle, or powerful, patter of rain. Butterfly wings, warm tea, and a deep, belly laugh. Those who smile the morning after crying themselves to sleep.

The people who walk with fearlessness; not in the absence of fear, but because they have walked through fire and come out the other side.

I threw myself into Kai's arms, my heart melting with relief. He pulled me tighter, burying his face into my shoulder.

I will never let you slip through my fingers ever again.

I know. But you might have to. The words pierced my heart, as if the inevitable things that I kept denying were creeping up on me.

I relished the feeling of his arms around me, his breath against the nape of my neck and all at once, I realized a million things, and they all crashed into me, nearly knocking the breath from my lungs. All too fast, too many in number for me to process them all. But the regret and guilt I bore for not listening to Kai and for falling for the enemy was drowned out by the realization that Kai didn't need to be an empath to know what I was feeling. He just knew. He knew *me*.

I also realized that everything Rowan had lied about. . .well, he'd lied about. Kai really *had* been in the tent with me after healing Spiritwolf. Rowan hadn't. He hadn't actually cared. He'd used me, and Kai kept telling me because *he* cared. He actually cared. And he had come after me after I had made the biggest mistake of my life. After Rowan, I vowed to never let down my walls for anyone ever again. But all along, Kai had been climbing them.

"Thank you," I murmured, pouring as much feeling and meaning into the simple words as I possibly could.

"Even through mistakes," Kai promised. "We stick together. That will never change."

"Thank you," I repeated. "Thank you Kai for not giving up on me even when I. . ."

"I'll never give up on you, Tala."

After another moment of holding each other, I pulled back and gave him a once over. "You're okay? The shrapnel is gone!"

He nodded, his mind not on what happened, but on me. "They removed them. Did a bunch of. . .things. But I'm okay."

My brows furrowed with worry. "Things?"

He waved it aside with a tired sigh. "They seem to think I'm the best lab rat around. I'd like to disagree."

He told me about how he escaped, and everything in between. He looked near collapsing with exhaustion. I laced my arm through his and led him over to the fire. "Sit. Eat. You need it."

He didn't argue, and while he ate, everyone filled him in on what happened, happily not addressing the fact that he had knocked them all unconscious with the dwam flute. They went over how they had blown up the cellar to get into the building to me, and how there was a small battle in whatever was left of the cellar.

Navy waved his hands excitedly. "And then Tala–"

I interrupted him with a cough. I wanted to be the one to tell Kai what had happened. It was. . .incomprehensible. I was struggling to understand that it really hadn't just been a crazy dream. But he wouldn't believe me unless I showed him.

I glanced over at Kai to find his eyes droopy and hardly holding on to his bowl. He looked close to falling asleep right there. I took his bowl and spoon and set them aside, then I pulled his arm around my shoulders. "Come on, up. You need to rest."

I left the others and helped Kai to the tent, where I helped ease him into the cot next to mine.

He pulled a blanket around himself, nestling into the pillow, letting out a deep breath. "I can't sleep. You know that."

He raised his brows as I lay beside him on his cot, propping myself up slightly with my elbow. "I do. But I think I can help with that, if you'd like. You need rest, Kai. Real rest. You said you'd pull me out of every nightmare as long as you lived. I'm saying I want to do the same for you, if you'll let me."

His tired eyes searched my gaze, but he stayed silent. So I placed my fingers on one of his temples, and he closed his eyes like I did. Just like I had the day I had pushed away his nightmares and memories, I calmed his heartbeat, his nerves. I took every part of his mind that was in pain and swaddled them with peace.

When I opened my eyes, he was asleep. Completely, deeply asleep for the first time in years. I lay there beside him for a long while, watching him. He had never looked so peaceful and serene before. I traced the worry lines at his brow, ran my fingers through his slightly curly hair, touched his pointed ear.

Great gamble. He was my best friend. He had seen me through my worst, and had given me my best moments. I couldn't imagine a future without him. And he made me feel safe, like no one else ever could.

But. . .was this feeling I had as I watched him sleep– what exactly was it?

My best friend, yes. But was it more than that?

The certainty that I would do anything to save his life. That I would have his back through anything. That I yearned for his gaze, for his touch. That the way he looked at me made me feel like more. That every waking moment I wanted to be held in his arms. That his embrace felt as if everything would be okay. Was that more than just friendship?

I didn't understand these feelings. I didn't understand why I was having them, what they were, or how to deal with them. But one thing I was sure of; these feelings I was more certain about than anything– whatever they were.

My dreams were scattered and chaotic, but most of them were my usual nightmares. King Rubarb's face, the voice of Queen Hersha, the sound of the lash. I tossed, turned, shivered, and whimpered in my sleep. Kai's voice woke me with a start. "Tala."

I was so tense my chest ached and my ears rang. But then Kai wrapped his gentle, strong arm around me, his steady heartbeat against my back and his body heat warming the chill in my bones, making my tense muscles relax. "Shh," he said firmly. "*You're safe.*"

I was only briefly aware of it before I fell into a deeper sleep without any more nightmares.

When I woke before dawn, his arm was still around me, like a shield of safety, his chest against my back, our breaths synchronized.

I lay there, trying to figure out what had woken me. For once, it wasn't my nightmares, and I had been deep asleep, completely relaxed and at peace with Kai. But something had woken me.

I reached out my mind, letting myself feel every one of the Renegade's minds. Everyone was still fast asleep in their cots, except for Mira.

I slid gently from Kai's cot so as not to wake him and pulled on my cloak as I padded outside into the gray dawn. Mira was sitting against a tree just outside of camp, hugging her knees. Anxiety and fear radiated from her like a flame, kicking me in the gut with such force that I nearly found it hard to breathe.

I crouched beside her. "Mira, what's the matter?"

She turned her ivy green gaze to mine, her lip trembling. "I had another dream."

I took her hands and cupped them in mine. "Do you want to tell me?"

She swallowed hard, staring off into the forest. "I–I'm not sure if I should. Tala, oh it was so awful!"

Her thoughts raced, and though I kept out of her head, I sensed that this had something to do with me. "Mira, you need to tell someone. Clearly, it's left you shaken. You shouldn't bear the burden on your own."

She looked at me as if I were breathing my last breaths. "Tala. . .y–you died."

My stomach clenched. "What? It's okay. Tell me."

She turned the color of snow. "We were in the cavern, or cell, where the dragon was. I saw her lying in chains, huge but weak and nearly dead. Were we all fighting mages, and then I turned and saw you w–with. . ."

I was certain I knew what was coming next, but I still took her face in my hands, my voice shaky. "Mira. Tell me."

"There was a sword. . ." her voice cracked. "And then you were bleeding and limp and–" she cut off suddenly, sucking in a breath. "You died."

I let go of her, ice tracing down my spine and denial drowning out everything else. "That doesn't mean it'll happen. We can avoid that. Change the future."

She shook her head, her eyes wide. "My dreams are never wrong. Never."

I swallowed the horrible taste in my mouth. Ever since the dragon had placed her consciousness within me, I knew deep down the inevitable. There was no avoiding it however much I wanted to.

I nodded, biting my lip. "Don't tell anyone," I pleaded. "Especially not Kai."

"You knew?" Mira asked, shocked. "You knew all along what would happen?"

I avoided her gaze, my breath shallow. "They can't know. Kai can't know. If it comes down to it, it can't be stopped. If he knows, then he'll do anything to keep it from happening."

Her eyes watered. "I can't just let you die. I won't."

"Yes, you will *if* it comes down to it," I told her. "Promise me. And promise me you'll keep Kai from stopping it. This isn't his burden to bear." Mira shook her head. I squeezed her hands. "*Promise* me. Please."

Her voice was impossibly small. "I promise."

I embraced her, trying to stay strong for her. "Thank you. I'm sorry, it's too much to ask of anyone. But if the mages are ever to be stopped, I can't get around it."

"Still," she said. "*If* it comes down to it. Until then, we will believe there is a way around it, like you said. We must believe."

I nodded, letting myself get pulled along with her current of hope and denial. "Sounds good to me."

We sat in silence together watching the sun rise. Orange, rose, and gold painted the sky like a mural of color with the occasional splash of light blue. Birds chirped announcing the arrival of day, and squirrels quarreled over their food.

"If Kai hadn't come for you," Mira broke the silence, "would you have died?"

I felt guilt pouring from her. "I don't know. But I would never have found myself after my memories were erased if it weren't for him, that's for sure."

"I'm sorry we didn't come right away," she apologized. "Kai was just so hurt and I knew he was going to die. I am certain the thought of you was the one thing that kept him alive. But I was sure that if we let him go after you, he wouldn't make it. I was going to go after you, I swear. I just wasn't sure how."

"Don't apologize," I chided her. "There is no reason for it. You and the others saved Kai's life. And you came. You got me out of there. Thank you."

Mira tilted her head. "Have you told him about what happened yet?"

I shook my head. "No. I plan to do it today. He needed to rest."

She smiled. "You should have seen him. On his deathbed, and all he cared about was finding you."

I gazed off into the trees, smiling to myself as I thought about his arm around me while we slept. "How did you know you cared for Oliver in a deeper way?"

Mira shrugged. "I just knew. It's something that just happens, against all odds. It's something that you just feel, both of you. You feel it in your stomach, your face, your hands, your heart– your soul, like a magnet. But even more so, I knew because I would do anything for him. And he'd do anything for me."

Butterflies fluttered in my gut. Kai had proven that over and over again, even when we were still near strangers. And I for him. Mira stared at me, her expression amused. "What?" I demanded.

"Another way I knew is that he filled my thoughts all the time. The first thing I thought of when I woke, and the last thing I thought of before I went to sleep at night." She raised a brow. "Want to know an observation that I've made?"

I nodded.

"In a fight, you two are lethal. But around each other, you melt like cream on a hot day."

I felt my face heat up.

"And I saw you in there," Mira continued. "Both of you actually asleep, actually at peace– in each other's arms."

I waved aside her comment. "Enough of this silly talk."

She grinned. "Fine." Then her expression turned serious. "How is the dragon?"

I sighed. "Growing weaker by the minute. I don't know how much longer she can hold on."

"We should come up with a plan and head to the palace as soon as possible."

"Yes, but," I added, "I think we should all take today to enjoy each other's company. Have a good time before we take on this mission. If it's my last–" I stopped. If it was my last day, I wanted to cherish it. I didn't want my last day to be spent fighting for my life. I wanted it to be with my friends. With Kai.

Mira nodded, understanding. "Okay. But remember, this isn't your last day. Neither is tomorrow. Not until it really comes down to it, okay?"

I nodded. "Okay. But remember, Mira. Don't let Kai stop it if it does. And if it happens. . .please tell my brother. I'd want him to know."

She nodded sullenly.

We headed back to camp to find the other girls, deciding to start off our day with a creek bath. Val, Navy, Oliver, Felix and Evian were eating breakfast and sharpening weapons. Kai and Aidilane stood just outside the supply tent, talking. Val looked up as we approached, asking, "So, what's the plan?"

"Not now," Mira told her. "We'll talk plans later tonight. Today we relax."

"Relax?" Evian exclaimed. "I was afraid you would never say those words." He happily marched back into the sleep tent with a yawn.

"Okay," Oliver shrugged. "I have enough munitions ready any way."

Mira invited Val to the creek with us while I went over to Kai and his sister. I interlocked my arm with Aidilane's and grinned at the two of them. "Good morning! Us girls are off to bathe. Kai, make sure the boys stay well clear of the creek until we return."

He smiled. "Oliver and I planned on going hunting. The others have their own occupations."

I let go of Aidilane briefly to embrace Kai. "How you feeling?"

"Much better. I forgot what its like to get decent sleep."

"Your wounds?" The burns on his face, hands and arms were beginning to heal, but I couldn't be sure about the others. Or where the shrapnel had been.

"You know already, don't you?"

"Yes, but I still want you to tell me."

"They're alright. Healing."

I pulled back from him and he let go of me, but I held on to his hand, closing my eyes. I felt for each burn, cut, and the sewn incisions where the shrapnel had been and all the internal bruising. The damage that the shrapnel had done to his insides and the affects the explosion had had on his lungs. I mended each one, weaving the damaged cells over with new ones until there was no evidence left of the explosion even on a molecular level.

I opened my eyes, smiling up at Kai. "Better?"

He held my gaze with his dark eyes, more relaxed without the pain. "Much."

Mira and Val jogged over. "Come on," Val said, taking my hand. "Let's go. I'm dying for a good dip in the creek!"

I laughed and followed them, Aidilane at my heels, surprised that the healing hadn't taken much of my energy. The creek was about a half mile from the camp, running through a thick copse of pines. We hung our clothes on the bushy branches of the trees to air out and waded into the water with only our underclothes, laughing and splashing each other. The crystal clear water wove around our knees and over the colorful rocks and pebbles, creating an illusion similar to a diamond, making it seem like the pebbles at the bottom danced.

We helped each other with washing our hair, using the soap bars that Navy had snagged from town, probably from an inn or bathing house. It was refreshing— I hadn't had a proper scrub in a while, and the water was cool, a wonderful thing in the summer heat. Val, Mira and Aidilane were beautiful elves. Aidilane with her luscious, wavy raven hair and her slender form. Val with her kinky, jet black, coily hair and curves. Mira with her silky, blonde hair highlighted by the sun, her sturdy hips, and graceful form. All of their muscles well developed. I felt self conscious in the midst of their beauty with my wiry limbs and many scars, my too long auburn hair, my freckles. But unlike among the women back at the palace, there was no judgement, no criticism. Mira, Val, and Aidilane treated each other and me like we were of equal beauty, and it made me feel at home.

Spiritwolf joined us at some point, splashing around in the water and lapping it up, her eyes wild with excitement. I was having such a good time that for a moment, I forgot about my worries. I was thankful that Kai had brought me back to myself. It was for the best. I had been blinded by my fear, ready to do anything to avoid dealing with it any longer.

But if Kai hadn't guided me back to myself, then I would be an empty shell serving Rowan. Just the thought made the bile rise in the back of my throat. Instead, I was here with my friends, my team. And we would face whatever came next together.

Chapter Nineteen

Kai

*T*wo *damaged people, trying to heal each other. It was love.*

"I'm no good at this, you know," Oliver complained

"I know." I stepped over a fallen log without a sound, while Oliver crunched and snapped twigs and leaves with every step. "That's why I'm teaching you."

"Teaching me?" Oliver repeated, panting. "I know how to hunt! I'm just not so good at it."

"You talk too much."

"What?"

"You talk too much. That's why you're no good at hunting."

"Oh. Well, I suppose you're right. I'm just more of a demolitions expert. I talk to myself sometimes, while I build things. But you didn't really need to know that." He laughed. "A lot of the time Mira helps me assemble my projects. We talk a lot. She tells me all about her childhood, and I tell her mine. What was your childhood like? Also, I think you're kind of dark. Like, mysterious. I know you're an assassin, but did you actually—"

I stopped and shot him a look. He swallowed hard. "Right. Sorry."

I slid an arrow from my quiver and guided Oliver's attention to the deer standing a few yards away. It was half hidden in a cluster of trees, so it took him a moment to spot it. It was a miracle Oliver's noise hadn't alerted it of our presence and scared it off. It was a doe. I set my arrow and drew back the string, aiming for the spot beneath the ribs so that with enough force, it would go through the lung and pierce the heart.

"Ready?" I whispered.

"Me? But you're—"

"I'm just here in case you miss the mark. Go on," I prompted. "Follow my line of sight and do what I'm doing."

Oliver fumbled around with his bow and then did his best to copy my stance and aim. "Do I—"

"Aim and release as you let go of your breath." My voice was hardly audible, but he seemed to have heard me. He took a deep breath and released the arrow. It soared and hit the deer square in the leg. In a heartbeat, I let my arrow fly, sending it into the heart of the creature. We headed over to it and pulled our arrows free. A clean kill.

"Good work," I congratulated him. "Just need to work on your aim."

"Really? Thanks!" Oliver exclaimed. "I didn't think you out to be a complimenting type."

"It wasn't a compliment. Just an observation."

Oliver laughed. "Fair enough."

We tied together evergreen boughs and placed the deer on it so we could drag it back to camp with ease. Although, I did most of the dragging. Just before we reached camp, Oliver stopped me with an outstretched arm, opening and closing his mouth nervously. I raised a brow. "Is there something you wanted to tell me?"

"Well," he stuttered. "I just wanted to say that I think Tala loves you."

I coughed, my face heating up, and pushed past him. "Right. Anything else?"

"Seriously." Oliver ran to catch up to me. "In case you haven't noticed, I thought I should let you know."

I whirled to face him. "Why?"

"Why?" He took a step back. "Well, I uhm. . .that's the sort of thing I'd want to know if I didn't realize it myself. And it's obvious you care about her. So I just thought that you'd like to know."

I let go of my breath with a quiet sigh. "She doesn't love me. She's not stupid." I led the way into camp, dragging the deer behind me.

After cleaning the deer, we set the meat aside. Felix offered to cook it, but we all decided the women would make a much better meal out of it than we could. Oliver told us in great detail about the seasoning Mira could make from all the ones Navy stole from town, and just his description made my mouth water. Yep, definitely leaving it up to the women.

Evian still napped in the tent, vibrating the walls of it with every snore. Felix challenged us to an archery contest, and we were still in the middle of it when the girls returned, their hair still dripping wet. They watched our little contest and laughed whenever one of us missed the targets. I hit the bullseye every time, and the selfish part of me hoped Tala noticed.

Then the girls prepared the meat, Mira adding her seasoning. They called me over with expectant expressions.

"Yes?" I asked.

"You know," Val wiggled her fingers, "do your thing."

"My thing?"

Aidilane laughed. "Can you cook the meat? It'll be faster than if we did it over a fire."

Tala crossed her arms, the corner of her mouth turning up. "Your *thing*."

I scoffed, shaking my head with a laugh. "So I'm your cooking spit now."

"Yep," Aidilane piped.

"Precisely," agreed Tala.

I sighed and got to work roasting the meat while the girls proved to the boys who were better archers. It seemed to take an eternity for the meat to cook all the way through, but I had to be careful not to burn it. When it was finished, Evian emerged mumbling about a "heavenly scent" and helped Felix and I slice the meat into reasonable pieces and dish them out.

I started a bonfire, reminding myself that this time, Rowan wasn't here. We ate and took turns telling riddles and solving them, and Tala weaved daisy crowns with Val while the sunset turned the sky orange. Then, Navy mentioned the violin he "found" and Aidilane perked up.

"I know how to play!" Then she tucked her hands underneath her. "I mean, can I?"

"Yeah!" Navy jumped up and ran into the supply tent. He emerged a moment later with the instrument in his hand. He handed it to my sister. "Here!"

She took it, delicately running her fingers over the graceful instrument, then set it on her shoulder, her chin on the chinrest, and lifted the bow. I'd forgotten how well she played the violin– she'd been the best at the orphanage, even better than kids older than us. With every pull of the bow against the strings, notes followed forth, creating a melody that made my soul feel light.

Next to me, Tala swayed to the music, the petals of the flower crown on her head rippling with the movement. Mira and Oliver got up, taking each other's hands, and danced in the firelight, step for step. Navy bounced around, and Val and Felix joined in the dance with delighted laughs. Evian watched on with a somewhat pleased expression.

I got to my feet, offering my hand to Tala. "We never did finish our dance."

She looked up at me, a smile etching the corners of her eyes. "That's right, we didn't." She took my hand and stood, placing a flower crown on my head. "But this time I won't trip over my feet."

"We'll see."

We glided around the fire, the moss beneath our feet cushioning our steps and giving a bounce to the dance that made me feel free. My memories brought forward our last dance, when we first met. Tala had been clumsy at first, but she'd learned swiftly, her graceful light footedness taking over. But this time, I didn't need to guide her. We danced as one, synchronized, the melody carrying both of us like leaves in the wind.

As twilight settled on the forest and Aidilane's music faded, I twirled Tala one last time. Her boot caught a tree root and she tripped, gravity pulling her backwards, but I caught her with my hand at the small of her back.

"You did trip."

"But not over my own feet!" she protested. "And for that I feel accomplished. That root had it out for me."

I gazed down at her, her auburn hair streaming back, grazing the earth. Her chestnut eyes reflecting the firelight, holding my gaze steady, and her hand on my arm. Her freckles were like stars across her face, resembling the night sky above us. I longed to lean forward and press my lips to hers, but I didn't. Last time someone kissed her, he'd betrayed her, and that wasn't something I could imagine being easy to get past. I wanted her to feel safe, and my longing for her was of no importance in comparison. Besides, there was no reason for her to love me. But I would always love her anyway. . . because her heart was a treasure to me, and as long as I kept it safe, nothing else mattered.

She smiled up at me. "Why are you looking at me like that?"

"Because you are deadly but charming, and that is the finest beauty."

I could hear the blush in her laugh. "Have I beguiled you, Kai of Moonland?"

Yes, you have. And it may someday cost me my life. But that life, however short, wouldn't have been worth living without you anyway.

The next morning before dawn, we gathered inside the cavern, sitting in a circle on the edge of the water. I shot a glare at the spot Evian had chained me just to settle the disgruntled feeling I got whenever I looked at him.

Tala stood in the center of our circle, looking slightly nervous to have everyone's attention on her. She gripped the hilts of her daggers tightly, but her voice rang clear when she spoke. "Are you all sure I should be leading this?"

"Yes," everyone murmured. Mira spoke up, "For sure. Tala, the prophecy was about you, and this is your mission. We're just your soldiers."

Tala swallowed hard. "Alright. Mira, do you still have the map we made based on your dream?"

"Yes, but it will only lead us to the city. The rest. . ."

"Okay." Tala nodded. "I've been considering the best way to go about this, and I think this is the best route." She paused, meeting my eyes. "There is very little people know about the Northland Kingdom, so there is no way to know what will greet us there, so we must be as prepared as possible. Oliver, pack as many of your explosives as you can. Harmless ones like smoke bombs and the other kind, too."

He nodded. "Sure thing."

Tala continued, unsheathing and resheathing her knives. "Today, we will follow Mira's map and then we'll make camp somewhere hidden, somewhere safe outside of the city. When night falls, Kai and I will infiltrate the city under the cover of darkness. We were trained to do this–"

"But have you actually done it before?" Evian interrupted, raising a doubtful eyebrow. "You're both just kids. You couldn't possibly have–"

"Yes," I cut him off. "We have. Many times over. More times than you are old. Missions like this were our lives, our purpose. We were at the bottom of society, but at the top of the food chain. Tala is correct– we are best cut out for this part of the mission. We live and breathe this– and yes, we are just kids. But our age does not define our maturity or skills."

Thank you, Tala transmitted. I gave her a nod.

She continued. "Kai and I will find the records and forge one to allow us all to enter the city without any trouble and we'll make sure to find out where the palace is. Then we'll collect mage uniforms to disguise us and bring them back to you. It shouldn't take more than a few hours as long as everything goes smoothly. Then, we'll all enter the city at the recorded time and find the dragon. Hopefully, Kai and I will be able to get information on the dragon's location, but there's no guarantee. We might have to wing it."

"Good plan," Val agreed. "It's as solid as it can be. Who will use the Sea Gem?"

Tala thought about this. "Whoever needs it most at the moment. It will all depend on whose abilities we'll need the most in whatever situation we might get into."

"Will I get to do something important?" Navy asked.

"You can help me with the demolitions," Oliver offered. "Help me make sure they don't go off until we want them to."

"Okay!"

"So this is the whole plan?" Felix asked. "Isn't it a bit. . .risky?"

"It's extremely risky," I agreed. "But it's our only option if we want to defeat these mages. They can't keep at what they're doing– the world *will* crumble."

"Right." Tala sighed, holding my gaze. "None of you have to do this. You all can walk away right now. This isn't your fight."

"Never," I told her. "Your fight is mine."

"Exactly," Mira added. "And it is our fight, too, Tala. These mages are destroying everything, and we won't just stand by and watch, even if it's the last thing we do."

Aidilane nudged my shoulder. "We got this, right guys? Let's think positively here. We *will* find the dragon and defeat the mages, but we will also make it out alive. All of us. Okay?"

Everyone nodded, murmuring their agreement, except for Tala. She smiled, but I saw the tension in her shoulders and the way her eyes drifted to the stones at her feet, as if she didn't believe it could be possible. I tilted my head, trying to draw her attention from whatever she was thinking about, and finally she lifted her eyes to mine again, immediately brightening her expression.

Don't you dare pretend you're okay for me, I thought.

She didn't respond, which pulled at my heart in a way I couldn't explain, almost as if she was hiding something from me.

We all went our separate ways to get ready. I sharpened my blades and helped Oliver, Felix, and Evian load up the wagon they'd acquired, and then I ducked into the tent to gather my bed roll.

I found Tala, sliding her blades into their sheaths at her wrists, waist, thigh and all sorts of other hidden places. Her hair was pulled into a braided bun at the base of her head, and she had on her usual black clothes and leather gauntlets, gloves, boots, and hood, and held her wolf mask in her hands, staring at it.

"Just like the first time we met." I announced my presence quietly, careful not to startle her.

She turned to me. "You mean the day you almost killed me?"

I grimaced. "It was also the day everything changed."

She nodded. "I haven't really thought about it that way. Things have changed so many times in my life that sometimes I don't even register certain things anymore."

"You say, 'Okay, it's just another thing,' and keep going, keep blazing through," I said.

"Exactly," she agreed softly. "Kai, I'm afraid I'm going to get everyone killed."

"You aren't going to," I chided her. "They are choosing to go on this mission. As am I. Let us help you, because this isn't your burden to carry alone anymore."

She rubbed her arms with a sigh. "Usually I carry my burdens alone. My life, my past. . .it's painful and gruesome, and I don't want anyone to know any of it. It's too much for people, too difficult. If they know, they'll leave." She smiled sadly. "I once had a friend, before the royal guard took notice of me. She was kind and caring and had a wonderful family. For weeks, we were inseparable. But, one day she asked me where I lived, what my family was like, and if she could meet them. I got so excited– she wanted to know me, the real me! I warned her it wasn't what one would expect, but she assured me that it was okay, that she wanted to really know me. So I showed her the stables and the stall where I slept, with the straw and the horses. I introduced my family, the dogs, cats, and horses. I showed her where I got the materials to sew my clothes, and how I got my food, stealing from the market. I told her about how much I hated the cold winter nights, how my hands and feet would turn blue and numb. I told her about the mean boys who would taunt me and chase me with their pig herding sticks and the names they'd call me. I told her everything." Tala's shoulders rose and fell with a stifled sigh. "She smiled and listened the whole time. But in the end, she was just a kid with a happy family. My life was too difficult, too painful for her. I never saw her again."

I sat down on the edge of her cot, looking up at her. "She just. . .left?"

Tala nodded. "But it's okay. Even so young, I understood. I didn't blame her. She was fortunate to have her innocence– it was unfair of me to rip that away from her. But it did make me realize that people can't really know me, not unless I want them to walk away. Most shy away from hard things, and I don't blame them. The only people who don't are the ones who also know what it's like to die a little inside. To be broken, and messy, trapped, and in pain. It's selfish of me, but I'm grateful for people like you and Mira, who know me completely and stay."

"And we're not going anywhere."

She tilted her head. "I'm glad I don't have to do this alone. I'm scared as hell, but knowing you and the Renegades have my back is reassuring."

"Are you ready for this?" I asked, pushing myself up off the cot.

"I'll miss this bed," she said longingly. "But yes. I'm ready. I have to be."

"Then lead the way, Princess."

Chapter Twenty

Jala

True love desires the heart, not the body.

I led Kai by the hand, through the rabbit trail that followed the path we were taking to the Northland border. The Renegades rode horses and the wagon on the path, but I wanted to show Kai privately, even though everyone knew already. So I pulled him away into the trees, Spiritwolf leading the way.

I warned him, "Please don't freak out."

"I'm not really sure what you could do to freak me out at this point."

We entered a clearing with fruit trees– beautiful, tall and slender white plants with sage green leaves and purple fruit that resembled plums back at home. The fruit was just out of reach, even for Kai, so after a moment's hesitation, I took my chance before I could overthink it and let my nervousness trap me.

There is no easy way to explain it– so I'll put it as it is. I shapeshifted, leaping into the air as a sparrow, flying up to the fruit in the trees, plucked one, and dropped it from my beak to Kai's hands.

I shifted back to my human form, and studied Kai's pale face, holding my hands up in a placating gesture. "I know, it's crazy. I didn't know I could do this until. . ." I recounted how when the Renegades had come to rescue me, and how things had gone sideways quickly. We had been miserably outnumbered. The panic had risen in me, bringing another part of me to life– perhaps because of the Mind Muse's meddling– and my instincts kicked in. I had shifted into a wolf, and in the nick of time, too. If not for my shapeshifting, we wouldn't have gotten out of there alive.

Kai opened and closed his mouth, and said, "You are an unending plot twist, Tala."

I smiled. "So you're aren't–"

"No," he interrupted. "Surprised, yes, but not freaked."

I let out a sigh of relief. "I thought you might wet yourself or something, like Oliver did."

Kai chortled. "Ha! The demolition expert wet himself." We laughed, but I made sure to tell him not to mention anything about it.

"I make no promises."

The journey to the Northland border went smoothly, but it took longer than we expected it to be because of difficult terrain. The Moon Range was a challenge to cross, and it was something we hadn't expected. Kai had mentioned the mountain range near the border but he hadn't told us just how difficult the mountain pass was. Sheets of rain soaked us the whole way through, with the occasional few minutes of hail. It was cold, windy, and oh so *wet*. I kept pulling my hood over my head when the gusts of wind would blow it off, and pulled the cloak Mira had packed tighter around me, but it didn't do much to keep the cold and wet out.

When we were finally out of the pass, we entered a sparse terrain of arctic tundra. The only trees around were yards apart and small compared to the trees in Moonland. Spruce trees, Aidilane informed us. Shrubs, bushes, and moss covered the ground, making it difficult to walk through without getting your foot or ankle caught and tripping. It was hilly, and even the surface of the ground was terribly uneven from the permafrost.

In front of us, the tallest row of hills stood, and just beyond them, we could make out the towers of a palace.

"Wait. . ." Mira squinted at her map. "Northland is a. . .city?"

"No, it's a kingdom!" Navy piped up. "Silly!"

Mira ignored him, pointing to the hills. "No, really. Those hills surrounding that city? That's the border."

Kai sidled up next to me, tilting his head as he stared out at the landscape. "You're right, Mira. That is the border. That city is *massive*. I think you might be right."

"According to my calculations," Oliver said, "That city is the size of an average kingdom. The Northland Kingdom is one gigantic city!"

We all exchanged glances. "Great Gamble," I murmured. "They are *powerful.*"

"To make their kingdom into one massive city is an undeniable demonstration of their power and wealth," Oliver agreed. Mira elbowed him in the ribs. "OW!" he complained.

"We don't need that, Oli," she chided him. "We need *encouragement*, not discouragement."

"Right." Oliver brightened. "At least we have each other."

We all stared at him, awkward silence filling the air. "Not helping," Val sighed.

Oliver shrugged. "What am I supposed to say? *Don't worry we'll be fine?* Or maybe, *It's okay! I'll let loose my little bombs!*"

Mira snorted, giggling. "Don't put it that way."

We all burst out laughing while Oliver looked utterly clueless. When we all calmed down, Aidilane sighed. "All that wealth was stolen from the other kingdoms."

"Wealth resulting in destruction isn't wealth at all," I murmured. "It's an abuse of power."

We pitched camp in the dark, at the base of one of the hills near the city, far enough from the border and from the roads to be safe from any watchful eyes. We ate, dried and warmed up, and it wasn't long before it was time for Kai and I to head out.

We didn't bother with saying farewells– saying goodbye suggested that we might not see each other again. Instead, we shared a fruit and gave each other encouraging nods. I commanded Spiritwolf to stay with the Renegades.

As Kai and I left, Mira shot me a look. I understood.

Don't die.

Kai and I made our way up the hill, hurrying from tree to tree to make sure we weren't seen from the city walls, although we both wore all black– except for my wolf mask– so the chances of us being spotted at night were low.

I led the way, navigating with my Keen to keep us in the right direction and to keep us from running into or tripping over anything. Shadow to shadow, thankful that the moon wasn't full. Just before we reached the city walls, we passed a small lake. Kai ignited a flame, illuminating the body of water.

"It's pink," I gasped.

Kai nodded. "The pink color is caused by the presence of salt-tolerant algae in the water. It's an interesting phenomenon."

I took one last look at the rose colored water in wonder before Kai extinguished his flame and we kept going.

The wall was made of stone and forged metal. Thick and slippery, without any footholds. I was thankful Kai and I brought our grappling hooks, otherwise it would have been impossible to scale the wall.

We tossed and secured our hooks and began our ascent. Slowly, with much difficulty. Our feet kept slipping, and the rope of our grappling hooks was slick from the never-ending drizzle. I prayed that our hooks would stay secure and not send us to our deaths far, far below.

Towards the top, the wind whipped around our legs, and we panted, our lungs aching for extra oxygen, my arms screaming in protest from pulling myself up and bearing the entirety of my weight for so long. Kai trembled with exhaustion, and I wasn't much better.

Just before we reached the top, I stopped, my boots scraping against the wall. I reached out with my mind to find out if anyone was on the wall. I didn't sense anyone. The coast was clear for now.

We clambered over the side of the wall to sit with our backs against the parapets that ran along the top of the walls to keep anyone from falling. We sat there out of sight for a minute, catching our breath. I adjusted my hood, making sure my hair wasn't peeking out, and wiped my damp gloves on my pants to try and dry them a little. Kai ran his fingers through his hair, the wet making it even curlier. He opened and closed his mouth, taking deep breaths with his eyes closed.

"Are you okay?" I asked.

He nodded. "I don't like being wet."

I stifled a laugh. "C'mon, fire elf. Let's go get some costumes."

We got up and cautiously made our way along the top of the wall, occasionally hiding behind crates when mages patrolled past. Finally, we climbed down onto one of the tower roofs, and then leapt from roof to roof through a section of the city towards the city gate security tower.

Kai was as much of an expert at this as I was. It was almost a game for us as we slipped along the rooftops, our footsteps silent on the shingles, and leaped each space between the buildings, landing on the next without a sound.

The Northland Kingdom, or city, was a vast one. It stretched further than I could see, and the lights from it shone from miles and miles away in the distance. In the direct center of the city stood the castle, its massive jeweled towers reflecting the light of the moon. Otherwise, it reminded me a lot of my kingdom– the mages were only human after all.

We used the city wall to guide our way to the tower, and when we finally reached it, I put the idea of a warm, soothing bath on this chilly night into each of the mage's minds, making it so overwhelming that they *had* to go bathe. One by one, they exited the tower without a worry, too focused on their need for hot water and steam to think about their stations or invaders.

"I will never get used to that," Kai said as we headed up the spiral staircase in the tower.

"Get used to what?"

"That you just make a man do something by sure will."

"It's more than that," I explained. "But it's difficult to put into words. I could never truly understand what it's like to ignite fire from my fingertips."

"It's exhilarating."

"I can imagine. But how do you just. . ." I wiggled my fingers at him and made a sound through my teeth.

He laughed and pushed my hands down as he passed me. "Like you said, it's difficult to put into words."

"We have a mutual understanding, then?"

"I believe so."

The room at the top of the tower was round, circular, with a glass roof that allowed us to see the stars. Shelves with scrolls, and multiple tables filled the room, a library of records, both old and new, tarnished and fresh. Ink and feather pens littered the table, as well as unused scrolls and paper. The candle that lit the room was half through, a white glob of wax that was slowly getting smaller and smaller. A wide window overlooked the city gate, in clear view of it and anyone or anything that went in or out. Fresh records of expected visitors and incoming patrols were also piled up on one of the tables. Kai and I sat down at one of them and forged our document, stating that a patrol of nine was expected to come in at noon to stock up and bring supplies back to their troops in the other kingdoms. I copied some of the signatures that I found on the other scrolls, and added official embellishments to make it convincing while Kai roamed the room, rifling through scrolls.

"What are you looking for?" I could feel him wrestling with himself inside, so many feelings surging through him and pushing him a million different directions. I paused what I was doing and turned to him, pulling off my mask. "Kai."

He avoided my gaze. "Just looking for a map or something that might lead us to the dragon."

My stomach twinged. I pushed the feeling aside. "What I meant was, what are you looking for inside?"

He stopped short. "What do you mean?"

"You're in turmoil, Kai. Don't think you can hide that from me when your mind is radiating it." I stood up and took a step closer to him.

He set his jaw, his defined jawline and dark eyes angling towards the floor as he went silent and still for a long few heartbeats. "I'm not sure how to be," he finally admitted. "With anything. Before Aidilane was free, my sole purpose was my job, to free her. Extinguish my targets, one step closer. One more person dead, another step closer. It was an unending game, a game I hated. But now that it's over–" he paused. "I hated my job, but it made me who I am. And without it. . ."

"You're not sure who you are anymore."

"Right. All that's left of me," he pressed his fingers to his temples, grimacing, "are these demons in my head. They haunt and pull at me, taunting and screaming. I can't shake them, and I can't bring myself to fight them because my past is unforgivable. How am I supposed to take care of Aidilane when I'm just a scrapyard of ghosts and shadows? I could see it in her eyes– she could hardly recognize who I was anymore."

"I don't mind your shadows, Kai," I murmured softly. "They look a lot like mine."

He met my gaze, his dark eyes softening. "After you've done the things I've done, you start to numb yourself to your feelings. It's the only way to survive when hell is ripping at your seams."

"Numb is easier than feeling," I agreed quietly.

"Even good things," he continued. "I don't let myself. It's too dangerous. But you?" He sucked in a shaky breath. "You make me. . .feel," he whispered fiercely, "and it scares me."

"Why?" My voice was hardly a whisper.

"Because trust. . .love. . ." his voice faded. "They're foreign concepts to me."

"Shall we learn together, then?" My words trembled, but I meant them all.

The candlelight flickered in his eyes as Kai slowly, cautiously leaned close, his gaze searching mine for permission. I didn't move or breathe as his lips neared mine, his light breath caressing my face. He stopped an inch from me, leaving a little room for me to choose if I really wanted this. The curve of his lip; his unblinking gaze. His nervous shallow breaths; his furrowed brow.

Despite my racing heart– I really did want this.

I closed the space between us, and suddenly nothing else mattered. His lips against mine, our hands lacing together– all was right with the world. He slid his hand to the small of my back and the other to the back of my head, pulling me closer.

He tasted like rain, his lips soft and his touch careful but passionate. It was the kind of kiss that would have brought me to my knees if he hadn't been holding me. Everything inside me unfurled, like a blooming rose bud. If our pasts were hell, he was heaven. This was the very edge, and I was falling.

Chapter Twenty-one

Kai

What is the definition of love?

There are many answers to that question. But I think that if I had to put it simply, love is when someone's wreckage is beautiful to you. Like a mosaic of shattered glass. Their scars are not a story of who they are, but who they have become despite all odds

Her head tilted to the side, our noses touching, her lips parting slightly against mine. Her body relaxed in my arms, melting the clump of ice within me. My mind stilled for the first time, filled only with the thought of her. She smelled like cinnamon, and her hair was like silk, finespun and delicate.

For the first few moments, I'd felt like an imposter.

You don't deserve her!

She deserves better!

Stop!

But just like night shifts into day, the screaming in my mind ceased as she met my lips and her tense muscles relaxed against mine, folding into me. Everything else faded away, replaced by the honey–sweet taste of her lips and the sound of her breath catching. And that breath was mine.

This human was all I needed.

When we finally let go of each other, Tala smiled up at me, pulling her mask back on, her voice husky. "Shall we finish what we came here to do?"

She finished forging the document and set it on top of the expected pile while I went through the stack of papers that told of the people going out of the city. I picked up the first one and read it, then showed it to Tala. She read it, her eyes widening with shock and surprise. "The King and Queen of Northland left two days ago?"

I nodded. "That's what it says. At least now we'll have a little less to worry about. The castle should be under lighter guard."

"This is good," Tala agreed. "Very good."

We put everything back the way it was when we first entered, and then headed downstairs. We had to work faster– we'd taken longer than expected. But it was worth it.

We made our way back along the rooftops, the rain picking up, soaking us again. In front of me, Tala gracefully scaled the roof, then leapt the space to the next one with a running jump. I went after her, scrambling on the slippery shingles when I landed, almost losing my footing.

We found and shadowed a group of mage soldiers making their way towards the gate, following them like circling hawks. Our prey took a shortcut through an alley just before reaching the city gate and that was when we swooped, talons outstretched. Tala took the liberty of taking that analogy seriously.

I dropped down onto the shoulders of one of the mages while Tala shifted into a hawk, diving down unto the mages in a furious flurry of feathers and talons. She attacked their faces while they shouted and swatted at her, pulling the hoods of their cloaks around their heads to no avail. Distracted, they didn't realize their unconscious companion lying at my feet, and they were too busy trying to evade the hawk's talons to worry about the assassin slipping through the shadows, picking them off one by one. When there was one man left standing, Tala shifted back into her human form and took him out with a kick to his head.

"Nine," I counted the cloaks and uniforms as we gathered them. "We have everything we need."

We bound the mages with rope and dragged them into a storage house beside the alley where they wouldn't likely be found for a while. Then, we put on two of the cloaks, hiding our clothes, faces and the other uniforms underneath them. We hurried to the group that the mages had been heading towards, leaving the city through the gate.

One of them eyed me as we slipped in among them as they shuffled out of the city. "Where are the others?"

"They're running late," I explained. "Too much to drink."

"Ah. Well they'll just have to travel on their own. Idiots."

Tala and I kept our heads low until we were through the gate and a ways down the road. Then we slowly, subtly faded to the background, hung back from the group and took the rear for a while until we reached a bend in the road. Once everyone had turned the corner ahead of us, Tala and I turned and ducked into the forest, disappearing from sight.

Mira was the only one awake, keeping guard, when we stepped into the light of the small fire she sat beside. "Well well," she greeted us. "It's almost dawn. What took you so long?"

I glanced at Tala. "The wall," we both said simultaneously.

"Ah." Mira got to her feet and took the uniforms from us. Tala let out a long, tired sigh as she stretched her arms above her head and smiled at me, her eyes glossy with exhaustion but shining. "It was much taller than it looked."

The corner of my mouth turned up. "Indeed."

"Mhn. . ." Mira shot Tala a quick look, so quick I hardly caught it. "Well, you two better eat something and take advantage of whatever's left of the night. I'll wake you both when dawn light arrives."

We obeyed, scarfing down what little food was left over from their dinner and then spread out our bed rolls next to each other, borrowing each other's warmth on the chilly night, our weapons in arms reach.

It felt like I'd just closed my eyes when Mira aggressively nudged my shoulder. "Rise and shine. Wake Tala."

Tala was curled in a ball, her face buried in my chest, her knees pressed against my abdomen. I gently stroked her shoulder for a moment, and then brushed a strand of hair from her face. "One last fight, Tala. It'll all be over when tomorrow's sun rises."

She opened her foggy eyes, focusing them on me through her lashes. "One last fight," she murmured.

Chapter Twenty-two

Tala

Sometimes all we desire is a way out. A way out of a responsibility, a way out of our circumstance, a way out of a problem, a way out of something difficult. Perhaps even a way out of something inevitable. Yet, at best, we are left with a reason to blaze on.

Even so, the reason may not seem enough. It may not seem worth it. And yet, we blaze on anyway, because the inevitable is unavoidable. Because oftentimes, we don't have a choice.

So pick up your sword; hold your head high. The flames burn, but they cannot destroy you, Soldier.

"Welcome back," one of the gate guards greeted us as we headed into the city. "How's it looking down there in hob gobbles? Still mangy and primitive?"

I hesitated for too long, so Kai answered for me, "Yes. Thank the gods we've nearly got everything under Northland control. Otherwise those worms would continue wasting perfectly good land and resources!"

"Indeed," the mage agreed. "Back to stock up?"

"Yes, and to get a proper meal."

"Good idea," the mage waved us on, calling after us, "The food in the lesser kingdoms will have your men falling left and right with malnutrition!"

"That was a passionate display," I commented to Kai with a pointed look.

He shrugged. "I've heard them talk. Not that I enjoyed it, but you seemed pretty speechless."

"I was," I admitted. "I don't understand how any creature could say things like that about their own species." I had told Spiritwolf to keep outside the city and a good way from the city wall. She had protested profusely, but I stayed firm. I refused to get her killed today. There was enough we could lose– I wasn't going to add to the stakes.

It felt wrong pressing through the enemy's city with my face fully exposed. I had gotten used to people seeing me without my mask, but this was a whole other level of discomfort. Every glance towards me sent my skin crawling.

As we headed towards the castle in the center of the city, I cradled the dragon's essence within me. *I'm coming,* I promised. *I'm so close. Hang in there just a little while longer.* She was fading, like a cooling ember, her consciousness flickering. I sent a burst of my energy to her, boosting her strength a little. *Stay alive,* I commanded fiercely. *Make this all worth it.*

Please.

By noon, we were halfway to the castle, doing our best to keep from drawing attention to ourselves. Mages and families filled the streets, mingling and making the city look like a good one, a normal one, if it weren't for its size and their evil ways. I was beginning to worry about how we were going to infiltrate the castle and find the dragon, when I sensed something.

I stopped dead in my tracks, and Navy bumped into my legs with an *oof!*

"What is it?" Kai asked as I stood there, my eyes wide and the hairs on the back of my neck standing on end. He took my hand, looking around guardedly. "Tala?"

I blinked, then whispered, "There's a tunnel system that leads to the castle. I can feel the dragon– she's underneath the castle."

"Underneath?" Mira repeated. "That would make sense. In our dreams she was in a cavern or something of the like. Underground."

I nodded.

"Do you know where the tunnels are?" Val asked.

I nodded again, shifting on my feet towards an alley. "This way." They followed me down the alley and into an old tavern. It was in shambles, and at first, I wasn't really sure why I was drawn to it.

We scrambled around, looking for anything, thankful that no one else was inside. Aidilane, Felix, and Val searched the back rooms, Navy stood watch, and the rest of us went through the main tavern area. Nothing.

Finally, I hopped over the counter, where all the old and empty drink fountains and bottles lay around, their contents long gone dry, as well as beer mugs and wine glasses. As I landed, one of my boots thumped on a creaky wooden hatch door. I swept away the dust and scraps with a cough, then slowly opened it. A tight spiral staircase leading down, down into the darkness. At the very bottom, far down, I thought I saw a small light.

Kai was already beside me, looking down over my shoulder, his jaw set. I waved the others over, and they gathered around silently. "It's too easy," Evian put to words what everyone was thinking.

"Not a single guard," Mira murmured.

"With a wall like they have, they probably assume no one would get this far inside the city in the first place," Kai pointed out.

I placed my feet on the first step. "Come on. Let's finish this."

Kai grabbed my arm. "I go first." He drew his blades and started down the stairs. I followed at his heels with the others a step behind me. When the daylight coming in through the hatch no longer affected the darkness, Kai lit a flame and used it to help us see and keep us from tumbling down the staircase.

The stairs were made of some kind of metal. Everyone managed to descend fairly quietly, but Felix struggled the most with it with his brawn build. It was like expecting a strong gorilla to step quietly.

I opened my mind to the others, allowing myself to feel them. Navy was frightened but excited to be included in this big adventure, naive to the extreme dangers that we risked. Val was concentrating on her little brother, carefully making sure that he didn't miss a step. Felix was embarrassed about being the loudest, self conscious about the noise he was making and anxious that we'd be caught because of him. Evian was mostly annoyed with Felix, but he was also running all his water bending drills through his head in case we needed them. Oliver was going over each of the things he brought from smoke and strobe bombs to deadly explosives, and was being extra careful not to jostle his bag too much. Mira was thinking about the what ifs on what was to come, and she kept looking at me, anxious. Aidilane was just scared, repeating *It's okay, I'm okay, everything's okay,* over and over in her head while putting on a brave face. And Kai, well, he was fully concentrated on what was around and below us.

When we finally reached the bottom, the only thing that greeted us was the candle that stood in a small alcove in the wall.

"For all their talk about the other kingdoms being primitive," Val said, "they don't seem to care much about their security."

"You wouldn't say that if you had to climb that wall," I pointed out. Muddy water pooled at our feet, not quite to our ankles, and the musky earth scent was overwhelming, making the small, dim space feel stuffy and claustrophobic. Kai led the way down the tunnel with his fire, and as we tramped along, I hung back with Mira.

"Remember," I told her quietly.

"Not unless I *have* to," she replied stubbornly, speeding up.

We reached a bend in the tunnel, and then another, and at the third, Kai quickly pressed himself back against the wall, extinguishing his flame with a frantic signal to be silent. I made my way back to his side and took his hand.

What is it? I transmitted.

So much for no security.

And that was when I heard it. Up ahead, voices echoed down the tunnel. I could sense the mages in the next tunnel, guarding a much, much larger cavern beyond that. The dragon was so near gone that I hardly realized she was there, but she was. We were so close. But between her and us, I could sense twenty seven other people.

I swallowed hard. *I'll lead them away from the cavern. Once they're gone, go in and see what you can do for the dragon.*

Okay.

I shifted into a golden eagle, my wingspan nearly grazing both sides of the tunnel as I swooped around the corner. The mages all hunched in groups, clearly bored, all heavily armed with both scepters, swords, and daggers. Most guarded both ends of the tunnel, but a few played cards by candlelight on the top of barrels, and yet some sat sharpening blades and practicing their magic. A hint of beer tinged the air, as well as body odor and the sense of hoping that the change of guard would come sooner than scheduled.

It took them a moment to register what was happening, my wings beating the air and the top of their heads with good, hard whacks. They all leapt up and began shouting.

"How'd that thing get in here?!"

"Are eagles even native here?"

"Shoot it!"

"AH WHY IS IT CHARGING US!"

I tore at them with my talons, snagging hair and flesh and circled over and over again, drawing them slowly down another tunnel. They chased and threw things at me, attempting to cut me from the air above them with their blades. They managed to nick my talon and wing, but I kept going. As I went, diving and scratching, I snatched their wands one by one until they were all in my beak before they could use more of the dragon's magic. Another tunnel, then another, and yet another until I knew for certain that the time it took them to get back to the cavern was enough for us to free the dragon. One more dive at the mages for good measure, sending them screaming and running all sorts of frantic directions. Then I shifted into a small owl and flew back to the others as fast as my wings would carry me.

I landed in the cavern entrance as I shifted back to my human form, panting. My shoulder had a pretty nasty gash, as did my shin and they burned horribly, but I had accomplished my goal.

I looked ahead of me, slowly stepping into the cavern. It was dimly illuminated by bioluminescent moss and lichen, and the sound of dripping water echoed around, bouncing from the stone like a melody. Glowing crystals and stalactite grew down from the tall stone ceiling like icicles, and towered high along the rock walls and floor. And in the center of the cavern, the dragon. I sucked in a sharp breath, a moment of shock, disbelief, and utter wonder making it difficult to breathe.

She was lying against the stone floor, her massive body chained by her ankles, neck, wings, and tail. She was the most wondrous, breath-taking creature I'd ever seen. Her scales reminded me of, but couldn't be compared to, the iridescent feathers of peacocks, starlings, and the shells of jewel beetles– as if they couldn't decide whether to be green, blue, or purple. Her wings faded out into silver with an opalescence that made the light reflect off of them with a million different colors. Her horns were at least as long as I was tall, sharp and dark as if made of onyx, as well as her talons and the spines along her back and tail. But her eyes were closed, and she was bleeding from too many wounds to count. Her breath was so shallow that I wouldn't have been able to tell if she was still alive if it weren't for her essence within me. A nauseating amount of her scales were missing, ripped from her to craft the wands and scepters the mages used, exposing bleeding flesh beneath.

How, I wondered, had they captured her in the first place? Where had she come from? I knew that dragons aged differently than humans and elves, so maybe she was still alive from back before humans and elves came to be, when the continent belonged to the dragons only.

But now, it didn't really matter. The deed was done. They'd imprisoned her and drained her. It couldn't be reversed. All that mattered now was that we healed what they broke.

Kai and the others stood around her, gaping up at her with wide eyes from a safe distance. I passed them and limped up to her, pulling my gloves off and placing my hands on her snout. She let out the faintest sigh, as if her body knew that freedom was so close.

Kai came to my side, awe and anxiety radiating from him. "She's. . ."

"Magnificent. Beaten down, but magnificent." I turned to him. "We don't have much time."

He set his jaw with a small shake of his head. "These chains aren't going anywhere. They're anchor chains– the largest, strongest kind. We can't move or break them. So I melted through a few of the main links, but that's all we can do. If she wasn't so. . ." His words trailed off. "If she was stronger, she might be able to get free from them now that I've melted some of the links. But even if we could remove them completely, there's no getting her out of here unless she's awake and strong."

My heart sank, dropping into the dark pool within me, sending ripples of dread through my veins. I frantically circled the dragon, trying to find a way. But I wasn't even halfway around her when the mages arrived.

"We're out of time!" I shouted to the others before I shifted into a wolf and charged the mages, teeth bared, and used my Keen to confuse their minds.

"She's the one that attacked us! The eagle!" one of the mages yelled, as he drew his sword. "Watch yourselves– the Demise is among us!"

Without their wands, they were forced to use their blades. The Renegades fought furiously. Kai was near me, his blades flashing and blasting the mages with flames. My mind raced as I shifted from one animal to the next and tried to figure out what to do. But I already knew what needed to happen. . .I knew the moment the dragon had placed her essence within me.

Evian used the Sea Gem to amplify his water bending and sent surges of water at mages, knocking them off their feet and slamming them into the stone walls of the cavern. Val used the air currents to buffer mages into the air and send them crashing back down again and to lift herself above the ground to gain advantage.

I lunged and bit and scratched, snapping bones and tearing muscle, using my teeth and claws as weapons, unleashing the relentless strength and wits of the beasts.

Kai and I slowly got separated in the fray, and I could sense the victory in mages' minds as they began to overwhelm us. The sound of clanging broad swords and daggers and Oliver's strobe and smoke bombs choked the air, and I found myself out of energy. I shifted back into my human self, drawing my longest daggers.

A mage clashed blades with me, nearly taking off my hands, but I kicked him backwards into another, and then leaped up onto the shoulders of a man and flipped him, disarmed another, and slashed with my blades.

Though I stumbled and took one too many wounds, I kept fighting for all it was worth and used my Keen to twist the mage's thoughts as best I could to derail them, but I couldn't do them all at once. I slashed and kicked and turned and ducked, jabbing a mage and slicing the leg of another and driving my dagger into one of their sides. I sent three mages down the tunnel, convincing their minds that they needed to find mice immediately. Others I caused to fight each other.

Kai and the others were on the other side of the cavern now, and I was cornered beside the dragon by six mages. Kai fought with such calm fury that only an assassin could have, the kind that showed just how much one should avoid being on his bad side. But even with his skills, I could sense his growing weariness, and the others were just as well off. Oliver threw another bomb, this time an explosive, and it took out eight of the mages with an ear shattering *bang!* and threw everyone else to the ground.

I recovered quickly and forced myself to my feet. Three mages got up near me and circled me, twirling their blades with dark eyes filled with hatred, black pits of death. Simultaneously, I felt the dragon letting go of life within me, and all at once, a million things flashed through me like a crashing wave.

If the dragon died, the mages would use her body– scales, horns, talons, bones– for their magic; they would be unstoppable. They would take everything and leave a trail of blood, death and desolation in their wake. The world would go up in flames. My brother and everyone in his kingdom would die. All those innocent people, *my* people, as well as everyone in Lowland, Moonland, and everywhere else. An invincible, wicked reign would come forth, built from the ashes and blood of the world's ruin.

The sense of duty within me was strong, but stronger yet was the instinct inside me that all wolves possessed.

Protectiveness.

I would protect Sabian, and all he had, all he loved. I would protect the kingdom I had grown up in, though outcast, it had been the closest resemblance of a home for me. The little barn, the stable, the keep, the town and the people in it. The cobblestone streets I would run barefoot on in the snow while I stole food from the marketplace. But most of all, the happy families that brought me so much warmth and joy to watch. The palace and the royal guard and the purpose I'd had with them there, the duty we'd shared. I would protect my kingdom— *save* it. I would protect my brother and Quinton, our home.

I would protect the Renegades. Mira, who had grown to be my best friend; her and her wise words. Oliver, who she loved. Evian. Val, and little Navy. Felix. All so willing to risk their lives to stop this war– to help me.

I would protect Kai. . .the man I loved, though I denied it for so long. The man who loved me. I would protect him and Aidilane.

I would protect my wolf pack and Spiritwolf, my family. Motherwolf and Alphawolf and all the others, who had taken me in and loved me as though I were one of their own, shielding me from the world around for a time.

The world was painful and harsh, cold and cruel. But life wasn't just pain, it wasn't just darkness. It was beautiful, too. For every sorrow, there's joy. For every suffering, there is peace. For every fear, there is love. For every tear, there is a laugh. For every darkness, light. Roses aren't all thorns, after all.

This beautiful world was worth protecting.

I knew that when the dragon had placed her essence within me, she had become a part of me, and I of her. The only way for her to be free was if I gave her my strength so that when her consciousness was in her own body again, she would be well enough to rise once more. To be free.

But the only way for me to allow her back into her own mind was if my consciousness wasn't there to hold her anymore. If *my* essence was no longer within me, tying me to this life.

I jerked my gaze to Kai, who was locked in combat with two mages. He kept glancing at me, his panic beginning to show in his eyes. I sensed his confusion. What were we supposed to do? Hadn't Tala known what she was going to do?

My heart tore apart knowing that our first kiss had been our last. That a lifetime with him wasn't my destiny. That I would never be one with him. That I would never be there to calm his restless mind again.

My soul fought against me, my heart tearing at its seams. But I was certain of one thing: My destiny was to be the reason the kingdoms saw peace once more.

I locked eyes with Mira. She shook her head, her eyes widening in denial as I let my daggers clang to the stone floor. I sent the dragon my last burst of energy, pulling from deep within myself, thrusting it into her essence with my Keen like an electric shock.

My knees buckled and gave way, but not before the sword was driven through my back and center. Its point jutted out from my belly, glistening scarlet with my blood.

Kai saw. He'd started running to me when I'd dropped my blades. Mira caught him and held him back, her face streaming with tears as she wrestled to keep Kai back. He screamed, "*TALA!*"

But his cry was so far away, as if he wasn't really even there. My vision tunneled, and the mage pulled the sword free with an excruciating grating. . .my bone? Spine even? I hardly registered the pain anymore.

I wasn't sure where I was. . .somewhere warm, or was that just my blood? It didn't really matter. The dragon was free, and she was rising, waking with a bellowing roar, ripping out of her chains and unleashing her wrath upon the enemy.

I floated through darkness for a while, dancing between life and death like I'd done so many times before. It was a familiar place, this darkness. It was the thing that had saved me the first time.

But there was no cheating Death this time. He had waited patiently for so long, snatching me up once in a while, then letting me go. This time, he wasn't letting go now, and I wasn't going to fight him.

Purpose is what drives you. Gives you something to live for. Sometimes you know your purpose, other times you don't. But it's what keeps you going. And when your purpose is completed, so has your time on this earth.

My purpose was completed. My story reaching its climax. And though it pained me to let go and leave behind the life and the people that I loved, I took Death's hand. He smiled at me before he led me away. . .

Away. . .

Away.

Chapter Twenty-three

Kai

Sacrifice. Possibly the hardest part of life.

I felt everything inside me give way as Tala crumpled to the ground. I pushed Mira off of me and ran to her side as the dragon rose and began shattering the chains and breathing blue fire at the mages. I didn't care.

I crashed to my knees beside Tala and gathered her up in my arms, pressing my hand into her gaping wound to try to stop the bleeding, but there was already a pool of blood beneath her and blood trickled from her mouth. Panic rose in my throat, choking me. I shook her, my heart skipping beats. *"No!* No, Tala! Dammit, *stay with me!"*

Around us, the dust was beginning to settle, the air quieting in the aftermath of the battle. The mages had all been crushed by the dragon or burnt to a crisp by her fire, their remains scattered around with the weapons. The Renegades slowly gathered around me, their shocked silence loud after the chaos of the fight.

The dragon crouched beside Tala and I, towering over us quietly, her powerful presence like a chill in the air. Her wounds were mending themselves, and her missing scales were slowly reforming, returning her to her full power and majesty. She watched as I cradled Tala, her blood staining my clothes. She wasn't breathing, her chest still and cold, and her pulse was gone.

I frantically, desperately shouted, "Someone do something!" but no one budged. I laid Tala on the stone floor and began chest compressions, but all I did was make her bleed more.

Mira put her hand on my shoulder, her voice shaky. "Kai. . .she's gone. It had to happen."

I whirled on her, my rage boiling over. "*What?* You knew this would happen and you *held me back*? This. . ." I shook uncontrollably. "This didn't have to happen. It *shouldn't* have happened!"

Oliver stepped in front of Mira. "Kai–"

I turned my back to them and took Tala's face in my hands, wiping away the blood. "I am *not* going to lose you now."

"It was the only way for the dragon to live," Mira tried to explain, her eyes bloodshot and her voice catching. "It was the only way to stop the mages. She knew it, and she knew that you would try to stop it from happening. She didn't want you to know, and she–"

"*No,*" I growled stubbornly, shaking my head. "No." She would have told me, and we would have figured out a way around it. She. . .

I surged to my feet, pointing an accusing finger at the dragon. "She died so that YOU could live!" I shouted, trembling with rage. "*You. . .*" I gripped the sides of my head, my throat letting out a choked sound as I crumpled back to my knees beside Tala's limp, pale form and took her soft hand, her graceful fingers limp against my own.

The dragon lowered her head, her nostrils flaring with her warm breath. Like the feeling of being plunged in cool water, her voice rang clear and crisp in my mind.

"*Young elf, her sacrifice was necessary. It has been written in the stars for centuries. Without it, the world would have fallen to calamity. My death would have brought ruin to the world, my power taken into wicked hands. This girl was born for this; it was her destiny. Her only purpose. She was never meant for anything less, or anything more.*"

I glared into the dragon's emerald eyes that were bigger than three heads. "She is much more than a sacrifice. She isn't just a tool, o–or a product of some prophecy. She is *Tala*, Stalkingwolf. A girl with the Keen, and waist long red hair that's softer than silk. Brown eyes that glow blue when she heals– that smile when she sees something beautiful. Her kindness, compassion. Her gentle touch, and strong, wiry limbs. Her courage, even when she's terrified. Her voice. . ." My voice cracked as I remembered that day at the palace, when I'd watched her sing to the blue bird, completely unaware that she was my target. "Her voice like a birdsong melody, silver tongued and seamless. Her inability to sit still, her nervous grip on her blades. Her quick wit and impeccable empathy. Her endearing presence, and her freckles." I sucked in a sob. "Her sacrifice wasn't written in the stars; *she* was. So what about her? What about the life she could live? Her purpose is far beyond this. And she was meant for so much more. *She is so much more.*"

I held the dragon's gaze steady. I didn't care if she burned me to ashes. Tala was dead; nothing else mattered anymore. No one could estimate the extent of the war I would wage on every single person who had ever hurt Tala, and if this dragon was the reason she died, she would surely be first on my list of vengeance.

The dragon's pupils were slits, like a cat or snake's, hunting its prey. She knew the things running through my mind, both the dark and the panicked. She could crush me with one stomp of her talon, or snap me up in her jaws like a rabbit.

"*I sense your fierce heart, young elf. Your devotion to this girl is striking. Loyalty is hard earned, but yours belongs to her, does it not?*"

I rose to my feet. "It does. And it always will." Then I ignited my flames and hissed, "She is lying here *dying!* And you waste time with–"

"*She is already dead,*" the dragon interrupted my outburst. "*She is in the Beyond now.*" Her eyes, like jewels, shimmered in the light as she shifted her sharp gaze to Tala's body. "*You ask about the life she could live, and you ask for much. To bring her back would cost a great price, young elf. And once paid, it cannot be reversed. Her sacrifice was required, her purpose brought to completion. In all reality, her life is over. So to bring her back, to allow her another life, someone's life must be given willingly.*"

After the moment of elation that there was a chance, my heart sunk again. Someone had to die to bring her back?

The dragon blinked, knowing the distress within me. *"No. Not a life in the way you perceive. A life as in something that makes one's life theirs."* She pointed a talon at the fire dancing at my fingertips. *"Your fire makes you an elementalist. It makes your life yours. It is a part of you, and if taken, would change the path of your life so drastically that it would be a different life entirely. Just like your heartbeat, your breath-your fire is a part of you. If taken, it would be the death of the life you now have."*

What she was saying dawned on me. To bring Tala back, I would have to give up my fire element.

My heart skipped a beat. I couldn't even imagine my life without my fire. Everything I did involved it. But I didn't hesitate.

I knelt back down beside Tala and pulled her onto my lap, cradling her in my arms. "My life isn't worth living without her. Tala is my heartbeat, my breath. There would be no life without her." I stretched out my arms and brought my flames to life. "Bring her back."

The dragon didn't have to ask if I was sure. She knew the certainty ringing clear in my voice, the willingness coursing through me and the memories that fed it. Tala's bluebird melody as she sang to the little creature. The moment in Moonwood, and the pure wonder in Tala's glowing blue eyes when the moon phoenix flew over our heads. Our dance in the great hall, but better yet, our dance by the fire in the Renegades' camp. The first time she'd woken me from my memories and the ghosts haunting me, her hair falling forward into my face and her gentle fingers against my temples, her eyes tight in concentration as she flooded me with peace. The night on the ship, as we reconciled and held each other.

Tala would not die today.

The great winged beast lifted her talon and touched a claw to my palm. My fire began tracing up her claws and around her talon, up her leg, illuminating her veins as it went. I wasn't controlling it. It felt as if it was being unraveled from me, like thread on a spool. It was uncomfortable in the way that stepping into the cold after being wrapped in a warm blanket was. But I didn't fight it. I let it go willingly, letting the dragon drain me of the element until there was none left.

Then she placed her talon on Tala, covering nearly her entire body with it, including the wound. The ember–like glow of my fire that the dragon stored in her veins began to ripple from her and to Tala's body, and for a moment, I tensed. Surely it was burning her?

But she was unharmed by it. Instead, like air, it surged around her and into her lungs. When the dragon moved her talon, stepping away, the gaping wound from the sword was gone, leaving only a wide jagged tear in Tala's clothes. Her pale, cold skin was warming, her color returning.

"Tala?" I whispered as my heart raced.

Her chest rose as she took in a wispy breath and her heart thumped with the first few beats. Finally, I could breathe again. I held her tighter, relief flooding me, making me lightheaded and dizzy.

I nearly sobbed when she opened her eyes, blinking groggily. "W–Wha..."

"Welcome back, Savior," I murmured, pressing my forehead to hers, my trembling finally ceasing, replaced by tears.

She took my face in her hands and searched my gaze. "How?"

I smiled. "You can't be a savior all by yourself, now can you?"

"What did you do?"

"He gave you life from his own," the dragon said.

Tala's eyes widened as she saw the dragon, alive, well, and free. It took her a moment to respond, but when she did, she spoke to me, her brows creasing. "What does she mean?"

"It doesn't matter," I chided her as I helped her sit up. "You'll have to save the afterlife for another time, Stalkingwolf. Your time is not yet over."

"I don't understand," she said.

"*You will. When the time is right,*" the dragon added, meeting my gaze. She knew that I didn't want Tala to know just yet. There was no need right now.

Tala got to her feet, reaching out her hand to the dragon, who pressed her snout to Tala's palm. "*Thank you, Princess of Highland.*"

I wiped my cheeks with the back of my sleeves. Crying wasn't something I'd done in a really, really long time. But Tala made me feel things that I usually didn't. And her death had torn me open, but so was the sight of her beside this great scaled creature, just in a different way. I was in awe. Her torn, bloody clothes. Ruffled hair, cuts and bruises, and dusty boots. But she may as well have been in a gown and tiara.

The sound of another troop of mages coming down the tunnel roused us all to draw our weapons again, our exhausted bodies tensing wearily. Tala backed up to my side as the dragon rose to her full height and turned to the entrance of the cavern just as the mages came around the corner, dragonscale wands and scepters raised. They all froze in their tracks, slamming into each other at the sight of the massive creature before them that was very much awake, unchained and furious.

By sheer force of will, the dragon shattered the wands and scepters like glass. She spoke sharply in everyone's minds. "*You have stolen what was not yours, and I have taken it back. There will be no more destruction by my power, no more bloodshed in the name of greed. Power has twisted your souls. That cannot be undone, nor can the pain you have caused. But now is the beginning of a new era. An era of peace. You no longer have a hold on this world. My suggestion to you? Run."*

And they did.

There was a still sense of wonder and strange calm afterwards. Tala sensed this, too. She turned to me, her brows scrunched. "It's. . .over. Is it really over?" Her pupils were dilated, eyes wide. She looked frightened.

I tilted her chin so she would meet my eyes. "It is."

"Then why do I feel so. . ."

"Like everything around you has suddenly come to a standstill and you're still spinning?" I guessed.

She nodded.

I took her face in my hands. "You just *died,* Tala. Full stop. You brought the war to a full stop with you. But you came back. Just like wildfires burn everything down to bring new life, through death you brought an end to this war and have given the world a new beginning. And," I added, "Your brother is waiting for you."

She inhaled sharply, and covered her mouth with her hand. "Sabian. . ." A tear escaped her eye. "I–I really did it. . .*We* really did it." She turned to face the Renegades. "And the prophecy didn't even mention you at all."

"It may not have," Aidilane said, "But history will."

"It sure did mention *him,*" Mira gestured to me with a knowing smile.

Tala exhaled, her eyes tired but shining. "It did. And history *will* remember you," she added. "All of you. This may be the end of the war, but it is the beginning of something beautiful for everyone here." Her voice wavered with the last few words, but I was the only one that noticed. I got the feeling she didn't believe the words were true for herself.

Suddenly, her eyes widened, and she jerked her gaze to mine. "Do you think Sabian felt it when I. . ."

The dragon answered for me. "*He did. He will surely be in pain now, certain of your death.*"

"You need to go to him," I told her, but my heart sank at the thought of her leaving. I was no longer of use to her– the war was over. Our mission was over. What we shared was. . .well, indescribable. But I wasn't from her kingdom.

She tilted her head at me, narrowing her eyes, knowing exactly what I was thinking. "I died with clarity. But I also died with a heavy heart, knowing what I was leaving behind. The only thing you have in Moonland is a warrant for your arrest. You aren't safe there, and neither is Aidilane." She took my hand and laced her fingers through mine. "And I wasn't given another life just for us to go our separate ways now, Kai. I'm not doing that. My last sinking thought as Death took my hand was that our first kiss was our last. But it turns out, it doesn't have to be. I've chosen what I want, and it's something I've never been more sure of. Come with me to Highland."

I squeezed her hand. "What will the other humans say?"

"Does it matter?"

I held her gaze. "No." *Not so long as you're with me.*

She smiled. "Come with me."

I bowed deeply, kissed her hand, and said, "If I can be of further use to her majesty, I'm honored. Though, it will be an interesting conversation with your brother."

She beamed, her eyes smiling. "Indeed it will be. But he also has the Keen, he'll know our truth, and he'll see you for who you really are now. He'll thank you for all you've done."

"So. . ." Mira sidled over to Tala's side. "Then is this goodbye?"

"No," Tala answered, a sad smile forming on her lips. "It doesn't have to be. You all could come back with me."

Mira shook her head. "I'm afraid not. We all have things to get back to now that the war is over. And I have a brother to hunt down. . ." She sighed. "But visit, okay? You'd better."

"You too. Don't be a stranger. You all will be welcome in Highland as soon as Sabian knows what you all did. You shall all be honored guests." Tala embraced Mira, who whispered something in her ear before stepping away and taking Oliver's hand, leaving Tala blushing with a laugh.

"I really wanna see your kingdom," Navy piped up, his voice thick with longing.

"You will," Tala promised, hugging him. "And there you won't have to steal to survive. I'll make sure of that. You'll all have a home there." Things she'd never really had there herself.

I watched her as she said her goodbyes, making heartfelt promises to everyone. If she could, she would have given them the kingdom itself. She was true royalty of most importance– purity, sacrifice, and courage of heart– not just by blood, but by every essence of her being.

I shook hands and patted the backs of Oliver, Felix, and Navy. I didn't with Evian, though. But I did dip my head slightly in respect, to which he nodded. Our dislike of each other was mutual, but we had worked together, fought for the same cause. We were brothers in arms to a degree, despite our indifferences. Besides, he'd helped Tala. And that was enough reason for me to have an amount of respect for him. He was, after all, my elder.

"Tell me what awaits you," Mira called after Tala as she climbed up onto the dragon's neck. "I will!" she replied.

I helped Aidilane up behind me, then sat down just behind Tala, taking hold of the dragon's spine scales as Aidilane wrapped her arms around my middle.

"*Hold on tight,*" the dragon commanded. "*After all you've been through, it would be a shame if you fell off.*"

Chapter Twenty-four

Tala

Somehow, we keep marching on, keep fighting. Fight after fight, trial after trial, our stubborn bodies just keep going. Our relentless souls refuse defeat, refuse to be finished until our stories come to a close. Even then, what lies beyond? What is it that steals us away from this world?

Is it rest? Is it a greater power? Is it the One who created, calling us?

Better yet– what keeps us tied to this world, keeps us fighting? Faith? Hope? Love? I believe that each of those are of utmost importance. However, similarly to them, the thing that keeps us here is something that cannot be measured or seen.

Reason. We each have a reason we're here. Whether that reason is to be the hero or villain in someone's story, we all serve a purpose in the great scheme of things. From the littlest things, to the greatest, all are equally as important. A sword cannot be forged without fire, just as it cannot be made without each small spark, each strike of the hammer.

We may not yet know what lies ahead, or what reason, what purpose is keeping us here. But one thing is for certain:

If you are still here, there is a reason. You still have a purpose to serve. Make your life worth living, leave a trail for those yet to come, and be great even in the little things. Make your story worth telling. Take this one chance you have, for it is your first, but it is also your last.

So make it count.

The wind whipped my hair back and filled my lungs with life. I couldn't believe I was actually alive again; at first I had been certain that I had reached what lay beyond. But Death had let go of me again. . .no. Life had stolen me back, snatching me away from Death greedily. This was not the doing of chance or luck. This was much, much more.

The landscape passed hundreds of feet below us– trees, towns, cities, borders, lakes, rivers, mountains. The remains from the war lay scattered around– panicked mages retreating home, chased by the other kingdom's soldiers, their wands and scepters shattered. The dragon's powerful wings beat the air, carrying us as if we were weightless. We were flying, and for the first time in my life, I felt free. I could reach out and touch the sky– I was certain of it. And the clouds that drifted just above our heads nearly brushed our hair as the sun lowered in the sky, turning the sky into an amber and rose gradient. I turned to look back at Kai and Aidilane. They looked just as amazed as I was.

"This continent has changed much," the dragon noticed.

This continent? I asked, confused.

"Yes, princess. Across the oceans, and many seas, there are places that have been long forgotten by most here. Those who remember are lying on their deathbed, or are already six feet under. It is a tragedy. However, I think it is for the best. The creatures here have done enough damage on this continent. They have destructive, despicable tendencies. It is best that the secret of the other lands stay between us."

I won't tell anyone, I swore.

"Save the elf."

I startled, feeling my face burn. But the dragon continued, *"It is alright. I understand it can be difficult to withhold such a thing from the one you withhold nothing from."*

Thank you. The other lands...they're where you're from, aren't they?

"Yes."

What are they like?

A moment of silence, then the dragon replied, *"One day, you will know."*

Kai tapped my shoulder and pointed down at the clearing we were passing over. "Tala, look." Spiritwolf and the rest of the pack ran under the dragon's shadow, letting out sharp howls in greeting and excitement. They sensed me here, and they sensed the kinship between them and the dragon. Unless you angered her, she was no one to fear.

The dragon's scales felt like glass beneath my hands, smooth and strong like crystal, shifting with her movements like the aurora borealis. I wasn't sure what to expect when we arrived. In what state would the kingdom be in by now? What state would Sabian be in? I knew he was alive, I could feel his heartbeat as sure as my own. But he had fought as King in a harsh war, and had felt his sister die. As far as he knew, I'd died with the war.

As we crossed over the Highland Kingdom border, Quinton's lights came into view. Fireworks whistled into the darkening twilight, lighting up the sky in all colors of the rainbow. Folk danced in the streets and sang songs to the music filling the atmosphere, celebrating the end of the war with drink and a multitude of festivities. Most of the city was merely a pile of rubble and ruin, wreckage leftover from the battles. But the people of Highland celebrated despite it on light feet with joy in their hearts. The war was over, and so was the pain and hardship with it. There would be much grief for the loved ones lost and the aftermath of the destruction, but the storm was over.

I smiled as I watched them, my heart filled with joy to see them so happy. It had been a long time since the folk could dance freely in the streets without fear. A happy tear traced down my cheek. The children down there had a chance at a life now.

As we circled over the palace keep, a shout went up. The dragon landed on the hill just a short ride from the keep, and I could sense the riders headed our way, sending a nervous feeling scittering through my insides.

Kai, Aidilane and I climbed down from her shoulders, and Spiritwolf leapt into my arms. Or least, she tried. Instead, she knocked me over. I laughed, rolling in the grass as she covered me in excited, relieved canine kisses. I embraced her tightly as I greeted the other wolves. They howled and lowered their gazes in respect. I wasn't quite sure why, but I sensed their respect and honor for me.

As the riders from the palace neared, I sent the pack away. *Don't be seen*, I told them. *Don't worry Spiritwolf. I will come see you soon.*

They obeyed, but Spiritwolf stayed at my side stubbornly. *I am no longer a pup,* she retorted. *You cannot chase me off. I will stay here where I am meant to be. At your side.*

I nearly argued, but the look in her eyes suggested there was no changing her mind. And I didn't want to send her away anyway.

I turned to the dragon and bowed, then pressed my palm to her snout. "Thank you, friend."

"You, human, are the one who should be thanked," she chided me. Then she dipped her head deeply and spread her wings wide. *"You have carried me within you as if I were your own. You gave your life willingly for the greater good and have spared the world from destruction. You have taken the right path, though painfully earned, you are worthy of the title Savior, and the title of many more things yet to come."* She rose from the bow to meet my gaze. *"You will be a magnificent mother one day, Tala. Fierce and protective. These qualities will one day save **your** world."*

I didn't understand what she meant, but I smiled. "I'm honored to have flown with you, Dragon."

Her eyes sparkled brilliantly. *"My name is Krystallo. I want you to have this as a token of my thanks."* She placed one of her scales in the palm of my hand, leaving me breathless. *"Do with it as you wish. Now, I must return to my land. I look forward to our next encounter."*

She turned and beat her wings, lifting into the sky with a flick of her massive tail. The light from the fireworks reflected off her scales, making her look like she was either transparent or glowing.

As she faded into the night sky, I transmitted, *Goodbye, Krystallo.*

Kai brushed the back of his hand with mine. "Tala."

I turned to find the riders approaching through the trees. The lead rider stopped the rest with a raised fist and slowly dismounted from his horse. He held out a lantern as he cautiously neared, and I knew immediately who it was from his gait and the way his head tilted slightly to the side as he concentrated on us.

Beside me, Aidilane ducked behind Kai, who began to draw his blades defensively. But I stopped him, grabbing his arm. "It's okay."

Kelgare's face came into view beneath his hood as he stopped and stared at me. *Tala?*

"'Tis I."

I ran into his arms, and he embraced me tightly, letting out the breath he'd been holding. "Great gamble. . .Sabian said you were dead. I thought that we'd lost you." He pulled back and held me at arms length to give me a once over. "Dear girl– you succeeded! You really did it!"

I smiled at him from underneath my mask. "So you were right along."

"I was, and I never doubted it." He turned his attention to Kai and Aidilane. "Isn't that–"

"Yes," I interrupted. "But. . .Well, it's a long story. Kai helped me. We helped each other. I could not have done this without him."

Kelgare raised a doubtful brow as he held out his hand to Kai, who took it tentatively. They shook, and Kelgare held on a moment longer. "Thank you."

I could feel the surprise radiating from Kai. "I was honored."

I introduced Aidilane, then Kelgare asked, "Was that a dragon?"

"Yes," I told him. "I'll tell you all about it on the way to the palace. I need to see my brother."

Kelgare led me through the corridor to the king's chambers silently. The corridors of the palace were quiet and still except for the music drifting up from the great hall.

When we reached the chamber, Kelgare put a hand on my shoulder. "Welcome back."

I silently slipped into the king's chambers. It was dark except for a few candles and the colorful light bursts from the fireworks coming in through the window. I padded towards it, where Sabian's form sat slumped in the window nook, his face in his hands. His soiled sword lay nearby, the king's crown tossed on the bed. Despair and grief poured from my brother, nauseating me. His hair was unkept and he still wore his damaged armor.

I stopped just a few feet from him and gently touched his mind. Lightly, like a breath.

He sucked in a sharp breath, but he didn't move. So I transmitted, *Brother.*

Slowly, he raised his head and turned, his weary eyes widening at the sight of me. "I–I'm dreaming," he whispered.

"No, you aren't." I took off my mask and took another step closer. "Sabian. Feel my mind. I'm really here. I'm alive."

Whatever was left of his composure fell apart as he covered his mouth with a sob. "Tala."

I closed the space between us and pulled him into my arms. "I'm here."

He wrapped his arms around me, and we sobbed into each other's shoulders until there were no more tears left to cry. Then we both collapsed on the floor, hand in hand. Sabian wiped the tears from his face, his brow scrunched in confusion. "How? I–I felt you, Tala. It was like a piece of me was ripped away. You were dead."

"I don't understand that part just yet either," I replied honestly.

"You stopped the war, Tala," he said breathlessly. "You saved us."

"Remember that elven assassin?" I asked. When Sabian nodded, I continued. "He ended up saving my life. Many times. None of this would have been possible without him. He's here now, too. And his sister."

Sabian blinked, amazement filling his gaze. "I want to hear it all, Tala. Every bit of it. I want to know how you're here, how you did it. But first, you need to know something."

He helped me to my feet as I held his gaze steady. "What is it?"

"The Queen," he explained. "Soon after you left, she ran away. Disappeared without a trace."

"What?" There was no doubting the relief in my voice. "Really?"

He nodded. "Tala, do you know what this means? You're heir to the throne."

"What are you saying?"

He turned and reached for the silver crown that graced his fireplace mantel, placing it in my hands. "The queen's throne belongs to you, now."

"*What?*" I stared at the jeweled crown in my shaking hands. "No, I can't be. I couldn't possibly be queen. Besides, what about the other princesses? Surely–"

"Princess Joy is too young to assume the throne, and Princess Teyqa has already refused it. She doesn't believe herself fit for the throne."

"Well neither am I!" I exclaimed.

Sabian shook his head. "Don't be ignorant, sister. You just saved the world. You sacrificed your life to end the war that was going to end us. You were selfless, courageous, and you didn't hesitate. You put the lives and well being of everyone in this kingdom before your own. That is the true quality of a sovereign, Tala. You taught me that, remember? There isn't a single being more fit for the throne than you."

I couldn't really breathe.

Behind me, Kelgare murmured, "For once, this is something you can choose for yourself, Tala. It isn't an obligation, or a duty, or the only way to survive. It is a *choice*. But, may add that your heart is something this kingdom needs. It has suffered greatly, and is but a pile of rubble. The people– we– need a queen who will help us mend and rise again. I cannot think of a person more capable of that than you."

My lip trembled and I let out a half hearted laugh. "I can think of many things I would change to make this kingdom better. I'd establish an orphanage– a safe haven for children without families, without parents. I'd make sure that each child on the streets is warm and clothed, is well fed... and is loved. And that's just the start– but I couldn't possibly be the right one for the throne. I grew up in the shadows, scraping to survive all my life. I was just an orphan stable girl, then a guard and spy. I was an outcast, a runaway. I was an ill slave after that, working for the king just to live– to live a life I would have rather left behind. How could I be a good queen if darkness is all I have known?"

"And yet, your light is brightest," Kelgare countered. "And that is why you would make a good queen. Because you lived in the darkness. You were amongst the lowest of this kingdom. You know what it's like. And you know from experience what would make this kingdom a better place because you have suffered the worst of its cruelty."

Doubt surged through me along with fear. "B–But how? All I know is how to serve, not to lead."

Kelgare's eyes smiled, the candlelight reflecting off them. "I doubt that very much, Tala. Tell us, who led you and the others on the mission?"

I opened and closed my mouth, but nothing came out. Oh.

"Exactly." Sabian took my shoulders in his hands. "Think about it, okay?"

I nodded, turning to leave. I felt flushed, shocked. After all that had happened, I was being handed the throne to the Highland Kingdom. I couldn't comprehend leading– let alone leading an entire kingdom. I'd only led the others on the mission because, well, I hadn't really had a choice. My life revolved around not having a choice. Stealing and scraping to survive, being a royal guard and spy, running away, living with my seizures. My torture and near execution, forced to serve the king with the very abilities that he'd sentenced me to death for having. Going on the mission had ultimately been my choice, but really, I hadn't had a choice. I was the only one that had a chance at stopping the war, and I wouldn't let my brother and his kingdom die if there was something I could do. I hadn't had a choice to carry the dragon within me, or to die. My whole life. . .it was written out for me centuries ago. I was merely a puppet being pulled by the strings of fate.

But now, I had a choice to rewrite my story. I had the chance to take hold of the pen and decide what my story would tell. For once, the fear within me wasn't terrifying. It was more like adrenaline coursing through me. This time, I wasn't being shoved off the cliff– I was taking the leap.

Just short of the door, I stopped. "Actually, I've made my decision."

"Last time, it was you that helped *me* dress," Princess Joy laughed. She helped me layer on the underdress for my coronation gown. "Your dress is almost finished being tailored."

"Yes," I recalled the afternoon before the ball. "I quite enjoyed seeing all your gowns and jewels. Thank you, Joy."

She peered up at me through my mask, her head tilted curiously. "I still can't believe you're becoming queen. I sort of wish I'd treated you better now. I mean, in order to become queen, you must be a blood heir. But why can't I know who you are under that mask?"

"Because King Sabian has a plan for the coronation," I explained. "I don't want to ruin it."

"Alright," she relented, turning to Aidilane who was rummaging through the princess's jewelry. "Do you know who she is?"

"I do."

Joy sighed loudly. "Fine, I'll stop asking about it. But really, how patient is a girl expected to be?"

"Patient enough," her aunt chided her. Princess Teyqa adjusted the silver pin in my hair as she smiled at me in the reflection of the mirror I sat in front of. "Remember, she is going to be our queen. You must treat her as such."

I laughed. "I can hardly believe it myself. Do you have any advice on how to be royalty?"

The corner of Teyqa's mouth twitched, and she leaned in to whisper into my ear, "Don't poison your son."

My heart skipped a beat. "You know?"

She nodded. "I finally came to terms with it when Hersha left. I am sickened by it, and more so for the girl the murder was blamed on."

For a moment, air escaped me. Then I remembered to breathe again as she held up another silver pin. "Do you fancy your hair like this?"

I studied myself in the reflection. My auburn–red hair was half up half down, braided around the back almost like a halo. Silver pins graced it, making it look like a sunset sparkling with stars. "I do," I replied in wonder.

"Good," the princess sighed, relieved. "I'm not the best at this, you know. But I am better than Joy."

"Are not!"

Teyqa laughed. "As you say, your highness."

Aidilane sidled up beside me. "You look like a queen."

"She will once that mask falls away," Teyqa murmured. "I'll go fetch your gown."

"Me too!" Joy piped, leaping up on her toes. "I want to see it first!" They raced to the door and out into the corridor.

I fiddled with my dragon scale necklace. I hadn't been able to decide what to do with the gift, so I'd made it into a necklace with the resolve that it would be safest with me. Aidilane held up different jewels, suggesting rings, necklaces, and an assortment of bracelets. Finally, I took her hand. "Why don't you wear them instead?"

She looked taken back. "Me? But I'm not royalty! And besides, you're going to be queen!"

I shook my head. "I have all the jewelry I need. Please, as your friend, I'm asking you: enjoy the jewels."

A brilliant smile broke free across her face and eyes lit up. "O–Okay."

I asked her, my voice shaking, "Is my back showing?"

"No, it isn't."

I sighed with relief. "Thank you." I didn't want the princesses, or anyone for that matter, seeing my scars.

A knock at the door startled us, and a servant entered. "King Sabian requests your presence on the rooftop gardens."

I pulled on a cloak, leaving Aidilane to her jewels and followed the servant up to the gardens where Sabian, Kelgare and I would train. Once there, the servant bowed and headed back down the winding stairs.

Out in the center of the garden were Kai and my brother, standing amongst the trees and plants. I didn't prod their minds, but I could tell they were having an important conversation. Finally, they shook hands and Sabian headed towards me, a smile spreading on his lips.

"You didn't scare him away with your kingly presence, did you?" I teased.

"I doubt there's much that could scare him away from you." Sabian's expression turned serious. "You did the right thing bringing him here. The Moonland crown has been on my tail about him and Aidilane, but they're safe here. There they wouldn't have lasted longer than a few days."

I nodded. "I hope Mira and the Renegades make it to the coronation."

"They will. You sent for them a week ago, they will have gotten your message a few days ago with plenty of time to get here. I've got a good feeling about it."

"Yeah?"

"Yes."

"I'm nervous, Sabian."

"Good. I would be concerned if you weren't."

I whacked his shoulder. "You know what I mean."

He nodded. "Remember what you told me when I became king? *Take it hour by hour, minute by minute. Do everything to the best of your ability, and ask for help and advice when you need it.* And remember when I told you you could be heir to the throne? You said *one day, maybe.* It's one day, Tala. And I'm so grateful and honored to rule this kingdom at your side."

I squeezed his hand. "Go get ready for the ceremony, your highness."

He grinned. "As you command." He winked and left Kai and I alone in the garden. The trees were bright with red and orange leaves, and the autumn breeze scattered a few of them across the ground.

Kai leaned on the parapet overlooking the swaying ocean of red, yellow and orange forest trees. He was dressed in the same clothes he'd worn at the ball, complete with his silver leaf headpiece.

I padded to his side and stepped up on the parapet, taking off my mask to look down on him. "So tell me, what happened in the cavern? People don't just come back to life."

Kai shifted, holding my gaze. "The dragon brought you back."

"Kai," I chided him. "Must I search your mind?"

His eyes smiled. "You really are ravishing when you're serious."

I put my hands on my hips and raised my brows. "I need to know."

His gaze dropped to my feet, and after a long moment, he held out his palm like he would when he was about to bring a flame to life. But no flames lit, even after a minute or two. Then he dropped his hand and his eyes met mine once more. I understood.

"You gave up your element to bring me back?"

"A small sacrifice."

I crouched in front of him on the parapet and took his face in my hands, my heart heavy. "Kai. . . That was no small sacrifice. Your fire was part of who you are. And you gave it up for me . . ."

Kai covered my hands with his. "It was well worth it, Tala. And every moment without my element is worth it as long as you're alive."

"Thank you," I whispered. "I was so afraid that that was the end of our story."

"I was, too. But now, you have a kingdom to rule."

I sighed. "I hope I'm making the right choice."

He shrugged. "I can't tell you. That is something you'll have to find out on your own. But I know you, Tala. And more than once, I've marveled at what a suitable queen you would make."

"Really?" I felt my face heat up.

"I may be a sneak, but I don't lie."

I raised a brow. "Anymore."

"Anymore," he agreed. "Remember, you got this far. Finally, you can start living your life."

He was right. My heart had been beating, my lungs breathing, but that isn't what defines life. I was merely surviving. I hadn't started living until a few weeks ago.

"That reminds me," I started. "I want you to be head of the Royal Guard."

He raised a brow. "You do?"

"Yes. You are most suited for the job. Sabian agrees. Will you accept?"

"I do."

"Good." I grinned. "Because you can't refuse your queen."

He laughed. "I suppose I can't. But I couldn't refuse you even when you didn't have a crown."

I sat down, letting my legs dangle on either side of Kai. "I don't have a crown just yet. But I have the feeling there's something you wanted to tell me?"

His dark eyes were soft as he took my hand and kissed it. "Have I told you how afraid I've been since our paths crossed?"

"Afraid?"

He tilted his head, running his fingers along my jawline gently, his voice low. "Fear is the thing that tells you you have something to lose; and every time I look at you, I'm terrified. I want to wage war on the creatures that broke you. I want them all to know that now that I'm at your side, there isn't a single being in the world who can get away with hurting you." He swallowed hard. "It's selfish of me to want you. But here I am, wanting you anyway. You make me soft, and for that I will forever resent you. Because the man I am isn't who you deserve. You are a gentle heart with the soul of a dragon and the mind of a wolf. You are a diamond– the most priceless mineral and the strongest gemstone, capable of splitting a single beam of light into a million. You deserve so much more. Far better creatures could love you. But now, they'll have to go through me."

He pulled something shiny from his pocket. Two rings; a dark band with a silver design, and a smaller silver one that was an exact reflection of the other ring's design. Unity rings.

Kai put on the larger one, and he took my hand. "I never want to lose you again. Tala, I want you. I want you to be mine." He slid the smaller ring on my finger. "But most of all, I want to be *yours.* "

I stared at the ring, hardly able to breathe, my heart skipping a beat. Overwhelming joy flooded me. I laced my fingers with his. "My heart is yours. But I only have half a heart to give to you. . .and I hope it's enough."

"So do I," he said, his voice hardly a whisper as our rings touched with a tiny *tink*. "But two halves make a whole."

Kai had been an unexpected twist to my story, a surprise in, at first, the worst way– but in the end, the best way. It turned out that surprise had been a miracle. He loved me, scars and broken pieces and all, and he didn't want to fix me. He just loved me. He was the man whose arms I felt safe in, who had made me feel safe for the first time in years. He made me feel as though I were enough. His kindness and gentleness despite the ways he'd been hardened. All his flaws and qualities– all pieces of my heart now. Our demons danced together, and we would have each other with our pasts, darkness, pain– everything that makes us– and not anything less.

He was the boy *I* loved. A bit messy, a bit ruined. A broken, beautiful disaster. Just like me.

We leaned into each other, our lips full of passion, taking in each other with every breath. We were no longer our own persons– we were each other's.

I pulled back for a heartbeat to catch my breath, and Kai picked me up and twirled me around. When he set me back down on my feet, he tucked a loose strand of my hair behind my ear. "You fit in well with Autumn."

I ran my fingers through his hair and pulled him into my lips again. He tasted like home.

"Oh thank the gods!" I squeezed Mira tight. "You made it!"

"Of course we did." She grinned. "I was thrilled to hear from you. I wouldn't miss this for the world. Everyone else is in the great hall. Now, let's get this gown on you, shall we?"

The gown was an eye-catching shade of emerald amongst forest green folds. It had silver lining along the edges of the layers and shimmering silver off shoulder sleeves. It suited my form impossibly well, but once Mira helped me tie the front corset top, I realized how low the back of the dress was, nearly to my waist, revealing my scars.

Mira noticed my anxiety and draped a silver, iridescent shawl over my shoulders. "There. Better?"

I nodded. "Thank you."

She adjusted the parts of my hair that had come undone while I was in the rooftop garden with Kai. Afterwards, she guided me to the mirror. "The vision of a true queen." Then her eye caught the glint of my ring. "I called it!" she exclaimed.

I laughed. "You sure did."

She crossed her arms. "I told you. When am I ever wrong?"

"Oh, never."

"I knew right from the beginning– you and Kai were meant to be from the start."

I blushed. "I just hope that my becoming queen won't push him away. You know? It's daunting. I would understand if he did."

Mira shook her head. "He'd be a total idiot, Tala. And I may not know him well, but Kai isn't an idiot. Now, let me see that ring!"

I held out my hand and she examined the silver, her eyes shining and maybe slightly jealous. "Don't blink," I said, "You'll be next."

Her face reddened. "Indeed I will be. If Oli ever takes the hint."

"He does. And he will when he's ready. And I'll put in a good word."

Mira tilted her head back with a groan. "Oh but you beat us to it!"

I giggled, nudging her with my elbow. "Only by a moment. You'll see."

The sound of the palace bells began to chime, signaling the beginning of the coronation ceremony. Butterflies fluttered around inside me, and my head felt light and starry as if I'd just had one too many glasses of champagne.

"This is really happening," I said breathlessly. "The past few weeks have felt like a dream, Mira. I'm not really sure any of this is real."

She took my hand. "Oh, it's real. Steady, soldier. It is your time to step out of the shadows and into the light."

That sentiment didn't really help calm my nerves, but I was thankful to have my best friend at my side as I put on my wolf mask and headed to the great hall. When we reached the massive carved doors,

Mira squeezed my hand one last time before letting go and slipping through the doors.

At the sixth chime of the bells, both of the doors were opened by the royal guards, revealing the Great Hall. Glittering chandeliers hung from the ceiling, lit with candles, and the coronation tapestries graced the walls with all their colors and splendor. The people of Highland filled the hall, along with the elegant music that drifted through the air from the quartet. Nearest the raised throne platform, the Renegades stood together, looking back at me in wonder along with everyone else. Aidilane and Kai stood a little ways apart from them, Aidilane draped in her jewels and Kai clad in his new head of guard uniform– or at least part of it. The clothes from the ball were still visible beneath. His eyes shone as he looked at me, his expression louder than words.

I opened my mind to his just in time to hear him think, *What a magnificent creature, my queen is. Bewitching.*

And with that, I held my head high as I glided down the aisle to the throne dais, where my brother the king, Kelgare, the princesses, and the bishop of Highland awaited me.

The last time I walked these exact steps, I was chained and facing a trial for a crime I didn't commit. Guards had prodded me, shoving me forward as I limped to kneel before the angry king and the manic queen. My head had been bleeding, throbbing from where they'd knocked me senseless, and my leg in agony from the wound from the trap, leaving a trail of my own blood across the cold marble floor. And the worst had yet to come.

But now, I strode the length of the hall to the dais, the train of my gown flowing along behind me. My steps didn't falter, but my heart did. It raced, and my hands trembled. My skin felt clammy, and every fiber of my being screamed and pulled at me, protesting against moving any closer to that dais with a vigor that nearly knocked the breath from my lungs. But as I reached it, I stopped, taking in a long, deep breath before stepping up onto it. I turned to face the gathered, swallowing hard. King Rubarb had stood here as he sentenced me to death, Queen Hersha just a step to his left with an eager grin on her face. But now, *I* stood here in my gown, undefeated. With a nod from Sabian, I reached up and took off my mask.

Silence met me as the crowd took in who I was. I heard a few light gasps from both of the princesses nearby. I couldn't breathe.

Sabian stepped to my side, his voice ringing loud and clear throughout the hall. "Before you stands Princess Tala of the Highland Kingdom, heir to the throne. My sister. Years ago, she was accused and sentenced for the murder of Prince Farley. But she was charged falsely, blamed by the criminal herself, Queen Hersha."

I felt a sob forming in my throat as the crowd began to murmur amongst themselves, but Sabian quieted them again. "As your king, I am not only obligated, but am honored to finally reveal the truth and bring justice to this kingdom and for my sister. Since birth, Tala has served the crown diligently, loyally, without question, even though her place as heir to the throne was denied and she was kept from a royal life. And even after being falsely sentenced, she served as King's Wolf. And after King Rubarb's death, as the Northland Kingdom ravished and destroyed us, she set out to find a way to stop them. And she did." Sabian gestured towards Kai and the Renegades. "Along with the help of these elves, Princess Tala stopped the magicians–"

"Mages," Navy called, earning a stern nudge from his older sister.

Sabian laughed. "I stand corrected. Mages. She cut off their power source, thus ending the war. The reason we all stand here today is because of her sacrifice, her willingness to serve, and her courage. She has lived for this kingdom, and vows to continue to do so as your queen."

He turned to the bishop, who stepped forward and placed a jeweled golden scepter in my hand. "Princess Tala, do you vow to rule with justice, truth, compassion, and fair judgment over the people of the Highland Kingdom?"

"I do." I was surprised at how strong and steady my voice rang out.

"Do you vow to uphold the traditions passed down through royal tradition?"

"I do."

"Do you vow to oversee and bring about the kingdom's prosperity and well being to the best of your ability and knowledge?"

"I do."

Quietly, the bishop instructed, "Now face me with your back to the people and kneel."

I hesitated, pulling the shawl tighter around my shoulders, but Kelgare leaned in and whispered, "Wear your scars with pride, for they tell the story of how you rose from the ashes. You turned pain into power— and that, my Queen, is true glory."

Strengthened by his words, I took a deep breath and let the shawl fall from my shoulders as I turned and knelt, revealing my back and scars, triggering a wave of emotion from many of the people gathered.

The bishop raised the silver, emerald and sapphire embedded crown, and slowly placed it on my head. Then, taking up a ceremonial sword, he touched the blade to my left shoulder, and then my right. "Rise, and face your people" he commanded.

As I did, the bishop proclaimed, "Hail, Queen Tala of Highland, Savior and keeper to us all."

"Hail," the people echoed, going down on their knees. "Queen Tala."

Years ago, I had been the one kneeling in my own blood and dust. Now, Highland knelt before *me*.

With the gentle weight of the crown on my head, the crown that my devastator had worn, now mine, I felt the shift in fate. I'd had a destiny, one I fulfilled, but Kai had brought me back. He'd changed fate with his own sacrifice, laced with mine. I could live now, in the light. The shadows didn't hide me anymore, they couldn't pull me back into darkness any longer. Death was a close friend of mine, but now he would keep his distance for a time. I didn't have to run anymore, I didn't have to spend my nights in fear. I had a life to live, a kingdom to rule, a man to love. . .and *I* was loved.

Tears welled up in my eyes as I looked on upon my people, the people I'd lived for, spied for, and fought for. It was worth it— every tear, every drop of blood— not because of the crown I now wore, or the palace I called home. But because of who I was now.

Pain does not create, nor does it destroy. It is capable of both, but we are the ones who must choose what we become despite it. Pain can form monsters, and it can form saints. One does not become stronger because of pain, but by how they pull themselves up time and time again despite it. What doesn't kill us simply teaches us. Sometimes, it breaks us. But what we choose to do with the pieces left behind determines who we really are.

For all the moments that I was beaten, defeated, almost gave up, I kept going because I didn't have a choice. But now, I stood in full gown, my scars exposed to the world, utterly grateful to the past versions of me who got back up again, who kept going to carry me through to this day despite the odds. Because now, I can heal. I can have Peace. I can have Joy. Love.

All because that little girl didn't give up, Spiritwolf transmitted to my mind. I was glad I kept going, not for what I did, but for what would come. And as I glided down the aisle at my brother's side to greet the people of our kingdom, Kai close behind me, I felt a trickle of energy in my mind, coming from the dragonscale dangling from my neck. I knew that I'd only scaled the surface of my power, and I wondered what my future would hold for me. I carried history, but the world that I'd shouldered was replaced by a kingdom, and I felt the relief that came with it. I wasn't daunted by my new position— not much can daunt someone who has survived hell. In a way, it was comforting. I had a place, and for once I was recognized in it.

But the thing that lightened my heart the most as I shook hands with my people and held their little children, was pride. Not in myself, but in little Stablegirl. Because if it weren't for her resilience through the cold, hunger, and loneliness and her joy in little things, I would not be standing here— let alone with a crown on my head.

I smiled at Kai, and he pinched the fabric of his new uniform between his fingers with a smirk. *I'm not wearing this on a day to day basis,* he thought.

You look better in black leather anyway, I respond, filling his mind with my words. *Head of Guard, but you'll always be my assassin.*

He arched a brow as he sidled in beside me, sliding his arm around my waist. *And you'll always be my Tala.*

I gazed at him, his dark, umber eyes deep, and my heart stuttered with the anticipation of what was to come. He was mine. This kingdom was mine. This life was mine. And I looked back on the pain and thought—

That was not my end. It was just the beginning.